SAVED BY VENOM

Grabbed #3

Lolita Lopez

Night Works Books
College Station, Texas

Night Works Books
3515-B Longmire Drive #103
College Station, Texas 77845
www.roxierivera.com

Publisher's Note: This is a work of fiction. Names, characters, places, and incidents are a product of the author's imagination. Locales and public names are sometimes used for atmospheric purposes. Any resemblance to actual people, living or dead, or to businesses, companies, events, institutions, or locales is completely coincidental.

Cover Art © 2015 P Schmitt/Picky Me Artist

Grabbed By Vicious/ Lolita Lopez – 2nd ed.

Saved By Venom

Lolita Lopez

Grabbed, Book Three

To escape her father's debt to a loan shark, Dizzy seeks refuge in the upcoming Grab. She'd rather belong to one of those terrifying sky warriors from the battleship *Valiant* than to the sleazy criminal who wants her as his plaything.

The years of constant war haven't been kind to highly decorated sniper Venom. Only the promise of earning a wife kept him going through deadly battles. Catching and collaring Dizzy fills him with incredible hope. Finally he has a woman of his own, a mate to love—and bind and adorn with his ropes.

After a brazen Splinter attack, the Shadow Force uncovers secrets about Dizzy's late mother that entangle her in a web of deceit. To save Venom, her father and an operative named Terror, Dizzy digs deep and risks it all.

Venom refuses to stand idly by while Dizzy's haunted past threatens the future they're trying to build. He finally has a reason for living—and he's not giving her up.

SAVED BY VENOM

Lolita Lopez

Chapter One

"**Y**OUR FATHER DID *what*?"

Cringing at her best friend's tone, Dizzy stopped folding the clothes she had chosen to pack. She turned her full attention to Ella, who gawked at her with wide eyes. With as much bravery as she could muster, Dizzy repeated, "Dad sold my lottery number to a councilman who plans to marry his daughter to some doctor from the colonies. I'm going to be Grabbed tomorrow."

Stunned speechless, Ella plopped down on the small bed. Pain colored her voice as she asked, "Why would he do that?"

They'd never kept secrets from each other and Dizzy saw no reason to start now. "There was some sort of problem with a shipment of cargo. He didn't share the details but apparently he needed a lot of money to make it right. Now he owes a huge debt to Fat Pete."

Ella gasped. "The loan shark who launders money for the Splinters?"

She nodded. "I guess Fat Pete is threatening to collect me as collateral for a loan Dad can't repay."

"That miserable bastard!" Ella wrung her hands. "Maybe I could come up with the money to help you."

Dizzy shook her head. "You don't have this kind of

money."

"I bet I could get my hands on it," Ella insisted. "Business owners pay a lot of money to put my face on their posters. They want people to see me wearing their clothes or using their products. Being a muse might not be the most respected job on this planet but it's profitable." Ella grasped her hand. "I can find a way."

"Doing what? Posing in lingerie?" Dizzy hissed the words. "Sure, the guys who run *SKIN* pay their muses a lot of money to take those pictures but it's not worth the risk. You know what happens to girls who get caught by the censors." She shivered with fear. "It's not worth it."

Ella rolled her eyes. "The pictures aren't even that risqué. What's so shameful about showing a woman in her undies?"

"Nothing," she agreed, "but it's not my opinion that matters. You know what the censor crews are like."

"It's ridiculous."

"It's The City." Dizzy's matter-of-fact reply ended their discussion. There wasn't anything more to say about the hypocrisy of the planet's capitol. With enough money, a person could get their hands on anything restricted by the government or buy their way out of trouble. Those without money? Well—they did without or went to prison.

Dizzy shoved aside the clothes and made a space to sit next to Ella. She made sure to sink down slowly, not wanting to aggravate the strange condition that plagued her with fits of dizziness and nausea and ear-ringing when she moved too quickly. Hands folded in her lap, she sighed. "Look, Ella, I'm just—I'm tired."

Her friend frowned. "How the heck can you think about sleep at a time like this?"

"No." She exhaled roughly. "I'm not sleepy tired. I'm emotionally exhausted." Dizzy absentmindedly touched the gnarly scars running along the curve of her throat. The awful memories of the day she had been nearly obliterated by the terrorist bombing outside the Harcos embassy swamped her. She pushed them aside and tried to focus. "You know I've been talking about leaving The City for a while now."

"Yes. We talked about getting you to the colonies, maybe Safe Harbor. That's still a possibility."

"It's not and you know it. After that mess at the old battery plant with the Sixers and the Splinters and their stolen weapons and food, the Harcos have basically blockaded the planet to prevent any insurgents from escaping. The fees for immigrating legally to the colonies are too high for a girl like me to afford."

Once upon a time nothing had been too expensive for Dizzy. She had been born into the lap of luxury and enjoyed the extreme wealth of her bank-owning father and successful businesswoman mother. The bomb that had taken her mother caused a panic and recession that ruined her father's bank, leaving them penniless and homeless.

"You could go into hiding until we get the money together for a visa."

Dizzy shook her head. "I can't hide." She glanced nervously at her window. "I swear there were two goons following me today." Then, with a resigned shrug, she added, "Besides, the colonies want skilled workers for their visa programs. I'm just a seamstress."

"Just a seamstress?" Ella scoffed. "You're the best damned seamstress in the fashion district. Your work is beautiful. You're committed to your craft. Don't ever say you're *just* a seamstress."

Dizzy couldn't deny that it felt good to have her friend, the most popular muse on Calyx, talk about her work that way. "It doesn't change things, Ella. I'm never going to find someone to sponsor me for a visa. Right now, I don't have the kind of money it takes to buy a visa or the connections to get one of the seats on the transport ships run by the Red Feather."

"What about Danny? You know, my friend the fixer? He's tight with the Red Feather." Ella grasped her hand. "I could make it happen."

"There's not enough time. Fat Pete expects Dad to bring him the money or me by Friday. That's two days from now! I'm not taking the chance."

"So you're going to let one of those awful sky warriors take you?" Ella shuddered.

"They're monsters, Dizzy."

"They can't be any worse than Fat Pete!" Dizzy swallowed hard. "The one that my mother…" Her voice trailed off as the sordid details of that assignation raced through her head. "Well…anyway. He seemed nice enough and he saved my life." She touched the scar on her neck again. "Maybe I can find one like him."

"I don't know." Ella nibbled her thumb. "They're so overbearing and so controlling."

"It's a cultural thing, I think. Maybe it won't be so bad." Searching for a positive slant to her crappy situation, she said, "I've seen some Harcos men around the embassy downtown. They're all big and scary but some of them are handsome in a rugged sort of way. I've heard they're good to their wives."

"If you call being leashed and collared *good*."

"I don't," Dizzy admitted, "but this is my only chance to get away from here. After the bombing, after losing Mom, I can't stand it here. Dad is so far gone now that he's wrapped up in the black market. I can't let him drag me down. This place is suffocating me. I've got to get out."

Ella squeezed her hand. "I know the nightmares are bad, Dizzy, but are you sure you want to trade all those problems for whatever the hell awaits you up there?"

"It can't be any worse than this."

Ella made a frustrated sound. "I realize you've been through a terrible, traumatic event, Dizzy, but you have no idea what worse really means. *I* know. I know what it's like to be cold and hungry and homeless and terrified that strange men are going to take you and rape you. Please." She gripped Dizzy's hand so hard it hurt. "Please reconsider. You don't have to do this."

"I do." Dizzy had settled her mind and there was no going back. "I'm going to run tomorrow morning and one of those sky warriors is going to Grab me."

For a long moment, Ella simply stared at her. Finally she exhaled slowly and said, "Then let's get you packed."

Dizzy relaxed. "Thank you for not fighting me on this."

"Oh, I want to fight you but we've been friends long enough for me to know when I can't win." Ella tugged her into a tight hug. "I'm really going to miss you."

Dizzy didn't even try to stop the tears that spilled onto her cheeks. "I'm going to miss you too."

"I hear that some women contact their families a few weeks after being taken. You have to promise me that you'll get a hold of me if you can."

"I will." Dizzy rubbed Ella's back. "I'll find a way to make it happen."

After ending their embrace Dizzy stood carefully and returned to her packing.

"What are you going to do about that?" Ella pointed to Dizzy's head. "You won't be able to run very far if it acts up and makes you sick."

"I know." She chewed her lower lip. "Hopefully I won't have to run long. I assume those men are rather fast."

"Definitely," Ella agreed. "You're only taking one bag?"

"That's all they allow." Dizzy glanced around the small studio apartment and all the things she was leaving behind. "I told the two Karraway sisters who live next door that they can have all the furniture. The newly married couple upstairs is going to take all the cookware and anything in the cabinets and pantry."

Ella eyed the closet teeming with colorful clothing. "Um...what about all that?"

Dizzy laughed. "You can have first dibs on anything in my closet."

"Yes!" Ella popped off the bed like an overeager puppy and darted to the closet.

"You have some of the best clothes in The City."

Dizzy snorted. "Hardly."

"Stop being so modest." Ella pulled out a coral-pink dress and held it up against her body. She used the mirror mounted on the door to check out her reflection. "I always get the most compliments when I'm wearing your creations. I still think we should have started our own business."

"If money grew on trees," Dizzy replied a bit wistfully. Joining Ella at the closet, she flicked through the hangers and selected all the dresses that were too small for Ella. "I want these to go to the shelter. The girls there will get some use out of them." She glanced at her workstation. "The fabric and supplies too."

"I'll make sure it gets there. What about your work? Are you taking anything with you?"

"My seamstress kit." She pointed to the leather messenger bag she carried everywhere. "I assume it won't be difficult to find fabric or thread up there. They must have a much better market system than we do. Hopefully I can find a store that will sell my designs."

"I'm sure that won't be difficult. One look at your sketches for your fall line and everyone will be clamoring for the chance to have your designs hanging on their racks."

Still hugging the pink dress, Ella leaned back against the wall. "Let's go out tonight."

"What?" Dizzy shook her head. "I can't."

"Why not?"

"I have to pack."

"I'll help you when we get back. What time do you run tomorrow morning?"

"Nine o'clock but I have to be at the square by eight. They're bussing us out to the woods for the Grab."

Ella made a face. "It's going to be ridiculously cold. Do you have anything suitable for that weather?"

"The paper they gave me at the registrar's office said that I'll be provided a uniform for running."

She made a *humph* noise. "It will probably be paper-thin and cheap."

"Probably."

"Come on, Dizzy." Ella begged with that high-pitched whine that she somehow made impossibly cute and endearing. "Please? We'll just grab a quick meal and a drink."

She frowned at her friend. "The last time I heard that we ended up at Hopper's underground dance club and barely escaped a raid by the secret police. No thanks!"

Ella rolled her eyes. "Whatever! You loved it. When was the last time you had that much fun? You know, other than the whole running-from-the-police-in-the-abandoned-subway-tunnels thing."

"No."

She checked her watch. "Look, it's nearly eight. Let's just listen to the Mouth and see what's going on tonight. If there's any chance that something might kick off we'll stay inside. Okay?"

Unable to deny Ella anything, Dizzy nodded reluctantly and knelt down next to her bed to fish out the small homemade radio she kept hidden there. Because the walls were shoddy and thin and owning a radio was an arrestable offense they took the device into the bathroom and turned on the shower for background noise. Ella climbed up to poke the antenna against the window for better reception. It took Dizzy almost a minute to find the pirate radio station that alternated channels to avoid detection.

"…hear that the League of Idiots will be holding a rally at tomorrow's Grab. Anyone who doesn't want their ass kicked by a bunch of muscleheaded sky warriors should probably steer clear of those festivities. If there's a book open on this, I've got ten bucks on the sky warriors, by the way."

Ella shot her an amused smile as the female DJ known only as the Mouth from the South described the dustup that would likely occur between the League of Concerned Citizens and the Harcos. The grassroots organization billed itself as a group of men concerned about the increasing number of Harcos ships orbiting the planet but most people understood that they were little more than a government-approved front for Splinter activities on Calyx.

Dizzy had met a few members of the league and all of them were batshit crazy. They were the type of people who seemed to *want* anarchy—and she simply couldn't understand it. The terrorist bombing that had taken her mother and nearly killed her had spurred intense rioting and chaos for weeks. She never wanted to experience true anarchy.

"We've also had reports from our friends by the sea

that the big beasties in the sky have been scouting land outside Blue Shores. Maybe those rumors of a military base in our backyard aren't so farfetched."

"Ugh." Ella made a face. "That's all we need, right? Then the Splinter terrorists would have a real reason to cause more problems for all of us."

Dizzy wondered if she was getting out just in time. The sky ships orbiting her planet were extremely safe— much safer than living down here where crazy people were blowing up buildings.

"Oh, and for all you night cats out there, I hear that a certain hopping spelunker is opening up the rabbit warren. First band starts at ten o'clock sharp. This one is a bringyour-own-booze affair."

Ella lowered the volume and shot Dizzy her most pleading look. "Please?"

"Well…" She wavered. The "hopping spelunker" the Mouth described was a girl everyone called Hopper. Like a lot of street kids, Hopper had spent most of her youth living and exploring the tunnels of the abandoned subway system below The City. As an adult, she made a living organizing parties that took place literally and figuratively underground to avoid the morality laws of The City.

And they were such good parties! Dizzy loved to dance. She didn't know when she might get the chance to do it again, especially not with some of the hottest bands on Calyx playing for a live crowd.

"Come on, Dizzy. Let me send you away in style. We'll consider it your bachelorette party."

"Well how can I pass up an offer like that?" Dizzy

pushed down the sadness threatening to overwhelm her. She didn't want to spend her last night on Calyx in tears and questioning her father's betrayal. She wanted to spend it laughing and having a good time with her best friend in the whole world.

"Great!" Ella jiggled the dress in her hand. "But I'm changing into this first!"

Dizzy rolled her eyes and pointed to the closet. "Don't forget the shoes."

"Score!" Ella disappeared into the small space. A moment later the dress she'd been wearing sailed through the air and landed on the bed. Snorting at her friend's utter carelessness, Dizzy picked it up and draped it neatly over the chair at her desk.

When Ella stepped out a few moments later, she looked effortlessly sexy. With that bee-stung pout and bewitching hazel eyes, she was a natural in her career as a muse. It was no wonder that companies lined up to have Ella showcase their products.

Once Dizzy had been in the same line of work. That was how they'd met as teenagers. Ella had been one of the muses Dizzy's mother had recruited to work for the agency she owned.

But the explosion that had killed her mother and brought the Harcos civil war to Calyx had taken away any possibility of Dizzy succeeding in that career. The scars on her neck weren't awful but they were noticeable—too noticeable.

Once recovered, she had moved behind the camera. There she had discovered her real passion. Designing clothing had provided her a steady income and a sense of fulfillment and accomplishment. She couldn't imagine how her life might have turned out if she hadn't had her scissors and sewing needles to fall back on after the bombing ruined her chances of being a muse and stripped her family of its wealth and influence. She was damn lucky not to be living on the streets.

"Are you ready?"

Dizzy considered Ella's question. In three words, Ella had captured her warring mindset perfectly. Was she ready?

"YOU READY FOR tomorrow?"

Jerking forward from the impact of Raze's unexpected whack between his shoulder blades, Venom choked on his mouthful of pretzels. Raze laughed as Venom took a long drink of his cold beer to clear his throat. Coughing, he scowled at his best friend and watched him drop into the empty chair across the small table. "A little warning next time?"

Raze held up both hands. "Sorry."

Placing his beer on the table, he loudly cleared his throat and considered his friend's query. "Sure. I'm ready."

Rather imperiously, Raze arched a dark eyebrow. "You sound rather relaxed for a man about to change his entire life with one silly race."

He frowned at Raze. "It's not a silly race. The Grab is one of our honored traditions."

"That often ends in heartache," Raze grumbled. "How many damn SRU calls have we been on in the last year with brides who want to leave their sky warrior husbands or for men fighting over a woman who got snatched away from her husband during the trial period?" He shook his head. "They've got to come up with a better way of screening these women than a damn lottery."

Venom didn't disagree with that. "The system isn't perfect but it's all we've got out here. If you want a wife and a family, it's the Grab or one of the matchmaking services from back home."

Raze's jaw twitched at the mere mention of matchmaking. Venom was probably the only man on the warship *Valiant* brave enough to say the word around him.

Years earlier, Raze's parents had used a well-respected matchmaking service to find him a pureblooded Harcos wife from Prime, their home planet. Unfortunately Raze and his bride had been miserable together. As a last-ditch effort to save their union, Raze had taken her on a vacation to one of the colonies but she had met and run off with an Earth-descendant scientist. Raze hadn't fought her on the divorce so they had parted amicably enough. Still, the many years since that rather humiliating experience hadn't dulled Raze's embarrassment.

With a loud grunt, Raze finally remarked, "You're probably better off jumping into a Grab, I guess."

"I hear the Grab next quarter still has some slots open." He eyed his friend carefully over his beer. "I know you've earned enough points to replace the ones you lost after your divorce. Your rank is high enough to push you to the top of the list."

Raze scrunched up his face and rubbed the back of his neck. "Do I look stupid to you? I need a damn wife like I need a hole in the head." He slashed his hand through the air. "I tried mating once. It clearly wasn't for me."

Venom experienced a pang of sadness for his friend. "That's not true. You and Shelly weren't mean for each other. It was a matchmaking mistake. You'd be a good mate."

Raze snorted. "Is that a proposal, Ven? Hell, why don't we ask Menace and Naya if we can throw in with their wedding and do a double ceremony?"

Glaring at his friend, Venom pelted him with pretzels. "That's the last time I try to be nice to you."

Raze snatched the broken snacks from his shirt and flung them at Venom's head.

"Boys!" The grizzly old bartender Brand shouted over the noisy din in the officer's bar. "This isn't a damn barn. Clean that shit up."

"Yes sir," they answered and quickly swept up the mess with their hands. Even though they both outranked the old man, they respected him for the decades of service he'd given to the land corps. There weren't many enlisted men who stayed in for life—or survived long enough to make that choice.

Still laughing, Venom settled up his tab and left the bar with Raze. While they waited for an elevator, Raze pointed to the news screen mounted on the wall there. "That is going to keep us busy."

Venom glanced at the scrolling images and the news ticker running along the bottom. His chest tightened at the announcement that the plans to build a base on Calyx were moving forward. It had been a rumor for the better part of five years but no one was sure it would ever happen.

Harcos' presence in the orbital space around the planet had grown over the last few years. It made sense to put in a ground installation—but the extremely pacifist and closed-off society down there on Calyx wasn't going to like it.

"Shit," he said softly. "We'll have to start training for policing protests and putting down riots."

Raze agreed with a grunt. "Maybe now Vicious will find me the funds I need to open a fourth SRU team for the *Valiant* and a third for the *Arctis*. We're going to need the manpower."

The elevator arrived and they stepped inside. Raze tapped the button for the floor housing his small apartment in the bachelor section of the officer housing wing. Venom, however, tapped the key for his new quarters on a floor for mated officers.

"How are the new quarters?"

He detected the tiniest hint of envy in his friend's voice. "Spacious. Quiet. The neighborhood's nice," he added. "Menace is right across the hall."

"You lucky bastard! The new guy who took your old place is in the sky corps. I swear he looks to be about ten years old and he is noisy as hell." They both laughed at his description. "I suppose I'll get used to him eventually. I got used to having you and Cipher on either side of me."

Venom snorted. "I don't know how you deal with Cipher's damn video games all hours of the night. When we shared quarters onboard the *Retribution*, I nearly strangled him over it."

"I thought about buying him headphones but I worry about damaging his hearing. He keeps that volume turned up so damn high." Raze smiled wryly. "I'd send him down to the surface to Grab a wife to keep him busy at night but I doubt she'd be much quieter."

Venom tipped his head back and laughed. "Probably not, boss."

The elevator arrived at Raze's floor. He stepped out into the hallway but turned at the last minute. Holding his hand against the door, he held Venom's gaze. "Look, I know I've been giving you so much shit about going down to Grab a bride but I really do hope you find the right woman tomorrow, Venom. I hope you find someone who will make you as happy as Hallie and Naya have made Vicious and Menace."

Venom blinked with surprise. "Thanks, Raze."

Raze whacked his arm twice. "Good luck." He backed away and winked. "Enjoy your honeymoon. Call me if you need pointers."

Venom fought the urge to shoot him the finger. The low hum of the elevator ascending higher and higher in the housing section of the *Valiant* accompanied his busy thoughts. By this time tomorrow, he would have a wife.

The very idea of it sent red-hot frissons of excitement streaking through his chest and gut. A wife. A mate. *His.*

Like most Harcos soldiers, he had never had anything that truly belonged to him. He had been taken away from his family at only five, stripped of everything he owned— even his name—and thrown into the most exclusive military academy to begin his many years of training. Amid the harsh, rigid hell of the academy, he had made many friends, some of them very close, but it wasn't the same as having a real family.

Even though he considered the men he fought beside his blood brothers, their bonds would never come close to the one he would share with the woman he would Grab tomorrow. The bond he would create with his new wife would be one born of love and tenderness, not the fear and loneliness of his childhood.

The promise of earning the right to a mate and family had been the only thing that had kept him going in the darkest days of the Sendarian siege. When the battle had been at its bloodiest and all had seemed lost, he had filled those hours of misery with daydreams of *her*. She was the nameless, faceless creature he'd conjured to comfort him in those awful times.

With her he would build a family. With her he would share his most secret desires for the future, for a life without war and violence. With her he could shed the hardness forced upon him by his position and rank and indulge his softer side. With her he would finally know love.

Venom reached his new quarters and locked the door behind him. Before heading to bed he made one last round of the generous space he had been allotted. He'd spent the afternoon getting everything ready for his new bride.

Naya and Hallie had been kind enough to guide him through the housewares and clothing departments in the retail section of the ship. Both had convinced him to purchase only the bare minimum to make his home inviting and comfortable so that he and his new mate could decorate and outfit their new space together when the time was right. He was glad to have their counsel because he wanted everything to be perfect.

After all the cautionary tales he had heard from newly matched friends, Venom desperately wanted things to go smoothly. As he undressed, his gaze flicked to the locked door of his playroom. In their culture, rough loving was the norm. Harcos women had different body chemistries than their Earth-descendant counterparts and required pain to find pleasure.

Locker-room talk had assured him that these women from Calyx could climax without applying any heat, so to speak, but it appeared that for many of them a rough touch or a little domestic discipline awakened a sensual side that their strict society had repressed.

His heartbeat sped up as vivid images of his woman, bound in his ropes and knots, flashed before his eyes. Would she beg him to take her, to make her come until she passed out from the sheer pleasure of it all? Would she enjoy the silken embrace of a rope harness on her soft skin?

The very idea of it made him hard as a rock. Groin tight and belly rolling with needy heat, he fell back on the wide, long bed and closed his eyes. Soon he would have his answers.

Chapter Two

T HE NEXT MORNING when he stepped off the transport ship and onto the snowy ground, Venom shuddered as a blast of frigid air smacked him in the face. The constant mild climate aboard the *Valiant* had spoiled him. The cold burn of the wind against his skin felt incredibly *real*. He savored the discomfort for a few seconds before flipping up the collar on his jacket and fishing a black knitted cap from his pocket. It was the first time since he'd been issued winter wear that he'd had a need to haul it out of his closet.

Though military regulations allowed the men of his rank to wear their hair longer, he still preferred to keep his head shaved clean. It wasn't much of an issue living on a warship but down here, with this wintry chill, it left him vulnerable to hypothermia.

With the knitted cap firmly in place he joined the throng of uniformed men moving toward the staging area. There were only seventeen of them running today. He and a sky corps pilot had the highest ranks and had been commissioned a day apart, the pilot before him. If they chose the same woman it could get tense.

He had overhead the man talking about wanting a dark-haired woman with full curves. Venom hoped he'd find a woman the complete opposite of the pilot's ideal bride to avoid any sticky situations out on the field. The idea of knocking out the lights of a slightly superior officer didn't sit well with him—but he'd do it if it came down to losing the woman he chose.

As they neared the staging area, Venom noticed an agitated crowd surrounding the fence protecting the spot where a hastily erected stage now stood. Instantly he went on alert. His trained gaze scanned the crowd. They were mostly men in their late teens to early forties. Some of them were probably family members but it was likely there were troublemakers among them.

The Splinters operating on Calyx often chose situations like this to agitate the locals. The terrorist cell had so far evaded the Shadow Force operatives tasked with shutting them down but a few important captures had been made in the last few months. Two months earlier, Venom had been on a rescue mission for Menace's wife that had gone to hell in a matter of seconds. They had managed to save her life but only barely.

She had averted a major crisis by recovering weapons stolen by the Splinters and sold to the Sixers, a gang operating out of The City. She'd also uncovered a nasty little bit of government corruption by finding piles of food supplies in the Sixer hideout. The two groups had been manipulating food supplies and costs in the capitol city and some of the outlying villages to foment revolution. Thankfully it hadn't worked.

But this? Venom eyed the noisy crowd with apprehension. *This could get ugly fast.*

"Ace?" He called out to the pilot leading their men to the starting line of the Grab. Using hand signals, he gave a quick order that the pilot received with a nod. Some of the soldiers in their group glanced back at him for instructions. "Let's keep it tight and keep our hands to ourselves."

A round of *yes sir*s circled the small group. They formed double lines and kept close together as they neared the shouting throng. Venom had no doubt his fellow soldiers would maintain their formation. The discipline drilled into them from childhood would allow nothing else.

Venom's ears rang with the nasty insults hurled their way. His jaw tightened but that was the only outward sign of annoyance he allowed. A fat, rotten fruit splattered on the back of a man in the middle of their group. The soldier tensed but didn't break formation. The man behind him brushed away the foul, soggy flesh. Their heads high and their gazes fixed forward, they kept walking.

As if sensing their group wouldn't be fazed by insults and rotten produce, the angry crowd changed their tactics. They chanted their filth even louder and moved in closer. Venom's hawkish gaze took in the changing environment.

"Easy, men," he said, his voice calm but clear. "Stay on track. Keep moving."

A split second later, someone jumped out of the crowd and slammed into his shoulder. Venom had just enough warning to brace himself for the impact as the heavy weight of his attacker took him to the ground. On instinct, Venom threw up his hand and blocked the falling blows. He put a hand to the man's throat and shoved hard.

Their gazes met and Venom's heart stuttered. Despite the grizzly beard and wild hair, he recognized his assailant. It was Devious, a member of his academy class he hadn't seen in more than ten years. The man had been one of the operatives chosen for the Shadow Force but he had been arrested and tried as a traitor. The transport ship carrying him to the Kovark prison system had been attacked and he had been freed and never seen again.

Until now.

Venom had never believed Devious would side with the Splinters but the evidence against him in his trial had been incredibly convincing. What if it had all been a show? Had it merely been the beginning of a deep cover?

Those questions wouldn't be answered today—or maybe ever. Schooling his features, Venom showed only fury. He punched Devious in the temple and cheek before flipping their positions. They grappled and slapped at each other. Briefly Venom felt Devious' fingers slipping under the cuff of his jacket and brushing the bare skin of his wrist. A moment later, the sensation vanished.

"Dev! Come on, man! Enough!" One of the protestors stepped forward to drag him out from under Venom.

At the same time, one of the soldiers taking part in the Grab snatched Venom by the shoulders and hauled him onto his feet. "Captain!"

"I'm good!" Venom shrugged off the soldier's hands. He kicked snow at Devious and spit on the ground near him. "This traitorous piece of trash isn't worth the disciplinary demerit."

A faint, mischievous smile curved the likely undercover agent's mouth as he wiped dirty snow from his face. "I'd rather be trash than a kidnapping, raping piece of shit like you."

Even though Devious said those things to stay in character Venom still flinched. Was that what people down here thought of them?

"Come on, Captain." The younger man tugged on Venom's arm. "They're waiting for us."

Venom cast one final glance at Devious before turning his back. Carefully and without rousing suspicion, he slid his fingers inside the cuff of his jacket and found the thin square now firmly fixed to the fabric liner. He assumed it was a data device of some kind and cautiously pulled it free to move it to a more secure location in one of the inner pockets of his jacket.

The intel secured, he rejoined the group and marched to the flimsy fence and the too-short gate. The security appalled him. When he reached the *Valiant*, he would let Vicious know how shockingly underprepared The City officials were for a full-scale riot. At the next Grab someone was going to get hurt.

As they filed onto the stage, Venom's issues with the security were overshadowed by his absolute rage at seeing the way the women chosen for this Grab had been prepared for the run. They huddled together in a small space in a muddy pit a few feet below the stage. Infuriated, he took in their shaking bodies clothed in thin cotton shirts and pants. Only a few of them had on proper shoes. They all looked miserable and frightened.

His heart ached at the pitiful sight before him. Was

this how all Grabs were done? He felt sure that wasn't the case. Vicious or Menace would have told him if their women had been penned in like livestock awaiting slaughter.

This wasn't right. On other planets, the populaces viewed the Grabs as a way for women to find a good, honorable husband and a comfortable living—but here? Now the screaming protestors outside the fence made sense.

He searched the shivering group of women for one who appealed to him. Choosing a wife on sight wasn't the most auspicious beginning for a mate bond but it was the only choice he had. He had come this far. He wasn't going back empty-handed.

The tightly packed group shifted as some of the women turned toward the stage for a better look at the men who would be chasing them very soon. A flash of white-blonde hair caught his eye. He was momentarily taken aback by the pale shade. It wasn't very common among the Earth-descendants on Calyx but it was the mark of a full-blooded member of the Harcos race like himself.

He zeroed in on the pale hair. The woman it belonged to found her way to the rear of the crowd. She was a tiny little thing, petite like Vee's Hallie but not as thin. The boxy cut of her bright-red outfit obscured her frame but he could see the faint outline of curves beneath the papery fabric. She wasn't quite as curvaceous as Menace's woman but she had a nice shape.

Their gazes clashed across the wide expanse between them. Her eyes widened with shock and she took three quick steps back. Something primal ignited within him at the sight of her fleeing. Like a prowling cat catching the scent of its prey, he had to chase her now.

Her panicked gaze darted from the stage where a member of The City's council read the official Grab rules and the gate that led to the snowy open field and the forest just beyond it. Fists curled at her sides, she sized him up before taking two quick hops toward the gate.

No doubt she had done the math. There was no way she could evade him. His legs were nearly twice as long as hers and he had on rugged boots. She had on shiny pink shoes that were wholly unsuitable for doing anything outdoors. They looked like the kind of thing a woman would wear with a dress.

He frowned at her lack of preparation and hoped this wasn't a sign of flightiness. Judging by the state of the other women, it seemed more likely that the officials running the Grab hadn't properly advised them what to expect. It was yet another issue he would be reporting to the Grab committee aboard the *Valiant*.

The snap of two blocks of wood slamming together startled him. A man opened the gate and the women rushed out of the pen. The clock started on their short head start. Venom didn't linger on the stage. He hopped down into the muck and trudged to the gate. A handful of the other soldiers and airmen followed him.

With his gaze fixed on the pale-haired woman, he watched her fight through the ankle-deep snow. His gut soured with worry. He glanced at his watch and read the temperature and windchill before hastily calculating the amount of time she had before suffering from frostbite. He made a quick estimation as to how long the women had been exposed to the elements. The numbers he arrived at didn't make him happy.

Around him the other men seemed to be doing the same mental calculations. There were grunts of annoyance as the seconds ticked down to their release from the pen. Antsy and on edge, they fidgeted and flexed to release some of the anxiety.

The moment the blocks clapped together again, Venom shoved off the slick, muddy ground and raced onto the field. He tracked the woman he wanted as he sprinted to intercept her. She was in the middle of the pack but seemed terrible at navigating. From what he could tell, she was angling for a section of the woods clear off the course. His lips twitched with amusement. He'd have to make sure to program her personal tablet with a map app for navigating the ship.

Venom noticed another man closing in on him. He shot the guy a hard look to warn him off the prize he had selected. The airman put up both hands to show he wanted no problems and pointed to a brunette nearing the tree line. "I'm after that one, sir."

"The blonde's mine." He kicked his pace into high gear and started to gain on the woman he wanted. She had disappeared into the dense woods. Panic gripped his gut.

Would she evade him now?

Considering the way she had been unable to even run in a straight line from the starting point to the forest, he doubted it. When he hit the tree line, he slowed his speed just enough to get his bearings. He scanned the snowy forest floor and found her tiny footprints. With a path to follow, he hurried after her.

Another minute into the pursuit, Venom spotted the bright-pink shoes discarded near a tree. His heart leapt into his throat. Didn't she realize how dangerous it was to run barefoot in the damned snow?

"Shit." Growling, he surged forward in search of her. He had to find her quickly and before she got frostbite.

So focused on finding her, Venom missed the telltale sign of a hunter's mark on the trees surrounding him. His boot hit the spongy trigger of a trap a millisecond before his brain alerted him to the mistake he'd made. With a chilling snap, two metal halves of the trap slammed shut on his leg.

"Fuck!" His pained shout ricocheted off the trees. Caught, he fell forward onto his knees and hands. His jaws ground at the excruciating bite compressing his leg. The reinforced webbing and nanofibers of his boots kept the gnarly metal snare from piercing his skin and crippling him but the terrible squeezing grip knocked the air right out of his lungs.

A wave of panic seized him. Despondence quickly overwhelmed him. He had two choices now. He could try to jerk the chain free and bust the trap or he could use the signal flare tucked into the pocket of his pants to call for help. Once the flare was lit he was officially disqualified from the Grab. Even if he had his collar around her neck, they would set her free and send him home empty-handed.

Either way, he had lost his reward. He had lost *her*.

DIZZY GASPED AT the terrible, pained shout that echoed in the forest. Birds scattered as the guttural groan tore the stillness. She slid to a stop in the freezing-cold snow and tried to slow her ragged breaths. Was that a man?

Was it *the* man?

She gulped hard and licked her lips. Glancing back in the direction of the awful sound, she tried to decide what to do. A sky warrior like the rugged, intimidating one who had been eying her would only make a sound like that if he was in big trouble.

The race officials had warned them that people hunted in these wounds. The gun laws out here weren't like the strict zero-tolerance laws in The City. It was rumored everyone in the sticks had a weapon. Maybe the sky warrior chasing her had been shot? Did he need help?

She warred with her conscience only a moment before exhaling roughly and turning back in the direction she'd come. Pressing a hand to her temple, she tried to gain control over the vertigo threatening to swamp her. She hated this damn sickness!

Running and playing had been nearly impossible as a child. She couldn't predict when the waves of nausea and dizziness would hit her but they usually happened at the worst times.

Like right now.

Bracing herself on a tree, Dizzy closed her eyes. She inhaled steadying breaths and performed a series of slow maneuvers that usually helped abate the uncomfortable swirling some. Today, thankfully, it worked. She managed to get moving again without feeling as though she was going to puke or fall flat on her face.

The sounds of a struggle met her ears. She heard rattling chains and grunting. Hiding behind a tree, Dizzy licked her lips and gathered her courage before sliding to the side and peeking out at him.

Seated on the snow, he gripped a long, thick chain in both gloved hands and jerked hard. Her eyes widened at his shocking display of strength. When her gaze moved lower, she gasped at the sight of the awful-looking trap closed around his lower leg. The snow around his leg remained white and pristine, so he wasn't bleeding badly. Even so, the injury he would sustain if the trap wasn't removed quickly would be a terrible one.

Trembling with cold and fear, she stepped out from behind the tree and revealed herself to him. His gaze snapped to her and she took a nervous step back. He let the chain fall from his hands. The tension eased from his face, softening his harsh features and making him look less vicious. They stared at each other for the longest time.

Finally Dizzy found enough courage to move closer to him. Her footsteps crunched on the firm, packed snow. He glanced at her bare feet and scowled. "Why the hell did you take off your shoes?"

Taken aback by his gruff tone, she froze in place. Squeaking with fright, she explained, "The soles were too slippery. I nearly face-planted on a tree stump and decided it wasn't worth the risk."

He grunted. "You'll care when you lose those toes to frostbite."

Her stomach trembled violently and she stared at her frigid feet. "Are you serious? Am I really going to lose my toes?"

His lips twitched with amusement. Was he teasing her? She couldn't tell. With a flick of his fingers, he motioned her closer. "Come here. Let me help you."

She took a few tentative steps toward him. "I think you're the one who needs my help."

His mouth settled into an irritated line. "My leg will keep. Now get over here and let me see your feet."

She frowned at him. "You could be nice about it."

He sighed loudly. "*Please.* Come here before you freeze to death or need your damn feet amputated."

Though that was hardly nice Dizzy felt sure that pushing him wasn't a good idea. She moved as close as she dared. Apparently that wasn't close enough, because the frightening sky warrior snatched her by the waist and hauled her onto his lap. She squealed with surprise and smacked his chest. "Let me go!"

"Not likely." He gathered her even tighter to his warm, hard body. "Now stop fighting and hold still."

"Like hell," she snapped and pushed at the ridiculously strong arm clamped around her waist. It was no use. His superior strength rendered her desperate shoving futile.

"Stop," he said with a laugh. "You're going to fall off me onto the snow. I'm trying to warm you up. Now behave or I'll toss you over my lap and spank that sweet little ass of yours."

Outraged, she gasped at him. "You wouldn't dare!"

"Oh, sugar, I would." His blue-green eyes glinted with excitement and something else, something she couldn't quite pinpoint. Arousal? Yes, she decided finally. The thought of spanking her bottom aroused him. She wasn't sure what to think about that.

His gloved hand moved down her legs to her feet. She couldn't believe how small her foot looked cupped in his massive palm. He brushed the snow and wetness from her skin. "Can you feel your feet?"

She nodded. "Yes."

He pinched and wiggled her toes. "And here?"

"Yes." She curled her toes under and tried to pull her foot away from him but he held tight.

"Unzip that pocket on my left leg." He gestured to the pocket in question with his head. "There is an extra pair of socks in there."

Fingers trembling from cold and nervousness, Dizzy did as instructed. She found the pair of too-big socks and handed them to him. He shook them out and quickly rolled them onto her feet. The tops brushed her knees and the heel was above her ankle but she didn't care how silly they looked. Her feet began to warm almost instantly. "Thank you."

He simply nodded and unzipped another pouch on his strange pants. He withdrew two clear plastic bags and two long, thin strips of plastic. "Evidence bags and zip ties," he explained. "I'm going to use them to secure a barrier around the socks. I don't want them getting soaked with melted snow."

She marveled at all the things he kept in his pants. "Don't these get heavy?"

He flashed a quick smile. The sight of his lips curving in that playful way did crazy things to her belly. "You get used to it."

Ignoring the wild tremors shaking her core, she asked, "Why do you need all these things?"

"I'm SRU." He slid the plastic bags over her feet. "Special Response Unit," he clarified. "We're small, focused, elite teams who respond to highly dynamic environments and situations."

"Dynamic environments?"

"Hostage situations, terrorist threats—dangerous stuff that requires some finesse and understanding." He tightened the zip ties around her ankles. Satisfied with his work, he pulled down the cuffs of the ugly red pants she'd been forced to wear. "What do you do?"

"I'm a seamstress." It seemed a silly occupation compared to his. "I design clothing for a couple of small boutiques in The City. Well—I *used* to design for boutiques."

His gloved hand caressed her cheek. The cold, slightly damp fabric rasped her skin as he slid his fingers under her chin and forced her to meet his unnervingly steady gaze.

"I'm keeping you."

She swallowed hard. Voice barely a whisper, she answered, "I figured."

Rather generously, he said, "My leg is still caught in this damn trap. If you really want to be free, if you truly want to reach that safe zone, you'd better get up now and start running." He pointed in a direction to the far right. "It's that way, honey. You were headed in the wrong direction."

She blushed with embarrassment. Map-reading wasn't a skill she had ever needed in The City. "Oh."

He pushed the long wisps of her chin-length bangs behind her ear. "What's your name?"

"Dizzy."

His eyebrows rose with surprise. "Dizzy? Is that your real name?"

She shook her head. "It's the only one I'll answer to. What's your name?"

"Venom."

"Really?" She studied his face to see if he was playing with her. "Are you serious?"

He chuckled softly. "Yes."

"Is that your *real* name?"

He parroted her earlier reply. "It's the only one I'll answer to, Dizzy."

Hearing her name in his gruff, low voice made her tummy flip-flop. She'd always been attracted to gentler, normal-sized men, the types who worked in the downtown government offices and had degrees from Capitol University. They had soft hands and easy smiles.

But Venom? Well, he was the complete opposite of the men she usually dated but something about him excited her more than any other man ever had. He had the harsh features so common in Harcos men. The square jaw, the straight nose, the hulking frame—he personified the race of alien warriors so perfectly.

Secure in his brawny arms, she allowed herself to imagine what it would be like to wake up every morning to
see those strangely hued eyes staring right back at her. Her
belly clenched tightly at the realization that this giant sky
warrior would be the one to take her virginity. Would he
be gentle? Would he show her pleasure?

White-hot currents sizzled through her core as his
gloved hand skimmed her jaw and neck. He cupped her
nape and gazed into her eyes. "What are you thinking
about, sugar?"

She dropped her gaze and tried to get a hold of her
crazy emotions. Clearing her throat, she said, "That we
really need to get that trap off your leg."

Before he could change the subject, she squirmed out
of his grasp and knelt down next to the gnarly trap. She
winced with sympathy as she moved her face closer and
studied the contraption. "Considering you've been chat-
ting me up for a few minutes, I suppose the injury isn't
life-threatening."

Venom snorted. "No, it's just painful. My boots are reinforced on the sides to prevent projectile and shrapnel
wounds."

She ran her finger along the weird fabric. The woven
fibers astounded her. "I think all that tugging and jerking
you were doing when I found you may have weakened the
fabric. The teeth of this thing are deep inside the boot."

"Yeah," he agreed gruffly. "I can feel it scratching at
my skin."

"Sorry." With her fingers on the cold metal now, she

followed the curve of the trap to the bottom. "Okay, I see the release mechanism."

"I tried it." He started to unzip his jacket. "I think it's stuck."

"Hmm," she hummed and bent even closer. Her fingers were smaller than his so she was able to wiggle them firmly into the spot near the mechanism. She pressed it a few times but nothing happened. When she pulled her fingers back, they were coated with rust. "I think I've found our problem."

Venom slipped out of his jacket and handed it to her. "Put this on."

"Thanks." She didn't even try to turn down his offer. The cozy, heated embrace of the jacket instantly soothed her shaking limbs. Venom reached over to zip up the front and turned down the collar. The arms were too long so she shoved them up around her elbows so she could work. "Do you have a screwdriver or a knife in your pockets?"

He shook his head. "We aren't allowed to bring any types of weapons to the Grab."

She slid down for a better look at the stuck mechanism. An idea formed. She tugged a hairpin from the spot just behind her ear and forced it open and flat. "I think if I can just clear away some of this rust…"

"Be careful," he urged.

"I am." She slid flat onto her belly for the best view and worked the pin into the tight space where the rust had accumulated. After a minute of scraping and stabbing, she pushed hard on the release mechanism but it wouldn't work.

Venom shoved aside her hand. "Let me try. Sit back first. Please," he added as an afterthought. "I don't want this thing to spring open and slam your face."

She touched her nose and grimaced. "Good call."

After she'd skittered out of the way, Venom sat up and shifted his weight. Gritting his teeth, he shoved hard against the release button. It took four tries before the trap finally jerked free. Venom sat back with a relieved exhale while Dizzy hurried closer to pry the jagged metal teeth from his boot. Small drops of blood dripped onto the snow as she pulled the trap out of his ruined boot.

"Are you okay? You're bleeding!"

"It's a minor wound." He leaned forward and unzipped the side panel of his boot. Sure enough, his sock was ripped and bloodied. Ugly scratches marked his skin but there were no puncture wounds. Satisfied by what he had seen, he zipped up his boot.

"I'll live."

Freed from the trap, Venom swiftly moved to his knees. Even in that position he towered over here. The full reality of her new situation hit her. This man, this blue-eyed giant, owned her now. She scampered backward and put some distance between them.

Venom held up his hands to show he meant her no harm. "Don't be afraid of me, Dizzy."

"I don't want to fear you but you're so—"

"Big?"

She nodded. "You could really hurt me."

"I don't want to hurt you."

"What…what do you want with me?"

"What do you want with me?"

She frowned at the way he had so neatly turned the question around to her. "I'm not the one chasing a woman through the forest."

He smiled. "No, but you came back to help me. If you'd really wanted to get away, you would have thanked your lucky stars that I'd been trapped and kept on running. Why did you come back, Dizzy?"

She swallowed hard and considered his query. Finally she admitted, "I don't have anywhere else to go."

The smile faded from his face. He crawled toward her, lifting his knees and planting them closer to her. His movements pushed aside the powdery snow and left trailing troughs. "Go with me. I'll take care of you, Dizzy. I'll provide a nice, comfortable home for you and all the perks of being an officer's wife. You'll want for nothing if you come with me."

The idea of belonging to this man, of having someone who cared for her and only her, tempted Dizzy a great deal. Since her mother's death, her father had been so forlorn and distant. There were times he looked at her as if he hated her, as if he resented that she had survived and her mother hadn't. Lately he only came around when he needed money or a favor.

Thinking of the way her father had betrayed and used her, she asked, "In exchange for what, Venom?" Her face grew hot as she found the courage to ask, "If I don't...I mean...if I withhold sex will you withhold food or clothing from me?"

His aghast expression reassured her more than his

words. There was no faking that offended reaction. "I
don't know what you know about Harcos men. Considering that protesting crowd outside the fence back there I
can only assume you've heard the very worst, but I swear
to you now it's not true. I would never punish a woman in
that way." She remembered what he had said earlier. "But
you said you would spank me."

Amusement gleamed in his strikingly hued eyes. "And
I probably will someday but not as a punishment."

"Why else would you spank someone?"

"Foreplay." He tilted his head. "Have none of your
lovers ever smacked your bottom in the heat of the moment?"

Face flaming now, she was forced to admit, "I've never
had a lover." Realizing how pathetic that sounded at nearly
twenty-three, she hastily amended, "I've had long-term
relationships. I've just never…you know."

"I see." He regarded her carefully. "May I ask why?"

She found the courage to meet his curious stare. "It's
not safe."

"Safe? You mean disease?"

She shook her head. "I mean that an unmarried mother doesn't last long in my world. The odds are even worse
for a child born out of wedlock. It wasn't worth the risk."

Venom crawled even closer, backing her right up
against a wide tree trunk. He pressed his hands to the bark
on either side of her head and pinned her in place. Lowering his head, he nuzzled her face. The very touch of his
skin against hers left her trembling. White-hot arcs
sparked through her chest and heat pooled low in her belly

as she inhaled his masculine scent.

"There's no risk with me." His rough, husky voice washed over her like sunshine, warming her right to her very core.

Gazing up into those pale eyes of his, she gulped. "I'm not so sure about that."

His mouth slanted in a dangerously sexy smile. "I'm not half as scary as I look."

She considered how frightening he was. "That's still pretty scary."

His low, rumbling chuckle spilled over her. Running his gloved fingers under her chin, he tilted her head back so she couldn't avoid his intense gaze. "We aren't in any rush. When I think it's the right time I'll take you nice and easy."

When *he* thought it was the right time? She started to remind him who made decisions about her body but he took her by surprise by capturing her mouth.

As if to prove he could be gentle when it mattered, Venom claimed her mouth with the most tender of kisses. Her eyelids fluttered as his skilled lips moved against hers. Gripping the sleeves of his uniform shirt, she held on for dear life as he deepened the kiss. His tongue swiped hers just briefly before retreating and leaving her desperate for more.

Vibrating with excitement and need, Dizzy tried to catch her breath. Had she ever been kissed like that? That was a resounding no.

Deciding she needed to kiss him again for comparison—you know, just to be sure—she found the courage to place her hands against his broad chest. She wasn't nearly tall enough to reach him, not even kneeling as they were, so she gripped the front of his shirt and gave him a little tug.

His lips twitched with laughter but he lowered his face, dipping down to meet her seeking mouth. She tried to take control of this kiss but the moment her tongue flicked out to touch the seam of his lips, Venom growled and wrapped his brawny arms around her. He swallowed her gasp of surprise as he darted his tongue against hers and cupped the back of her head.

The commanding strength of him left her shaking inside. She grew very aware of how easily he could overpower and hurt her—but something about the way he held her convinced Dizzy that he would never harm her. He cradled her so gently in his strong arms, almost as if he feared breaking her.

Though his needful, insistent kiss stole her breath away it wasn't rough. He took his time tasting her mouth and seemed to relish the experience. She began to wonder how long it had been since he had kissed a woman. As harsh as their society was reputed to be, she doubted there was much time for romance or sweetness up there in those big sky ships.

Almost reluctantly, Venom eased off the kiss. He pulled back just enough to stare down into her eyes. "I'll be a good mate to you." He sensually nibbled her lower lip, biting down just enough to make her throb in all the right places. "I'll show you pleasure unlike any you've ever imagined, Dizzy."

She didn't doubt that for a second. He had only kissed her and already she tingled with such incredible arousal.

"Give me your answer. Right now. Right here. Will you take my collar?"

"Yes," she answered instantly. There was nothing for her in The City but a nasty loan shark and a debt waiting to be collected. After a kiss like that and a glimpse into a sensual world she had always wanted to experience, she wanted to know all the secrets he promised.

Venom produced a thin white leather collar from the front pocket on his uniform shirt. He pushed aside his jacket and swept her hair out of the way. She knew the moment he spotted the scars on her neck. His brow furrowed. "What's this, sugar?"

Self-conscious, she touched the bumpy patches that had been hidden from view. "I was wounded in the embassy bombing."

Shock tightened his features. He slid his gloved fingertip along one of the scarred ridges. "You're lucky to be alive."

"That's what they tell me."

He slipped the collar around her neck and buckled it. "Too tight?"

She shook her head. "Do I have to wear this all the time?"

"You can take it off when you shower."

He said it as if that was a big concession. Not wanting to argue with him right now, she decided she would bring up the issue later and try to find a better compromise. Wearing this thing around the clock was a no-go for her.

Already the stiff edge of the collar rubbed against her scars in the most irritating way.

Venom rose to his full height. Mouth agape, she tipped her head back and stared up at him. Holy shit but he was tall! When he turned his back on her and crouched down, she frowned with confusion. A second later, he instructed, "Hop on my back. I'm carrying you to the processing station."

The heat radiating from his huge body enticed her. Though she felt a bit ridiculous, she did as she was told. There was no way she could walk in the makeshift shoes he had crafted out of socks and plastic bags.

When he reached up and tugged her hands away from his shoulders, she followed his lead and loosely looped them around his neck. She wound her short legs around his trim waist. He slipped his hand back and gave her bottom a reassuring pat. "I won't drop you."

"I trust you."

His lips brushed her hand. "That's a good start."

Though Venom was intimidating and little more than a stranger to her, Dizzy had made her choice. She had entered the Grab to escape her fate as Fat Pete's plaything and fallen into this sky warrior's welcoming hands. All she could do now was hold on tight and try to make the best of it.

Chapter Three

THE MOMENT THEY cleared the processing station and had Dizzy's passport and documents in order, Venom grabbed her small suitcase from the luggage area and carted her to the waiting transport ship. There were already a handful of couples finding their seats in the rows lining the sides of the ship. He found a spot in the corner and lowered her to the floor. Her slight weight had been easy to bear and in truth he rather liked having her pressed so tightly to his body.

A medic hurried over with a heated blanket. Venom quickly removed the slightly damp jacket and wrapped the hot blanket around her petite body before pushing her into an empty seat. Pointing to her feet, he told the medic, "Check those. I'm worried she may have injured herself running through the snow barefoot."

Frowning with concern, the medic hastily cut off the bags and socks with trauma shears he ripped free from a loop on his pants. He scrutinized her pink feet, pushing her toes apart and pinching them to check her capillary refill. Dizzy's teeth had finally stopped chattering so she had no trouble answering the medic's questions.

Another medic brought Venom a protein bar, two bottles of water and a pair of socks. "I cannot believe how

poorly prepared these women were for the Grab." The
second medic's disgust was evident on his taut face. "Their
council should be ashamed for sending them out there like
that. We're just damn lucky I was able to scrounge up
enough extra socks between you men and the pilots."

"I appreciate it." Venom had the utmost respect for
the medics. Though they were far from frontline combat
now these men had all proven themselves in battle, often
risking their own lives to reach wounded soldiers. It didn't
surprise him in the least that the medics had gone through
every gear bag and pocket on the ship in search of clean,
dry socks for these women.

When Dizzy was given a thumbs-up, Venom pushed a
bottle of water and the energy bar into her hands. He
dropped his bottle of water on the seat next to her and
knelt down in front of her to put the new pair of socks on
her cold feet.

"I can do that."

"I'm sure you can." He pointed to the food and water.
"Eat. Now."

Her pouty lips settled into an irritated line. "Are you
always so bossy?"

"Yes."

Even though she narrowed her eyes at him, she
couldn't stop the little smile tugging at the corners of her
mouth. With a dramatic sigh of annoyance, she opened
her bottle of water and took a long, slow drink. She didn't
try to stop him from rolling the new socks onto her feet.
He fought the urge to caress her soft skin or stroke his
hands up her bare calves. This wasn't the place to explore

her body—the body that now belonged to him.

Settling into the seat next to her, Venom tried to gain control over his skyrocketing lust. When she had admitted to never having a lover he had been deeply and shockingly affected. He had never been the kind of man who cared about that sort of thing. There were some men who would only accept a so-called pure wife but he wasn't one of them. It hadn't ever made sense to him that a man was expected to be skilled in the arts of lovemaking but a woman was expected to come to her husband as pure as snow.

He sneaked a glance at Dizzy. She was just so damn beautiful! Wisps of pale-blonde hair curved around her jaw and neck. Warm and cozy inside the heated blanket, she'd gotten some color back into her face. The pink shade highlighted the apples of her cheeks. Those full lips and her honey-brown eyes enthralled him.

Soon, he would have her small body pinned beneath his in their bed. He'd stare down into those big brown eyes before claiming her mouth, before claiming her. Faced with the knowledge that he would be the first man to know her body, Venom would be a liar if he said he wasn't excited by the prospect of sharing something special with her.

But the fear of frightening or hurting her struck him cold.

The women from Calyx were so small compared to the women from the other planets where his people had initiated Grab schemes. On the *Valiant*, they had run into problems with medical care because of pharmaceutical formulations. As far as he knew, those issues had been resolved.

But their differences in size made him a little nervous. Vicious had been frank and honest when Venom had worked up the courage to inquire about how things worked behind closed doors. The general had assured him that with a little patience and a hell of a lot of foreplay things went beautifully.

Venom glanced at Dizzy again. She deserved a tender introduction to the pleasures to be found in his bed. Though he preferred to be in total control in the bedroom, he would be willing to hand her the reins for their first few weeks together. That meant keeping the door to the playroom locked. One look at the ropes and cuffs and she would probably have a panic attack. He wanted a happy wife, not one who fled every time he walked through the front door.

Her nervous gaze jumped around the ship's interior. Wanting to ease her anxiety, he reached for her hand. He had taken off his gloves and tucked them into his jacket while she was being checked by the medics. Feeling her silky skin beneath his rough fingertips made the simple action of grasping her hand feel so intimate.

"The display mounted up there tells us how long we have until liftoff." He pointed to the screen in question. "Since this is your first time flying and going into space, you'll probably want to stop drinking that water now." He eyed the half-empty bottle. "Your stomach is likely to rebel."

Her eyebrows arched. "Is ascending that rough?"

He shook his head. "Not in these transport ships but your body isn't used to the extreme forces. There will be a few minutes of discomfort as we climb higher and higher. When we bust through the upper atmosphere you'll experience ten or twenty seconds of weightlessness before the gravity boosters kick online. If you get sick grab one of these." He gestured to the puke bags tucked into the overhead compartments. "Once we're in flight our pilot Zephyr will probably open the observation window. You might like the view."

Instead of fright on her face, he saw only curiosity. "It must be amazing to see the things you've seen and to experience the things you've experienced."

He started to tell her that she wouldn't like to relive most of the awful things he had seen during his career but he stopped himself. She had probably never traveled farther than the woods where she had been Grabbed. He'd crossed the galaxy and visited dozens of different worlds, some beautifully lush and tropical and others frighteningly cold and harsh. He had seen alien life forms with his two human eyes that she likely had never even seen in books.

"Now that you're mine, you're going to experience all sorts of amazing and wild things."

A coy smile played upon her mouth. "Is that a come-on or a promise?"

He chuckled at her teasing. "Both."

The screen blinked with a one-minute warning. A member of the flight crew walked up and down the aisles checking seat belts and ensuring that anything that might go flying during weightlessness had been secured. The crewman tapped a button to alert the pilots things were a-okay and took his seat.

Beside him Dizzy gripped the arm of her chair and his hand. She put on a brave face but he sensed the prospect of rocketing off her planet's surface into the great unknown with a stranger might have finally hit her. The sounds of sniffling and muffled sobs met his ears as other women began to cry. Whether it was from the fear of flying or the stress of their new situations he couldn't say. Either way his heart ached for them.

Sure, he looked like a mean bastard but like most men of his race, he had a serious soft spot when it came to women. Harcos men tended to breed sons more than daughters, even when mixing with other human races from around the galaxy. Females were few enough that they were considered precious. From birth Harcos men were taught to respect and honor and protect them.

The screen blinked yellow and then red before turning bright green. Dizzy's fingers tightened around his. He caught her gaze and shot her a reassuring smile as the transport ship rose slowly and vertically. As it gained speed it tilted until the front of the vehicle pointed toward the sky. The ship rattled harder and harder as the vibrations from their fast ascent shuddered through it.

With her head firmly against the seatback, Dizzy clamped her eyes shut. He watched her face for any signs of trouble. When she grimaced his gut clenched with worry. She lifted a hand to her left ear and began to rub the spot.

"Swallow," he urged. "It will help your ears pop."

"It's not that." Her voice was barely audible over the rushing burn of the thrusters shoving them higher and higher into the atmosphere.

She ripped her other hand free from his and massaged both ears. He noticed the way she swallowed rapidly, her throat moving in rhythmic bursts as she tried to lessen the pain that was surely stabbing at her brain. Feeling useless, he rubbed her thigh through the heated blanket. "It will only be a few more minutes."

When her hand moved to her throat and her eyes flew open in a panic, he reacted without hesitation. Grabbing one of the sick bags, he flicked it open and shoved it to her mouth. She wasn't the only woman making use of one. The terrible sounds of sick women filled the cabin. It wasn't the most romantic start for the new couples.

As she retched into the bag Venom glanced toward the opposite seats where one of the medics now sat. He caught the man's eye. The medic nodded and pointed to the sign. Venom read his silent message clearly. As soon as they were in space, he'd come check on Dizzy.

Eventually Dizzy pushed away the bag. He secured the top and tucked it into the refuse slot in the overhead compartment before grabbing a wet wipe. As he dabbed at her mouth she continued to rub her ears and grimace. The expression on her face told him she was in an immense amount of pain.

An uncommon amount of pain, he realized with a thud. Something wasn't quite right. Glancing at the medic, he noticed the man wore a concerned look. They both checked the screen. Any second now, they would lose gravity. It would be another minute or two before Dizzy could get any medical attention.

But when the moment of weightlessness occurred, Dizzy's eyes rolled back in her head and she went totally slack. The tight seat belt harness caught her full weight as she slumped forward.

"Dizzy!" Venom slid his arm under her sagging body and lifted her into a sitting position. Totally unconscious, she didn't respond. Panic seized him. "Dizzy!"

Floating with finesse, the medic had disregarded the sign and swam through the air. He gripped the bar lining the ceiling as the gravity sign began to blink. He caught his full weight and swung his feet for a soft landing.

The moment they regained gravity, Venom was out of his seat belt. "What's wrong with her?"

"That's what we're going to find out, Captain." Exceedingly calm, the medic called for backup. Still unconscious, Dizzy was carefully taken out of her seat and placed on a stretcher. Venom followed the medics as they carted her to the small exam-and treatment area off the main cabin. He knew better than to ask stupid questions or get in the way of the medics. Standing back, he chewed his thumb and watched the men assess her.

For a brief moment, she opened her eyes and struggled against the straps holding her onto the exam table. Venom stepped forward and put a hand on her shoulder. "Sugar, it's okay. Be still. Let them help you."

One of the medics flashed a light in her eyes. That was when Venom noticed her eyes were literally jumping as they tracked the movement of the light beam. He had never seen anything like it.

"Hit her with a sedative and an antiemetic." The lead medic gave his order and then turned to Venom. "It's vertigo but I suspect there are other complications we can't see. She needs a full scan." He touched the scars under her collar. "Any idea what this is?"

"She said she was in the embassy bombing."

"Shit." The medic punched the video communication link. "I need to speak to the captain."

A moment later Zephyr's face appeared on the screen. "What's wrong? They're telling me one of the brides is sick."

"Affirmative. How close is the *Mercy*?"

"Not close enough," Zeph replied. "They pulled the medical installation out of its lower orbit for repairs and maintenance. The *Valiant* and her medical bay are closer but it's going to be two hours at least. I'll ask for emergency clearance for docking but it could be three hours if we don't get it. Do I need to radio for a dart?"

Venom's chest tightened. The darts were small, incredibly fast spacecraft used for immediate evacuations of critically ill patients.

"Negative," the medic replied. "Her vital signs are good. We'll keep her sedated. She has a stable airway. I would have preferred a quick transport to the *Mercy* but it's not serious enough for a dart crew."

"Keep me updated."

"Will do, Captain." The medic tapped the screen and shot Venom an apologetic look. "Hope you didn't have big plans for your honeymoon."

Venom didn't find the man's attempt at humor very funny. Sick with worry, he stared at Dizzy's unconscious form on the too-big exam table. He was taken back to the memories of Menace's wife Naya bleeding out on that dirty warehouse floor. After she had survived a tricky and very long surgery, she had looked so frail and pale in the hospital bed aboard the *Mercy*. He didn't like the thought that his first few hours with Dizzy had required medical intervention. He prayed this wasn't an omen for their relationship.

After the longest two hours and seventeen minutes of his life, Venom followed Dizzy's stretcher into the *Valiant*'s infirmary. To his surprise Vicious and Raze waited in the lobby area. He was glad to have his friends close by when the medics forced him to stay behind as they wheeled her into a trauma room for proper assessment.

Raze grasped his shoulder. "Are you all right?"

Venom nodded. "I'm worried about her."

"From what I could see, she's a pretty little thing. What's her name?"

"Dizzy."

Raze's lopsided smile eased some of Venom's tension. "Dizzy? Really? And she has vertigo?'

Venom groaned and rubbed the back of his neck. "I didn't even think that's why her family gave her that nickname. I just assumed it was short for some longer name."

Vicious chuckled and slapped his back. "She'll be fine. We can treat simple ailments like that. If her people weren't so stubborn and would accept our offers of hospitals and clinics, she could have had that fixed as a child."

Vicious wasn't saying what they were all thinking. The rules of the Grab required medically defective brides who couldn't be fixed to be dropped back on their worlds. That specific clause was written so broadly and could be interpreted so many different ways that it caused problems for quite a few couples. Vicious and Hallie were currently among them.

As far as Venom knew Hallie still hadn't conceived. He had heard from Menace that the pair had been dragged in for testing. Apparently Vicious had been so furious about the way it upset Hallie that he'd threatened to retire immediately if anyone on the medical advisory board so much as looked at Hallie the wrong way again. There were rumors that General Thorn, a five-star general and member of the war council, had intervened and gotten the couple a waiver.

Venom wouldn't be that lucky. He didn't have friends and mentors on high like Vicious. If Dizzy couldn't be fixed…

Fuck that. His thoughts turned angry. They would have to take her from his cold, dead hands. He had claimed her. He had collared her. He wanted *her*.

Clearly trying to keep his thoughts occupied, Raze asked, "How was it down there? Cold as hell?"

"Freezing," Venom replied and followed his friends to a seating area. He glanced at Vicious. "I'm going to write an official report for you and the rest of the Grab committee. What I saw down there today was appalling."

Vicious' jaw tightened. "Tell me."

As he described the women in their thin outfits and without proper footwear, Vicious' expression grew dark. Hearing about the poor security didn't make Raze very happy.

"I told you something like that was going to happen, Vee." Raze shook his head. "I know you all think I'm paranoid and a worrier but that populace down there is ripe for rebellion. Once we start building this new base the shit is going to hit the fan.

Repeatedly. We have to increase our SRU teams and get our military police better trained in riot procedures."

Duly chastised, Vicious nodded. "Come to my office in the morning. Clear your schedule. We'll get on this immediately."

Risk, a trauma surgeon who had worked the front lines for years, came out of the exam area and approached them. Venom jumped to his feet. "How is she, Risk? Can you fix her?"

"Calm down, Venom. You'll get your honeymoon. Just not tonight. We're prepping her for surgery. It will be minimally invasive—lasers and sound waves." Risk touched his ear and the area behind it. "We'll go in here and work on the vestibular system. If you want to see the scans I can walk you through the procedure."

Venom waved his hand. "No, I trust you to do what's necessary."

The surgeon pulled a white bride's collar from the front pocket of his scrubs. "We had to take it off for the procedure. It's an airway issue."

Venom gripped the collar. He shot Risk a warning

look. "Your men better not get any funny ideas about my woman. I'll kick every ass in this place if one of you tries to claim her while she's uncollared."

Risk held up his hands. "Easy, Venom. We have no intention of taking your bride. Everyone knows that she belongs to you."

Venom nodded but he wasn't totally convinced. The competition to get on the Grab lists every quarter was harsh. The rules of their society made it possible for any man to steal away a new bride within the first thirty days that she was on the ship.

"I'm having them scan this area on her neck." Risk touched the spot on his own skin. "The suturing there isn't as primitive as what I'd expect from someone on her planet. I have a feeling she's been treated by us before."

"It wouldn't surprise me." Venom noticed Raze and Vicious' confused looks. "She said she was caught in the embassy bombing. I think she took some shrapnel to the neck and shoulder."

"That's what it looks like to me," the surgeon agreed. He extended a tablet and a stylus. "You know the drill. Scan your chip and sign if you give consent for her treatment."

Venom did what was necessary. "How long will it take?"

"We're waiting on some blood test results to check for any allergies she may have to our pharmaceuticals." He glanced at his watch. "I'd say you've got a three-hour wait before you're called back to recovery and four before they get her into a private room. I don't expect that she'll need to stay in the hospital longer than a night."

Venom didn't like the idea of being separated from her for so long but there was nothing else to be done. "If she wakes up before I see her, let her know I'm waiting. I don't want her to think I've abandoned her up here in this strange new place."

Risk's expression softened. "I'll make sure she knows you're here."

Alone with Vicious and Raze, Venom sank back down onto his seat. He tucked the collar back into the front pocket of his shirt. His fingers brushed something small and hard. So consumed with worry for Dizzy, he'd totally forgotten about his run-in with Devious. Hell!

Meeting Vicious' gaze, he said, "Man, this place sure could use a visit from the janitor."

Surprise contorted the general's face. Understanding the silent code for the Shadow Force operatives on the *Valiant* and the guard ship *Arctis*, he said, "Well, there have been some issues with the cleaning crews since Orion shuffled the order of things aboard the *Valiant*."

Venom got the message. Terror, the head Shadow Force operative in this sector, had been punted to the *Arctis* eight weeks earlier. Orion, the sky fleet admiral and the commander of the *Valiant*, had been furious when Terror had contravened a direct order to carry out one of his secret missions. The admiral had thrown Terror off the ship under threat of venting him into space if he didn't comply.

"Let me call down to the janitor's station and see what we can do." Vicious rose from his seat and left in search of a secure connection. As far as Venom knew, Pierce—another covert operative—was still aboard the *Valiant*. He had caught a glimpse at the man a few weeks earlier.

Raze shot him a questioning look. Even though he trusted Raze with his life he didn't dare divulge whom he had seen or what he had been given. "I can't, Raze."

"I understand." And he did. There would be no weirdness or bad blood between them over this secret.

When Vicious returned, he lowered his voice. "They're sending a cleaning crew. It might be a while." He checked his watch and frowned. "I wish I could stay, Venom, but I have a meeting with Orion in twenty minutes." Vicious squeezed his shoulder. "Keep me updated on your bride. I hope the surgery goes smoothly." With a smile, he added, "Expect a dinner invitation from Hallie in the next few days. You know how she is about these things."

"Thank you for coming. I appreciate it."

After Vicious left, Raze drew Venom into a conversation about how they would conduct riot training and which soldiers might be good for SRU recruitment. His mind drifted from the task at hand to Dizzy. Was she in pain? Were the surgeons going to be successful? Would she suffer with troubling side effects?

"Ven?" Raze spoke loudly and broke through his thoughts.

"Sorry. What did you say?"

"I asked what you thought about extending an invite to Mayhem to try out for the team."

Venom was taken aback by the suggestion. "Has he

been cleared for duty?"

Raze nodded. "I watched his fitness trials last month. He's in exceptionally good shape. That bionic leg is amazing. Unless he's wearing shorts, you'd never know he lost the real one in an explosion."

Venom rubbed his jaw. "He'd be the first amputee on an SRU team. Our work environments are less than ideal. Do you think he'd be at a disadvantage?"

Raze shrugged. "Everyone on the team has strengths and weaknesses. I don't think Mayhem would put us at risk if that's what you're asking. He's a damn good soldier. He's fought like hell to get cleared for active combat duty again and should be given the chance to show what he's capable of doing. He proved himself at Sendaria. I wouldn't think twice about having him on the Alpha squad."

"I wouldn't either. I worry about the others in SRU. They might not be so accepting. The competition is fierce to make our teams. Mayhem will have to meet or exceed the standards of every other man who tries out for a spot. We can't have the men whispering behind his back that he got special treatment because of his leg."

"He won't," Raze promised. "He'll understand that we'll be riding him harder than the others. He knows what's at stake for all the other injured soldiers suing to be allowed back into combat duty rotations. I have no doubt that he'll excel at every level of the tryouts and training."

"Then let's put him on our shortlist."

Movement near the entrance of the medical bay caught Venom's attention. He spotted Pierce pushing a janitor's cart. Dressed in green coveralls with his cap pulled low, he was easy to overlook—and that was just the way these Shadow Force guys liked it.

Because of his SRU work Venom knew most of the operatives working this sector. They often overlapped on missions and shared intel but their identities were a secret he closely guarded.

Venom picked up an empty coffee cup that had been left on one of the tables in the waiting area. He carried it to the trash can in the corner but purposely dropped it. When he bent down to retrieve it, he swiftly pulled the memory device from his pocket and tucked it into the empty paper cup. He dropped it in the trash and returned to his seat. Briefly he met Pierce's gaze before glancing to Raze.

"So what do you think about increasing our team sizes by two men?" Raze stretched out his legs and carried on their conversation. There were enough medics and other soldiers filing in and out of the infirmary to require them to keep up appearances while Pierce cleaned the lobby.

"If we're going to be handling crowd control or heading off riots, we're going to need the extra bodies." Venom ignored Pierce's progress and turned his full attention toward Raze. As the second-in-command of the SRU in this sector Venom's opinion mattered. "After what I saw today I'm concerned about the next Grab. There were enough citizens outside that flimsy fence to cause serious issues. Zeph and his ship's crew would have been able to cover us from above and provide a place for retreat but it would have been tense until more ships arrived."

"It may be time for us to take control of security at the Grabs." Raze looked less than excited by the prospect.

"It's going to agitate them. It's probably what the Splinters want."

"Probably," Raze agreed, "but we can't put innocent women in harm's way and our soldiers and airmen too. They need to know they're protected. And frankly I don't give a shit what the people down there think. They're getting a hell of a lot more out of our treaty than we are. Think of the small number of brides they've sent to us and the huge amount of resources we've sunk into protecting their backward little planet." Raze shook his head. "To hell with their feelings."

Venom eyed his friend with some surprise. "No, no, no, Raze. Tell me how you *really* feel."

Near the trash can, Pierce snorted while changing out the bag and wiping down the silver can. Venom had to give it to him. When he played a part he played it well.

"All I'm saying—" Raze stopped as Risk entered the waiting room.

Venom leapt to his feet. Even though Dizzy's procedure was probably considered minor his stomach clenched like a fist. He hated that her first experiences with him were so miserable. "Doc?"

"The procedure went perfectly," Risk said with a reassuring smile. "We inserted some drains to keep fluid from building up again in that area. We'll want her to come in periodically for scans to ensure that she's not forming new calcium deposits."

"Is she still sedated? She's not feeling any pain?"

Risk shook his head. "She's out like a light. We'll keep her sedated until it's safe for her to sit up and move around." He checked his watch. "Probably eight or nine hours.

Feel free to grab lunch or run errands. We'll take care of her."

"No." Venom's hand brushed the pocket holding her collar. "I'm staying with her."

"I'll grab some things for you from your quarters," Raze offered. "I'm your emergency contact, right? I have access to your new space so it's no problem. I'll get Cipher to bring you lunch so you can stay with your bride."

"Thanks, man."

"No problem." Raze backed away. "I'll be back in an hour or so."

When Raze was out of earshot, Risk stepped closer. "When we scanned your wife's neck we found some of our synthetic blood vessels in place. They're all in perfect working condition so don't worry about that. We ran the serial numbers. It looks like she was patched up on the *Indefatigable*."

Venom frowned. "That's the warship we replaced when we were deployed here."

The surgeon nodded. "They were the ship in orbit when the bombing happened. One of the medics working in the OR was on that rotation. He remembers about two dozen citizens of The City being brought onboard for treatment. He didn't remember her but it was a mass casualty incident so that's not unusual."

"I'm surprised the officials in The City allowed their

wounded to be evacuated and treated."

"That's the thing," the surgeon's tone grew almost conspiratorial. "All of the victims who were brought here worked at the embassy or had a connection to some of our men stationed there."

"But Dizzy would have been just a teenager. She couldn't possibly have worked there."

"Exactly," the surgeon said. "When we ran her blood samples, the computer kicked back a rather surprising result."

His heart sped up as he feared the very worst. "And what was that?"

"Half of her DNA is Harcos. *She's* one of *us*."

Venom stared at Risk as he tried to process that information. "But that's—"

"Impossible?" Risk shrugged. "Before today I would have agreed. I mean, she's much too old to have been part of the current Grab scheme on her planet. Clearly her mother had access to our men two decades ago. The Harcos blood in her comes from her father's side."

Did she know what she was? Surely she would have mentioned it in the woods. He had glimpsed her passport and the photos of her parents. The man in the picture didn't look anything like a Harcos male. He had the smaller, leaner stature of these Earthdescendant humans.

"Her things were on the stretcher. We've got them in the private room they're prepping for her stay tonight. Maybe there are some answers in there. It's possible she has a father among our active ranks or our retired servicemen. He might not even know she exists. She might even have property rights."

The doc's statement caused a flutter of panic in Venom's core. What if she wasn't eligible for the Grab? Any man who had served could exempt his daughters from the ritual. Would her father—if he was still alive—try to break their union? Venom's gut soured.

"Obviously I won't say anything to anyone, Venom. The confidentiality of the medical branch protects the two of you. She'll have to be told of the results of her blood test but that doesn't meant the two of you have to share it with everyone else."

Venom nodded and thanked Risk for fixing Dizzy. As he waited for a medic to escort him back to the recovery area, Venom tried to make sense of this new piece of information. He didn't know what to do about it. Dizzy had said she had nowhere else to go but if she had a father out there somewhere...

He couldn't bear to think about the possibilities.

The squeaky wheels on the janitorial cart made him wince. He lifted his gaze to Pierce's and saw a great deal of interest there. No doubt Pierce had heard everything. So much for secrets.

Chapter Four

DIZZY CAME AWAKE to the strangest beeping sounds. A little woozy and shaky, she blinked rapidly and tried to figure out where the hell she was. Before her mind cleared away the fuzzy thoughts preventing her from making sense of her surroundings, a familiar face appeared above her. Icy-blue eyes, so dark with concern, peered down at her.

Venom.

The memories of her strange morning came flooding back. She remembered the frigid cold, the deep snow and the panic that had gripped her as she rushed into the forest. The phantom sensation of those muscular arms of his wrapped around her and his tongue insistently dipping between her lips caused her belly to wobble. Still a little confused she reached up to touch her neck, fully expecting to feel his white collar there, but encountered only naked skin.

"It's in my pocket, sugar." Venom eased onto the bed, his hip against hers, and brushed his bare fingertips along her cheek. "You're in the infirmary aboard the *Valiant*, the battleship where I'm stationed." Lifting her hand, he kissed the back of it. "You scared me, Dizzy."

Scared him? Hell, she had terrified herself. Never in

her entire life had she felt such stabbing pain. Passing out cold had been a blessing because the searing-hot ice-pickthrough-the-brain sensation had finally stopped.

Looking up into Venom's taut face, she read the worry clearly. "Sorry."

"For what?"

"Scaring you." Her voice sounded a bit gravelly so she cleared her throat.

"You don't have to apologize for that. Are you thirsty?" He reached for the small blue cup and matching pitcher on a rolling tray.

"Very." Her mouth was so incredibly dry. Realizing she was flat on her back, she started to sit up but Venom's huge paw gently flattened against her chest. Her questioning gaze flicked to his face. "What are you doing?"

"Easy," he said calmly. "You're not supposed to sit up too fast. Let me handle it."

She was too groggy to argue with him. He flipped out a panel attached to the side of the bed and tapped at some sort of screen. Though most technology was forbidden on her planet, the area of The City where she lived had been teeming with illicit and black market goods, including handheld tablets with touchscreens like that panel.

Slowly the bed began to incline. She expected to experience pain or dizziness as she shifted positions. Her brow furrowed as she felt...nothing. There was no swooping in her belly or aching behind her ears. It struck her quite suddenly that she could hear *everything*. That annoying ringing that normally plagued her when she woke had vanished.

"Venom!" She snatched his hand. "I can *hear*!"

The flash of fear that had crossed his face when she grabbed him faded quickly. Grinning down at her, he cupped her jaw. "You couldn't hear well before the surgery?"

"Not always," she said. "I had this awful tinny ring in my ears whenever I moved fast and especially in the morning." She touched her forehead in wonder. "I'm not dizzy."

He ran his thumb across her lower lip. "You're still Dizzy though."

She rolled her eyes at his lame joke. "Funny."

He chuckled softly and picked up the cup of water. Carefully he pressed it to her mouth. "Small sips. You might be a little queasy after the anesthesia."

She dutifully followed his directions and swallowed tiny drinks until her parched mouth and throat felt better. "Thank you."

He set aside the cup and slid back down onto the bed next to her. Taking her hand in his, he explained, "When you passed out on the transport ship, the medics sedated you and gave you some medicine so you wouldn't be sick again."

She groaned and glanced away in humiliation. "I'm so sorry I caused such a scene."

"Don't," he whispered gently. "You're not the first person to get sick or pass out on a flight. It happens all the time."

She cast a skeptical eye his way. "Really?"

"Yes."

Feeling marginally better about embarrassing herself, she reached up to touch her left ear. Venom's hand shot out with lightning speed to stop her. "No."

She frowned at him. "Why can't I touch my ear?"

"You have tiny incisions. They're already healing but you shouldn't touch them."

She gulped nervously. "What did they do to me?"

"They used a thin probe, like a fine wire, to bust up the obstructions that were causing your dizziness and nausea and that ringing in your ears. They did it with lasers and sonar waves." He glanced at the partly open door. "I can ask one of the surgeons to explain it to you."

"Later." She was certain the doctor would come in to speak with her eventually.

"They inserted some drains to make sure fluid and deposits won't build up there again. You'll have to have them checked periodically but the docs expect you'll have no issues in your recovery."

"When can I leave the infirmary?"

"I'll take you home in the morning. You could leave now but I want them to keep you overnight just in case." He gazed at her with such intense desire. "I've waited a long time for you. I don't want anything else to go wrong."

Though his voice was naturally gruff, he spoke with such tenderness. She still couldn't quite reconcile this big menacing soldier with the genuine kindness he showed her. Since pulling her onto his lap out there in the snowy forest, he had treated her like some kind of precious prize to be protected and cherished.

"How long have you waited to enter one of these

Grabs?"

He wrapped some of her pale hair around his thick finger. "Years. Over ten," he clarified.

Her lips parted in shock. "Ten years? But—why wait so long?"

"I wasn't…" His jaw tensed. "It wasn't the right time for me to bring a woman into my life until recently. This new deployment here above Calyx is long-term and stable. It's relatively safe here, all things considered and a good place to start a family."

The longing in his voice cut through all her anxiety over the rather rash decision she had made back in the forest. She wasn't silly enough to think it was going to be easy to build something real with Venom—but she didn't doubt that he was sincere about all the things he had promised her when he knelt in the snow.

Venom traced the ugly scars on her throat. "Why didn't you tell me you'd been treated on the *Indefatigable* after you were wounded in the bombing?"

She shrugged. "I assumed it was obvious. How else would I have survived these types of injuries? I mean, there are some underground doctors in The City but none of them have trauma training."

He ran his fingertip along a gnarly bump. "Do you know who brought you onto the ship?"

She shook her head. "I don't have any memories of my time in that ship's hospital.

They used heavy sedation to force accelerated healing on me. They dropped me back on Calyx in my father's care while I was still sedated. I think they had me up here for like a week."

Venom looked annoyed. "They just sent you back like that? What if you'd had complications?"

"There was a medical team in The City center but I recovered without any problems."

He let his hand fall from her neck. "Did your mother work in the embassy?"

"No. Why?"

"I wondered why you were extended the courtesy of our medical care. I understood that most of your people who were injured in the bombing refused our offers of aid. Did they take you because you were so young?"

Dizzy hesitated and picked at the edge of the crisp gray sheet covering her lower half. She didn't want to lie to him, not at the very beginning of their relationship. However bizarrely it had begun it felt as though it had long-term potential. She didn't want an untruth between them this early in the game.

Finally she sighed and admitted, "My mother was having an affair with one of the men at the embassy. One of your men. I didn't know it until about a week before the bombing when I heard my parents arguing about it. I started following her to see what made this other guy so special that she'd break up our family and then...well." She touched her neck. "I woke up back in my bed at home almost ten days later."

"I see."

Feeling the need to defend her mother's memory, she added, "My mom was a good woman. She loved me and she was such a great mother to me. She fought to have a career and was incredibly successful at it. Everyone loved her and—"

"Dizzy." He spoke firmly but gently. "I'm not judging her." He tapped her hand. "Did you know who the man was?"

She frowned at him. "Why are you asking all these questions about my mom's affair?"

"I'm sorry." He held up his hand. "I shouldn't pry. It's the tactician in me. I want to know all the angles."

"Look, even *I* don't know all the angles behind that story. Frankly I don't want to know them. Whatever my mother was doing was really none of my business. She's gone now. None of that matters anymore."

Venom remained silent for a few long moments before tipping her chin. "You hungry?"

"What?" His question took her off guard.

"It's almost dinnertime. Would you like to eat?"

She hadn't had a bite since breakfast with Ella. The thought of her best friend sent pangs of sadness through her. Venom must have seen it on her face because he asked, "What's wrong?"

"My friend," she said. "I just realized I'm probably never going to see Ella again."

"Why would you think that?"

"Well…I understood that most brides who are taken never have contact with Calyx."

"That's not true. We try to establish contact between new mates and their families whenever possible. So long as your friend passes a background check I don't have any issue with you maintaining regular contact with her."

"How?"

"We have a mail service now. Paper letters," he explained. "We have couriers who route them to your planet. There's also a new face-to-face visitation program. Relatives and friends from Calyx go through a background check for approval and then we bring them to the observation deck here on the *Valiant* or the *Arctis* for the initial meeting. We hope to progress to overnight and then forty-eight hour visits in the near future."

After all the terrible things she had heard about the brides taken in Grabs, Dizzy was taken aback by the consideration put into the visitation policy. "That's nice."

"The top sky and land corps commanders in this sector, General Vicious and Admiral Orion, are trying to be more sensitive to the needs of the new mated couples."

"Mated?"

"Married," he clarified. "We call them mate bonds or life bonds on my planet but you call them marriages."

"We do things a bit differently," she said with a smile. "You know, dating instead of chasing. That kind of thing."

"Chasing and dating aren't too far apart." His teasing grin made her smile. "We're doing wedding ceremonies now. Vicious married a woman from Harper's Well in a proper Calyx-style ceremony. It was the first official one on this ship. They did the rings and everything."

"Really?"

"Yes." He tilted his head as if to study her. "Would you like to try something like that?"

"Um…"

"When you're ready, we can discuss it." He slid off the

bed. "I'm going to get us dinner. Don't move."

She gestured to her surroundings. "Where would I go?"

"I meant don't try to get out of bed or move around too much. You're supposed to take it as easy as possible for the next few hours."

Considering how good she felt and how grateful she was for no longer having that stupid sickness, she wasn't going to tempt fate by going against doctor's orders. "I'll be a very good girl."

Venom's eyes narrowed briefly. Something fierce and primal sparked in those paleblue irises of his. He bent down and kissed the top of her head. "I'll be right back."

When he was gone she sat up a little straighter in the bed, adjusting her position slowly and cautiously. She was still taking in the strange surroundings when the transparent door slid open again. It wasn't Venom who came into the room but a darkhaired, green-eyed doctor in a bright-blue uniform quite unlike the ones the other soldiers wore.

He smiled warmly. "My name is Risk and I'm the surgeon who treated you today."

Her eyebrows rose sharply. "A surgeon named Risk?"

He laughed as he moved closer to her bed. "My class at the academy was a bit wild."

"Your class?"

Risk nodded and pulled up a chair next to the bed. "When we're accepted into one of the military academies they take away our birth names and assign us numbers. Later, when we graduate, we earn a new name at the pinning ceremony."

"That's awfully tough."

"It's part of the process of building us up into strong men."

Building them up? It sounded like a way to break them down but she didn't want to offend him by saying that. "Thank you for fixing me."

"It was my pleasure. I rather enjoy working on these simpler cases. It's a nice break from the traumatic injuries I typically treat."

She could only imagine what kind of awful things this man had seen as a doctor in their gruesome battles. He turned his rectangular tablet toward her. The bright screen was filled with the most amazing animated images. "Is that me?"

"It's all you—your brain, your auditory system, your eyes." He tapped each one with a blunt stylus to enlarge them. "Other than the issues you presented with when you were brought into our emergency unit you're in perfect health. Would you like me to explain the procedure I performed?"

"Yes."

Risk walked her through the surgery and explained in detail how she had developed the condition and the way it had been exacerbated by the bombing. When he was done, Risk caught her marveling at the tablet in his hands and extended it toward her. "Here. Check it out."

She hesitated before taking the device. "Thanks."

"Venom will give you one in a few days."

"Really?"

He nodded. "Everyone uses them here. You'll be

amazed at how much you can do on it."

"Like what?"

"Do you like reading?"

"So much." She perked up at the very idea of having access to books.

Risk leaned closer to tap at the screen. Suddenly a digital library appeared in front of her. He touched a title and pages appeared. "You can pack thousands and thousands of books onto your tablet and organize them any way you'd like."

"Wow. *Wow.*" She didn't know what else to say as she flipped through the digital pages. "It's been years since I've been able to read a whole book."

Risk shot her a strange look. "What do you mean?"

"When I was a kid we had a private library that my parents kept locked up and hidden away from visitors." She decided to skip the parts about her family losing everything. "Later, when I went out on my own, I started buying my own books but they're so expensive. I usually visit the library or hit up the secondhand shop a few streets over from my apartment. All of the books I get that way have been censored."

"Censored?"

"There might be entire paragraphs that are blacked out. Sometimes they cut out the offensive lines. It's like looking through a window."

"That's ridiculous. What's the point of reading a book if the best parts are missing?" He moved in a little closer. "What kinds of books do you like to read? I heard they recently added a romance section in the library for the wives. Apparently it's very popular—and steamy."

She caught his playful tone and smiled at him. "Why do I get the feeling that if I kept browsing your library, I'd find a whole section of romances?"

Risk laughed. "I won't dignify that accusation with a response."

As Dizzy tapped the screen to exit the library, she wondered if it would be possible to use the device to help her design her clothes. "Is there a way to draw on this thing? I saw the way you used that stylus to make lines while you were explaining my surgery. Is there a way to freehand draw?"

"Sure." He took the tablet from her. "There are all sorts of applications you can download. The virtual store-front is fairly intuitive when it comes to searching. Once you're comfortable with your device you'll have no problem finding what you need." He turned the tablet toward her to reveal a blank page with a long stripe along the bottom and pressed it back into her hands. "How about this one?"

She studied the screen. The wide, clear drawing space could be enlarged or minimized. The stripe along the bottom offered dozens of tools to create different effects. "This would definitely work."

"Were you an artist back in The City? If you are, there's another wife here, Hallie, who is very talented. She's part of the wives' group that meets a couple of times a month. You'll meet her in the next few days at one of the mandatory information sessions."

"Like an orientation?"

"Basically," Risk said. "They used to just have you gals come on the ship without any type of support. Hallie, the general's wife, has changed all that. The women who arrive on the *Valiant* attend a couple of mandatory meetings to learn about their rights and living on this ship and in our society."

Dizzy thought this Hallie woman sounded like quite a force. "I have rights?"

Risk snorted with amusement. "Of course."

"The paperwork they made me sign before the Grab and after made it seem like I was basically going to be property of the man who caught me."

"The legal language is rather harsh," he agreed. "Ownership in our world isn't the same as it is in your world. To us owning a woman is the greatest responsibility—and a cherished gift. It takes a hell of a lot of valor points to earn the right to take a mate and reproduce so we take our roles as providers and protectors very seriously."

She thought of the way Venom had treated her so far. There was no way he had been faking his concern over her illness or his relief when she'd woken up without pain or ringing in her ears. "Do you know Venom well?"

"Fairly well," Risk remarked. "We were one year apart at the academy. I've always served in the field hospital that accompanies his battle group. I was even caught in the Sendarian siege."

She frowned. "What was that?"

A haunted look crossed the surgeon's face. "Sendaria is a planet that we mine quite extensively for our preferred fuel source. A little over ten years ago we were engaged above the planet with the Splinter faction. This was when they were much larger and better equipped. They caught us by surprise and hit three of our sky ships."

"What happened then?"

"We went down hard and were totally cut off on the ground. We managed to make it to the heavily fortified city surrounding the main mining camp. Vicious—our general now—was the highest-ranking officer to survive and he took control. Our orders were to secure and defend those mines—whatever the cost."

Dizzy swallowed hard. "And what did it cost?"

Risk had a faraway look. "Too much. In the months we were cut off from reinforcements and supplies, we lost nearly eighty percent of our forces. It was…bleak at the end."

She remained still and quiet as he relived what appeared to be truly awful memories.

As if giving himself a mental shake, Risk inhaled a sharp breath. "We showed the best of ourselves during that siege. Vicious proved he could make the hard decisions when it counted. Menace showed that he could make a weapon out of damn near anything. Terror stopped at nothing to get the recon we needed. Hazard and Zephyr risked their lives a number of times on extremely dangerous missions to bring in what few supplies they could squeeze through the enemy blockade."

"And Venom?" She had to know what had happened to him during that siege.

He hesitated and then seemed to choose his words carefully. "Venom volunteered to take up a position outside the city."

"Why?"

"He's a highly skilled sniper. It was where he was needed." She didn't have to ask what they had needed him to do.

"He saved a lot of lives by putting his on the line."

And taking so many more...

"Have I upset you?" Risk studied her carefully. "Please don't think badly of Venom."

She reeled back with some surprise. "Why would I think badly of him?"

"Your people are all pacifists."

She rolled her eyes. "We're not *all* anything. I'm not naive enough to think that war isn't sometimes a necessity. An ugly one but necessary nonetheless." She touched the scars on her throat. "We did nothing to provoke those monsters who blew us up that day. You can't reason with people like that. I don't pretend to understand what you Harcos have endured in this war but I would never think badly of any soldier fighting to protect people like me."

"I'm glad to hear that." Risk sat forward in his chair. His gaze turned professional.

"Have you considered having those scars revised?"

She put a shielding hand to her neck. "What do you mean?"

"Our surgical techniques typically minimize scarring." Risk pushed out of his seat and moved onto the bed so he could examine her more closely. "I can see that the surgeon who was working on you was rushed. You weren't given the usual follow-up treatment that would have prevented these thicker ridges."

He carefully tilted her head to the side to expose the old injuries better. There was nothing even the least bit flirtatious or unprofessional about his touch but it felt wrong to her.

Because it isn't Venom touching me.

The thought struck her suddenly and left her feeling a bit unsettled. She didn't harbor any feelings of resentment or anger toward Venom for catching and collaring her as his bride. If anything she felt such gratitude toward him. He didn't know that he had basically saved her from becoming a loan shark's plaything but she sure did. He had even made it possible for her to receive medical care that would vastly improve her life.

In the forest she had chosen to take his collar. At the processing station she had willingly signed her name on that contract. She had given herself to him—and having Risk's hands on her now, no matter the context, felt uncomfortable.

Risk must have sensed it because his hands fell from her neck. "I should have asked before touching you."

"It's okay. I'm just not used to being touched by men."

"You only have to get used to one man touching you—Venom. I seriously doubt he'll allow any other man to touch you."

"No, he won't." Venom's rough, deep voice boomed from the doorway. "And if you intend to continue operating, Doc, you'd best keep those hands of yours off my woman."

Dizzy held her breath as she glanced between the two

men. Risk's playful wink told her that he thought Venom's bark didn't have much bite behind it. She wasn't so sure.

Venom looked awfully serious as he strode into the room carrying two covered trays. He shot the surgeon a pointed stare as he slid their dinners onto the table next to the bed. "Is this type of hands-on treatment something they taught you in medical school?"

"No, it's a little something I picked up in a different sort of operating theater."

Venom glared at Risk. "I don't find that the least bit funny."

"No, you wouldn't." Risk rose from his seated position. "I am her doctor, Venom."

"Don't forget that I've seen you *play doctor* at the officers' club," Venom grumbled testily.

Dizzy wasn't quite sure what Venom meant by that remark but it drew a laugh from Risk. The surgeon shook his head as he stepped away from the bed and retrieved his tablet. "We'll discharge you in the morning, Dizzy. A medic will come by periodically to check on you. That last dose of pain meds you received will wear off as the evening progresses. I don't expect you to feel any discomfort but if you do let us know."

"I will." Arms crossed, Venom answered for her. She glanced at him with a look of utter frustration but he didn't even acknowledge her. Instead he trailed Risk to the door and shut it firmly behind him.

When Venom got close enough to the bed, she reached out and whacked his arm.

"You know I have a voice, right?"

Venom seemed startled by her smack. "Yes. And?"

"And I can answer questions for myself and decide who can and can't touch me."

"You may answer questions but *I* decide who can and can't touch you."

His reply stunned her. Until this moment, he had been uncommonly compromising and quite unlike the stories she had heard of these Harcos men and their dominant, commanding natures. This version of Venom—the haughty, arrogant man standing over her—seemed to fit the stereotypical sky warrior mold much better.

She recognized this was one of those moments where she had to be strong and stand up to him. "No."

His eyes widened. "Yes."

She sat up straighter. "No, Venom. I'm a grown woman. I've lived on my own since I was eighteen years old. I've supported myself and made my own decisions for five years. I don't need you barking orders at me."

"I didn't bark at you."

She gaped at him. "Out of everything I just said you're focusing on that?"

An irritated expression tightened his features. "As long as you wear my collar I decide who can and can't put their hands on you."

She pointed to her bare neck. "I'm not wearing your collar now."

"Well, that can be easily fixed." Venom reached into his pocket and retrieved the white leather strap.

When he leaned down to put it on her again, she ducked to the side and blocked him. "No."

"Dizzy."

"Venom."

He made a low, growling sound but didn't attempt to manhandle her or force the collar on her. "You belong to me."

"Yes, I do," she answered calmly. "That doesn't mean you get to boss me around, Venom."

Confirming that she belonged to him seemed to ease some of the tension in his clenched jaw. Still, he remained stubbornly stuck on the touching issue. "Actually it does mean I get to boss you around, Dizzy. That's how it works here."

"Not for us," she retorted quickly. Swallowing nervously, she continued, "I liked the way you took command out there in the forest and the way you made sure I was safe and warm—but I'm not going to have you dictating my every move."

"I don't intend to dictate your every move."

"But you intend to tell me who I can be friends with?"

His forehead creased in confusion. "When did I say you couldn't make friends?"

"You said that Risk couldn't touch me."

"Damn straight," he said roughly. "You can be friends without him pawing all over you."

"Wait." She started to see where they had misunderstood each other. "When you say touch, you mean, like, in a sexual way. When I say touch I'm thinking, you know, a handshake or whatever."

"I see." Venom visibly relaxed. "Dizzy, you need to understand something about me. I survived some of the bloodiest battles of this war to earn the points to take a wife. I'm not sharing you with any other man."

"Share me?" He wasn't talking about sharing her time. She recoiled at the very thought of being shared with another man in bed. "Why would you share me?"

"I wouldn't—but some men do." He shifted as if uncomfortable. "Some men here swap wives or invite their friends to enjoy them in various games and in the bedroom."

Dizzy didn't like the sound of that at all. What other couples did behind closed doors was their own business but she wasn't about to let someone who wasn't her husband touch her like that. "You sure as hell aren't sharing this wife."

A slight smile curved his mouth. "You don't need to worry about that. I'm not into that kind of thing." Placing his big hands on either side of her, Venom leaned down and captured her mouth in a gentle kiss. "You're mine— and *only* mine."

Thinking of how lucky she was to have been Grabbed by a man who didn't want to share her spurred Dizzy to snatch his white collar from his hands. She fastened it around her neck a little looser than he had when he'd first put it on her. He looked terribly pleased by her action. "What about you, Venom? Do you belong to me?"

"From the moment I first spotted you," he admitted huskily and swept his fingertip down her cheek. "There was no one else for me."

She marveled at his unwavering certainty. What had he seen in her that he liked so much? Was it simply her pretty face? What would happen to their relationship when her looks faded or his infatuation with her dissipated?

He tapped her cheek. "What's got you worried, sugar?"

"What happens when the newness wears off?"

The lines around his mouth crinkled. "We start building something *real*—and that's when the true fun begins."

Chapter Five

A S HE PEERED down into her big brown eyes, Venom finally managed to muscle down the irrational jealousy and extreme possessiveness overwhelming him. When he had first entered the hospital room he had been sure Risk was kissing her. It wasn't until he took a quick step into the room that he had realized the surgeon was merely examining her neck. Even though it had been innocent he'd been gripped by the urge to grab Risk and toss him across the room.

After the little tiff they had just shared, Venom felt sure Dizzy would not have approved of a physical altercation. He reminded himself that she'd willingly taken his collar again. She didn't seem the least bit tempted by Risk, charmer that he was.

"Listen," Venom said as he sat down on the bed, "you need to be aware of the realities up here."

"Okay," she answered a bit nervously.

Not wanting to scare her, he took her smaller hand in his. "Women are incredibly scarce and the Grab criteria are very strict. To level the playing field they put certain rules in place."

"What kind of rules?"

"Our mate bond isn't fully legal until a period of thirty

days has passed. At the end of thirty days we'll sign another set of contracts affirming our intention to remain together. If another single man with enough points spots you outside my—*our*—quarters or if you're without a proper escort, you can be taken."

"Taken?" Her worried gaze darted to the door. Was she thinking of all the men roaming around the infirmary?

So much for not scaring her...

"It doesn't happen very often but we've had a few cases where brides were snatched from their mates."

"I see." She bit her lip. "That must make for some awkward run-ins around the ship."

"To say the least," he said with a chuckle. "We've had population issues for quite a while now. There aren't nearly enough women from our own planet to go around so the matchmaking services back on Prime are swamped and extremely expensive.

They're so far beyond what most of us soldiers and airmen can afford."

"So that's why you have the Grabs?"

"Partly," he agreed. "They've been a tradition of ours for hundreds of years. When we were a conquering race we took brides from the native populations to cement treaties and build trust. Now it's truly become a necessity. Even though your planet agreed to the Grab treaty, they're being very stingy with the numbers of women they make available to us."

She made a soft clicking sound, alerting him to her annoyance at something he'd said. "You make it sound like women are just lining up around the damn block to be chased and taken by a stranger. The numbers are small because the government doesn't want to agitate the populace. The only women getting Grabbed are poor women. If you've got money or connections you can avoid the lottery. Unless you want more riots you guys are just going to have to practice a little patience and wait your turn."

Dizzy's fiery response left him speechless. In the short time he'd known her it was his first time seeing this passionate side to her—and it turned him on something fierce. "Do you know how pretty you are when your cheeks get all pink like that?"

She rolled her eyes and pinched his biceps. "Coming on to me doesn't change the facts, Venom."

"No," he agreed with a smile, "but I was hoping it might distract you enough to let me sneak in another kiss."

Her cheeks turned an even darker shade of that rosy hue. "You'll have to find another tactic."

"Sweetheart, that's quite a challenge to issue to a master tactician." He was still considering the myriad ways he might coax a kiss from those pouting lips of hers when she glanced around the room a little anxiously. "What's wrong?"

She dropped her gaze to the thin sheet covering her. "Um…is there a bathroom nearby?"

He silently cursed himself for being so inconsiderate. "I'm sorry. I should have made sure you were comfortable before heading out to find dinner." Jerking back the covers, he bent down to scoop her up but her hands flew to his chest in protest. "What are you doing?"

"I'm taking you to the bathroom."

"I can walk."

"I know." He cradled her slight weight in his arms and lifted her off the bed. She stiffened and gripped his shirt. "Easy, honey. I'm not going to drop you."

"You don't have to do this. I'm not an invalid. I can take myself to the bathroom." Irritation made her voice sound harsh and tight.

"You were under anesthesia earlier today to treat a condition that made you dizzy and caused you to pass out. I'm not taking any more chances with you." He hugged her a little tighter to his chest as he carried her across the room. "You're mine to protect and care for now. I won't have you falling and getting injured over something as silly as walking to the bathroom."

She didn't argue with him but those pursed lips of hers told him he was getting very close to crossing one of her lines. Inside the bathroom he slowly lowered her to the floor and kept an arm around her shoulders to steady her. When he started to lift the loose hospital gown, she grasped his wrist in a death grip. "Don't even think about it, Venom."

He met her angry gaze and was taken aback by the embarrassment reflected in her eyes. Not wanting to upset her even more he carefully stood to his full height. "I was only trying to help."

Her grip on his wrist loosened. She ran her fingertips along his forearm in a soothing gesture. "I know, but I need some privacy."

He didn't understand why she found it so embarrassing to accept help from her mate when she was clearly still feeling the effects of the sedatives but decided not to push his luck. He started to tell her there wasn't much that made him squeamish anymore, not after so many years on the front lines, but thought better of it. Something told him she wouldn't find that comforting in the least.

Cupping her face, he said, "I'll be right outside the door. When you've finished call for me and I'll help you stand."

After her silent nod he left the bathroom and shut the door. Leaning against it, Venom closed his eyes and felt the tension he had been carrying leave his body. Reassured that she would heal and recover, he could look forward to starting their new life together. Though he had expected to spend their first night as mates in much different surroundings, he decided that he could tamp down his desire and need for one more night. After all, he'd waited this long for a wife.

The muted sound of a high-powered flush followed by Dizzy's shocked shriek jerked him right out of his thoughts. Spinning on his heel, he shoved the door aside and strode into the bathroom to find Dizzy hugging the far wall. She gnawed her plump bottom lip as the guilt of going against his orders played on her beautiful face. Apparently she hadn't anticipated the automated system.

Crossing his arms, he sighed. "I thought I told you to call for me when you were done."

"I didn't want you to see me like *that*."

He frowned at her with utter consternation. "Dizzy, I'm your mate. I'm supposed to care for you."

She wrung her small hands. "And I'm seriously thrilled by the idea of having someone take care of me— but shouldn't there be some mystery in a marriage? I really, really don't think we need to get *this* close, you know?"

He snorted with amusement. "All right. I'll let you have this one." Crossing the room to retrieve her, he said, "When I give you an instruction in the future you need to follow it. I'm not the type to be bossy just because I feel like it. This new world of yours operates under different rules and I need to know you won't accidentally get your-self hurt."

Her expression turned serious. "I understand."

"Good." Scooping her up again, he carted her to the sink and set her down on her feet. He slipped one arm around her waist and braced her body with his even though it put him in an awkward position. When she didn't move her hands toward the faucet, he realized she was looking for knobs. "It's motion-activated."

"Oh." She let him guide her hands under the faucet to wet them before tugging them over to the automated soap dispenser. A foamy blue blob landed in her palm. Gently holding her wrists, he smashed the foam between her palms and helped her work up a rich lather.

Curled around her like this, Venom couldn't ignore the effect her warm body had on his. Someday very soon, he intended to have her beneath him like this—but very naked. He could just imagine how her snug pussy would feel wrapped around his dick. The very idea of the breathy, pleasured sounds she would make as he rubbed her clit and plowed her pussy had his cock stirring to life in his pants.

He shifted his hips back a bit so she wouldn't feel the evidence of his arousal jammed up against that tight little ass of hers. The last thing he wanted to do was make her think he was a sex-obsessed barbarian.

Their gazes clashed in the mirror mounted over the sink. The flush to her cheeks betrayed her enjoyment of his nearness. He found her reaction rather enticing and decided to see just how interested in him she was.

When he guided her wet hands under the air dryer, he dropped his mouth to the exposed curve of her neck and planted a couple of soft kisses on her pale skin. She shivered as he skimmed the side of her throat, just above her collar, but didn't try to evade him or pull out of his embrace. No, she pressed back against him in a silent invitation to continue.

Not about to pass up an opportunity to get closer to her, Venom swept aside the long pale strands of her hair and nipped playfully at the spot where her neck curved into her shoulder. She whimpered softly, the kittenish mewl traveling straight to his throbbing cock. Licking the spot he'd reddened with his teeth, Venom relished the sight of her marked skin. Spanking had never been one of his favorite bedroom activities but the idea of Dizzy's flesh all hot and pink from his hand made his balls ache.

"Uh, Captain?" A medic called through the closed bathroom door as he knocked hesitantly. "Is everything okay with the patient? Her vital signs are outside the acceptable parameters, especially her heart rate and blood pressure."

Venom chuckled quietly as he kissed Dizzy's cheek. He had forgotten all about the small patches dotting her chest and upper arm that transmitted vital signs to the monitors in her room and at the medic's station. Raising his voice, he answered, "We're fine. Thanks for checking."

"All right. Uh—maybe you could try to get her back in bed. I mean, you know, to rest, sir. Not to—"

"I got it."

"Right. Uh—I'll just go now. Let me know if you need any help with her, sir. Medical help," the medic added quickly.

Venom laughed at the medic's fumbling but Dizzy looked absolutely mortified that the man had thought they were fooling around in the bathroom. He settled his hands on her shoulders and kissed the top of her head before holding her gaze in the mirror's reflection. "We're mates, Dizzy. It's perfectly fine for us to enjoy each other's company."

"I know." She sounded as though she was trying to convince herself. "Where I come from couples don't talk about these kinds of things and they sure as heck don't joke about them with other people."

His earlier plans to ease her into his lifestyle were on target. Taking her to the officers' club would definitely have to wait. Massaging her shoulders, he said, "If something makes you uncomfortable or embarrasses you, tell me. I'll stop and we'll reassess the situation." He pressed his lips to the side of her neck one more time. "Let's eat."

He picked her up again and took her back to the hospital bed. While he adjusted the incline, she touched his arm and asked, "Can you bring me my bag?"

"Sure." He retrieved it from the chair by the door and brought it over to her. Not a fan of the one-bag rule, he said, "I'm happy to make arrangements for anything you left behind in The City."

"Thanks but there's nothing left." Dizzy unzipped her small suitcase and retrieved a leather messenger bag. She dug around inside it until she found a pink hair tie that she used to secure the pale-blonde tresses away from her face. "I chose the things that meant the most to me and gave away the rest. It wasn't like I had much anyway. I lived in a tiny studio apartment, so there wasn't much room for extras."

He listened carefully for any sadness in her voice but didn't detect any. She honestly seemed okay with jettisoning her possessions before jumping into the Grab. Something she'd said earlier about only poor women being pulled into the lottery came to mind. Perhaps she hadn't had much in the way of worldly goods in the first place. The desire to shower her with pretty things hit him hard. "Anything you need or want I'll find for you."

She shot one of those dazzling smiles his way. "Thank you."

As she set aside her bag, he lifted the tabletop attached to the bed into place and secured it. He picked up the trays of food and explained, "I wasn't sure what you liked so I got a tray of hot things and another tray of cold things."

When he lifted the lids she sat forward with interest. He started to drag a chair closer but she pointed to the foot of the bed. "Why don't you sit there? I've got my legs crossed, so there's plenty of room."

He considered her suggestion and figured it would work fine. Bending down, he removed his boots and made a mental note to see the uniform shop about another pair.

He had a backup set in his closet but would need to break in another pair just in case.

Hopping up onto the bed, he realized that sitting with his legs crossed wouldn't be as easy for him as it evidently was for Dizzy. The nimble little sprite seemed awfully flexible. The sight of her so comfortably contorted spurred some terribly dirty thoughts. He was suddenly very glad for the table between them that shielded the obvious hardon pressing at the front of his uniform pants.

"I think you're going to have to drape your legs on either side of the mattress, Venom."

He loved the way she said his name in that gentle, sweet voice of hers. "I think you're right, sugar."

One side of her mouth lifted to form a quirky smile. "That *sugar* thing seems to be sticking."

He picked up one of the cutlery sets and handed it to her. "You don't like it?"

"I didn't say that." She opened the protective packaging and tugged free a fork. "The first couple of times I thought maybe you couldn't remember my name."

Her mischievous grin sent little darts of excitement right through his chest. The more relaxed she became around him the more of the real Dizzy he glimpsed—and he really liked her. "Your name isn't an easy one to forget."

She made a little laughing sound. "My real name is

way worse."

He'd been tempted to dig through her bag and peek at her official paperwork while she'd been sedated but it felt wrong to go through her things, even if they technically belonged to him now that she was legally his property. "What is it?"

She shook her head. "You first."

"My name is Venom."

"No," she said. "The name you had before the academy."

Before the academy? "I take it Risk filled you in on our naming conventions."

"He mentioned that you lose your birth name when you enter the academy and earn another name when you graduate."

"It's a way to build unit cohesion and brotherhood. The boys we were when we joined the academy disappear at the front doors. We're all the same and all on equal footing. No one is richer or poorer. We're just numbers."

Her expression turned sad. "That sounds terribly hard for a little boy."

He shrugged. "It's not easy but it's our way. Someday our sons will climb the same stairs to the academy's front doors that I climbed and my father climbed and his father before him."

Dizzy went perfectly still at the mention of someday having his sons. It wasn't a secret that Grabs were meant to promote procreation of strong, healthy boys to fill the ranks. It was one of the reasons why only the bravest, toughest soldiers were granted the right to take wives by earning valor points. It weeded out the weak and the less deserving.

But he had only just Grabbed Dizzy that morning and already he was talking about sons. *What the hell is wrong with you? You're going to scare her.*

While he had been dreaming of starting a family for years, Dizzy was in her early twenties, still very young to be considering a family of her own. Would she balk at the idea? Would she follow Menace's wife's lead and petition for a birth-control implant?

"I shouldn't have said that. I don't want you to think that the only reason I entered the Grab was to get you pregnant."

Shit. That sounded even worse, didn't it? He could just hear Raze laughing at him and encouraging him to keep digging.

"What I mean is that I want more than just children with you. I want the whole package."

She studied him for a few discomfiting moments before finally saying, "You've probably just jinxed us."

Bemused, he asked, "Jinxed? How?"

Her mouth slanted rather impishly. "You're all puffed up about the idea of having sons. We'll probably end up with a dozen girls."

Dizzy's playful reply set him at ease. Maybe they weren't so far apart when it came to that issue. "If they're as pretty as their mother I'll be a very proud father."

She waved her fork at him. "There's that flattery again."

"Is it working?"

"Maybe." She rolled her top lip under to squash a grin. Turning her attention to the food, she asked, "What do you want?"

"You go first."

"Um…" She poked at a few dishes before choosing a green salad loaded with fresh vegetables, a serving of steamed veggies in a tart sauce and some of the fruit. She gestured to the salad. "I can share this."

He shook his head. "I had one with lunch." Eyeing her choices, he pushed some of the grilled steak her way. "You should have some protein."

She pointed out the bright-red beans on her salad. "These are protein."

"I meant meat." He remembered Vicious telling him that Hallie had been hesitant to eat what she wanted. Food insecurity was a real issue on Calyx and women tended to be underfed and malnourished. He gave Dizzy a scrutinizing glance. "You should probably have more protein in your diet."

She made a face and shoved the dish back toward him. "I don't eat meat."

He gawked at her. "What do you mean? How can you not eat meat? It's delicious."

"I'm sure it is but it's not for me."

Venom couldn't wrap his head around the idea of any person choosing to forego a juicy steak. "Why not?"

She wrinkled her dainty nose. "That's not a story you want me to tell over dinner." When he sat there waiting patiently for her to continue, she rolled her eyes and said, "When I was a kid my dad sent me to spend a week with his sister on her husband's sprawling farm. It was the fall, during the annual hog slaughter. Let's just say that seven days of watching *that* cured me of any meat cravings."

He had never witnessed such a thing but had always assumed the process from pasture to table wasn't particularly nice. Even though it didn't bother him to consume meat, he didn't want to upset Dizzy so he started to set aside the steak he loved so much.

Her warm fingers clasped his wrist to stop him. "It doesn't bother me to watch other people enjoy meat."

He cast a skeptical glance her way. "You're sure?"

"Yes. My best friend chows down on slabs of meat in front of me all the time. It's not a big deal."

Though it was selfish he experienced a wave of relief. The idea of having to sneak his favorite foods wasn't one he relished but he would have done it for her. "We'll have to make sure there are other protein sources in our kitchen for you."

"Can you get fish up here?"

"Sure."

"I don't mind eating fish occasionally, especially the fresh stuff they catch down in Blue Shores. We used to go down there every summer for vacation. It was a beautiful place. So much cleaner and prettier than The City."

The peek into her past left him with so many questions. From what he knew of the society down on Calyx there weren't many people who could afford a summer getaway. Had she come from a wealthy family? Why was she living in a tiny apartment if her family had money?

And then there was the issue of her father. Did she realize the man she called Dad wasn't her biological parent?

Tucking into his meal, he made pleasant conversation and hoped not to rouse her suspicions. "Your father enjoyed the sea?"

She shook her head and swallowed her tiny bite. "He couldn't stand it so he spent most of his time at the casino there. My mother loved the ocean and the beach so we would have girls-only days on the sand. She said being at that seaside hotel reminded her of the happiest summer of her life."

"And what summer was that?"

"The one where she and my dad made me," Dizzy said with a sweet smile.

His gut clenched. She clearly had no idea what her mother had truly meant and he wasn't about to be the one who burst her happy little bubble. Not yet at least. The truth would come out soon but he had to find an easier way to deliver it.

Speaking to Risk as soon as possible jumped to the top of his list of priorities. He didn't want the surgeon to reveal the information about her DNA before he had a chance to prepare her. Dizzy needed a little time to get used to being his mate and living in this new society before he started tearing into the wall of secrets between her and her parents.

"Can we visit Blue Shores?"

He didn't miss the hopefulness in her voice. "Sure. It will have to wait a few months. We can't possibly get the travel clearance while I'm on honeymoon leave but I'll file the permits and work it into my schedule."

"I think you'll like it there." She stabbed her fork through some of the leafy greens. "I want you to see it the way it is now, just a sleepy, easy place, before they build that monstrosity of a base down there."

Venom heard the distaste in her voice. "We need a land-based center of operations for this sector. From what I understand, the Blue Shores community welcomed the possibility of a base there and the financial incentives that come with it."

Her shoulders bounced. "They're not like the rest of our settlements on Calyx. They're a fairly autonomous group out there. They were the first to break away when our ancestors were given the planet by your people. Long before the settlers who founded Connor's Run," she added. "You'll understand more about them when we visit. They're just…different."

A thrill of excitement rippled through him at the thought of going on vacation with Dizzy. He'd never really had a true vacation. Oh, he took mandatory leave like every other soldier, but he generally coordinated with Raze or Menace or some of his other SRU buddies to hit up one of the pleasure ports. Sex, gambling, sports, films—it started off fun enough but by the third or fourth day he started to dread getting out of his bed. It was so…empty.

Of course, going on vacation with Dizzy meant he would have a much better reason for not wanting to get out of bed. Technically they were in bed now and Venom didn't want to budge. He eyed the reclining chair where visitors were supposed to sleep.

Not a chance in hell…

Chapter Six

A SHORT TIME later, Dizzy anxiously eyed the closed bathroom door. Any second Venom would step out of there freshly showered...and then what?

She twirled some of her hair around her finger and thought about the dinner. In some ways it had been very much like a first date. Except that it had taken place in a hospital bed while she was half-dressed and looking like a hot mess.

As she played with her hair, the scent of the shampoo provided by the hospital wafted toward her nose. It wasn't unpleasant but it was a bit too stringent and manly for her tastes. Surely they had stores that sold feminine soaps and shampoos? She hoped so—otherwise Venom was going to have to get used to snuggling up to a girl who smelled like one of his comrades.

Thoughts of snuggling with her giant sky warrior left her feeling a bit lightheaded. It wasn't the sickness that made her feel that way. No, it was the memory of Venom's thick, corded arms wrapped around her in the bathroom while she washed her hands. Even though he had shifted away from her she'd still felt the very hard—and very big—evidence of his attraction toward her nudging her backside.

When he had dropped those ticklish kisses on her neck she'd nearly fallen into the sink. Her knees had gone all wobbly and her tummy had trembled wildly. If a couple of kisses and a hug did that to her, how the hell was she going to survive Venom making love to her?

And he wanted to make love to her so badly. There was no doubt in her mind about that.

When he had accompanied her into the bathroom for her shower she'd been sure he would try to finagle his way into the stall with her. He had surprised her by giving her some privacy and space. Though he wouldn't leave the room he'd turned his back and kept his arms crossed. A few times she'd caught him sneaking peeks in the mirror but she couldn't fault him for that. Had the tables been turned she would have wanted to get a glimpse of his naked body too.

Even though he was obviously trying to be respectful of her need to recuperate he couldn't hide the burning lust darkening his blue eyes every time he looked at her. Considering how long he'd waited for the chance to have a wife she couldn't really blame him for being so hot. That he'd shown this much restraint proved his self-control.

Her experience as a young woman living alone in The City taught her to be wary of men who were so kind and gentle. Usually they had ulterior motives. But she didn't think Venom was one of those men.

Talking with Risk had given her some insight into the man who had snatched her from the planet's surface. He had survived so much to earn the points needed to enter a Grab. He seemed to want nothing more than to take care of and love her. After being emotionally and physically abandoned by her father after her mother's traumatic death, the idea of having someone to lean on for support was incredibly enticing.

She wasn't silly enough to think that it was going to be smooth sailing between them—they'd only just met, after all—but she had a growing hope that life with Venom could be very good.

First they would need to deal with that bossy streak of his. She felt conflicted when he gave her orders. She naturally rebelled at the idea of being told what to do by anyone…but she would be lying if she denied there wasn't some tiny part of her that found Venom's commanding nature rather exciting. There was something about that gruff voice of his that made her shiver inside.

The bathroom door opened and Venom exited in a small cloud of steam. Her eyes nearly popped out of her head at the sight of his half-naked body. She had to clamp her teeth together to keep her jaw from dropping. It was rude to stare but she just couldn't help herself.

Oblivious to the way he affected her Venom strode into the hospital room and dropped his neatly folded uniform onto an empty chair. He wore only black shorts and when he bent down to adjust the boots he'd left under the chair she got a rather enticing view of his taut backside. The sight inspired some rather naughty visions of this gorgeous man between her thighs, thrusting into her and showing her all the secret delights of a marriage bed.

A wicked thrill raced through as she ogled his massive and muscular body. He straightened up and walked to the end of her bed. She took in his broad chest and toned arms. Tattoos marked the right side of his body, swirling around his arm right down to his knuckles and arcing up the side of his neck. His left side remained bare. She had heard they reserved the left side, the side closest to their hearts, for telling the stories of their families while the right side told of their military history.

"Do they bother you?" As if self-conscious, he ran his hand over the dark ink.

She was surprised to see such a tense set to his square jaw. "No. Why would they?"

"Some of your women don't like them."

"I think they're beautiful." At his funny face, she added, "You know, in a manly sort of way."

Laughing, he walked over to the side of the bed. She took advantage of his closer position to reach out and touch one of the tattoos. He inhaled a sharp breath and she instinctively pulled back her hand, worrying she'd crossed some line. Grabbing her wrist, he dragged her hand back to his arm. "I want you to touch me. It surprised me. That's all."

With his fingers wrapped loosely around her wrist, Dizzy traced the symbols on his skin. How long had it been since a woman had touched him like this? Too long if his heavier breaths were any indication.

Her finger moved to a series of squares with slash marks through them. He had them rolling up his biceps and onto his back. "What do these symbols mean?"

Venom didn't answer her immediately. Seeming reluctant, he explained, "They mark my confirmed kills as a sniper. Every box equals five."

"Five?" Her astounded reply escaped her lips before she could stop it. There were just so many of them on his skin. She didn't have the stomach to add them up.

"Yes." The harsh, pained whisper of his voice cut her to the bone. She could feel the cold waves of regret and discomfort radiating from him. Venom dropped her wrist and took a step back. "I'll put on a shirt."

"Stop." She reached for him, clasping his hand and tugging him down onto the bed. He watched her with a mistrusting eye, almost as if he feared what she would say next. Fully aware this was a chink in his emotional armor, she wanted to tread carefully. "I can't even pretend to understand what war is like."

"You probably understand better than most brides." His thick finger moved aside the thin collar circling her neck to touch the gnarly scars dotting her skin.

"Maybe," she said uncertainly. "Venom, I don't know you that well—but I don't think you're a monster. I think you're a highly talented soldier who did his duty. I won't judge you for carrying out orders."

"Maybe not," he said quietly, "but these tattoos will be a constant reminder of the things I've done and of the lives I've taken."

Searching for the right words, she swept her palm over the markings on his hard biceps. "This is your past, Venom." Her hand moved to his left arm where the skin remained pristine. "This is your future. That's all that matters to me."

He swallowed hard, his throat moving, before taking

her hand and dragging it down to the space above his heart. "*You* are my future. This is *our* future."

The huskiness to his voice made her chest tighten. Since surviving the bombing Dizzy hadn't really allowed herself to think too far ahead. In the back of her mind, she secretly doubted there was a future. Terrorists like the Splinters wouldn't stop with one bomb. No, they were biding their time and waiting for the next opportunity to strike.

She had allowed herself to plan as far ahead as next month. Thinking in short-term bursts—tomorrow or next week—didn't make her nervous. After all, she had design and production deadlines that had to be met—but day-dreaming about five years down the road? Never.

Sitting there with Venom, Dizzy allowed herself to imagine for the briefest of moments what her life could be like in a year or two. She remembered all the things he'd talked about wanting with her, especially a family, and liked the possibilities that flashed before her eyes.

"Have I gone too far?" Her hulking sky warrior stared at her so intently. "Is it too soon to talk about our future?"

She shot him a bemused glance. "Venom, you snatched me out of a forest and put your collar on me. Moving too fast happened around five minutes after I left that cold, muddy pen."

"Fair enough," he said with a short laugh. He brushed his fingers through her loose hair. "When you think about the future, what do you think about?"

"Security." The answer came swiftly. "I'm so tired of being afraid."

Compassion softened his expression. "I'll protect you."

She figured if any man in the universe could pull off that promise it was Venom. "Yes, I think you will."

Feeling braver than ever, she leaned forward and planted a kiss right on his mouth. He reacted with some surprise at her aggressive move. In the short time they had been together she had been too shy or uncertain of him to let down her guard. Not anymore.

When she looped her arms around his shoulders, Venom relaxed and slid his hand to her nape. Cupping the back of her head, he took control of the kiss she'd initiated. With any other man it would have annoyed her to lose power but there was just something so damn intoxicating about the way Venom naturally assumed the dominant role.

And the man could kiss!

As he had back in the forest when he'd left her shivering with desire, he quickly wowed her with his skill. His tongue flirted with hers before delving deeper. She had never allowed the few men she'd dated to get very far with such passionate kisses. Considering she had sworn off sex before marriage to protect herself, she tried not to cross that line. Too many steps on the wrong side and it might prove too difficult to stop.

But all those old worries and roadblocks fled. Held in Venom's strong arms she was powerless to deny him the erotic kisses he seemed intent on sharing with her. Nor did she want to deny him. God, she wanted it *all*.

When he sucked just the tip of her tongue she nearly died. Her heart fluttered wildly and she whimpered with need. He nibbled her bottom lip until her face flushed and she throbbed all over. Overheated and panting, she clung to him and wished he'd keep going.

A man cleared his throat very loudly from the doorway of the hospital room. Dizzy tore away from Venom in shock but he didn't seem the least bit fazed. He forced her to meet his calm, assured gaze. His playful wink lessened her embarrassment at being caught making out like teenagers.

"Venom," Risk said with teasing censure in his voice, "if you can't let her rest, I'll have to banish you to the waiting room."

Venom grunted and sent the surgeon a daring look. "I'd like to see you try."

Laughing, Risk walked toward the bed. "The dozens of sedatives at my fingertips might even the odds."

Venom cracked a smile. "You always did like to play dirty."

"I prefer to think of it as playing smarter." Risk reached toward the neck of her hospital gown. In a movement so fast it startled her, Venom gripped the surgeon's wrist. Instead of looking annoyed, Risk rolled his eyes. "Would you calm the hell down? I'm removing her life-sign patches so you two won't be setting off alarms all night. The medics have other patients who need their attention."

Venom released the doctor's wrist. "I'll do it."

"Fine." Risk shrugged and reached up to tap away at the screen mounted on the wall next to her bed. "I'm stopping your vital signs checks. You've been stable since surgery so there's no point. We'll get another read during your discharge exam. We also need to complete your intake exam in the morning."

"What does that entail?" Her belly lurched as the possibility of painful procedures awaited her.

"Nothing scary," Risk replied. "We were able to take samples for all of the necessary tests while we prepped you for surgery. We need to go over your medical history to make sure we haven't missed anything small. That's all."

"Oh." That didn't sound so bad.

Venom carefully peeled the small silver squares from her upper arm and chest. "It will be quick and painless. We'll be out of here before you know it."

The idea of being alone with Venom made her heart race. When she had queued up to run in the Grab that morning she'd dreaded the idea of being alone with one of these scary Harcos males. Now she couldn't wait for Venom to take her away to his home.

Risk headed to the large window looking out toward a central station where medics and doctors congregated. When he tapped the glass it changed from transparent to opaque to provide them privacy. "That's *amazing*."

Venom chuckled. "I can't wait to show you around our quarters. You're going to love the technology."

Risk watched them with interest. Whatever he saw made him smile. "I'm off shift soon but I'll see you two in the morning." Pausing in the doorway, he pointed at Venom. "She's still my patient, so behave yourself, Captain."

Venom held up his hands. "I'll keep my big paws

above the sheet."

Risk snorted and shook his head. "It's not your hands I'm worried about, Ven."

Venom balled up the stickers he'd peeled from her skin and tossed them at Risk. The surgeon displayed his whip-fast reflexes by catching them midair before they pelted his head. Still laughing, Risk chucked the small ball into refuse bin on his way out the door. "Have fun, kids."

"But not too much," Venom grumbled and slid off the bed. "Do you sleep with the lights on or off?"

"On," she admitted. "Ever since…"

"The bombing," he said with an understanding smile. "That's all right. It won't bother me to keep them dimmed." He adjusted the lights to their lowest setting before returning to the bed and moving the sharp incline to its flattest setting. When he put his knee on the mattress to join her for the night she looked at him as though he was crazy.

"What is it?"

She pointed out the obvious. "We're not going to fit."

"Sure we are," he replied, undaunted. "We're going to have to get very close—but we'll make it work."

He seemed rather excited about getting very close. Dizzy wasn't so sure getting *that* close was such a good idea tonight. Deciding a buffer between their bodies was the best option, she scooted all the way to the other edge of the mattress and rolled onto her side, presenting him with her back. She tried to ignore the way his body heat called to her, urging her to snuggle against his naked chest and inhale the now-familiar scent of him.

"I don't think so, sugar." Venom's huge hand cupped her hip. With one good tug he dragged her onto her back. "I didn't get my foot caught in a damn trap only to spend the night staring at your hair."

When his head dipped toward hers she put her hands against his chest. The futile gesture made him grin. They both knew there was no way she could stop him from kissing her right now. Not that she really wanted to stop him.

"Relax." His husky voice soothed her. "I'm not about to make love to my mate for the first time in a hospital bed."

The anxious ball of nerves in her belly stopped bouncing. "No?"

"No." He brushed his mouth against hers. "But I have a few ideas of how we might enjoy ourselves."

She gulped at his wickedly inspiring words. "Oh?"

"*Mmmhmm*," he hummed his reply while skimming his lips down her throat.

She nervously bit her lower lip as she remembered the doctor's orders. "You promised to keep your hands above the sheet."

Venom lifted his head. Those pale-blue eyes of his sparkled with mischief. "Is that a dare?"

His devilishly sexy grin made her toes curl. "No."

His deep, rumbling laughter echoed in the stillness of their room. "It sure sounded like one."

"You don't strike me as the kind of man I should be egging on with dares."

"Oh, I don't know about that." He ran his fingertip

along the rounded neck of the hospital gown. "Maybe you could dare me to put a big smile on your face."

She squeezed her thighs together as heat pulsed between them. "I really don't think I'm brave enough to do that."

"Lucky for you I have enough bravery for the two of us." Oh, she didn't doubt that.

Venom claimed her mouth in a slow, sensual kiss. He didn't seem to be in any rush as he traced the seam of her lips with his tongue before flicking between them. With gentle pressure, he coaxed her to accept his invasion. Eyes closed, she relished the way his big, hard body curled around hers.

It seemed wicked to let this man she had known for less than a day kiss her like this but she couldn't find any reason to stop him. The idea that she belonged to Venom freed her from all the pressure to deny herself any pleasure. The rules were very different up here in Venom's world.

All those carnal delights she'd yearned to experience were no longer off-limits. As long as he'd waited for his chance to have a mate Venom wasn't going to abandon her after he had his first taste. After everything he had shown her today she believed she could trust him.

With a soft sigh she wound her arms around his wide shoulders. Her fingertips ghosted over his shaved head and encountered the rough stubble. Cupping her face, Venom plundered her mouth, leaving her breathless and aching all over. Her breasts became so incredibly sensitive that the thin fabric of the hospital gown sliding against her nipples forced them into tight, throbbing peaks.

As his searing kisses grew more intense she tightened her hold on him. His hand left her face to follow a slow trail down her neck, over her collar and toward her breasts. He palmed her flesh through the gown and she hissed with need.

"I can't wait to get you home." He growled the words as he dragged the sheet down to her knees. "Tonight I'll make do with my hands but tomorrow I intend to discover every single inch of your body with my tongue."

Was that a promise or a threat? She couldn't tell but it did wild things to her already overheated body. His hands felt so good gliding over her curves. She couldn't even imagine what it would feel like to have his tongue circling the stiff point of her nipple instead of the fingertip currently tormenting her.

When he tugged down the front of her hospital gown and bared her breasts, she inhaled a shuddery breath. Her belly clenched as white-hot arcs of desire sizzled through her body. Venom made a hungry sound before sucking her nipple between his lips. She arched into the unexpected and deliciously naughty sensation of his tongue fluttering over the sensitive peak. "Oh!"

He noisily released her breast and dragged his mouth across her chest. He flicked her nipple with the tip of his tongue before suckling her long and hard. "Do you like this?"

"Yes." She breathed the word as fire raced through her core. Feeling a bit lightheaded, she wondered if her old sickness was returning. When Venom pinched her nipple she experienced another wave of it and realized that it was all him. *He* was making her feel *that* good. "Please don't stop."

His gruff laughter vibrated through her chest. "Be careful what you ask for, sweetheart."

Holding her gaze, he ran his hand along the curve of her hip down to her knee before sliding his hand along her inner thigh. Eyes wide, she clamped her legs together, trapping his hand there. This playful kissing and petting was one thing but she was worried where opening the door to naughtier play might lead. "I don't think we should—"

"Hush," he admonished gently. "When we're in bed together, I'm in charge. I decide what we should and shouldn't do."

Her eyebrows shot to her hairline. He wanted to be in charge of sex? "I don't know about that."

"I do." He regarded her carefully. "I realize you've only known me for a short time but do you think I would do anything to harm you?"

"No." There was no doubt in her mind that Venom would rather suffer excruciating pain than to ever see her harmed.

"Then what's so wrong about trusting your mate—your husband—to control this?" When she didn't answer immediately, he asked, "Are you afraid?"

Was she? After taking a moment to consider, she answered honestly. "Yes."

"Of me?"

"A little," she admitted with a nervous swallow.

"You're right. I don't know you. I think you're a good, honest man—but I've known women who were fooled and hurt. I don't want to be one of them."

"Believe what I show you, Dizzy." Venom nuzzled their mouths together. "You are the most precious thing in the universe to me. If we were attacked right now I'd lay down my life to save yours."

He spoke as if delivering a vow. Peering into his handsome face, Dizzy felt her inhibitions fading. She wanted this. She wanted *him*.

Grasping his wrist, she eased the tension from her thighs and let them fall apart. His breath caught in his throat as she slowly moved his hand along her skin. When their hands disappeared under the gown, she whispered, "Show me, Venom."

Chapter Seven

VENOM'S HEART RACED at Dizzy's whispered invitation. He sensed it had taken a hell of a lot of courage for her to ask him and he wasn't about to disappoint her. He had meant what he said earlier about claiming his wife in a hospital bed. The infirmary was too busy a place to share something that should be incredibly special for Dizzy.

But that didn't mean they couldn't have some fun tonight. He wanted to ease some of her anxiety and fear of him. What better way to do that than to show Dizzy just how good he could make her feel?

Her heavy, excited breaths fanned his naked chest as his fingers crept along her thigh. When he touched her panties her grip on his wrist tightened. He dragged his fingers up and down the fabric shielding her sex. Already the thin cotton was soaked. His dick ached to be buried in her wet sheath but he muscled down the primal urges threatening to overwhelm him.

"Look how wet you are, baby." He couldn't wait to get his fingers on her slick heat. When he hooked his finger around the damp fabric and started to tug it away from her body Dizzy clamped her eyes shut. He watched the furiously red blush race across her face.

Deciding not to call attention to her embarrassment, Venom peppered kisses along the swell of each breast. She had the sweetest tits, not too small or too big, and so incredibly sensitive. He traced a pink bud with his tongue before suckling her. He really wanted to get his mouth on another, even pinker part of her but doubted he could control himself if he allowed himself even the shortest taste.

"Venom!" She bucked against him and he smiled against her breast. He bit down gently—just enough to make her gasp—before easing his tongue over the area he'd nipped. "*Oh.*"

He loved hearing the soft sounds she made and wanted to hear more of them. Gripping her underwear, he jerked them down to her knees. "I hope you didn't pack too many of these."

"A week's worth. Why?"

"It was wasted space." He left her panties there, just above her knees, and cupped her bare pussy. "You won't be wearing them anymore."

Her scandalized expression made him smile. "I have to wear undies!"

"Says who?" He kissed her before she could come up with an answer. "They'll only get in the way."

"Well…"

"When I want you I don't want anything to slow me down." He dipped his face until their noses were touching and their breaths mingling. Dragging his fingertips up and down her pussy, he said, "I don't want anything between me and your hot cunt.

Understand?"

She gulped at his brazen command. "Y—yes."

Kissing her, he took his time exploring her virgin sex. He traced her labia before parting them ever so gently. When his fingertip tapped her clitoris she sucked in a shaky breath. "Ven—Venom."

"That's it, sugar." Thrilled by her response, he urged her on while slowly massaging the swollen nub. "Do you like the way this feels?"

"Yes." She hissed the word and lifted her hips. The elastic waist of her panties would only stretch so far, so her legs had very little movement. When she tried to lift her hands she realized the hospital gown had been trapped beneath his hip. The taut fabric restrained her in arms in place.

Ready to set her free, Venom watched her face for any signs of panic but what he saw surprised—and enthralled—him. Her breaths quickened for a few seconds before she dragged a long, steady stream of air into her lungs. He felt her body relax beneath his and witnessed the flush of arousal spread across her skin.

His rock-hard cock swelled even more at the realization that she enjoyed being controlled in this way. Was she aware of her desire or was this new for her?

"You like being restrained." It wasn't a question. He stated it as simple fact rather than opening the door for argument.

She licked her pouty lips. "I...I don't know about that."

To prove his point, Venom lifted his hip just enough

to allow the gown to slip free. When she tried to wiggle away from him, he grabbed her wrists and dragged them over her head. Pinning them to the pillow, he hooked his leg over hers and used the weight of it to hold her down.

Almost immediately her eyes took on that hazy smokiness that was so exceedingly rare in the pleasure women who worked the sky ports. The highly paid prostitutes would act out any fantasy for the right price but only a small number of them actually craved true submission. It was one of the reasons he'd stopped visiting them on furloughs. The encounters left him feeling cold and empty.

But what he felt right now while holding down Dizzy burned him right up. She looked at him with such wonder and desire. Her shuddery breaths betrayed the way restraint aroused her. Even so, she seemed a little uncertain. Was it the guilt of enjoying the way he held her down? Was it the fear of behaving in a way her culture deemed deviant?

Maybe Dizzy didn't know what she needed. Maybe she needed him to show her.

Still gripping her wrists, he used his other hand to further his exploration of her slick heat. She whimpered when he dipped the tip of his middle finger into her molten, wet core. He penetrated her by torturously slow degrees, pushing in until his knuckle was buried inside her.

Always mindful of hurting her, he watched her face for any sign of discomfort. "Is this okay?"

Apparently unable to speak, she bit her lip and nodded. He didn't push any deeper or try to thrust in and out of her just yet. Instead he massaged her clitoris with his thumb. He drew lazy circles around the little pearl while kissing her into submission.

Gradually Dizzy surrendered to him. Her head rolled side to side as he rubbed her clit and held her in place. "Venom... I..."

"Do you touch yourself when you're alone?" He caught her off guard with his question. Wanting to coax an honest answer from her, he thrust his finger up into her and then slowly retreated. "Do you do this to yourself? Is this how you make yourself come?"

"I...I don't."

He slanted his head to study her. "Honesty, Dizzy. I always want you to be honest with me when we're together. It's the only way for us. If we're going to build something real we have to start on a solid foundation of truth."

To her credit, she didn't avert her gaze even though she was clearly discomfited by his question. "No," she said finally. "I don't do *that*. Not...not inside me."

"But you rub your clit," he guessed.

She swallowed again. "Yes."

"Do you like what I'm doing right now?" He continued to fuck her with one digit while stimulating the bundle of nerves with his thumb.

"Yes." She answered him breathlessly. Already her pussy gripped his invading finger. The honeyed wetness dripping from her snug cunt told him she loved what he was doing—but it was nice to hear her admit it.

"Tell me how you like to touch yourself."

Her lips parted in shock at his blunt request. She started to turn her head but he thrust up into her deeper and a little harder. Gasping, she rocked her hips as much as possible in search of more stimulation. Working up the courage to be truthful, she directed, "Faster."

He rewarded her bravery with another kiss and by giving her what she wanted. "Like this?"

"Yes." Her pussy fluttered around his finger. Side to side, he strummed the little button and pushed her closer and closer to the edge. "Please. *Please.*"

Touching his forehead to hers, Venom tightened his grip on her wrists while concentrating his stimulation solely on her swollen clitoris. Eyes squeezed tightly shut, she breathed faster and faster while his thumb swirled over the pink nub. Her nipples were hard peaks now and they enticed him with all sorts of erotic possibilities.

Already he dreamed of fashioning a rope corset that would squeeze and support them. Then he'd clamp her stiff nipples with clips and maybe even attach light weights. How hard would she come when he flicked the weights or tugged on a chain between the clamps? Would she scream his name? Would she beg for more?

"Venom!" With a strangled cry, Dizzy climaxed. Awed by her beauty, he watched her shatter beneath him. He sensed she was holding back, probably out of fear of being heard, but he didn't push her for more. Not tonight at least. Once he had her in their quarters he wouldn't let her hold back anything. He wanted it all from her.

When her shudders lessened Venom eased off his sensual torment. Dizzy pressed her face against his neck as the aftershocks of her orgasm rippled through her. He gently cupped her pussy and loosened his clasp on her small wrists. Still panting, she nestled into him in search of his warmth and his strength. He cradled her in his arms and made sure she received the reassuring affection she needed after her first orgasm with him.

Was it the first one she had ever shared with a man? The possessive need to be the *only* man who had ever seen her come undone like that surprised him. Never before had he felt that kind of primitive jealousy.

Dizzy's soft hand glided along his biceps to his nape. When she sought a kiss, he met her halfway. Her enthusiasm made his cock pulse even harder. He'd grown so aroused by touching her and watching her come that his dick throbbed almost painfully. Though he wanted nothing more than to stroke himself to completion, he set aside his needs to focus on her.

But as Dizzy's hand slid back down his arm to his chest, Venom got the impression she wanted to have her turn at exploring him. Hoping to encourage her confidence with him, he allowed her to touch him however she pleased. Her hands swept over his pecs and down his abdomen a few times before coming very close to the waistband of his shorts.

There was no way she had missed his massive erection. It tented the front of his shorts. No doubt she had recognized how much larger he was than the human males on her planet. Was she having second thoughts about letting him be her first?

Their gazes clashed as she curiously caressed his hard length through his shorts. He held his breath when her fingers traced him. Grasping him through the fabric, she mischievously flicked her tongue against his lips. "I want to touch you."

"You are touching me." He growled his response as the tether on his control remained tenuous at best.

"Without clothes," she clarified, her voice wavering with nervousness and excitement.

He pushed down the front of his shorts and released his cock from its fabric prison. Taking her hand, he brought it down to his rigid shaft. "I'm all yours, sugar."

Her sweet mouth curved with a playful grin. She nipped at his lower lip and wrapped all ten of her fingers around his thick length. He bit back the curse word that burned the tip of his tongue. Heat speared his belly as she idly stroked him with both hands. Up and down, her curled fingers caressed his hot flesh.

When one of her hands moved even lower to cup his sac, Venom nearly came. He clamped down on the overpowering urge and managed to hold his climax at bay. Her soft fingers massaged his balls while her other hand continued stroke him from the base to the blunt crown. Precum oozed from the slit there. The copious, glistening fluid slicked her fingers.

"Am I doing this right?" She sounded so unsure of herself.

"Hell yes." He punctuated his gruff reply with thrusts into her stroking, fondling hands. "Tighter. And faster, baby."

"Like this?" She followed his orders perfectly but seemed too timid to move her hand as quickly as he wanted.

"I won't break." He wrapped his hand around hers and guided it up and down his shaft at a quicker speed. "You can be rough with me."

Hoping to encourage Dizzy's curiosity and confidence with him, Venom kept her hand trapped beneath his to show her what he liked. The hand cupping his sac massaged him a little harder, just the way he wanted it. He dipped down to claim her sweet mouth, stabbing his tongue between her pliable lips and swallowing her excited whimpers.

He had never imagined something as simple as a hand job could feel this damn good. It occurred to him that it was the connection between them that amplified every sensation. He realized that in all of his adult life he'd never allowed himself to truly *feel* anything with a woman.

Like so many soldiers, his first time had followed his pinning and graduation ceremony at sixteen. Highly skilled women who worked in the pleasure sector were usually brought in to initiate the new graduates as a kind of reward and good luck send-off before they were rushed onto the front lines. There was nothing romantic or gentle about those encounters. It was sex devoid of emotion or intimacy.

Even later when he had discovered his love of rope bondage he'd simply sought out prostitutes who allowed that kind of thing. Very few of them had actually found any excitement or fulfillment in being tied up in his intricate knots and harnesses. For most of those women it was an added fee to be pocketed and nothing more.

So he'd erected a wall around himself, refusing to allow emotional entanglements. Before he had sworn off visits to the pleasure sectors at various sky ports, he would get in and out as quickly as possible. There was no softness or intimacy. The most foreplay that occurred happened during the fee and scene negotiations.

Right now with Dizzy, Venom allowed himself to *feel*. He allowed himself to indulge his protective instinct and welcomed his growing affection toward her. He eagerly awaited the chance to take this long, erotic journey with her, to discover what made her come the hardest or scream his name in pure ecstasy.

"You're so hard." Her awed whisper sent electric jolts through his chest. His muscles started to tense. Balls tight, he sped up their caressing hands to increase the friction where he needed it most. Her lips touched his neck, planting ticklish kisses on his skin. "Come for me, Venom."

Dizzy's whispered plea flung him right over the edge. Groaning her name, he went rigid as his blazing-hot cum rocketed through his cock. His climax punched the air right out of his lungs. The ropy bursts of seed spilled onto her thigh and belly, drawing a surprised gasp from her.

As he shuddered against her, Dizzy sought his mouth for a deep kiss. She caressed the back of his head and the knotted muscles between his shoulders as he recovered from his orgasm. He reveled in the tender comfort she offered him. "Thank you." Drawing back so he could peer into her eyes, Venom asked, "For what, sugar?"

"For being so gentle and easy with me. You could have taken this all the way. You're so much bigger and stronger than me that you could basically force me to do anything you want—but you haven't. You kept the promise you made in the forest."

"I never break my promises, Dizzy. Especially not to you," he added before kissing her. "I am bigger and stronger than you but I would never, ever use my size to intimidate or hurt you." Horrified by the very idea of it, he instructed, "If I ever make you uncomfortable, you need to tell me. I don't ever want you to be afraid of me."

"I'm not afraid of you." She studied him for a moment. "I'm curious about you. I'm attracted to you. But I'm not afraid of you."

"Good." He relaxed at the knowledge that he'd put her at ease around him. "Wait here."

Venom slid out of bed to retrieve a couple of wet wipes from the nearby cabinet. When she realized he was going to clean up her belly and thigh, she twisted away from him. "I can do that."

"I'm sure you can." He dragged her onto her back so he could wipe away the evidence of their heavy-petting session. "I made this mess. I'll clean it up."

The corners of her mouth lifted with amusement. "Does that extend to housework as well?"

Venom laughed. "Sure does." He leaned down to peck her cheek. "I didn't Grab you so I could have a house slave. I've lived on my own enough years to be fully capable of doing my own laundry or cooking dinner."

"You cook too?" She straightened her hospital gown and scooted over to the edge of the mattress to make room for him. "I might be even luckier than I thought."

"You have no idea." He crawled back into bed with her. This time she didn't try to turn her back on him. Instead she rolled onto her side to face him. For a long while, he simply enjoyed staring at her. He took in her bright eyes and full lips and that paleblonde hair spilling around her shoulders. The vision of her bare breasts, nipples hard and flushed, tormented him. The sweet sampling of her had whetted his appetite for so much more—but not tonight.

He allowed himself one final kiss before rubbing her arm. "Get some sleep, sugar."

She answered him with a silent nod and shut her eyes. Following her lead, he let his eyelids drift together. The exhaustion of a long day finally got to him. His emotions had vacillated all over the place today. Excitement, arousal, panic, fear, lust, desire, jealousy, protectiveness—he'd felt them all multiple times and it had worn him out physically and mentally. A good night's rest was definitely in order.

But every time he started to succumb to the lull of slumber Dizzy fidgeted next to him. At first he assumed she was trying to get comfortable. He imagined her bed back on Calyx was smaller and softer than these big, hard hospital mattresses.

When she rolled onto her other side he hoped she'd found a comfortable spot. A few minutes later she squirmed again and flexed her feet. She blew out an annoyed breath amid her restless search for sleep.

"Dizzy, is something wrong?"

She didn't answer him immediately. Eventually she admitted, "I can't sleep like this."

He frowned. "Like what?"

Sitting up, she rubbed her face between her hands. He sensed she was embarrassed to reveal something to him.

"Tell me how to help you."

"I have a weighted blanket at home. I couldn't bring it because it was too big and bulky for my bag. I...I can't sleep without it."

She sounded so humiliated to admit that she had a special blanket. If anyone else had heard her confess that, she might have been met with laughter or teasing. He knew better.

"Dizzy, honey," he touched her arm, "it's okay. Don't be embarrassed. It's not as uncommon as you'd think."

Her gaze whipped toward him. "Really?"

"Sure." He slid his arm around her shoulders and tugged her down into his waiting embrace. "Men who suffer from siege shock often have trouble sleeping. They actually sell weighted blankets and sleep masks programmed with the sound of rainfall and crashing waves in the commissary."

"This didn't start with the bombing. I've always been like this. My dad was the one who figured out that I needed constant pressure to sleep normally." She snuggled against his chest. "He actually rocked me to sleep every night until I was almost seven."

Her father must have loved her a great deal to be so dedicated. If he was aware that she wasn't biologically his it made him an even better man in Venom's mind. Among his people stepfathers rarely showed any interest in the offspring from their wives' first marriages. It just wasn't done in his culture.

Thinking of her father reminded Venom that he was going to have to bite the bullet soon and tell her what he'd learned from her blood tests. It wasn't a discussion he looked forward to having with her.

"Let's try this, Dizzy." Venom shifted her in his arms until her neck rested on his biceps. He hooked his leg across her thighs and wound his upper arm across her chest. He made sure his weight wouldn't crush or harm her but allowed enough pressure to soothe her. "How does this feel?"

"Better," she said, her voice devoid of the frustration that had earlier plagued her.

"Good." He brushed his lips against the top of her head and let them linger. If she needed one, he'd get her a weighted blanket in the morning. He suspected she would sleep just fine with him holding her.

"Briarlina."

The strange word she spoke so unexpectedly confounded him. "What?"

"It's my real name." She ran her finger over his forearm as if scribbling on him.

"Briarlina."

"Briar? Like the thorn patch?"

"Yeah," she said with a short laugh. "Now you know why I prefer the Dizzy nickname."

It was an awful name but he wasn't about to tell her that. "It's...different."

She snorted softly. "That's one word for it."

His lips twitched at her good-natured reply. "Is it a

family name?"

"My mother's name was Lina."

"And your father was Briar?"

She shook her head. "My dad's name is Jack."

What about her biological father? Briar wasn't a name he had ever come across during his many years in the corps but that didn't mean it hadn't been given to one of the men a generation above him. Maybe that was a good place to start.

"My birth name was Ehjay. It means first in our ancient tongue."

"First?"

"I was the first son in my family. They don't waste names on boys. We're named in order of our birth and earn our real names later. Venom is *my* name. It's the one that means something to me."

"But what happens to the boys who don't make it into the academies or who can't cut it in the programs?"

She had touched upon one of his society's greatest shames. "Everyone knows they're failures because they keep their birth names."

"That's harsh."

"That's life in the Harcos world."

He heard her intake of breath as she started to say something. Whatever it was she decided to keep it to herself. Certain it would lead to an argument, he chose to let it go for now.

"Get some sleep, sugar." Smiling at the thought of all the ways he planned to keep her busy tomorrow, he added, "You're going to need it."

Chapter Eight

AFTER THE BEST night of sleep she'd had in years Dizzy stood in front of the small bathroom mirror and dabbed on a little lipstick. She could hear Venom pacing outside the closed door, his heavy boots hitting the floor in a steady rhythm. She still marveled at the way he moved so quickly considering his huge size.

Her face grew hot as she remembered a certain big part of him that she'd held in her hands last night. She didn't quite know where that burst of courage to be so brazen had come from. Something about Venom drove her toward wantonness. He hadn't seemed the least bit fazed by the way she enjoyed being held down while he teased her with his fingers and mouth. Her reaction appeared to excite him a great deal.

From the moment her father had admitted to selling her lottery number, Dizzy's greatest fear had been the sexual side of the relationship she would be expected to form with the man who would Grab her. She had always been a practical sort of girl. Making a marriage work on less than auspicious beginnings hadn't frightened her but the rumors of the types of bedroom games these sky warriors enjoyed had.

Had she been wrong to worry about what her new

husband would want in bed? If the way Venom had rocked her world last night was any indication she was going to be a very happy, very satisfied wife.

"Dizzy?" Venom rapped his knuckles against the door. "Are you ready yet?"

She wasn't but she could hear the impatience in his voice. Slightly amused by his typical male behavior, she reached out to open the door. It seemed that men weren't much different from one end of the galaxy to the other.

With a tap on the door's edge, it retreated into a wall pocket to reveal Venom leaning his arm against the frame and looking bored as hell. His expression quickly morphed from one of impatient waiting to one of utter desire. He raked his gaze up and down her body before taking a step toward her. "How many of these dresses did you pack?"

"Ten." Feeling a bit nervous, she smoothed a hand down the front of her dress. "Do you like it?"

"Like it? You look amazing." He fingered the delicate ruffle outlining the modest neckline. "I want you to wear dresses like this every day."

His appreciation for soft, feminine things amused her. She considered their drabbut-functional surroundings and the fact that the ship was so heavily populated by men. No doubt it was a novelty for him to see something pretty. She had never been a fan of pants anyway so dresses were her usual daily garb.

"Lift your skirt."

She reared back at his unexpected instruction. "What?"

"Show me what's under your skirt."

"No." Remembering the order he had given during their heated tryst last night, she gulped nervously. Had he been serious about that? Judging by the look on his face? Yes.

"Dizzy." There was a slight warning edge to his voice as Venom invaded her personal space and backed her up against the counter. His boot moved between her feet and his knee slid between her thighs, preventing her from squeezing them shut.

"What are you doing?" Her breathless question didn't faze him.

He lowered his face until they were at eye level. There was nothing angry or irritated in his expression. He looked calm and collected as he stroked her jaw. "I'm not the sort of male who requires complete and total submission from his bride. There are very few orders I will ever give you— but I expect the ones I give to be followed."

Dizzy considered him for a moment. What he was asking wasn't the worst thing in the world, was it?

With trembling fingers she grasped the bottom of her skirt and pulled it up to reveal her simple cotton panties. "I didn't realize you were serious about not wearing undies. I thought maybe it was something you said to be dirty in the heat of the moment, not because you meant it."

Venom cupped her womanly heat through the thin cotton. "You'll soon learn that I mean everything I tell you." He gave the waist elastic a little tug and let it snap back against her belly. "Take them off."

"What? Now? But I'll be out in public and…" Her

voice died off as his unwavering gaze caused a naughty little thrill to rush through her core. With a dramatic huff she pushed her underwear down her hips. "I don't know why you're so insistent about this."

She only got them as far as her thighs before Venom dropped down to his knees and dragged them the rest of the way down her body. Her pulse was sprinting so hard that she felt a little lightheaded as Venom pocketed her undies. He shoved her skirt up and tucked it into the front of her bodice.

"Ah!" Dizzy gasped as Venom pressed a soft, ticklish kiss to her bare mound. His lips danced between her belly button and the dripping vee between her thighs. He got dangerously close to kissing a certain throbbing part of her but refused to give her the satisfaction of finally feeling his mouth *right there.*

"You," he carefully penetrated her with his middle finger, "belong to me." He smirked triumphantly as he encountered the wet evidence of her arousal. "You like belonging to me, don't you?"

There was no point in denying it, not when he could feel her inner walls clenching his thick finger. "Yes."

"And you want to please me, don't you?"

She licked her lips as she stared down at the ruggedly sexy sky warrior kneeling before her. "Yes."

"I want to know that when I have a craving for this sweet, tight cunt of yours that all I have to do is lift your skirt." He swirled his fingertip around her swelling, pulsing clitoris. "You seem to be forgetting that my pleasure is your pleasure."

Oh, that wasn't a mistake she would make again. Rocking her hips, Dizzy hoped to encourage Venom to continue doing these wicked, wicked things to her. "Please…"

"Not now, sugar." He gave her pussy a playful pat and tugged her skirt back into place. "That aching that you feel? That's your punishment for wearing panties without permission."

She wasn't just aching between her thighs. She was aching all over. Dizzy considered flirting with him and pleading a little—but his alpha nature wouldn't be won over by batting eyelashes.

He traced the fitted bodice of her dress. "This deep green is a nice color on you."

Trying to ignore the clamoring need so deep within her, she said, "Ella says green makes my eyes pop."

He tilted his head as if to consider her eye color. "She's right. Did you make this?"

"Yes." She had designed the simple fit-and-flare dress last fall. "It's been my bestselling design this year."

"If other women look this beautiful wearing it I'm not surprised they're flying off the racks."

She blushed at his compliment. "Thank you."

Smiling, he bent down and kissed her forehead. "Risk will be here soon to complete your exam."

"I'm almost finished." She turned back to the small toiletry case. While she searched for a pair of earrings, Venom picked up her lipstick. She glanced at him and offered a teasing grin. "I don't think that color would look very good on you."

He laughed and dropped the lipstick into the case. "No? Well, I suppose you'll have to take me to Naya's shop and pick out a better color."

"Naya?" She threaded the simple hoops through her earlobes.

"She's the mate of Menace. He's a close friend."

"Oh." The mention of a woman running a shop surprised her. She had assumed these sky warriors were like the men on her planet with their desire to keep women at home regardless of whether or not their wives wanted to be there. "What does she sell?"

"She's only been open a few weeks but she focuses on importing goods from Calyx. She ran a pawnshop back on your planet, so she has a fairly extensive list of contacts willing to ship in clothing and housewares."

Dizzy's hand went still as his words finally registered. "Wait. You said her name was Naya?" Venom nodded. "And this pawnshop of hers was in Connor's Run?"

Venom's eyes narrowed. "Yes. Why?"

"I think we have a friend in common. Ella was a street kid and she ran with a crowd from Connor's Run before making it to The City. She always talks about a girl named Naya whenever Danny stops by for a visit."

Venom eyes widened. "Dankirk? The Red Feather fixer?"

Dizzy swallowed nervously. Had she said too much? He must have seen the worry on her face because he soothingly rubbed her shoulders. "It's all right, Dizzy. We've worked with Dankirk on numerous occasions in the last couple of months. We have no issue with the Red

Feather up here. In fact we support many of their humanitarian missions."

She relaxed. "Oh. In that case, yes. Ella is very close with Danny. If this Naya is the same girl I'm thinking of I can't wait to meet her. She's the reason Ella survived her time on the streets to become a muse."

"A muse? You mean a model?"

"We call them muses, but yes." Dizzy turned back to the mirror to check her reflection one last time. "She's incredibly successful. Right now she's building a shelter for street girls."

Venom threaded his fingers through her hair. "Are there a lot of girls living on the streets in The City?"

"Yes." Dizzy packed away her things. "Ella was actually a second-generation street kid. Her mother was a teen prostitute so it's amazing that Ella managed to fight her way off the streets and make something of herself."

"Yes, it is." Venom kissed her neck. "As soon as the next visitation list opens I'll put Ella's name on it. I can tell how much you already miss her."

Touched by his offer, she stroked his arm. "Thank you, Venom. I really appreciate that."

"I know how much I depend on Raze for support. I don't want you to feel alone up here or cut off from your old life."

"Raze is your best friend?"

"We've known each other since the academy."

"He's here on this ship with you?"

"We work together in SRU. He's technically my boss."

"That's not awkward?" She couldn't imagine having

Ella as her boss. She figured they'd snipe at each other all day long.

"Not in the least," he answered. "We've worked together so long we almost share a sixth sense."

"I suppose that comes in handy with the kind of dangerous work you do."

"Very," Venom agreed. At the sound of the main door opening, he glanced toward the empty bed. "I think Risk is here." He motioned toward her toiletry case. "Are you done with this?"

"Yes."

He picked it up and gently pushed her toward the door. Risk tapped away at his tablet and greeted them with a smile. "How are you feeling this morning, Dizzy?"

"I feel great." She took the toiletry case from Venom, slipped it inside her suitcase and zipped the large piece of luggage shut.

"No more lightheadedness or nausea?"

"No."

"Did you have any headaches last night or pain anywhere in your body?"

"No."

"Good." He pointed to the bed. "Hop up there and let me get one last set of vital signs before I send you on your way."

She did as directed. Risk extended one of the small silver stickers toward Venom. "Since you bit my head off yesterday, why don't you put this one on her?"

Venom snatched the adhesive-backed square. "I didn't bite your head off. I only asked that you respect my boundaries as her mate and master."

Dizzy's astonished gaze snapped to Venom's face. "My *master*?"

His lips settled into a tight line as he peeled away the clear backing on the vitalsigns detector and placed it on the underside of her wrist. "It's just a term, Dizzy. I realize it has a negative connotation in your world but it's not like that here. When we get home I'll explain it to you."

The firmness in his voice made her eyebrows arch. "Is this where I nod my head like a good girl and say *Yes Master*?"

Risk chortled noisily behind Venom. Her mate—*master*—eyed her carefully. Leaning down, he planted his hands against the mattress on either side of her hips and didn't stop leaning in until their gazes were level. His masculine scent swirled around her and the insane amount of body heat he produced radiated right through her.

"Well, Dizzy," he said finally, "I suppose that depends on how badly you want to be rewarded once we get home."

The dangerously sexy glint in his eyes made her tummy flutter wildly. She had a feeling his idea of a reward included her naked and totally at his mercy. If last night's glimpse into Venom's skills as a lover were any indication of what she could expect, Dizzy wanted him to *reward* her long and hard.

Rather than overreacting without all the information, she decided to wait and let Venom explain this whole master thing to her. Hopefully it was a simple cultural difference. After all, he had said that he didn't want a house slave, right? So far, he had stood by his word to her and broken none of his promises. She doubted he was going to start now.

Toying with one of the buttons lining the front of his uniform shirt, she whispered, "All right, *Master*."

Venom's lips twitched as he tried to fight a smile. There was no hiding his pleased response to her teasing reply. The tender kiss he pressed to her forehead reassured Dizzy. If he really *was* controlling or mean, he wouldn't show her such patience and gentleness. He would have been a raging jerk right out of the gate.

Risk stepped closer to finish his exam and Venom reluctantly stepped aside. He checked the incisions behind her ears and palpated her neck for any swelling. After asking a few more questions, he peeled off the life-signs detector and tossed it in the trash. "You're good to go, Dizzy. I'd like to see you in a week for another head scan to ensure that you're healing properly internally. Externally your incisions are nicely knitted together but I'd recommend treating them gently when you're washing your hair." He exchanged a glance with Venom. "We'll also chat about your test results from the intake exam."

She frowned. "Should I be worried?"

Risk waved his hand to dismiss her worries. "No. I didn't see anything in the preliminary results that should concern us. I'll take another look when the final report is in just to be sure."

"Oh. Okay." Her panic subsided. Considering the state of The City and the lack of good medical care and even sanitation in some of the slums, she could only imagine the awful diseases and toxins she'd been exposed to during her short life.

"If you experience any pain, swelling or pressure in the area where we operated, I want you to come see me immediately. All right?"

"Sure."

"I'm medically disqualifying you from space-to-surface travel until I've had a chance to do two follow-ups on your surgery. Obviously if we had to abandon ship, you would have to take the risk but for pleasure travel?" He shook his head. "I don't think it's worth the chance of rupturing the drains we installed." Risk glanced at Venom. "Since we're talking about pressure, no inversions or suspensions where she might shift upside down for at least two weeks, Captain."

Venom nodded. "Understood."

Inversions? Suspensions? Her curious glance at her new husband went unanswered. Maybe this was something else her *master* was going to tell her about when they reached his private quarters.

Risk held out his tablet. "Sign here, Venom, and she's all yours."

Watching Venom scrawl his signature on the tablet screen to take possession of her from the hospital drove home her new and very unequal standing here in his world. So far he'd treated her with respect and showed that he valued her—but his legal system reduced her to nothing more than property. She didn't like it one bit.

Venom grabbed her suitcase in one hand and held out

the other. "Ready?"

She slid off the bed and placed her hand atop his huge palm. He wrapped those long, thick, calloused fingers of his around hers and pulled her tight against his side. "Take me home, Venom."

VENOM COULDN'T WAIT to get Dizzy out of the infirmary wing and safe inside his quarters. He sensed her rising anxiety after the way he had stupidly uttered the word *master*. Risk's mention of suspension and inversions hadn't helped matters any. He wanted to sit her down and have a candid conversation in a more comfortable and private environment.

Though he had no intention of forcing her to follow the old ways of his people, he *did* want to slowly introduce her to the concept of surrendering to his dominant side. He believed she would find a great deal of pleasure in submitting to him—but it had to be on her own terms. There would be no pressure from him. Venom wanted that gift of submission to come freely and without strings attached.

As they exited the infirmary and crossed the waiting room to the elevator bank, he noticed Dizzy gawking at her new surroundings. He tried to imagine seeing all of this from her perspective. It would be a daunting experience to be thrust into this gleaming technologically advanced world.

"I know it's a shock, Dizzy, but you'll get used to it." He slid his arm around her slender shoulders and gave her a reassuring hug. "As soon as Risk clears you for travel and I can free up some vacation time, I'll take you back down to Calyx so you can get your feet on solid ground again."

She smiled up at him and snuggled in closer to his side. The simple act of seeking his protection and support made his heart stutter. Building trust between them was his number-one priority. He needed Dizzy to know that he'd do anything for her and that she could count on him to provide for all her needs—physical, mental or emotional.

When they stepped into an empty elevator he took her hand and touched it to the navigational screen. "We're in this section of the ship. Our living quarters are way over here."

She bit her lip. "I'm really bad at reading maps."

He chuckled softly as he remembered the way she'd gone in the complete opposite direction of where she needed to go during the Grab. "Don't worry. Navigating the *Valiant* is foolproof."

"I'm not so sure." She studied the navigational screen with a great deal of skepticism.

Venom tapped the underside of her wrist. "They implanted your ID chip while you were sedated. This thing is like the key to the ship. It will allow you in and out of our quarters. It provides a method of payment when you need to shop." He waved her hand near the ID reader until it beeped. A second later a route appeared on the navigational screen. "Now you have a map to get home."

He let her examine the display for a few moments before gently nudging her forward. "Go ahead. If you make a mistake, I'm right here to help you."

She hesitated before tapping the screen and choosing the next appropriate floor. "Is this right?"

"Yes." He gave her ponytail a playful tug. "When we hit the next main floor, I'll take you through the shopping and food courts so you can get a feel for what's available."

"What about fabric and notions?"

"Notions?"

"Sewing supplies," she clarified.

"Oh. Well—I have no idea," he admitted. "I'm sure Naya can arrange an import order for anything you can't find in the shops here."

Before Dizzy could answer, an eardrum-piercing squawk blasted them from above. Startled by the sound, she jumped and squeaked with shock. Immediately concerned about her newly sensitive hearing, Venom clapped his hand over her left ear and smashed the other against his chest to muffle the noisy alarm. He thought of the healing incisions behind her ears a second too late but figured they were all right. He'd been on the receiving end of the fast-healing and quick-dissolving sutures enough times to be reasonably assured he hadn't just hurt her.

"It's an abandon ship drill." He raised his voice so she could hear him. Dropping the suitcase, he reached over to the navigational panel in search of an option to mute the damn alarm.

"Now hear this. Now hear this…"

"Yeah, I fucking hear you," he growled. These damn drills were annoying as hell but they served a necessary purpose. The new brides coming onto the ship every quarter had to know how to save themselves if the *Valiant* was ever attacked and abandon ship orders were given.

The elevator dinged pleasantly as they reached their destination. When the doors parted, Venom's mouth settled into a grim line at the two faces that greeted him. Pierce and Torment didn't seem the least bit surprised to see them. Suddenly he doubted the abandon ship drill and their elevator ride occurring simultaneously was a coincidence.

Was this about his run-in with Devious? If it was, these two Shadow Force operatives had the world's worst timing. Venom would never shirk his duty but he had much better things to do this morning than sit in an interrogation room with a couple of spooks. More importantly he doubted Dizzy was going to enjoy sitting alone in a waiting room while he was grilled.

Torment stepped inside and moved his wrist in front of the ID scanner, followed by Pierce. The doors shut and the alarm immediately stopped within the confines of the elevator. Venom lowered his hand from Dizzy's ear but she didn't make a move to leave the security of his embrace. She seemed to have picked up on the danger the two men presented.

Pierce smiled at them but Torment remained his usual sunny self. His dead-eyed stare unnerved Venom so he could only imagine how much it scared Dizzy. She gripped the front of his uniform and glanced up at him with much worry in her dark eyes. He tried to put her at ease by rubbing the spot between her shoulder blades but he was certain the stiff set of his jaw wasn't helping matters any.

He decided there was no point in lying to her because the truth about the two men would soon be evident to her. "Dizzy, these men work for a special branch of the corps. This is Pierce and that's Torment."

She gulped. "Special branch? You mean like the secret police?"

Pierce tried to ease her fears. "We don't roust people out of their beds in the middle of the night for beatings over publishing political papers but we perform similar functions."

"I see." She pushed even tighter against his side. Venom soothingly petted her upper arm. "I suppose you two didn't corner us in this elevator to congratulate Venom on Grabbing me."

"No, we didn't." Pierce picked up Dizzy's suitcase. "You have some very interesting friends and family, Miss Lane."

Pierce's remark sent a cold chill through Venom. This wasn't about Devious at all.

On instinct Venom pushed Dizzy behind his body. He kept his hand curved along her hip. "What's this about, Pierce?"

"We just have a few questions for your bride."

Venom didn't like the sound of that at all. Trying to remain calm he considered the two Shadow Force operatives. Pierce wasn't the kind of man who would ever harm a woman. He had committed a major infraction and earned a disciplinary demerit for allowing Naya to record a message before Terror dropped her on Calyx to run a covert operation. Whatever he wanted from Dizzy, Pierce would be gentle and respectful in his handling of her.

But Torment? Venom warily eyed the Shadow Force interrogator. The man had a dark and deadly reputation. He was a cold son of a bitch who excelled in extracting information from Splinter terrorists. The medics who had treated some of Torment's suspects had told Venom stories that turned his stomach. There was no way he would allow Torment to put those cruel hands anywhere near his Dizzy.

"Do I need a lawyer?" He doubted they were bringing Dizzy down to the hidden Shadow Force operations center for a friendly chat.

"We just have a few questions about some of Dizzy's acquaintances back in The City." Pierce offered a relaxed smile. "We have no issue with her at all."

"Unless she's uncooperative," Torment rasped.

Venom's hold on Dizzy tightened. He fixed the interrogator with a daring glare. "Watch your step, Torment. This is my mate—and you *will* show her respect."

Torment inclined his head in silent acceptance of the warning. Dizzy gripped the back of his shirt. He hated that she was being frightened like this. His protective instincts flared.

Despite Torment's position in the Shadow Forces and his ability to make life very uncomfortable, Venom wouldn't hesitate to knock the leaner, slightly shorter man flat on his ass if he lifted one finger in Dizzy's direction. He'd witnessed Menace nearly lose Naya after Terror and his men overstepped their bounds. He wasn't going to give them the chance to put Dizzy at risk.

The elevator opened onto an empty hallway that wasn't even on the navigational screen. Torment led the way and Pierce stepped aside with a gesture for them to follow the interrogator. On edge, Venom clasped Dizzy's hand and scanned the hallway for any threats. With Pierce trailing them, they followed Torment to one of the doors lining the opposite side of the corridor.

Torment pushed open the door and entered the brightly lit interrogation room. At the sight of the table and two chairs, Dizzy stopped walking. Venom hated to force her into the stark space but it had to be done. The sooner they got this over with the better. He pulled her across the threshold and walked her to the nearest chair.

"You can wait outside, Venom." Torment slapped a stack of folders onto the table.

"Like hell," Venom snapped. He grabbed the chair, pulled it out and sat. Winding his arm around Dizzy's waist, he dragged her down onto his lap. "Ask your damn questions so I can get my wife out of here."

Pierce looked awfully amused as he placed Dizzy's suitcase next to the table and took the seat across from them. "Direct and to the point as always, Ven."

"Let's just get this over with, Pierce." Venom let the irritation he was feeling at being blindsided by these two fill his voice.

"Fair enough." Pierce picked up one of the folders and opened it up in front of him. He lifted his gaze and smiled at Dizzy. "Let's talk about the Grab."

"Okay," she said uncertainly. "What about it?"

"This is the original list of lottery numbers pulled for

the Grab." Pierce whipped out a sheet of paper from the files he'd likely obtained from a spy within The City's government. "Your number isn't on it." He retrieved a second sheet. "Yet curiously it's on this revised list that was posted as the official lottery results."

Shock tore through him. He shifted her on his lap so he could see her face better.

"Dizzy, is that true? You weren't selected for the Grab?"

She swallowed hard. "Not exactly."

"She bought her way onto the list. Didn't you?" Pierce already knew that answer.

Didn't she realize that she'd broken one of the treaty laws? Didn't she understand how suspicious it looked for a woman to buy her way onto a list that would allow her to gain access to the *Valiant* and possibly a high-ranking member of the military?

Pierce slid another sheet of paper across the table. "We know that you sold your number to this council member. I need to know how you did it and why." He peered intently at Dizzy. "From all accounts, you had a rather nice life down there. You were living independently and enjoying a growing profile as a designer. Why does a young woman with so much success and prosperity ahead of her throw her name into the ring to be Grabbed?"

Venom wanted to hear her answer. What had she said back in the forest? *I don't have anywhere else to go.* Why would she tell him something so obviously untrue?

She fidgeted as a blush of embarrassment stained her neck and face. "I didn't sell my number. My dad did. He owes a lot of money to a loan shark. He needed the money or else Fat Pete was going to collect me as collateral."

Venom's gut soured. He felt the shame radiating from her and tried reconcile all the details she'd let slip about her parents last night, especially the ones about her father, with the picture that Pierce was painting. Dizzy had described her dad as loving and kind but the man had risked losing her to a loan shark.

"This man?" Pierce opened another file and retrieved a photo of a morbidly obese man in his late fifties.

She nodded. "They call him Fat Pete. He controls all of the sharking action in Low Town."

"Was your father being threatened by this man?"

"Well, yeah, I mean he *is* a criminal."

"Your father or the loan shark?" Pierce turned the question around so quickly.

She glared at him. "My dad is a black market dealer. Most of the cargo he moves is medically related. I'd hardly call providing antibiotics criminal."

"I suppose that depends on which side of the law you're standing," Pierce replied.

To keep Dizzy from lashing out at Pierce and causing herself trouble, Venom gently stroked her arm. He understood how difficult this was for her but she couldn't understand how much worse it could get if she refused to cooperate.

"Why does your father owe Fat Pete money?"

Picking at nonexistent lint on her dress, Dizzy shrugged. "He didn't tell me and I didn't ask. My dad has separated that side of his life from mine for years. I think it was over lost cargo or maybe shipping arrangements that fell through."

Pierce stared at her for a few unnervingly long seconds. Was he trying to read her? Venom wondered what they thought she knew.

"Tell me how your father exchanged your lottery number."

"I don't know how *he* did it. I know how *other* people have done it."

"And how is that?"

"It's not that hard. There's always some rich girl with a pulled number who wants out of the Grab and a family with a daughter who has a clean number that needs the money. If you know someone who knows someone—"

"Like maybe a fixer by the name of Dankirk?" Pierce narrowed his eyes.

Dizzy exhaled with frustration. "You seem to know the answers to all these questions already. Why are you even wasting your time by asking me?"

Pierce sat back and looked utterly relaxed. "I'm just trying to make sure I have all the ends tied up before I make a recommendation about your future on this ship." Venom's back went ramrod straight. "Are you threatening to take away my mate?"

"Whoa." Pierce held up his hands at the snarled question. "Calm down, Venom.

There's no need for you to come across this table, okay?"

Dizzy found the courage to ask, "Are you going to arrest me?"

"Do we need to?" Pierce countered.

"No." She pushed back against Venom's chest, as if desperate to retreat from this uncomfortable situation. "I didn't break any laws."

"No, but your father did and you failed to report them. We're not partial to lawbreakers up here. However," Pierce drew out the word, "we're willing to take into consideration that you were under an extreme amount of emotional duress. We don't believe that you're a terrorist sympathizer trying to gain access to the ship or her crew."

"A terrorist? Are you *insane*?" Dizzy's angry outburst made Pierce's eyebrows rise. She grabbed the front of the white bride's collar and dragged it down. "Do you see what those monsters did to me? They killed my mother. Do you really think I would ever work with slime like that?"

Pierce stared at the scars on Dizzy's neck. "No, I don't think you would knowingly work with them. Our intelligence tells us that Fat Pete has ties with the violent Sixer street gang. It's very likely they're using him to launder money for the Splinter terrorist cell on Calyx. Your father just paid him a very large sum of money…"

She put her hand to her mouth as if she might be sick. Recognizing that this might be a trick to get her to implicate herself, Venom covered her hand with his own. "Don't say another word, Dizzy."

"We're not after her." Torment finally deigned to speak. "You don't need to worry."

"You seem to forget that I was there in that warehouse when Menace's woman took three bullets to the stomach. I watched her bleed out on that filthy floor and nearly lose her life. You'll have to excuse me if I don't believe a damn thing you say, Torment."

"Believe this." Pierce retrieved a small communications device from his pocket and showed it to Venom. "We briefed Terror when Dizzy's background check flagged her as a possible risk. He secured a pardon from our Shadow superiors and the War Council. It's been signed by Vicious and Orion so you can be assured it's legit."

Venom lowered his hand from Dizzy's mouth but gave her a look to stay silent until he'd read the legal document offered to him. The sight of Vicious and Orion's signatures calmed him. After the mess with Naya neither the general nor admiral would ever allow another woman to be harmed or railroaded on their watch.

"What are the terms of this deal?"

"The usual," Torment replied. "She cooperates fully and convinces me that she's told the whole truth. When we're done here we release her into your custody and won't bother her again unless we have follow-up questions."

It was the follow-up questions that had Venom concerned. How often would they want to pull her in for questioning? Would they come for her when he was on duty?

Pierce would make sure he was notified but Torment? No, he shared Terror's views on their covert work. There was no cost too high to safeguard the Harcos nation.

Dizzy shifted nervously. "What do you mean by releasing me into Venom's custody? That makes it sound like I'm his prisoner."

Torment made an amused noise. "For all intents and purposes, you brides are prisoners of the men who catch you. They just call you their mates to soften the shock a bit."

Venom glared at Torment. "She is *not* my prisoner."

Torment shrugged. "We'll agree to disagree." The master interrogator trained his gaze on Dizzy. "To answer your question—when we're done here, Venom can choose to keep you or send you packing. It's an indulgence he's earned for his years of brave service. Don't make him regret it."

Her small hand gripped his. "I would never do that."

"Then let's get back to the interview," Pierce said, pulling them back on track. "Let's talk about your mother."

Venom swore inwardly. He had a sneaking suspicion his choice to delay telling her about the blood test results was about to bite him in the ass big-time.

Chapter Nine

DIZZY BLINKED AT the man called Pierce. "My mother is dead. There's not much to say."

"I disagree. I think there's plenty to talk about when it comes to your mother."

Dizzy couldn't believe this guy. Wasn't it bad enough that he had just humiliated her in front of Venom? What more did he want from her? He'd already insinuated she might be a terrorist sympathizer.

Torment, the scary-looking one, remained stock-still in his position behind Pierce. The man's deadly vibe made her legs tremble. She wasn't dumb enough to tangle with a guy named Torment. By the looks of him he had earned that name in ways she refused to even imagine.

Dragging her gaze back to Pierce, she asked, "What do you want to know about my mom?"

"Where was she born?"

The question seemed innocuous enough so she didn't feel bothered by answering it. "She was a colony girl. She came from Jesco where her parents were professors at the university there."

"What would make a colony girl leave behind the freedom of the colonies for your planet?"

"Love," Dizzy answered simply. "My mother was a

free spirit. She won a lot of pageants and beauty contests as a teenager. She wanted to be a muse. What you call a model," she explained, remembering the term Venom had used. "Apparently my grandparents weren't very supportive. They wanted her to get an education and make something of herself but she wanted to travel and enjoy life. She got a job working as a stewardess with Cross Colony Air and that's how she met my father."

"And how long did she work as a stewardess?"

"Um…six years? I think she was around my age when she left that job and started her muse agency in The City."

Pierce tugged another photo from his stack of folders. "Let's talk about this man."

Her gaze settled on a surveillance photo of her father leaving one of the known gambling dens in Low Town. "My dad?"

"Sure."

Her brow furrowed as she considered all the paths this part of the interview might take. "What do you want to know?"

"How did he meet your mother?"

"Oh. Well…he was on vacation in Safe Harbor and Mom had a layover there. They met on the beach there and had a whirlwind romance. A few weeks later she resigned her post with Cross Colony Air and married my father."

"Because she was pregnant with you?"

"Yes." She wondered at the odd way Pierce had asked that question. Was it because his culture took a negative view on pregnancy outside marriage?

Pierce thumbed through his paperwork. "Your father was a very wealthy man. You enjoyed a very nice lifestyle until the recession."

Her fingers skimmed the scars on her neck. "After the bombing the recession hit. Dad's bank suffered badly. They were overextended and heavily invested in real estate near the embassy and Up Town sector. Within a few months of the explosion Dad was bankrupt."

As if sensing how hard it was for her to dredge up the darkest time in her life, Venom caressed her arm. If they had been alone he probably would have kissed her tenderly and spoken soft words to her. The intense scrutiny of the secret police duo kept Venom from showering her with the affection she'd grown accustomed to receiving from him. Instead he remained silently supportive of her. It was more than enough and gave her the courage to keep going.

"After we lost the house I got my own small apartment. I couldn't work as a muse anymore. Not after…" She gestured to her neck. "But I'd always been very good at designing clothes. Dad gave me some cash to get my business started. I've been supporting myself ever since."

Pierce consulted another folder. "Your mother owned and operated a muse agency."

"Yes."

"And your parents were very high in society down in The City?"

"They were."

Pierce showed her various photographs of her parents at political parties and cultural events. "Do you know any of the people in these photos?"

She studied them and pointed out faces she recognized like the former mayor and a chief of police. "I don't run in those circles anymore so I haven't seen any of these people in years."

"After his bankruptcy what did your father do to make money?"

Dizzy frowned at Pierce's odd pattern of questions. "Is this some kind of interrogation tactic? You know, get me talking about one thing and feeling comfortable and then blindside me with something else?"

Behind her Venom laughed quietly. "Sounds like you need to work on your game, Pierce."

"My game is just fine, thank you," Pierce grumbled. "Tell me about Jack's current line of business."

"You already know what he does." She let loose a resigned sigh. "He's a fence and a black market dealer."

"Do you receive money from his illicit activities?"

She carefully answered his question. "I'm not sure whether the money to start my business or pay my first few months of rent for my apartment came from legal or illegal sources."

"That's fine." Pierce sat forward. "So—tell me what you were doing at the embassy the day of the bombing."

She swallowed hard. "I was following my mother."

Pierce looked interested. "Because?"

Did he know or was he just fishing? Remembering that the deal required absolute truth, she couldn't very well hold back the facts she'd already told Venom. "I followed my mother because she was having an affair with one of your men."

"Did you know the Harcos man?" Torment asked the question this time and he was anything but gentle in his delivery.

"No."

His eyes narrowed with skepticism. "No? You'd never seen or met this man?"

She shook her head. "I heard my parents arguing about him earlier that week. It was the first indication I'd ever had that things weren't perfect in their marriage."

"How long was your mother seeing this man?"

"I don't know."

His eyes narrowed even more. "Would you recognize him?"

Venom shifted beneath her. His fingers tightened around her arm. Was he worried they were pushing her too hard? "I doubt it. I only caught glimpses of him. It's been years."

"You don't think it's the slightest bit suspicious that your father, a man with underworld contacts, sold his only daughter into a Grab when his wife had been conducting an affair with a Harcos male?"

Dizzy didn't like Torment's tone. "What are you getting at?"

"What color was your mother's lover's hair?"

Venom cleared his throat but Torment didn't seem the least bit interested in easing up on his rapid-fire questioning.

"His hair?" Dizzy's shoulders bounced. "Why in the world does that matter?"

Torment seemed irritated. "Was it the same color as yours?"

"The same color as mine?" She started to touch her hair but stopped. A strange sensation invaded her chest. All her life people had remarked on the white-blonde color of her hair because it was so very rare among people in The City. Her mother had always claimed it was very common among the Earth settlers who had founded the colonies on the planets surrounding Calyx.

Chest constricting, she asked, "What exactly are you trying to insinuate?"

"I'm not insinuating anything." With an exasperated exhale, Torment stared over her shoulder to Venom. "You didn't tell her."

"Tell me what?" Dizzy twisted on Venom's lap for a better look at his face. Outwardly he looked calm—probably the effect of years of frontline battles—but he had a grim darkness about his expression. "Venom?"

His right eye twitched. She sensed he was waging an internal struggle. He tenderly touched her cheek and confessed, "Your blood tests before your surgery had some unexpected results. They showed that your father is one of us."

"That's not possible. They have to be wrong." Her clipped, rushed reply came even before she'd processed what Venom had said. She simply refused to believe it.

"They weren't wrong. Our medical tests are highly sensitized and accurate. Your father is not the man you think he is."

His words bounced around in her head but she

couldn't make sense of them. Her brain seemed to be on the fritz as she tried to reconcile twenty-three years of her life with the earth-shattering bomb Venom had just dropped. "My father is Jack Lane."

His expression softened to one of pure compassion. "Jack Lane is the man who raised you, yes, but your biological father is a Harcos male."

Dizzy shoved at his chest and rose to her feet. "No. That's not true." She narrowly evaded Venom's clutching hand and glared at the men who had been interrogating her. "This is some vile trick."

"This isn't a trick." Torment gestured to the sea of photographs on the table. "Look at your mother. Look at Jack Lane. They're both dark-haired." He pointed to her head. "That hair? It's a dominant trait in females bred by Harcos males."

Her stomach threatened to erupt. She didn't know what to believe anymore. She just knew that she had to get away from here. Spinning toward the door, she shouted, "Let me out of here."

"We're done. This interview is over." Venom's chair scraped loudly against the floor as he shot to his feet and hurried to her side.

"This interview is over when I say—"

"We can reschedule," Pierce interrupted Torment's outburst.

Reschedule? These guys were out of their damned minds if they thought she was *ever* going to talk to them again. They were such liars. Somehow they'd manipulated those test results. She refused to believe anyone else was her father. It wasn't possible. It simply wasn't.

Wordlessly Venom retrieved her suitcase and placed his hand against the small of her back. He led her out of the interrogation room to the elevator. The silent ride was excruciatingly uncomfortable. Anger surged through her but she couldn't pinpoint the source. Her mother? Her father? Those two jerks back there who scared her with their intrusive questions?

She glanced at Venom. Stiff-jawed and stoic, he drew her ire. "So much for your promises to protect me!"

Venom eyed her carefully. His jaw tensed and relaxed a few times. "I failed this time. I won't fail you again."

The shame in his voice tore at her conscience. Venom wasn't the one who deserved her fury. He had been nothing but nice to her. She wasn't exactly happy that he'd kept the test results from her but she figured he had a reason for it. Considering the way she'd just reacted, he had probably wanted to avoid upsetting her.

Gripped by guilt, she reached for his big, scarred hand and interlaced their fingers. He seemed surprised by her quiet gesture of apology. His icy-blue eyes reflected a mixture of hope and trepidation. "That was wrong of me. I shouldn't have lashed out at you."

Venom bent down and kissed the top of her head. "You're upset and you're in pain. You're feeling betrayed and confused. Making me the target of your jumbled emotions takes the heat off the people you're really angry at—your parents."

His wise, patient reply only made her feel worse. Other men probably would have snapped right back at her about being childish but not Venom.

As tears burned her eyes, she asked, "Is it really true?"

His unwavering gaze convinced her even before he spoke. "Yes."

Dazed by the realization she had been lied to for years, Dizzy barely noticed all the people and the shops as they crossed the bustling marketplace sector of the ship. They stepped into another elevator that took them to a quiet residential floor. She should have been excited to cross the threshold into her new home but all she could think about was locking herself away in the bathroom to have a good cry and try to sort out the lies from the truth.

But Venom seemed to have other ideas.

The moment the door was secured, he tossed aside her suitcase and snatched her by the waist. Her shocked gasp echoed in the dimly lit space of the entryway. Using his strength and size to his advantage, Venom lifted her up until she had no other choice but to wrap her legs around his waist. With the wall at her back, he supported her slight weight easily with his massive, muscular body.

Her heart thundered at the way he had so unexpectedly manhandled her. She was suddenly very aware of how gentle he had been with her since putting his collar around her neck. He could hurt her so easily—but he wouldn't.

He ducked his head and tried to kiss her but she turned her face. She wasn't in the mood for kisses right now. "No."

"Yes." His lips brushed her cheek before seeking out and finding just the corner of her mouth. "I thought I was protecting you by holding back the facts. I see now that I should have let Risk tell you as soon as you were awake."

She moved her head a fraction and peered into his soulful eyes. "Why didn't you let him tell me?"

He sighed heavily, the hot burst of air buffeting her neck. "You had been through so much. First you'd endured that terrible Grab with the freezing temperatures and all that snow. Then you were sick and needed surgery. I didn't want to distress you by revealing that your biological father wasn't the man you'd known and loved for so long." He touched his forehead to hers. "I am so sorry that Torment was the one who broke the news to you. I cannot even imagine what you're feeling right now."

Her heart softened toward Venom. "I don't really know what I'm feeling right now."

"It's normal to be confused." He trailed his rough fingertip down her cheek. "You don't have to sort it all out right now, Dizzy. Take some time to process your feelings."

She tilted her head and gazed at his handsome face. His expression had taken a haunted turn. "You sound like you've been where I am right now."

The corners of his mouth drew taut. "I've been in some terrible mental places, Dizzy. I know what it's like to feel betrayed and confused and guilty and angry and sick all at once. It's exhausting and painful." He slid his finger under her chin and tipped her head back. "Don't make the mistakes I did. Don't hold this all inside. It's okay to let it out and to acknowledge that whatever you're feeling in this moment is perfectly normal."

His advice calmed her a little. She tried to imagine

what kind of hell he'd been through after the many battles he'd survived—and the lives he'd been forced to take as a sniper. "I hope someday I learn to be as strong as you."

He blinked with surprise. "Sugar, you *are* strong. You survived a terrorist bombing. You had your neck ripped open by shrapnel but you fought like hell to live. Then after your mother died and your father lost everything, you didn't curl up in a ball and cry. No, you struck out on your own and made a go of it a world where very few women are independent or have careers." He brushed her bangs away from her face. "Don't you see how strong you are?"

"I don't feel very strong right now." Dizzy rested her hands on his shoulders. "I feel colossally stupid. Torment was right. I look nothing like my father. Everyone always commented on my hair but I never thought…"

As her voice trailed off Venom kissed her cheek. "I know, sweetheart. I know this is hard for you to accept."

"I don't think I do accept it yet." She ran her hands along his shoulders. "How am I supposed to believe that you're telling me the truth about the blood tests when that means that the two people I loved the most and trusted to tell me the truth were lying to me from the day I was born?"

"This is why I wanted to wait to tell you after we'd built more trust between us."

"I don't think my reaction would have been much different, Venom." She pinched the collar of his uniform shirt between her index finger and thumb. The desperate need to speak to her mother overwhelmed Dizzy. There were so many questions that needed answers. "Why didn't she tell me the truth?"

Venom didn't answer immediately. "She probably thought she was protecting you in some way. It couldn't have been easy for her to face a future as an unmarried mother. When you were born, the relations between our two races weren't nearly as friendly as they are today. She must have had her reasons."

"And my dad?" She refused to think of him as anything else. Blood or not, he'd raised and loved her from birth. "I can only imagine what you must think of him, especially after all that nonsense about the loan shark, but he wasn't always like this. I swear, Venom."

"You don't have to convince me of anything, Dizzy."

She doubted that was true. She'd seen the disgusted look on Venom's face when she'd revealed the details about Fat Pete and the black market dealings. She hated that her father's gambling was out of control and that it had put her in danger, but she'd never doubted for one second that he loved her.

Until now.

"Sometimes…sometimes," she continued after a slow breath, "when my dad looked at me after the bombing, he had this strange sadness in his eyes. Sometimes it looked like anger. Do you think…I mean…was he thinking that I wasn't his and he didn't want to be saddled with me anymore? I used to think that he was angry I had survived instead of my mother—"

"Stop." Venom silenced her by placing his fingertip to her lips. "Don't do this to yourself. Speculating is just going to make you hurt more." He caressed the span of skin just above the bridal collar she wore. "I don't know that it's possible but I'll try to find a way for you to communicate with your father. He may be on the restricted list because of his current occupation. If he's not I'll call in some favors. You need to speak to him face-to-face."

The pain in her chest eased. "You'd do that for me?"

"I don't want this hanging over you for the rest of your life. You need answers. I promise you I'll do everything in my power to get them."

Suddenly all the crazy emotions she had been feeling bubbled to the surface. Venom's kindness and affection was the very last straw. Once again he had stunned her with the lengths he was willing to go for her. He was proving to be exactly the kind of man she had always wanted. She refused to believe any man could be this good and this gentle but Venom seemed intent on proving her wrong.

Loud, ugly sobs erupted from her throat. The last twenty-four hours had been among the most jarring of her life and she just couldn't hold back the tears any longer. Venom whispered sweetly and gathered her to his chest before stepping away from the wall where he'd been bracing her body and carrying her farther into his home.

A few seconds later, he sat down on a couch. Holding her even tighter, he cradled her on his lap and let her have a good cry. His strong arms felt so good wrapped around her shaking body. She tucked her face against his neck and inhaled the comforting male scent of him. His hand swept up and down her back as she wept, the sobs growing softer and more spaced apart.

"I'm sorry," she said when her pathetic crying jag finally ended. Wiping at her face, she refused to meet his intense gaze until he cupped her chin and made her look at him. What she saw reflected in his bright-blue eyes stole her breath.

"Never apologize for feeling something, especially when it's this raw and this real." He swiped his thumb across her wet cheek. "We haven't had a chance to discuss the Harcos way of lovemaking yet but there will be times when we're together where you will feel emotionally exposed and vulnerable. I have to know that you're being honest with me and showing me everything so I can properly guide you through these experiences and protect you from harm."

She gulped at his description of being exposed and vulnerable. "Is this where you tell me about that master thing?"

He held her gaze for a long moment before exhaling long and slow. "No." His lips touched her forehead. "This is where I help you clean up your face and then make you breakfast."

"And then?"

He traced her lower lip. "And then I'm going to show you what being your master means."

A sizzling arc reverberated through her belly. "Maybe we could skip breakfast and get right to the good part?"

Venom's sinfully sexy smile made her thighs clench together. "Not this morning, sugar. You're going to need your strength."

Oh. My. God. She trembled to think what sort of decadently intimate things Venom had in store for her.

Tugging his uniform shirt out of his pants, Venom used the bottom of his soft undershirt to clean the wet streaks from her face. "Now—tell me how you feel about eggs." His mouth curved in a teasing grin. "Does that cross the line for you?"

She didn't take offense to his playful remark. "I love a nice fluffy omelet."

"Good." He gently shifted her off his lap and helped her stand. "I'll give you a tour of our home and then I'll make you breakfast."

He bent down and captured her mouth with one of those toe-curling kisses he was so damn good at. As Venom towed her along behind him to view the kitchen, she wondered if her heart was going to beat right out of her chest. "Then we'll make this union of ours official."

Chapter Ten

VENOM SAT ON the edge of the bed and waited for Dizzy to emerge from the bathroom. He'd already stripped down to his boxer briefs. His palms rested on his bare knees as he tried to rein in his sprinting heart rate with steady, controlled breaths. In his many years as a sniper, he'd learned to manage the adrenaline rush of battle to ensure his shots were always perfect the first time.

But this? Waiting for his new mate to come to him so he could claim her? None of his old tricks were working.

His fingers trembled against his thighs as he slid his sweaty palms up and down his legs. His blood pressure spiked when he considered all the different options he might employ to show Dizzy what he was capable of as her new husband and lover. More than anything, he wanted to reassure her that she could trust him in an intimate setting like this.

He let loose a rough snort at the realization that this petite beauty with her big brown eyes and pouty lips had him more riled up and out of control than a horde of Splinters rushing the Sendarian gates. The nervousness rippling through his gut stemmed from his desperate need to make her first time perfect. Well—as perfect as it could be. When it came to sex, perfect wasn't a possibility.

Without a doubt, something would go wrong.

But he could damn sure make certain Dizzy enjoyed the hell out of their first tumble in the sheets. There might be a little discomfort for her but he'd make sure she experienced true pleasure at least three or four times.

He was still mulling over how many orgasms she might like when the bathroom door opened. His heart leapt into his throat. He swallowed hard at the sight of Dizzy in a soft pale-pink nightgown. It was a vast improvement over the rather ugly hospital gown she'd been forced to wear last night—but it made her look so incredibly innocent.

Guilt speared him. She had waited to be with a man of her choosing—and now he'd taken her from her planet and dragged her into his world where she was classified as his property and expected to give him healthy babies, preferably sons, to fill the ranks. What was she feeling right now? Dread? Resentment? Disappointment?

He was reminded of Torment's remark about the brides being little better than prisoners of the men who Grabbed them. His gut soured at the very idea of Dizzy considering him her warden. His nature and upbringing drove him toward dominance but that didn't mean he had the right to dictate the moment she would surrender her innocence.

His anxiety levels skyrocketed. Had he overstepped the line? Was he rushing this? Was he rushing her?

She hesitantly stepped out into the bedroom. Her eyes widened at the sight of him nearly naked. He silently cursed his decision to strip down to his boxers. Should he have stayed in his pants and shirt? Would she have been more comfortable?

She took a couple of small steps toward him but didn't get close enough for him to reach out and touch her. He held perfectly still as she assessed the situation. Her gaze roamed his body before jumping to the large bed and then back to him. Wringing her hands, she asked, "Do I get on the bed now or…?" He held out his hand. "Come here."

She clasped his fingers and allowed him to drag her between his widened knees. Placing his hands on her slim hips, he stared into the dark irises that had ensnared him the moment he'd dragged her onto his lap out in the snow. Leaning forward, he dotted kisses along the neckline of her nightdress. "I said I would show you what being your master means but there are many ways for me to do that without making love to you."

She swallowed and the white bride's collar encircling her neck moved up and down. "There are?"

"Yes." Was that a hint of disappointment in her voice? "We need to discuss what mastering means in my culture first."

Her hands drifted to his shoulders. "I'm really hoping it doesn't have the same slave connotation it has back on my world."

"No." He decided not to tell her that there were some couples, especially back on Prime where pureblood marriages were still very common, whose mates embraced relationships with complete exchanges of power. There was no point in scaring her when such an arrangement had no chance of ever happening within their mate bond.

He wasn't that kind of man.

"That's good to hear."

He let his hand glide from her hip to her belly and then up toward her breasts. Cupping her hot flesh through the thin fabric, he brushed his thumb over her nipple. Almost immediately the little nub tightened to a stiff peak. Her body's reaction to his touch pleased Venom immensely.

"In our world, a master has the same meaning as husband does in yours. When we talk about mastering our mates, we're talking about creating a deep and unbreakable bond." He traced the hard peak of her nipple through the fabric. "It's about trust and respect."

"What about love?" She asked the question in a nervous rush of a whisper.

He moved his hand to her face, running his thumb across her bottom lip and brushing his fingertips along the patch of skin just in front of her ear. "I've never been in love."

"Neither have I." Dizzy reached up and laid her hand against his. "But something tells me you're going to change that."

His heart skipped a few beats. "I hope so, sugar."

Her sweet smile warmed his heart. She glanced over his shoulder and her brow furrowed. "Venom, where does that door lead?"

He didn't have to look back to see what door she meant. It was the only one he'd purposely avoided showing her during the earlier tour of their quarters. Deciding now was as good a time as any to have *that* discussion, he stated, "It leads to our playroom."

"Our what?"

"It will be easier if I show you." He stood and captured her hand. She matched his steps as they crossed the bedroom. After unlocking the door with a wave of his wrist near the scanner, he pushed it open and tugged her along behind him. The lights automatically brightened. Because he didn't plan for them to stay long, he didn't fiddle with the temperature controls to the room.

Four steps inside the playroom, he stopped but held tight to Dizzy's hand. Fearing the worst, he looked down at her. The expression on her face surprised him. It wasn't horror or terror reflected on her features but curiosity.

As if feeling his interested gaze, she glanced up at him. She licked her lips a bit nervously before asking, "So when you say playroom, you mean...sex."

"Yes."

"I see." She moved away from him. At first, he suspected she might try to bolt for the bedroom. To her credit, she indulged her curiosity of the space. She opened one of the drawers where he kept a selection of vibrators and anal toys. Almost as quickly she slammed it shut and refused to meet his amused gaze.

Walking to the wall where he'd arranged his ropes and striking implements, she simply stared at them. He could only imagine how very strange the floggers and many lengths of looped rope must have looked to her right now. She felt one of the rougher ropes among his collection. He didn't miss the fleeting distaste that spread across her face. That was definitely a rope that would be dead last in his rotation.

When her gaze drifted to the ceiling and the rein-forced hooks and rings, she stopped walking. Her mouth slanted and she pointed toward them. "I guess this is what Risk meant when he mentioned inversions and suspensions."

"Yes." Venom cautiously approached her. She was putting on a brave face as she explored the playroom but he sensed one wrong move would cause her to flee. "I'm not like most men of my race. I don't find much pleasure from domestic discipline but I've always gravitated toward bondage and restraint. We'll try out impact play to see if it's something you enjoy but it likely won't be something we do very often."

"Impact play?"

"Spanking, flogging, whipping—"

Air hissed between her teeth. She narrowed her eyes at him. "If you think you're going to whip me—"

"I don't." He dared to clamp his hand on her shoulder. "Everything we do in here or in our bedroom requires your consent. All you have to say is no and it's off the table."

She relaxed under his touch. "Okay."

He took down his softest, lightest and shortest rope and handed the small coil to her. She hesitantly accepted it. "I enjoy rope bondage—and I hope you'll learn to enjoy it too."

Swallowing, she glanced up at him. "Bondage?"

"Restraint," he clarified.

"You mean like the way you held me down last night

while we…?"

"Exactly like that," he confirmed. "Did you like what we did last night?"

She refused to meet his questioning gaze. "You know I did."

"There's nothing shameful about liking to be held down by your lover, Dizzy. Whatever makes you feel good is perfectly acceptable."

"I suppose."

He suspected she believed what he said was true but decided not to push her. In time she would learn to be more accepting of her desires and needs. Instead he took one end of the rope from the small coil in her hands. He expertly formed a knot and then teasingly rubbed it along her exposed collarbone. "You'll learn to crave the sensation of rope hugging your bare skin."

"Oh, will I?" She arched one of her bow-shaped brows.

His mouth curved with amusement. "Well—I *hope* you'll learn to crave it."

She didn't stop him from gliding the knot down toward the neckline of her nightgown. "Why do you like ropes?"

He searched for the right way to explain it to her. "I like the way they look crisscrossing skin. I enjoy the slow, methodical work of planning the ties and knots and rigging it all together." Quietly he added, "I enjoy knowing that the woman in my ropes is completely at my mercy."

Dizzy breathed a little harder. "It excites you to be totally in control?"

"Yes." He dipped his head to get a better look at her

face. The tips of her ears were bright red now and she seemed desperate to hide her eyes from him. "Does it excite you to think of surrendering control to me?"

She didn't answer him at first. Instead she rubbed her fingertip over the rope clenched tightly in her hand. "It shouldn't excite me—but it does."

He tipped her chin and forced her gaze to meet his. "Why shouldn't it excite you?"

She shrugged. "I don't know. It's just…it's not right."

"Says who?"

"Well…"

"Dizzy," he interrupted her gently, "what other people or society deems right and wrong ends at the front entrance of our quarters. *We* decide what is right and wrong for *us*. If you enjoy being tied up by me and I enjoy tying you up, we're going to do it. If you like giving up control when we're in bed so I can drive you crazy with pleasure, we're going to do that. This is *our* mate bond and we'll set the parameters of what is or isn't allowed within our union."

With a look of quiet consideration, she mulled it over while fingering the rope. When she finally lifted her face, Dizzy wore the oddest expression. She tilted her head back a bit bravely and said, "Tie me up."

He reeled back with surprise. "What? *Now*?"

"Yes." She looked as though she was trying to maintain her courage.

Worried about pushing her too far, too fast, he hurriedly said, "Dizzy, I didn't bring you in here to pressure you. I only wanted you to see what the playroom is and explain what I hoped we might someday enjoy together."

"I know that." She placed her hand against his bare chest. The searing touch of her fingertips on his skin branded him as hers forever. "You're going to be my first and I want to know what it's like to do things *your* way."

Venom studied Dizzy for a solid minute. "Are you sure?"

"Yes." There was no hiding her nervousness but that was to be expected considering all that she was about to experience for the very first time. "Unless you don't want to tie me up…"

"Dizzy, I've wanted to bind you in my ropes since that first moment I caught sight of you." He threaded his fingers through her white-blonde hair. "I need you to understand that you can change your mind at any time."

"I understand."

He hoped she did but he would be watching her carefully. At the first sign of discomfort or panic, he would end their first foray into bondage.

Bending down, he kissed her tenderly and took the rope from her hands. "Go into the bedroom and wait for me."

Biting her bottom lip, she nodded and carefully backed away from him. He enjoyed the sight of her swinging hips as she padded silently from the playroom. Left alone, he faced the wall of rope and formulated a plan for Dizzy's introduction into the sensual world of bondage.

WHAT THE HELL is wrong with me?

Dizzy couldn't decide if she was crazy or stupid. She

nervously paced the spacious bedroom and waited for Venom. Had she really just asked him to tie her up? *Are you insane?*

She must be losing her mind. Maybe that space sickness she'd read about in the pamphlets the medics had given her was a real thing. Surely she had to be coming down with some sort of space crazy to invite Venom to restrain her with rope. There was no other explanation for her brazen request. Unless...

No. Definitely not. There was no way she really wanted to be tied up. Was there?

Except... Well.

She *did*.

Dizzy couldn't explain it but something so stunningly primal had happened to her back in the playroom. As Venom had described wanting to restrain her with his ropes, she'd been overwhelmed by the most intense desire to feel squeezed and embraced by the intricate loops of knots and bonds. She remembered the way it had felt when he'd held her down while giving her an orgasm. Safe. Secure. Thrilling.

When he had spoken about the reasons he enjoyed rope bondage, she'd seen the primitive spark in his blue eyes. He *needed* this as much as she craved it. The way he had instinctively known how to help her sleep last night should have been her first clue that Venom understood her needs better than anyone.

For so many years, she'd considered herself broken with her bizarre need for deep pressure when trying to sleep. It wasn't *normal* and different wasn't something that people down in The City liked.

But maybe all along she'd simply been waiting for a man like Venom to show her what she needed. A man who understood how to nurture her and provide for all her needs—even the seemingly silly ones like needing to be feel secure and embraced at all times.

The sound of Venom's advancing footsteps spurred her heartbeat into overdrive. She gulped and licked her lips and watched him emerge from the playroom with three coils of rope looped over his brawny forearm, two of them were a deep-red shade and the other a creamy white. In one hand he held some shiny clips and a knife.

"In case I need to cut you lose in an emergency," he explained calmly. "I can grab some scissors from my play kit, if you'd prefer."

She shook her head. "I trust you not to hurt me with that."

"You probably shouldn't put so much trust in me," Venom gently chided. "We've only known each other for a day."

He was right, of course. "It feels longer."

He laughed. "Has spending time with me been that terrible?"

She cringed. "No, I meant—"

"I know what you meant," he interjected with a smile. Leaning down, he pecked her cheek. "I feel the same way. It's hard to explain but it *does* feel as if we've been acquainted for far longer than a day."

She watched him lay out the ropes on the bed. "How do you know which ones you want to use? Is there, like, a method or something?"

He seemed surprised by her question. A pleased smile stretched his mouth. "You really are interested in this."

"Of course I am." She frowned at him. "What did you think? That I was just going along with this because you wanted it?"

"No. I could tell that you were curious about your reaction to being restrained by me last night but I wasn't quite sure whether you were truly interested in being bound in rope."

"I am." She was able to admit it now without blushing too much. It seemed a strange thing to request but Venom made her feel safe asking for it.

"To answer your question—there are a few things I consider before selecting a rope from my collection. I consider what I plan to do with it first and that narrows down my choices. If I planned to suspend you from the ceiling, I would choose a stronger rope. Tonight, I plan to create decorative restraints so I've chosen something a bit softer and with some give."

"Decorative?"

He grinned. "You'll see soon enough."

Oh, she had no doubt. Picking up the closest coil of rope, she felt its weight. Her gaze was drawn to the bright-orange strip of cloth tape a few inches above one end of it.

"What's this?"

"I color-code my ropes to keep track of the lengths."

"Why do you need different lengths?"

"Six feet is good for making restraints. A dozen or so for harnesses." He examined her with a scrutinizing eye.

"Actually, as petite and thin as you are, I might need to cut some of them down a few feet."

She toyed with the end of the rope. He'd sealed it with some sort of clear gel. "What's this?"

"It's to keep the ends from fraying." He rubbed it between his fingers and gave an unsatisfied grunt. "I don't particularly like this stuff but I've yet to find a way to seal the ends that works long-term."

She studied the rope for a moment. "Why don't you just whip-stitch it?"

"Probably because I don't know how to sew," he replied with a snort. Giving her suggestion careful consideration, he asked, "Do you think it would work?"

"Yes."

"I may have found something to keep you busy for the next few days. Do you have all the supplies necessary?"

"I have a sewing kit in my bag." She rubbed the rope between her fingers. The fibers were soft but strong. "These aren't synthetic like your uniform fabrics."

"I'm not fond of most of the synthetic ropes that are available. I'm always careful to purchase ropes that won't burn skin too easily. We probably won't use the rougher braided types. They have their use but not with you." He reached out to touch her arm. "Your skin is so delicate and pale. I'd hate to mark or burn you too much."

She bit her lip. "Does that happen a lot?"

"It can if your master isn't careful and pulls the rope too quickly or too tightly." He shrugged. "Some subs like that sort of thing."

"Subs?"

"Submissive women," he clarified.

The description put her on the defensive. "I am *not* submissive."

His lips danced with amusement. "All right."

She glared at him. "I have a career and live independently. I'm not submissive to anyone."

"You're confusing submission in the outside world with submission to me." He closed the distance between them with one smooth step. Winding his arm around her waist, he dragged her against his body. "And you *are* submitting to me. You're surrendering control to me. You asked me to tie you up knowing full well that I can do *anything* I want to you once you're bound and helpless."

His words should have scared her—but they didn't. They aroused her so badly she had to squeeze her thighs together to lessen the pulsing right behind her clitoris.

And Venom knew it. He watched her face so intently. Smiling triumphantly, he lowered his head and claimed her mouth. "Make no mistake, Dizzy. I want your submission." He teased their lips together. "And you're going to give it to me." Was she?

Yes. The answer was nearly immediate.

Venom took the rope from her hands and set it aside. He grasped the bottom of her nightgown and dragged it over her head. Gripping the gown in his hand, he allowed his approving gaze to roam her naked curves. Last night she had been mostly clothed but now she stood here totally exposed and vulnerable. She hadn't been blessed with a knockout figure like Ella's and started to feel self-conscious about her small breasts.

Almost reverently Venom sank down to his knees. As tall as he was, they were eyeto-eye now. The dangerously hungry glint to his eyes sent rippling shivers of delight through her core. When he cupped her breasts, she sucked in a sharp breath. They seemed even less impressive palmed in his big hands.

It didn't seem possible but Venom appeared to read her mind. "I know what you're thinking."

She doubted it. "Oh?"

He leaned forward and nuzzled his mouth against the swell of her right breast. "You're thinking that you're inadequate." The pointed tip of his tongue traced the dusky-pink bud framed by his thumb and forefinger. "And you're dead wrong."

"Ah!" Her hands flew to his shoulders as he suckled her gently at first and then with harder tugs. He released her nipple and rubbed the slight roughness of his chin across her highly sensitive skin. The moan and shiver he elicited from her brought a knowing smile to his handsome face.

"Look at the way you respond." He pinched her left nipple with just enough of a bite to make her rise up on her tiptoes. The movement pressed her breasts even closer to his mouth and he took advantage of her position to suckle the nipple he had just tweaked.

Dizzy whimpered at the wicked sensations vibrating right through her. She had never felt *anything* like this. Last night had been amazing but she realized now that Venom had only shown her a teasing glimpse of the sensual possibilities he offered.

"Bigger isn't always better, sugar." He squeezed both of her breasts. "Wait until you see how gorgeous they're going to look bound up in my ropes."

She exhaled roughly. "How are you going to do that?"

He kissed each breast lovingly. "Patience."

She didn't have much of that left. She had been waiting so long for this moment. For years she had denied the erotic awakenings of her womanhood in a desperate attempt to protect herself. Being forced into a Grab and taken by Venom wasn't exactly the way she had planned this moment happening—but she suddenly couldn't imagine it going any other way.

Venom's strength and his commanding nature soothed her anxious nerves. He wouldn't fumble his way through this or leave her unsatisfied at the conclusion. Oh, she expected there would be some discomfort and assumed things might not go *exactly* according to plan but that was all right. She wanted to take this journey now.

With Venom.

He swept his hands up to her shoulders and massaged them. "When we're playing with ropes, you have to be completely honest with me, Dizzy. Don't hold anything back because you fear disappointing or upsetting me. If you don't like the way something feels or if you feel faint or in any way unwell, you have to tell me immediately. Understood?"

"Yes." The serious edge to his voice convinced her that he wanted to know the absolute truth, even if it meant she didn't like the ropes after all.

"You need to stay relaxed. Don't tense up when I'm

binding you." He stood slowly and walked around behind her. With his hand on her back, he carefully pushed her forward a few steps. "Stand tall and straight. We're going to begin now."

Gathering her hair in his hand, he coiled it up high and secured it with a couple of the clips he'd brought in from the playroom. With her hair out of the way, Venom peppered ticklish kisses along her shoulders and the very back of her neck. She giggled and squirmed as the feathery touch of his lips made her tummy flip-flop. His low, rumbling chuckle warmed her like sunshine.

She heard the rustle of rope and the thudding *thwap* as the long length of creamcolored line hit the floor. Glancing over her shoulder, Dizzy watched Venom unfurl his neatly coiled rope and folded it in half. He held the looped middle and advanced toward her. "Eyes forward, sugar. Head up and neck straight."

She swallowed and did as directed. At the first touch of the rope against her skin, Dizzy closed her eyes. Something told her this was a moment she was going to want to remember again and again. The rope kissed her skin as softly as Venom had, the smooth fibers gliding across her body without enough pressure to mark or burn.

He slipped the looped rope under her breasts and pulled it tight in the middle of her back. The easy tugging motion told her that he was making a knot there. Suddenly she wished there was a mirror so she could watch him work.

"All right?" He slipped a finger under the rope. "Not too tight?"

"It's fine."

He made a quiet approving noise and slipped the looped rope back around to her front, this time above her breasts. "Today you're only getting one simple loop under and above your breasts, but as you become accustomed to the ropes, I'll start adding more pressure and more intricate work."

When he stepped in front of her, their gazes clashed. His eyes had gone all smoky with desire and excitement. His cheeks were a bit ruddy too. Venom couldn't hide his arousal in boxer briefs but it was the intense set of his jaw that drew her attention most. She marveled at his focus as he created the beautiful rope work adorning her body.

She could hardly breathe as he weaved and tucked the rope under the two loops he had already created to form a sort of halter-top. He slid around behind her again to tighten the rope. She shivered a little as he wound it around her waist a couple of times, pulling it taut but not so tight that it bit into her skin.

He stepped back to survey his work. Something wasn't quite right. The touch of a frown played upon his lips. "You look unbalanced." He rubbed his jaw. "I'm going to bind your thighs."

His gaze flicked to hers just fractionally before moving to the bed. It was a look that told her he would stop if she wanted him to—but she didn't.

Venom picked up one of the shorter coils of rope and knelt in front of her. Prickly goose bumps raced across her skin as his bare fingertips glided along the outer curve of her leg. He took his time wrapping her left thigh with the braided rope and weaving the line through the belt-like adornment on her waist. When it slipped down the other side, he looped the rope around her right thigh.

Mesmerized by the skilled movements of his fingers, she watched him form knots and loops and braids. "It's beautiful." Her soft voice seemed to startle him. She bit her lip. "Sorry."

He reached up and brushed his thumb across her pout. "It's fine. I'm not used to talking when I'm working."

"Have you…" She stopped herself and decided not to go there.

But Venom cocked his head and seemed intent on following the thought. "Have I…?"

Avoiding his gaze, she asked, "Have you done this with a lot of women?"

Venom's fingertips skimmed her cheek. He drew her gaze and shocked her with the sincerity shining in his pale eyes. "I've been with other women, yes—but not as many as you're likely imagining. What I shared with those women—well, it won't come close to what we'll share. I've never been with the same woman more than once. Last night was the first time I slept with any woman."

"Really?" She hated the hopefulness coloring her voice. It was such a silly, romantic thought but she wanted to be some kind of first for him. She wanted to be as special to him as he was going to be to me.

"Really." He captured her mouth in a gentle, easy kiss. "You and I—we're breaking new ground here, sugar. We're building something new."

Venom sat back on his heels and traced the lines of

cream and red rope crisscrossing her body. He circled a couple of knots before resting his hands on her hips and turning his attention toward her breasts. They were supported by the ropes, almost like a bra. Her nipples were flushed and peaked and aching for his touch.

He gave it without request. Teasing at first, his tongue flicked against the pink buds before sensually laving them. When he suckled her, she sighed and lifted up on the balls of her feet, pressing her breast to his mouth and silently urging him to continue to stoke her passions. She made a disappointed sound when he released her nipple and merely caressed her hips.

"Tell me how the ropes make you feel."

"Warm," she said the first word that came to mind. "Secure. Safe."

"Good." He sounded so pleased by her response and she was filled with the most unexpected sense of happiness. "You seem less nervous and more relaxed."

"Do I?" She considered her emotions for a moment and realized he was right. The ropes hugging her body eased the anxiety she had been feeling about what awaited her with Venom.

"Yes." He brushed his lips against her belly. Her sharp inhale made him chuckle. The heady look they shared made the pulsing ache between her thighs grow nearly unbearable.

Venom slid his hand down her body to cup her bare sex. He lifted his face until their noses were nearly touching. Their breaths intermixed as his fingers parted the petals of her pussy and tapped onr finger against her throbbing clitoris. He held her gaze as his finger glided toward the source of her damp heat.

She made a little whimpering sound as his thick finger gradually penetrated her. He brushed his thumb side to side across her clit before capturing her lips in a long, slow kiss. Carefully he pulled his hand away from her sex so she could see the glistening wetness on his skin. "See how excited you are?"

"Yes."

He shocked her by licking her wetness from his finger. His low groan made her lightheaded. "You taste so damn good."

His comment surprised her. "I do?"

A corner of his sensual mouth lifted with amusement. "Yes, you do. Have you ever let a man—?"

"No," she interrupted him before he could finish what she was sure would be a very dirty sentence. "*No.*"

Now he was the one who looked surprised. "Not even once?"

"I never got that far with any of the men I dated." Her face was so hot now.

"There's a first time for everything, Dizzy." He grinned as she gulped hard. "I seem to remember promising you that I was going to explore every last inch of your body with my tongue." His fingers returned to her soaking-wet sex. "And I think I'm going to start right about here."

Chapter Eleven

DIZZY FOCUSED ON the tight embrace of the ropes wound around her body as Venom swept her off her feet and placed her on the bed. He crawled over her, grasping her small wrists in his big hand and dragging them over her head. As he had last night, he held them down while plundering her mouth with ravenous desire.

Nearly delirious with need, Dizzy arched into him and matched his increasingly passionate kisses. His tongue stabbed between her lips and danced with hers, setting her alight with a wildfire of lust. "Venom," she whispered. "Venom, please…"

"Patience, little one." His gruff voice and the tender pet name thrilled her. "We have all day and all night to enjoy this."

She didn't know if she could survive a night and day of feeling like this. It wasn't only her intimate parts that throbbed mercilessly. Her head ached and her body vibrated with a harsh heat.

"I won't restrain you to the bed right now but I will soon." He grazed his teeth over the sensitive flesh at her collarbone. "You'll love every second of being immobile and at my mercy."

Her shuddery breaths came faster as she imagined be-

ing tied down to the bed while Venom hovered over her.
His hands would be free to do whatever they wanted to
her body—and it excited her so much.

What is wrong with me? Two days ago she would have
been horrified by the very idea of a man restraining and
making love to her. Now she desperately wanted to know
what it would feel like to be helpless and forced to feel
pleasure—but only because Venom was the man taking
control.

Eyes closed, she relished the wicked sensations caused
by Venom's lips as they dotted kisses down her chest and
along the curve of her belly. He licked a slow circle around
her navel before dragging his tongue right down to the vee
between her thighs.

Lying flat on the bed, he shifted her thighs apart and
pushed her feet until her knees were bent. His long, thick
fingers spanned her inner thighs as he gazed upon the
most secret part of her. She didn't dare lift her head to
watch him. Just feeling him looking so intently at her bare
pussy made Dizzy so incredibly nervous and embarrassed.

"Oh!" Dizzy gasped when Venom carefully parted her
tender folds. The cool air of the room felt positively chilly
against her superheated flesh. She started to close her
thighs but his hand pushed her knee to the side.

"No." His firm command made her heart race. "You
keep them open—or I'll add more rope and solve the
problem my way."

"But—"

"No." He said the word calmly but sternly. "I won't be
denied access to my prize. Your body belongs to me now

and I mean to enjoy it."

The raw arrogance of that statement was breathtaking but Venom said it without a hint of cruelty or meanness. Claiming ownership of her seemed as natural to him as if he were discussing the weather. He had caught and collared her in the forest, so obviously she belonged to him.

His assertion of dominance over her didn't inspire the flare of anger it should have. Instead she made the delicious realization that enjoying his prize—her body— meant pleasure for her. His threat to add more restraints piqued her interest. It was so wrong, and she was definitely playing with fire, but Dizzy decided to see what would happen if she pushed back at Venom.

Lifting her head, she pressed up on her elbows and met his patient stare. He seemed to be waiting to see how she would react. "What happens if this prize decides she doesn't want to be bothered?"

"Bothered, huh?" He rubbed his mouth against her mons. "If the prize can't tell the difference between being bothered and having her world rocked, she may lose the choice to choose."

"Oh really?" Flirting with danger, she slowly closed her thighs until Venom applied pressure to keep them open.

"You might want to reconsider, sugar."

"I've made my choice." She snapped her legs shut and squeezed her knees together.

He clicked his teeth and pushed up into a kneeling position. "Remember you asked for this…"

Her mouth went dry as he picked up the last coil of

rope and the knife. He touched a button on the edge of the knife and the gleaming blade shot out of the handle. With a quick measure, he swiped the rope with the frighteningly sharp blade to cut two shorter lengths. After closing up the knife he tossed it onto the bedside table.

Dizzy's heart jumped into her throat when Venom trapped her legs between his on the mattress. The playful glint in his eyes allayed her panic. Whatever he was about to do with those two ropes wouldn't hurt her.

Taking her left wrist in his hand, he looped the rope around it to make a strange sort of cuff. A long length of rope dangled from the end. He did the same thing to her right wrist before sliding back down the bed until her bound thighs were easily accessed. It was then that she realized what he had in mind.

"Yes," he said as if reading her thoughts. "I think you're going to enjoy this." His mouth slanted with amusement. "Enjoy me *bothering* you, that is."

Oh there was no doubt he was going to *bother* her, all right. She giggled as he pushed her left knee up toward her shoulders, only stopping when her decorated wrist was in the correct position. He stunned her by how quickly he lashed her wrist to the braided loops of rope encircling her thigh. She was still giving her left wrist a trying tug while he did the same thing to her right one.

With her arms bound to her thighs, Dizzy finally accepted that she was in a rather precarious position. Her feet were up in the air now and her thighs forced wide open by the tension of her arms. She wiggled her hips but there was no getting loose.

A ripple of wild, erotic excitement zipped through her core. Dizzy licked her lips and tried to slow her erratic breaths as Venom planted his hands on either side of her head and flicked his tongue against her mouth. He nibbled her lower lip and nuzzled their noses together. Holding her gaze, he murmured, "If it gets to be too much, just tell me to stop and I'll set you free."

Set her free? Dizzy suspected she was going to find more freedom in Venom's bonds than she'd ever known outside them.

His instruction given, Venom nipped and pecked and licked his way back down her body. Using those broad, tattooed shoulders, he pushed her thighs even wider apart. He peered at the slick heat of her arousal. "You are so damn pink."

"Ah!" She rocked her hips as his thick finger glided through her labia. He separated the petals of her pussy so gently.

"So wet," he murmured. "I'm dying to taste you."

That was all the warning she had before Venom's skilled tongue began to torment her. He traced the ruddy lips of her sex and her swollen, pulsing clitoris and then penetrated her with the tip of his tongue. She keened loudly and curled her fingers into her palms. "Venom!"

He growled hungrily against her pussy and lapped at her in earnest. Side to side, his tongue waggled across her clitoris. He sucked the throbbing bud between his lips until she thought she just might die from the sheer pleasure of it. The vibrations deep in her belly grew stronger and brighter as Venom ravenously attacked her pussy. The ropes hugging her body amplified the wondrous sensations he evoked.

Venom's fingertips bit into her thighs but he didn't try to prevent her from moving. She understood that it was his excitement that caused his grip on her to tighten. Her hips moved with a rhythm that seemed innately primal. His fluttering tongue forced her closer and closer to the edge of something wondrous and wild.

And then it happened.

Head tipped back, Dizzy cried out as the powerful waves of ecstasy exploded from deep within her. "Venom!"

He groaned against her aching, pulsing clitoris. Her climax started to ebb but he didn't let up the swirling motion of his tongue. He increased the pace, flicking the stiff tip of it against her overly sensitive pearl. She tried to squirm away from him but Venom held fast to her thighs. She couldn't escape. She had no choice but to accept whatever he gave her.

Like a tightening coil, another orgasm began to build inside her. She gulped deep, shuddering breaths as Venom found a pace that made her limbs tremble. Glad for the ropes binding her and supporting her, Dizzy surrendered to the erotic frissons of delight rushing through her belly and chest.

"*Unnnnhhh!*" Her hips came up off the bed as the powerful spasms gripped her. Venom's hands slid under her backside, cupping her bottom as he feasted on her honeyed flesh. She didn't think she could take another second of his incessant licking—but it wasn't up to her.

Venom had taken the decision out of her hands.

Seemingly intent on making her pass out from the rapturous spasms of another orgasm, he worked her into a frenzied state. She collapsed against the mattress in a boneless, panting heap after the third climax that he tore from her.

Shaking wildly, she whimpered his name as he penetrated her virgin entrance with his tongue. She gasped with shock at the unexpected feeling. He did such wicked, wicked things to her. "Venom! *Oh!* No more. No. *No!*"

"Yes." His rough, husky voice thrilled her. He lapped at her clit another minute or so, not fast enough or with enough pressure to send her reeling into another climax. No, he seemed to simply be enjoying himself.

Venom peppered noisy kisses along her inner thighs and wiped his mouth on her belly. Pushing up on his knees, he pulled the knots on the short lines hooking her wrists to her thighs. With her arms free to move, she placed her hands on his forearms and glided her palms up to his bulky biceps.

"Are you all right?" He eyed her carefully.

"Are you kidding me?" Overcome with a mad case of the giggles, all Dizzy could do was laugh. "That was *amazing*. I had no idea. None."

"If you think that's amazing you'd better hold on to me." He moved into position between her thighs. "We're just getting started, sugar."

She gripped his muscular arms as panic shook her. Now that the moment was upon her, she lost some of her courage. "Venom…"

"I'll go slowly." He captured her mouth in a wonderfully sweet kiss. "It will probably hurt but we'll take our time." His hand followed a sweeping motion from her hip to her thigh. Touching the ropes spiraled there, he asked, "Do you want these off now?"

She shook her head and wound her thighs around his waist. "Leave them."

His boyish grin made her tummy wobble. Leaning down, he kissed her again before shifting to one side and reaching between their bodies. She followed his hand with her curious gaze. His massive cock stood erect and ready and jutting against her lower belly.

Fascinated, she watched him stroke the rock-hard length of his erection. A few glistening drops fell from the tip onto her skin. She had no experience in these sorts of things but she wasn't naive or uneducated. She knew that they were risking pregnancy, even if they only made love once.

He tilted his head. "What is it? Your expression just turned so dark."

She swallowed hard. "What happens if I get pregnant?"

He didn't look the least bit fazed by her question. Actually he seemed rather excited by the idea. "I get to spoil you for nine months while you give me the greatest gift imaginable."

"*Oh.*" She hadn't been expecting that answer.

He caressed her face so tenderly. "You're my mate. You're my wife. I've waited so very long for the chance to have you and to build a family. But," he massaged her earlobe between his fingers, "I can withdraw from you, if you would prefer. It's not foolproof but it's the best I can offer." His mouth drew tight. "Unless you want me to stop this now."

"No." She ached at the very idea of being denied this experience with him. She locked her ankles behind his butt and dragged him in a little closer. "Don't stop, Venom. *Please.*"

His eyes flashed with such adoration and desire. Falling forward onto his elbows, Venom kissed her like a starving man. He drank from her lips as if she offered the sweetest succor. Overridden with lust, she clung to Venom as their tongues dueled.

His hand rode the outline of her breasts and followed the gentle slope of her belly. He palmed her pussy, cupping the searing heat of her while his tongue darted against hers. With much care, he began to prepare her for that huge cock of his. First one finger and then two speared her slick sheath. She squirmed with discomfort at first but the unfamiliar sensation of being filled slowly faded. It was replaced with a desperate ache that begged to be assuaged.

Dizzy wanted to touch Venom. With the rope cuffs still hugging her wrists and the long trails of rope dangling across her skin, she reached down to grasp his stiff erection. As they had last night, her fingers didn't even come close to touching when wrapped around him. How they were going to make this work she didn't know. Other men from his sky warrior race had Grabbed women from her planet and had children with them so there had to be a way.

Venom's shaky breaths rippled across her lips as she dragged the ruddy crown of his cock through her intimate folds. His jaw tightened as she swirled the very tip of him around her swollen clitoris again and again. "Dizzy." He growled in a warning tone. "I'm trying to hold back and go easy on you but—"

"I need you now." She might not have his experience but she knew what she wanted. "I want to feel you inside me."

Venom crashed their mouths together and removed the fingers buried deep in her passage. His blunt crown nudged her opening. A quicksilver flash of fear pierced her chest—but there wasn't time to indulge it.

Venom thrust forward with one swift movement. It wasn't particularly forceful but it was enough to make her hiss with pain. He froze instantly but didn't retreat. She clawed at his shoulders as her virgin passage protested the sudden invasion of his toobig cock. Her earlier bravado fled. She was wrong. A petite woman like her and a giant like Venom couldn't do this. "I can't!"

"You can." His calm voice penetrated the haze of pain and panic. "You are."

As if to prove he was right, Venom pushed forward fractionally. It hurt but it was that sort of inevitable discomfort that she willingly accepted. If she wanted Venom to make love to her, she had to deal with this part of it. Surely it would get easier.

Venom didn't try to go any deeper for some time. He remained right there with only the tip of his cock buried in her snug pussy. Proving that they did have all the time in the world to make love, Venom lowered his chest so he could claim her mouth with sensual kisses. His big, strong hands massaged and caressed her breasts while his tongue danced wildly with hers.

As her body learned to accept his, Dizzy relaxed a little. She gripped his shoulders and rocked her hips just the tiniest bit. His cock moved inside her—and it felt *good*.

"Oh." Her sigh of enjoyment gave Venom permission to continue. He slid forward and retreated by slow degrees. His testing thrusts grew more deliberate and deep. She moaned against his lips and ran her hands up and down his broad back. Their foreheads touched as Venom began to rock in and out of her passage.

"Baby, you feel so damn good." His cheek twitched and his breaths were labored. "Your pussy is so tight. So wet. So *hot*." He changed the angle of his penetration. "Do you like this? Does it feel good?"

She bared her neck as her head lolled from side to side. "*Yes.*"

It felt so good. Incredibly good. Unbelievably good. His cock stroked places inside her that she hadn't even known existed. Her body on fire, she rose up to meet his plunging thrusts. Their mouths mated as he drove into her again and again.

"I want to feel you come with my cock buried in your cunt." Venom growled the filthy words. "I'm going to make you come again."

"I can't." It was the second time she had told him that—and the second time she was certain he would prove her wrong.

"You will." His fingertips found the pink button that brought her so much pleasure. He swirled the rough pads of his fingers around the sensitive nub, gathering her wetness to ease the stimulation. He whispered gently as he increased the pace and force of his thrusts. "Give me what I want, Dizzy." He nipped at her neck. "Come for me, baby."

"I—"

"No." His heady gaze made her belly clench. His fingertips moved faster as he strummed her clitoris in a way that made her toes curl. "Come."

She didn't dare tell him no again. Clasping his neck, she held on for dear life as Venom's pounding cock and dancing fingertips carried her right to the very edge again. Locked into a staring match with him, Dizzy witnessed the triumphant grin that made his eyes shine brightly when she finally lost her ability to hold out a moment longer.

"Venom!"

"That's it, sugar. Come for me."

She came so hard she feared passing out again. The earlier orgasms he had given her couldn't compare to the body-shaking, belly-trembling bursts of utter bliss that rocked her now. His thick, pounding cock amplified everything she felt a thousand times over. It was too much—but she didn't want him to stop.

He didn't. Venom gripped the front of the ropes binding her breasts like a bra and started to take her harder and faster. She sensed he was holding back and was thankful for that. Even though she wanted everything he could give her, she understood that her first time wasn't the right time.

"Dizzy!" He drove into her so hard that she scooted across the sheets. Pressing his cheek to hers, Venom went rigid and jerked. Damp heat filled her as he spilled his seed against the entrance to her womb. At the same moment, he marked her neck with his teeth, nipping a spot just above her collar. The surprising bite of pain crossed the wires in her brain and felt like pure pleasure.

Blazing-hot tears dripped from the corners of her eyes onto her cheeks. She wasn't quite sure why she was crying but she couldn't stop. Venom kissed her so tenderly and with such sweet affection. Still buried inside her, he slid his arms around her smaller body and dragged her onto his chest as he rolled onto his back. "It's all right, honey."

"I'm so sorry." She felt so incredibly silly. "I don't know why I'm crying."

"It doesn't matter. Let yourself feel it. We can sort out the whys later."

She marveled at his wisdom. All the things he had seen in his military career had no doubt shaped him into the wise, patient man he was today. She decided to take his advice and simply honor her emotions, however weird and confusing they might be.

Sometime later, Venom gently shifted her onto her back. He wiped her wet face with the sheet and kissed the trails of tears down her cheeks. They shared lazy kisses as he toyed with her hair and caressed her naked breasts.

"Can you sit up long enough for me to untie you?"

She nodded. "I think so."

He helped her into position at the edge of the bed. Sitting there with her feet dangling inches from the floor, she felt so incredibly small. Venom's world definitely hadn't been designed for women like her. She figured the furniture was probably the first of many things about this new life of hers that she would find odd or ill-fitting.

He slowly and carefully peeled the ropes from her body as if unwrapping a gift. Every time a loop of the braided line lifted away from her skin, Dizzy experienced the strangest buzzing that went straight to her head. She marveled at the red lines crisscrossing her body.

Venom knowingly touched her cheek. "Feeling a bit lightheaded?"

She rubbed her cheek. "Yes."

"Some people call it a rope high," he explained. "Let me get these ropes off your thighs. I'll get you something to drink and then I'll hold you. It will help."

And it did. Reclining against his pillows, Venom cradled her against his chest. His strong arms held her close and he draped one of his heavy legs across hers. She relished his body heat and the comforting thud of his heartbeat beneath her ear. He brushed his fingers through her hair and kissed her forehead.

"I can only imagine what you're probably feeling, especially about the ropes, but we won't discuss that right now. Maybe tomorrow. We need to put some distance between the experience and the discussion. It's easier that way. Better," he added. "Do you understand?"

"Yes. Honestly I don't think I could even find the words right now." Her brain was so fuzzy it was hard to even carry on this conversation.

"Are you in pain? I can get you something if you are."

"I'm sore," she admitted. "But I'm not hurting." Pensive, she ran her finger along one of the tattoos marking the right side of his chest. "I'm glad it was you."

He didn't need her to elucidate. He understood exactly what she meant. "I hope you never doubt how much I cherish being your first."

"I don't." Even if something totally unexpected happened and their relationship didn't make it Dizzy would never regret choosing Venom. The memories they had created just now were memories she would carry with her forever.

"What do you say to a nice hot soak and then a nap?"

"That's a very tempting offer."

Venom untangled himself and slid off the bed. He scooped her up into his arms and kissed her. Smiling up at him, she asked, "Is this when I start calling you master?"

Laughing, he strode toward the bathroom. "Not until you think I've earned it…"

Chapter Twelve

WATCHING DIZZY DOZE, Venom fought the primal urge to wake her for another round of lovemaking. The primitive instinct to mark, claim and bind her to him forever was a hard one to ignore. He replayed their morning session for the thousandth time. Had it really gone that well?

Apparently he had been worried about nothing. They had clicked so beautifully. The chemistry they shared in the bedroom was just as good as the chemistry they had outside it. His fear that she would find his brand of lovemaking upsetting or disgusting had been totally unfounded.

Venom caressed her naked breast. The sheet had slipped down in her sleep to bare her curved flesh. Her nipple was soft and pink but he didn't give in to the desire to playfully tweak it. She needed to rest, not be awoken from a deep sleep by her insatiable new mate.

The marks from his ropes had long since faded. They had been so lovely and he had traced them with his fingertips during their bath and later when she cuddled up against him before falling asleep. He imagined all the ways he would wrap her in his ropes. Her reaction to being bound had assured him that she was ready to explore that side of their relationship. No doubt it was going to a wild ride.

Unable to sleep a moment longer, Venom carefully slid away from her and tucked the sheet and covers around her slim body. He ducked into the bathroom before grabbing a pair of shorts and hopping into them. Gathering up the ropes, clips and the knife, he carried them into the playroom.

Like every boy who graduated from the academy, tidiness had been drilled into his brain. If he had to choose between sliding into bed with Dizzy after a romp to hold her or promptly coiling his ropes, Dizzy would win every time. He put away the knife and the clips first. She hadn't asked what the clips were and he hadn't volunteered the information. He could just imagine the look on her face if he said the words *nipple clamps*.

"What are you doing?"

Venom glanced at the doorway and frowned at the sight of Dizzy wearing his undershirt and leaning against the frame. "Losing my touch, apparently."

Confusion marred her pretty face. "What?"

"I didn't hear you sneak up on me."

"Oh. Sorry." She toyed with the bridal collar and slipped her finger underneath it to rub her neck. "Maybe you should get me a bell or something."

He laughed. "I don't think you would like the places I would want to dangle them."

She playfully narrowed her eyes. "No, I'm sure I wouldn't."

Venom opened one of the cabinets and took down

some prepackaged wipes. "I'm cleaning up from our play earlier." He waved one of the packets. "These wipes are to clean the ropes. Every now and then I give them a good wash but this is easier on the fibers."

"Can I help?"

"Sure." He handed her one of the wipes and a length of rope and gave her instructions. She sat on the closest piece of furniture—a spanking bench—while she worked. He didn't have the heart to tell her that the place where she had just put her plump bottom was the same place he someday intended to use to make it nicely pink and hot.

When she finished wiping the first rope, she gave it back to him and opened a second wipe for the next long length. She watched him coil the rope into his preferred flat figure-eight coils for hanging on the wall.

"I can teach you how to do this."

She shook her head at his offer. "I can barely tie my shoes, Venom. You really don't want me messing with two dozen feet of rope. You'll have a mess on your hands."

"You design and sew dresses. Surely you aren't that uncoordinated."

She shrugged and held out the red rope. "You would think, right?"

He took the rope from her outstretched hand and made quick work of coiling and hanging it on the wall from one of the many pegs he had installed. She had already cleaned the shorter lengths remaining, including the two he had cut to fashion simple wrist cuffs. He tucked those into a drawer for later and wound up the shortened rope.

When he turned back around, she was inspecting the playroom again. She looked damn good wearing his shirt. He liked the flirty, feminine dress and nightgown she had worn but there was something terribly endearing about the sight of her in a piece of his clothing. It lent a comfortable sort of feeling to their relationship.

"Do you feel like you might be ready to talk about the ropes and being bound?"

She shook her head. "I'm not up for a conversation that deep right now." Her worried gaze skipped his way. "Is that okay?"

"Of course," he assured her. "I always want the truth from you, Dizzy, even if you think it's something I don't want to hear. For what it's worth I didn't think you would be ready to talk about how the ropes made you feel. There's no pressure here. Hell—you might not even know what you're feeling when we do sit down to talk about it."

"I don't feel pressured. A little confused," she admitted. "Until I sort all that out, I need you to know that I enjoyed it immensely and want to do it again."

"I'm glad you liked it. You looked so incredibly beautiful all wrapped up for me."

She blushed and broke the gaze they shared. Glancing around the room she asked, "Other than the ropes, what is your favorite thing to do in here?"

He wasn't going to give her that answer so easily. "Why do you want to know?"

"I want to know what you like."

"Just because I like something doesn't mean you have to like it," he carefully reminded her. "The last thing I want is for you to agree to something because you think it will make me happy. That's not the way our relationship is going to work."

"I understand that, but how am I supposed to learn what I like if I don't try everything?" Her gaze darted around the playroom. "Well…maybe not *everything*."

He wondered what it was that had made her amend her reply. "My second favorite thing to do in here doesn't require any special equipment."

She hesitated before working up the nerve to prod him for more information. "And what is it?"

He held out his hand. "Come here and I'll show you."

Dizzy crossed the floor to join him. He tangled his fingers in her gorgeous hair and dipped his head to claim her mouth. She whimpered at his display of dominance and desire but didn't try to break free from his punishing kiss. Her soft hands landed on his waist.

Gripping the fabric of his shorts, she lifted up on tiptoes and tipped her head back to allow him greater access to her sweet mouth. Venom took his time loving her, dipping his tongue between her lips and flicking it against hers. She mewled like a kitten when he tightened the fingers curled in her hair. Maybe she wouldn't be averse to even rougher loving at some point.

Tearing away from her intoxicating mouth, Venom studied her face. Her flushed cheeks and smoky eyes convinced him of her aroused state. Tracing her silky pout, he gave her another reminder. "You can always say no to anything I propose or ask me stop if you change your mind. Do you understand?"

"Yes."

He let his hands fall from her body before giving his order. "Get on your knees."

Her eyes widened slightly at his unexpected direction. She slowly lowered herself to the floor. The sight of her kneeling at his feet made Venom's heart race. Heat streaked through his chest as he gazed down at the erotic vision she presented wearing only his shirt.

"Take off the shirt."

She peeled out of the garment and set it aside. He zeroed in on her perky breasts. Already her dusky-pink nipples had puckered to form tight peaks. It wasn't a chill making her body respond that way. It was excitement.

With a bit of nervousness playing upon her face, she licked her lips and waited for his next instruction. He brushed his fingers along her cheek. "Take off my shorts."

With trembling fingers, she leaned forward and dragged his shorts down his legs. He stepped out of them and watched the way her breaths had grown shallower and quicker. Fully aware of how uncomfortable she seemed to be with frank language, he softened his question in a way that wouldn't make her blush furiously. "Is this your first time to put your mouth on a man?"

"Yes." She bravely placed her palms against his thighs and smiled up at him with such enthusiasm lighting up her eyes. "But I want to try."

Certain she was going to test his control, Venom slipped his hands behind his back and used his body and the wall to trap them. "Take your time. Explore me."

"What if I do something wrong?" She looked so serious.

"Sweetheart, there aren't many ways this can go wrong. It all feels good." He caught her eye. "Except teeth."

She leaned forward to press a tender kiss to the spot just below his navel. "I'll try to keep that in mind."

Venom held his breath as she wrapped her fingers around his aching dick. She lightly stroked his heated flesh and seemed to be studying his anatomy. One of her hands slid down to cup his sac. As if remembering his lesson about the way he liked things, she used a firm touch while fondling and caressing him.

Her pink tongue flicked out and swiped the crown of his cock. He bit back a low groan when she continued to paint his shaft with her slick saliva. She peppered ticklish kisses on his ruddy erection while continuing to cup and massage his balls. For a firsttimer, she had damn good instincts about what would make him feel good.

When she finally sucked just the tip of him between her lips, his knees threatened to buckle. He swore softly and clenched his fingers behind his back. With the head of his cock buried in her mouth, Dizzy glanced up at him with uncertainty. The strikingly erotic image of her punched the air right out of his lungs.

Wanting her to know that she was doing everything just right, Venom tugged his hands free from the prison where he'd placed them and lovingly caressed her cheek. "That's so good, sugar."

A pleased smile brightened her face. With renewed confidence she took a little more of his length between her lips before pulling back to swirl her tongue around the head of him. Venom threaded his fingers through the long, pale waves of her hair. His toes curled against the hard floor as he tried to fight the temptation to thrust into her mouth. His primitive needs were hard to suppress but he managed it.

Deeper and deeper she swallowed his shaft. When she tried to take even more of him he tapped her cheek and shook his head. Frowning, she pulled off his erection and wiped at her mouth. "Did I do something wrong?"

"No."

"Why did you stop me?"

"You don't have to try to take all of me. You get points for enthusiasm but don't push yourself, sweetheart."

"But I want to make you feel good."

"You are," he assured her. Giving her a quick anatomy lesson, he explained, "It's this top area here that has the most sensitivity. Everything you've done so far feels fantastic."

She studied his cock for a few seconds, almost as if formulating an attack plan. When she wrapped her lips around him again, he didn't try to stop the growl from escaping his throat. He wanted her to hear what she did to him.

Using her tongue to massage the highly sensitive underside of his crown, Dizzy sucked him hard and faster. He became lightheaded watching his cock gliding in and out of the hot, wet alcove of her mouth.

So what if she lacked the skill and finesse of the women in his past? Sure, he had been on the receiving end of some stellar blowjobs from women who worked the sky brothels but they paled in comparison to the unbelievably pleasurable experience Dizzy created.

Dizzy shared this incredibly intimate experience with him because she *wanted* to and because she *liked* him, not because she was counting down the minutes until their session ended and the credits would be deposited in her account.

When she looked up at him while bobbing up and down on his erection, Venom nearly lost it. The wicked little minx had figured out a workaround for her inability to take all of his impressive length. She stroked the base of his thick, long shaft while using her heavenly mouth to drive him fucking crazy.

"Dizzy," he said her name on a sigh. His balls were drawing up against his body in answer to the buzzing sensation building in his stomach. Curling his fingers in her hair, he warmed, "I'm going to come."

"*Mmmm,*" she hummed excitedly around his shaft. The delicious vibrations made his damn toes throb.

"Stop," he urged, certain she wouldn't want him to spill his cum in her mouth.

But she wouldn't be stopped. With the wall at his back, he couldn't retreat or tug his cock free from her mouth. To his surprise—and pleasure—Dizzy dragged him a little deeper and gazed up at him so adoringly.

With one look, Dizzy obliterated his control. The crashing wave of climax drenched him in pure ecstasy. His cock swelled between her stretched lips a second before the first burst of intense pleasure rocked him. Dizzy made a shocked but thrilled sound when his seed splashed her tongue. She hungrily drank him down, lapping and sucking at his cock until he sagged against the wall.

His legs trembled as he tried to stay upright. Dizzy kissed his thighs and belly as his breaths finally slowed and the numbness in his toes and fingers ended. "Did I do all right?"

"All right?" With a laugh that sounded more like a groan, he slid to his knees in front of her. "Sugar, if this is your first try I may not survive your second or third attempts."

Giggling, she wound her arms around his shoulders. "Maybe next time you should be seated or in bed. I thought you were going to fall on me at the end. I didn't know how the heck I was going to climb out from under you."

"Good point," he conceded. "Next time we'll move it into the bedroom."

He captured her reddened lips in a long, steamy kiss that left her shuddering in his arms. Grasping her hair, he tugged her head back and exposed her neck to his nibbling mouth. She moaned when he grazed his teeth across her sensitive flesh.

He glided his hand down her naked front and dipped it between her thighs. Just as suspected, she was soaking wet for him. Concerned she might be sore after their earlier lovemaking, he concentrated his fingertips on the stiff nub hidden there instead of penetrating her.

Her fingernails bit into his shoulders. "Venom."

"One good turns deserves another," he murmured.

Loving the way she responded to his intense kisses, Venom rubbed her clit until she shattered in front of him. She came hard and fast but he knew she had so much more passion just waiting to be released.

Without a word of warning, he tossed her over his shoulder and carried her out of the playroom. She squealed with excitement and shock as he dropped her on the bed and crawled over her.

"Venom! What are you doing?" Fits of laughter followed her question as he gave in to the urge to tickle her sides and sensually torment her breasts with his mouth. "Oh!

No! No!"

"Yes." He loved the silliness they shared together.

"Venom, we can't keep doing this all day." Even as she protested his sexy intentions, she bucked her hips in the most wanton way.

"Sure we can." His kisses meandered down her body in a zigzagging path that finally ended right on her clit. Holding her thighs open, he gazed longingly at her pink, dewy center. "In fact I might not ever let you out of this bed again."

Chapter Thirteen

S EATED IN A quiet corner of the busy food court aboard the *Valiant*, Venom checked his watch for the twentieth time but saw that it wasn't time to pick up Dizzy from her first meeting of the wives' club. He still had half an hour and had already finished all the errands he had planned to tackle.

After draining the last of the icy juice he had ordered, he chucked the cup in the closest receptacle and decided he would head by the uniform shop now rather than waiting to take Dizzy with him. He doubted she would find the endless racks of uniforms very interesting anyway.

As he crossed the bustling marketplace, he noticed a number of other newly mated men sitting at tables or kicked back in benches in the plaza there. Most of them were drumming their fingers against their thighs or anxiously bouncing their feet. No doubt they all missed their new mates as much as he did.

They were all likely sharing his same fear that some asshole who didn't have enough points would stake out the entrance of the wives' club to make a play for an unescorted woman. The two policemen hanging out there would deter any man crazy enough to think he could snatch a woman leaving the support group. Venom would have preferred to have an SRU team guarding the door but it would have been overkill.

Ducking inside the uniform shop, Venom was instantly greeted by one of the staff members of the military-run store. Like every other male working in the retail sector of the *Valiant*, the young soldier who came over to help him had suffered a brutal injury in battle. There were many things their advanced technology and medicine could fix—but growing back limbs wasn't among them.

The young man had two of the newest bionic arms but he had chosen not to wear the skin-like covering that many were favoring these days. He bared the metallic limbs with pride and Venom respected him all the more for it. Many men who were medically disabled by the military left the service for civilian life but some chose to remain in the corps in support positions. Mayhem's recent lawsuit would hopefully increase the opportunities for wounded soldiers but Venom had a feeling it would be a long, slow slog for these men.

As he waited for the soldier to return with the right-size boots, Venom wandered over to a display of tactical pants. He kept hoping they would do a redesign of their most popular line but it didn't seem to be a top priority. Venom would have given anything to have the oversized pocket on the right thigh replaced with two or three thinner, longer ones.

A soft whistle caught his attention. The fine hairs on the back of his neck stood on edge as the warbling sound dragged him right back to Sendaria.

Suddenly Venom was hunkered down along a cliff

overlooking the only road into the mining camp where their force was besieged. Covered in improvised camouflage—brush and mud and debris—he controlled his breaths and remained perfectly still while watching the slow-moving column of Splinters. He had been cut off from any support for days and fully expected that he would die before nightfall. The insurgents heading for the gates had to be taken out—but it would mean revealing his position.

And then he had heard that odd little whistle. It had taken him nearly a minute to finally spot Terror flattened against one of the large boulders overlooking the road. Somehow the tenacious Shadow Force operative had made it to Venom's forward location from the bogged-down base of operations within the mining camp. That one whistle had filled Venom with the sweetest sense of relief. If he was going to die, it wouldn't be alone.

But they hadn't died that night. They had fought—valiantly—and survived to fight another day.

A blur of movement near the dressing room tore Venom from the flashback. Without looking to see if they were the right size, he snatched a pair of pants from the shelf and crossed the store to the dressing rooms. The space was eerily silent. To know that Terror was so quiet and motionless that even Venom's heightened senses couldn't pick him out sent an icy ripple down his spine.

Only one of the dressing room doors was unlocked. Venom stepped inside and caught the slightest hint of Terror's antiperspirant. As Venom shut the door, Terror stepped out from behind it and into the light. The harsh brightness of the dressing room illuminated the crags and puckers of the scars marking Terror's face.

Terror's lips slanted. "You up for a quickie or has that pretty new mate of yours worn you out yet?"

Venom snorted. "No and no."

"Pity," Terror replied and leaned back against the wall. "I'm surprised you didn't get roped into babysitting at family day aboard the *Arctis*."

"Technically I'm on call." He tapped his watch screen. The timekeeping device doubled as a communication unit. "The SRU teams on the *Arctis* were already scheduled for an escort mission, so Raze has our team on standby in case the police have any problems."

"It's highly unlikely anything will kick off. It's a bunch of farmers visiting their daughters. Unless someone sneaked a pitchfork by the ground team…"

Venom chuckled softly. "I've seen weirder shit happen."

Terror hummed in agreement. "How is the new bride?"

"She's perfect."

"Perfect, huh? That's not what I heard." He gestured toward his head.

"It was a mild medical issue that was easily fixed. She's fine now."

Terror studied him. "You look about as smitten as Vee was when he took Hallie. What's it been? Five days?"

Venom nodded. "Five amazing days. Clawing my way through the Sendarian Siege was worth it, Terror."

Terror's eyebrow lifted. "She's that good in the sack?"

Venom punched Terror in the arm. "That's my mate you're talking about so watch your step."

Terror rubbed the spot he'd hit. "Torment said you were touchy when it came to the girl."

"Yeah, well, Torment has a good whack upside the head waiting for him. He had no right to drop that bomb about Dizzy's biological father on her like that. It was wrong. It hurt her."

"I know it did." Terror actually sounded as if he regretted causing Dizzy pain. "It should have been handled more delicately."

Venom's eyes went wide with surprise. "Man, it sounds as if Menace kicking your ass and your exile to the *Arctis* is making you soft."

Terror didn't dignify that with a response. Instead he offered up a bit of advice.

"This thing with your mate's biological father? Let it go, Venom."

He frowned. "What? Why? She has the right to know who her father is."

"I'm not arguing that fact. But if her father wanted her to know he existed he would have done something about it by now."

Venom took a step forward. "You know who he is."

"I do." Terror exhaled slowly. "But I can't tell you. His files are classified and the only reason I know his identity is because there are no private DNA profiles when it comes to my clearance." Terror squeezed his shoulder. "Tell her to let it go. You don't want this man interfering in your life, Venom."

He rubbed the back of his neck. "That's not my decision to make."

"The hell it isn't." Terror's hand dropped to his side. "She belongs to you. She follows the orders you give her. Just tell her that her father's profile is classified and there's nothing more that can be done."

Venom decided not to get into an argument with Terror about his assumptions about how a man should treat his mate. "But that's a lie. She could file a grievance. One of the doctors onboard could petition to reveal the records because she needs to know her medical history."

Terror shook his head. "This is a box you don't want to open, Venom. If you follow this path you might be the one who gets hurt."

"I trust that Dizzy will make the right decision for us."

"I think you're playing with fire." With a wave of his hand, Terror ended the discussion about Dizzy's parentage. "Talk to me about Devious."

"Oh, so that's what this rendezvous is all about," Venom said as he rested his shoulder against the wall. "I didn't think you would risk sneaking back onto the *Valiant* over a DNA test."

Terror chortled. "What risk? Orion likes to bark loudly but there were no teeth behind his threat to vent me into space."

"You hope."

Terror shrugged. "I've gotten out of worse spots unscathed."

Venom didn't doubt that. "What do you want to know about Devious?"

"How did he look?" True concern darkened Terror's expression.

"Tired," Venom answered. "Haggard. I suspect being undercover for that fucking long wears on a man."

"Yes, it does." A far-off look crossed his face. "Believe me when I say that there are men undercover in far worse places."

Venom shuddered to think of the backwater shitholes where the Shadow Force had stashed their operatives. "What's he doing down there?"

"He's climbing the ranks of the Splinter force. After we framed him and drove him out of the corps, he was taken right in by them. He's been building rapport with them for over a decade. He's a well-liked and very highly respected member of their organization."

"It has to be tough to play both sides." Venom worried that Devious might be in too deep. Of course, Terror probably worried the same thing.

"I've never doubted him. Not once." Terror reached into the pocket of his uniform shirt and retrieved the small chip Devious had slipped to Venom that morning of the Grab. "Thank you for bringing this to us. It's loaded with invaluable information."

"I'm always happy to help, Terror."

Terror clapped him on the shoulder. "I know you are."

Venom considered the tiny chip Terror had tucked back into his shirt. "Should I be worried?"

"Not any more than usual," Terror calmly replied. "The Splinters are planning a big move but we will make sure it fails."

"And if you don't?"

Terror's lone eye narrowed. "We won't—but just in case you might want to hurry up and get that beautiful new mate of yours pregnant."

The warning came through loud and clear. Whatever the Splinters had in the works could bring the front lines of the battle to Calyx. It would mean months—maybe even years—away from Dizzy. The very thought of being separated from her and forced back into the thick of the bloody, brutal war made his stomach churn.

"Speaking of your little mate," Terror glanced at his watch, "I think it's time to queue up to collect her. You wouldn't want one of those skinny flyboys to sneak in and snatch her right under your nose." Then, just to goad him, Terror added, "I heard Risk was quite taken with her. I saw that he was on the list of speakers for their meeting today. Maybe he's hoping to privately examine her."

"I'll break every damn finger on both of his hands," Venom grumbled and reached for the door.

Terror laughed but stopped him from leaving. "Hey, are those Series 7 pants?"

"Yeah." Venom slapped them against Terror's chest. "But they still have that janky fucking pocket on the right side."

"What? Still? Damn." Terror took the pants and shook them out to study them. "Fuck it. I'm taking them." With a lopsided grin, he remarked, "Looks like I found a way to get into your pants after all."

Venom groaned at the corny comment and smacked Terror's arm. "I'll see you around, man."

"For your sake, I hope not. I'm rarely the bringer of good news."

They shook hands and Venom exited the dressing room. He found the soldier with his boots searching the store for him. After a quick apology, he purchased the boots and headed out to pick up Dizzy.

Terror's parting words rattled round in his brain. He hoped like hell his run-in with the Shadow Force operative wasn't a portent of things to come.

FINALLY GETTING THE hang of the tablet Venom had given her, Dizzy took notes as the different speakers took to the small stage. Every now and then she stopped tapping at the screen to rub the irritated spot on her neck where her collar chafed her scars.

She hadn't been very excited about coming to the meeting. Venom had practically dragged her through the door to get her here but now she understood why he was so adamant that she attend. The brief chance to interact with other women from her planet who had gone through the strange experience of being Grabbed was priceless.

After finding a seat, she had glanced through the pamphlets in her welcoming packet. Not long after, the program had started. So far the segments had been interesting.

First, General Vicious, a frighteningly huge and harsh-faced man, and Admiral Orion, an equally as tall and intimidating officer, had taken the stage to welcome them. Vicious certainly embodied his name. He had a loud, booming voice that made everyone pay attention, but there was an unexpected gentleness and kindness about him. From the looks of utter adoration he shot his wife Hallie, it was clear the man loved her like crazy.

He was quick to remind them they had rights aboard the ship and encouraged them to report any sort of abusive behavior immediately. The admiral reiterated that point as he talked about designated safe havens around the vessel. Dizzy got the feeling something terrible might have happened in an earlier batch of new brides. She sensed the general and admiral wanted to do everything possible to make sure the women living aboard the ship were protected.

After the discussions about their legal statuses as new wives concluded there were presentations about shopping and entertainment and even the education programs available. Risk gave a quick talk about the various medical services, including couples counseling, offered in the medical bay.

Dizzy tried to imagine the look on Venom's face if she suggested they seek counseling. He wouldn't like it but he would go. They might have only been together for five days but Dizzy knew there was nothing he wouldn't do to make her happy—even if it meant going through the discomfort of discussing his shortcomings with a third party.

Not that he had displayed any so far…

"It's Dizzy, right?"

A woman of similar age with dark skin and jet-black hair slipped into the seat next to Dizzy as the meeting reached its end. Women were milling around them, talking and enjoying the refreshments offered.

"Yes." Dizzy noticed the brilliant-blue color of the other woman's collar and the gorgeously stamped letters adorning it.

"I'm Naya." She held out her hand. "I'm mated to Menace. He's a friend of Venom."

"Oh!" Dizzy couldn't believe her luck. "He told me about you."

"Good things, I hope," she said with a laugh.

"Yes."

"This is going to sound weird," Naya began, "but we have a friend in common. She actually got a message to me through a man named Dankirk."

"Ella?"

Naya grinned. "Yes! I hadn't talked to her in years but I guess she was asking Danny if he knew any of the women aboard the *Valiant*. She's worried about you. I promised her I would look after you until you get used to it here." She hesitated. "If you plan to stay, I mean. If you're not happy I can help you extricate yourself from the bond you're in…"

"Thanks but I don't have any plans to leave the ship or Venom."

"I'm glad to hear that. Venom always struck me as a really nice guy." Her mouth quirked with a playfully frustrated smile. "He seems much more open to compromise than the big lug who Grabbed me."

"Big lug? Are we talking about Menace?" Hallie plopped down on the empty seat on the other side of

Dizzy. "I'm Hallie."

"Nice to meet you," Dizzy said while shaking her hand.

"How are you feeling?" Hallie asked. "Vicious said you were sick and needed surgery. I thought about popping into the hospital to visit and welcome you onboard but they discharged you pretty quickly."

"I feel great. Better than ever actually," she admitted.

"That's good." Hallie smiled genuinely. "You'll find that the medical teams here are amazing." She glanced at Naya. "They brought her back from the brink of death."

Dizzy's eyes widened. "What happened to you?"

"It was a family thing that got a little messy. Thankfully there was a dart—one of their super-fast ships—to transport me to the *Mercy*. It's basically a flying hospital. They're really wonderful there." Naya dismissively waved her hand. "So—I hear you're a designer."

"I am." She hesitated. "Or, I guess, I was. I'm not really sure how it works up here."

Hallie inhaled a noisy breath and stretched out her short legs. "It's complicated. The men here are willing to make a lot of adjustments for us but the working thing is a sticking point for all of them."

Dizzy frowned and glanced at Naya. "But I understood you own a business here."

"I do but I'm what they consider a 'special case'." She made air quotes around the words. "Because I nearly died on a mission that saved a lot of lives, they gave me a sort of dispensation to do whatever the hell I want. Menace is easygoing when it comes to the working thing and doesn't mind in the least—but he's definitely in the minority around here. By and large, these men are *extremely* traditional."

"Not Venom," Dizzy said confidently. "I'm sure he'll support my decision to continue designing dresses and other clothing."

"I hope so," Naya said carefully.

"He will." Dizzy remembered his assertion that he hadn't Grabbed her to be his house slave. Surely he understood that she loved her work as much as he loved his.

"If you do decide to keep designing, you come see me, okay? I've got plenty of space in my shop for your clothes. I can get any fabric you want." Naya reached into her purse and withdrew her tablet. "Did Venom teach you how to share between tablets?"

"Um…yes." Dizzy tapped her screen until she found the little icon for sharing. "This way, right?"

"Yeah." Naya smiled and touched their tablets together to start a transfer. "Danny was able to get Ella to a spot where she could call in with a message for you. If you want to send her a message, you'll have to go through official channels."

"There are instructions for submitting messages in the handouts from today's meeting," Hallie reminded her. "Venom can walk you through the process."

When the file finished transferring, Naya tucked her tablet back into her bag and stood. "I have to get going. Menace and I have an appointment in the medical bay."

"Oh right!" Hallie grinned up at her friend. "Today is the big day, huh?"

Naya's mouth curved in a bright smile. "Yep."

Confused, Dizzy asked, "The big day?"

"Tattoos," Naya clarified. Touching her chest, she explained, "Menace is having our new family crest applied today. I'm having his initial put on my wrists."

"Women are encouraged to get tattoos too?" Venom hadn't mentioned anything about that.

"It's very common here," Naya assured her. "Hallie had hers done after her wedding but I'm having mine done before we officially tie the knot Calyx style."

What would it be like to have Venom's mark on her body? Dizzy discovered the idea thrilled her more than she ever could have anticipated.

"You're invited to the wedding tomorrow evening," Naya added. "They don't do pretty paper invitations up here. It's just a message in your inbox."

Hallie frowned. "They're so romantic up here."

"Right?" Naya laughed and patted Dizzy's shoulder. "It was nice to meet you. Come see me sometime. Menace and I are right across the hall from you. Maybe we could get together for dinner or something?"

"Sure. Sounds great."

"Fantastic." Naya flicked Hallie's arm. "I'll drop by to show you the new tattoo later. I hope it meets your artistic standards."

Dizzy wasn't quite sure what that inside joke meant but Hallie explained it as Naya sashayed away, her slim-fitting skirt hugging her knockout curves to perfection. "I drew their crest."

"Oh. You're an artist?"

"I do small commissions for friends and colleagues of my husband." Hallie studied her. "Would you let me draw you?"

"Sure. Why not? Sounds fun." Dizzy had lived around artsy types for so many years. She had a sneaking suspicion she would bond with Hallie over art paper and charcoal.

"Kitten?" The gravelly, rumbling voice of the general interrupted their pleasant conversation. He stood off to the side, hands clasped behind his back as he waited for his wife to acknowledge him.

Hallie smiled at him, the warm brightness in her eyes reflecting her deep love for this man. "Vicious, have you met Dizzy yet?"

The general's light-colored eyes landed on her. He let the tiniest hint of a smile crack his harsh face. "Ma'am."

Hallie rolled her eyes and climbed to her feet. "He's such a social butterfly."

His lips settled into a thin line but Dizzy didn't miss the little twitch of amusement that played upon them. Holding out his hand, he wiggled his fingers. "I massaged my schedule a bit to make room for lunch. Unless…?"

Dizzy caught his questioning gaze darting her way. "Oh don't miss lunch on my account. I'm sure Venom will be here soon to pick me up."

Hallie gave Dizzy a quick hug. "It was so nice to meet you. I'll give you a call tomorrow, okay? We'll figure out a time to get together."

"I'd like that." Dizzy stepped aside and watched Hallie and Vicious leave hand in hand. Alone, she gathered up the handouts and her tablet and started across the room.

When she neared the exit Venom stepped through the doorway. His alert gaze scanned the space and finally stopped upon her. He strode toward her, his powerful legs eating up the distance between them. She thought he might swing her up in his arms but he stopped himself from indulging what he truly wanted.

Sliding his hand to her nape, he dragged her tight to his chest and bent down to capture her mouth in a gentle, easy kiss. "I missed you."

She laughed. "Venom, it was two hours."

"It was the longest two hours of my life."

"I doubt that very much."

He tapped the point of her nose. "I've got a way we could kill another two hours."

Her belly flip-flopped wildly. "I'm intrigued."

He laughed and slipped his arm around her shoulders to steer her out of the room. "I bet you are."

They made their way to an empty elevator and stepped inside. They chatted about the meeting and the two new friends she had made. Venom seemed genuinely happy that she had hit it off with Naya and Hallie.

"I know that no one can replace Ella but I hope you can find good friends here."

"I think I'm off to a promising start with those two. Naya invited me to drop by her shop whenever I'd like. She even offered me some space in her shop."

Venom shot her a strange look. "For what?"

"My dresses."

He turned so he could peer down into her face. "What

dresses?"

She couldn't read his expression. Was he angry? "The ones I plan to design and sell."

"I see." His jaw tensed. "You didn't think that I might want to be consulted before you made a decision like this?"

"Well…I thought you wouldn't care. I mean—this is my job. It's what I do. I design, sew and sell dresses. I'm a seamstress, Venom."

"No," he countered somewhat gruffly. "You *were* a seamstress. Now you're my mate."

Her hackles rose at his insinuation that she could only do one thing or the other. "I can be both, Venom. Lots of women juggle multiple roles. Besides, it would be nice to have the extra income."

He stiffened. It was almost as if she had verbally slapped him. "I may not earn a salary as large as Vicious or Orion but I make damn good money sticking my neck on the line every day. It's more than enough to support us."

Dizzy frowned. "Did I say anything about your salary being too small? Hell—I don't know how much money you earn. Don't you think I need to know that?"

He avoided answering her pointed question. "We don't need the extra income you would receive from selling a couple of dresses."

"So what? I'm supposed to just sit at home and wait for you to get off work every day?"

"Yes."

She rolled her eyes. "You can't be serious. You know that's ridiculous."

"So now my culture is ridiculous?"

"Stop putting words in my mouth, Venom. I don't know what your problem is but I'm not going to stop designing and sewing."

"You can design and sew for yourself but that's it. You will not sell your dresses for money."

Her eyebrows arched to her hairline. "Are you forbidding me from working and earning a living?"

"Yes."

Her mouth gaped at the harshness in his voice. This version of Venom was a man she hardly recognized. Had she been that badly fooled over the last five days with him? Was this the *real* Venom, this obstinate, uncompromising jerk?

"Naya has a shop."

"You're not Naya." He pointed out the obvious. "She's a war hero. She nearly died and saved thousands of lives."

Dizzy couldn't even find the words to reply to that. What he said was bad enough but what he *didn't* say hurt even more. He had just made it perfectly clear that he considered her *less* than Naya. She wasn't brave or heroic. She was just a woman who designed frilly dresses.

She backed away from him until the elevator wall stopped her retreat. "Is that really what you think of me?"

His brow furrowed. "What do you mean?"

Before she could explain how he had hurt her feelings, Venom's watch beeped loudly. He growled with irritation and studied the screen. "Shit." He smacked the navigation screen of the elevator and changed their destination. "This discussion will have to wait."

She didn't want to wait. She wanted to hash this out now but something in his voice told her this wasn't the time. "What's wrong?"

"There's a hostage situation aboard the *Arctis*. My SRU team is deploying and they need me." He rubbed his jaw. "You'll have to wait in the office I share with Raze. There isn't time to take you back to our quarters."

"Okay." She was taken aback by the fierce glint that had suddenly overtaken his blue eyes.

In a few short minutes, she had witnessed three different sides to Venom. There was the gentle, sweet lover she had come to know and crave. There was the harsh, traditional male who wanted her to live within the pretty little box his culture created for wives. And then there was this man—the brutal warrior who had survived so many horrific battles.

The elevator doors opened up into a noisy hallway. She heard a man shouting orders and the sounds of boots slamming against the floor. Venom gripped her hand and dragged her down the hall. One wall was see-through and gave her a clear view of a dozen men gearing up in frightening uniforms and loading up with weapons.

A great big bull of a man stepped into the hallway. "Ven, this isn't a daycare."

"Not in the mood, Raze." Venom's feet didn't slow and she had to scurry to keep up with him.

Raze? She glanced back over her shoulder to stare at her husband's best friend. The soldier had the broadest chest she had ever seen and was a good two or three inches taller than Venom. He didn't seem happy to see her trespassing in this very male domain.

Venom unlocked a door and tugged her into a nicely appointed office. He carefully steered her into a chair. "Don't move. I'm locking the door behind me. You stay here and you'll be safe." His fingertips traced the front of her collar. "Don't forget what I told you about the men who snatch brides. This isn't the time to go exploring the ship."

"I understand." The very idea of it terrified her.

Venom's hard expressions softened some. "I know you're mad at me about what I said in the elevator." He pressed a tender kiss to her forehead. "We'll figure it out."

Not wanting him to run off into a crazy, dangerous situation with an argument between them, she grasped the front of his uniform shirt and jerked him down for a real kiss. He groaned softly against her mouth and deepened the kiss, flicking his tongue against hers before reluctantly breaking away. Dizzy stroked his cheek. "Please be careful."

"I will, sugar."

And then he was gone, rushing out of the room and locking her into the office to await his return.

She prayed he would come back to her in one piece.

Chapter Fourteen

"**I** S YOUR HEAD in the game or do I need to pull you off this mission?"

Venom glanced at Raze. His question bordered on insult as far as Venom was concerned. He had never, not once, allowed his personal issues to cloud his judgment. "I'm here. My head's right."

Raze's pointed stare bored into him like a drill bit. "I realize I should be a good friend and ask you what the hell is going on between you and that blonde pixie you Grabbed—but we don't have time. We're hitting the deck of the *Arctis* in less than three minutes."

"I'm fine. It's under control." Venom didn't try to hide his irritation with Raze's incessant prodding. "Let it go, boss."

"All right." Raze seemed reluctant but did as asked. He turned his attention to Cipher, the brilliant engineer who was as deadly with his algorithms as he was with a weapon. "Intel?"

"The subject is a twenty-seven-year-old male named Ben from Grogan's Mill. He appears to be the ex-boyfriend or fiancé of Kate, the woman he's currently holding hostage at gunpoint. He faked his papers to get onto the transport ship for family day and posed as the victim's brother. He's shot and killed one policeman and wounded three bystanders. The medics can't reach one of the victims. He's critical and needs immediate transport."

Venom studied the intel screen strapped to his forearm. Cipher sent a live feed of the situation to their devices. He zeroed in on the injured man, another visitor from Calyx, sprawled facedown on the floor. Two small but growing blood pools framed his still body.

Ben, the hostage-taker, clamped a sobbing, nearly hysterical woman to his front. The subject had kicked over a couple of tables to form a fortified position so Venom quickly assessed the space for areas with higher vantage points. He had a sinking feeling this call was going to end badly and wanted to narrow down the possibilities for a perch.

"The subject is boxed in?" Venom noticed the policemen guarding the exit points and the perimeter of the *Arctis* food court.

"Yes," Cipher confirmed.

"So let's take some of the pressure off," Raze ordered. "We need to give this guy some breathing room and see if we can get him to talk. Priorities are the hostage and the wounded bystander. Ven?"

He didn't have to ask what Raze wanted. If talking the subject down failed, they would have few choices to end the situation. "I'm on tactical options."

"Cipher, run intel on this guy and this woman. Find someone who knows them. I need to know the score between this couple."

"Working on it already, boss."

Venom gathered four team members and quickly laid out three tactical plans. Once they docked with the *Arctis*, they deployed to the food court with maximum speed. Venom quietly signaled his men to take up a perimeter around the victim and the subject, replacing the policeman who had kept the situation contained.

Smiling broadly and projecting friendliness, Raze cautiously approached and made himself visible. "Ben, my name is Raze. I'm a member of the Special Response Unit and I'm just here to talk."

"Stay back!" Ben shouted as his wild-eyed gaze darted around the cavernous space. "You stay back or I swear to god I'll put a bullet through her brain right now."

"Okay." Raze moved back a few steps and held his hands up in front of him. Still smiling, he said, "We're hanging back and giving you some space but I need to get some medics in there to retrieve that wounded man."

"Stay back!" Ben's shout echoed in the evacuated food court.

"Ben," Raze said calmly, "I hear you, man. Okay? I know that you're feeling cornered but I need you to understand that I cannot help you out of this if more people die. Let me send three men out to grab this wounded man and then we can talk about what I can do for you."

Venom's adrenaline amped up as he prepared to move forward with extricating the wounded man. Fierce and Threat sidled up next to him with two of their heavy-duty shields. The mic attached to his uniform and tied in to the earbud he wore allowed the team to communicate. "We're in position, boss."

"Copy that." Raze continued to negotiate with the hostage-taker. "Ben, this guy is badly wounded. He's bleeding everywhere. Let me send my guys in to drag him out and then we can talk about what you want."

"What I want?" Ben snarled furiously. "What I fucking want you took from me!"

Venom eyed the growing blood pool on the floor. The witness reports stated the injured man had been hit in the legs and arms. They weren't immediately fatal wounds but that much blood loss presented a serious problem. He glanced at Fierce and Threat who nodded with understanding. This wasn't going to be an easy extraction but it had to be done.

"Ben, I hear you. I understand you. But Ben, I need you to look at this man you shot. He's not one of us. He didn't take anything from you. He's one of your people. He's innocent. He has family. Please let us help him."

Venom watched as Ben's panicked gaze darted from Raze to the small team he headed and back again to the boss. "Yeah. Okay. They can take him." He lifted his weapon menacingly and pressed it against the woman's temple. "If they try anything stupid she's dead. You understand?"

"Yes, Ben, I understand you." Raze tried to build rapport with the hostage-taker. "My team is going to slowly walk out, grab the injured man and retreat. Then we can talk. Okay?"

Ben nodded jerkily. He swung the poor woman he held around, putting her body between his and Venom's advancing team. The sight of a man using an unarmed woman as a shield sickened Venom but he pushed down his disgust to focus solely on the job at hand—rescuing the injured man.

Safe behind Fierce and Threat's shields, Venom gripped the wounded man under the arms and dragged him out of the line of fire and beyond the perimeter to the medics who waited. Two bloody streaks marked the path they had taken.

After handing off the injured man, Venom silently delivered orders to his men with a series of hand signals. They fanned out to take their new tactical positions. As Venom moved to the spot he had picked, he caught sight of Terror. The Shadow Force operative wore a murderous expression. Venom was reminded of his friend's quip about farmers and pitchforks. Clearly somewhere the security chain had been broken.

"Thank you, Ben. You're a good guy. I can tell you don't want anyone else to get hurt." Raze thought nothing of the sort but he was damn good at telling gun-wielding subjects whatever they wanted to hear if it mean a peaceful resolution.

"Boss," Cipher's voice carried across the team's earbuds, "we've got a problem. The female hostage is thirteen weeks pregnant. Her husband is a fighter pilot and he's arrived at the perimeter. He says this Ben character was her childhood sweetheart but he was wrapped up in that League of Concerned Citizens group and she broke up with him right before she was Grabbed."

"What's this league?" Raze asked the question they were all thinking.

"Shadow Force suspects they're a front for the Splinters."

"Great." Raze's grumbled answer mirrored Venom's feeling. An armed and highly agitated man with possible ties to a terrorist group holding hostage a woman pregnant by the Harcos male who had taken her away from him? This had shitstorm written all over it.

"Ben, let's talk about what I can do to help you, okay? Because, man, you're looking a little boxed in here. I have a feeling this day didn't go quite the way you had anticipated but it's all right. I can help you."

"You can't help me." Ben glanced around nervously. "I'm on my own now."

Now? Venom wondered at Ben's choice of words as he moved into position. *Is there an accomplice lurking in the crowd? Maybe an inside man?* It would explain how he had been able to board the transport ship with a fake ID and get his hands on a weapon once aboard the *Arctis*.

With the practice of so many years staring down a scope, Venom picked a spot beside a column and behind a fake potted tree. His rifle felt so natural in his hand. He treated it as an extension of his body. Painfully aware of its deadliness, he treated the rifle with the respect it deserved. This wasn't a weapon to be used lightly. This was a weapon of last resort.

But the tactics Raze attempted with the crazed man weren't working. The minutes ticked by as Raze tried to build rapport but Ben couldn't be reached. He grew more agitated and panicked. This man, this Ben from Grogan's Mill, had boarded that transport ship earlier in the morning with one sole purpose—he wanted to kill this woman and then take his own life.

"Boss, I have the solution." Venom stared down the scope at the gun-wielding subject.

"Understood." Raze continued to attempt to reach Ben through negotiation. "Ben, put the gun down and talk to me. Let me help you find a way out of this situation."

Ben gripped the gun even tighter and brought it back up toward the female hostage's face. "There's no way out of this."

Venom's finger itched against the trigger. Ben had already killed one man and attempted to kill three others. Venom wasn't going to give this bastard the chance to hurt that woman or her baby.

"There is, Ben," Raze hurriedly assured him. "But you have to lower your weapon."

The subject swallowed and scanned the room. He let his arm fall and pulled the gun away from the woman's face.

"Thank you, Ben. I appreciate your cooperation. You need to remember that if that gun comes up again, you're going to force our hands. Do you understand?"

Ben nodded. "Yeah. I get it."

"Good. Ben, tell me what I can do to help you."

The man perked up suddenly. "You can stop taking our women!"

Was this a politically motivated hostage situation? Venom couldn't wrap his head around this guy. First, it seemed as though Ben had taken the woman and shot up the place because his love for her had been twisted into something cruel and dark.

Now Venom suspected someone in that stupid league of his or even a Splinter member had wound this poor jackass up, shoved a gun in his hand and pushed him onto that transport ship on a suicide mission. There was no end to the list of people who wanted to cause problems between the Harcos warriors and the people of Calyx.

"Ben, that's a demand that goes above my pay grade. If I had the power to save Kate's life by ending the Grabs, I would do it in a heartbeat."

"Bullshit."

Raze kept that smile of his plastered in place. "It's not bullshit."

"You expect me to believe an officer like you doesn't have one of our women chained up in your bedroom?"

"I don't have a mate anymore. The one I did have for a short while was from my home planet. She came to me of her own volition. I didn't need to steal a woman to find a bride."

"That's because you're a real man," Ben remarked. "You're not like these other cowardly dicks who come down and take our women."

"I understand your frustration, Ben."

"What happened to your wife?" The arm Ben had clamped around Kate slid down a little as his grip loosened.

Venom didn't take his eye off the scope but he could imagine that vein in Raze's temple jumping at the very mention of his first mate.

"She left me." Raze spoke the words calmly and without any hint of the embarrassment and pain his old friend still felt. "For a man from the colonies. For one of you."

"Because you beat on her?"

"No," Raze said with a sigh. "No, she left me because I failed to understand her needs."

"Yeah?" Ben flicked his wrist but kept the gun still pointed at the ground. His arm tightened against Kate's throat and he curled his fingers in her hair. He pulled hard enough to make her cry out in pain. "Then you know what it feels like to have your damn heart ripped out of your chest and stomped on by the woman you loved."

"Ben! You don't need to do that. Kate isn't the one you're angry at, remember? It's us." Raze touched his chest. "It was men like me who forced her into a Grab and stole her away from you."

Venom's cheek twitched as he watched Raze deliberately drawing Ben's anger—and his gunfire. Despite the bulletproof vest his friend wore, that hard head of his would make an easy target. He kept his weapon trained on the subject and his finger at the ready. Their rules of engagement required him to wait for Raze to give the final okay to take a kill shot—unless a member of the team or a victim was in immediate danger.

"Ben—this isn't her fault."

"It is! She *wanted* this. She traded her number with her sister. She *abandoned* me." Ben let loose a guttural sob, the very sound so painfully raw that it made Venom flinch. With a rough shove, he pushed the woman to the ground. The gun remained pointed toward the floor as Kate managed to get up on her knees.

Weeping, she begged, "Ben, *please*."

"You humiliated me, Kate. You ran out and left me. I loved you."

Hugging her middle, Kate pleaded, "Ben, don't. *Please. I'm pregnant.*"

The moment her condition registered, Ben's eyes turned cold and dead. Venom recognized the signs that the subject was shutting down. He focused solely on the target, no longer thinking of Ben as a red-blooded man in the grips of a breakdown. He thought of him simply as violent, dangerous thing that needed to be neutralized.

Venom didn't hear whatever Ben uttered so maliciously and nastily at Kate. Time seemed to slow as the gun lifted toward the woman's belly. He didn't hesitate or wait for Raze to make the call. Venom squeezed the trigger—and ended the standoff.

Fierce and Threat rushed in with Raze not far behind them to secure the gunman and sweep the hostage to safety. Venom inhaled deep cleansing breaths as the old feelings of dread crept along his spine and gripped his throat.

Even though he tried not to think about the growing tally of lives he had taken in the call of duty, Venom couldn't stop the number that danced around in his head. In his early days of training to be a sniper, it was a count that would have inspired awe in him. Now? It made his stomach pitch violently.

Across the controlled chaos, Venom met Raze's steady gaze. His best friend understood better than anyone the burden Venom carried. After a call like this, the team would debrief and then Venom would usually go spend some time with Raze to talk and decompress.

But Dizzy was anxiously awaiting his return—and he had no idea how the hell he was supposed to face her after taking another man's life.

DIZZY FIDGETED NERVOUSLY as she waited for Venom to return. Terrible images rushed through her mind. Logically she understood he dealt with dangerous situations like these on a regular basis but that didn't make it any easier to accept. She massaged her temples and wondered why the hell she couldn't have been Grabbed by a damn clerk or something.

Was this how it would be once their honeymoon was over and Venom returned to his usual duty rotation? Would she be left to sit alone in their quarters and worry about him while he was out saving the world?

Their earlier argument in the elevator made her chest ache. She liked Venom so much but that nonsense about her not working was something she couldn't accept. He had to realize that cultural differences went both ways. She was already making huge concessions for him to accommodate *his* culture. The least he could do was make one or two for her.

Annoyed with the constant throbbing under her collar, Dizzy gingerly touched the inflamed area where the leather strip rubbed against her scars. It was driving her completely batty. Venom and his people considered these collars to be as good as wedding bands but she couldn't stand another minute of wearing it.

Locked inside the office, she figured it was safe to re-move the collar marking her as Venom's property. She sighed with relief as she peeled the collar away from her skin. In the last few days she had tried everything to cut down on the irritation but short of not wearing the collar, nothing had worked. She hadn't wanted to hurt Venom's feelings but this damn thing had to go.

Spinning in the desk chair, Dizzy scanned the large of-fice Venom shared with Raze. It was an extremely manly space and so very bland. Everything in the room was a shade of gray. She found it oddly disorienting.

Her gaze dropped to her bag. She thought of her tablet and the message Naya had transferred to her device. Feeling homesick, Dizzy dug her tablet out of her bag and located the message from her friend. There was no video like the sample messages Venom had shown her when teaching her how to use the device but Ella's voice came through loud and clear.

"Dizzy! I'm not sure how long I have so I'll make it quick." Ella's voice turned serious. "Look, I ran into your dad. He looked like he was about to cut out of town and go underground. Something isn't right about that debt he said he owed to Fat Pete. Yesterday, I ran into some of his knee-breakers. They were asking about you and I blew them off. I have a weird feeling about it. I'm heading out to Blue Shores until the smoke clears."

After Dizzy's run-in with Pierce and Torment, she didn't know what to believe anymore. She suspected the two Shadow Force operatives knew much more about the deal that had forced her father to sell her lottery number but they weren't going to share that information with her. Was her dad in serious trouble?

"Anyway, I realize that none of that helps you now—but I thought you needed to know. I'm not sure what's going on here but I'm worried about you." Her voice grew sad. "I miss you so much. I can't wait to see you again. Naya said that there's a visitation program and you better put my name at the top of that list!" With a smile in her voice, she added, "I hope you're doing well and that his new guy of yours realizes how damn lucky he is to have Grabbed you."

As Ella's voice faded away, Dizzy experienced a crushing wave of sadness. The last five days with Venom suddenly seemed rather dreamlike and almost unreal. Hearing Ella and thinking about her father dragged her back to a reality that she had been avoiding. It was so easy to allow herself to be swept up in the romance and excitement of her new bond with Venom—but that didn't mean her life on Calyx simply stopped existing.

What was the real story between her dad and Fat Pete? What in the world could the underworld player possibly need so badly from her father?

Dizzy didn't want to think about the stupid blood test that said Jack Lane, the only father she had ever known, wasn't her biological parent, but it was impossible to avoid now. How in the world was she going to bring up *that* topic with him? It would a painful conversation and one she would give anything to avoid.

Footsteps in the hallway outside the locked office door

caught her attention. Dizzy glanced at the door. Was Venom back?

The door handle rattled as someone tested it to see if it was locked. Her heart leapt into her throat. Venom knew the door was locked so that definitely wasn't him on the other side of the door. Standing perfectly still and holding her breath, Dizzy listened for any signs that the person on the other side of the door had left.

Beeping sounds terrified her. Someone was trying to unlock the door using the keypad out there. Visions of an oversexed sky warrior breaking into the office to steal her pushed Dizzy into a panicked state. She scanned the room for a place to hide and picked Raze's big desk.

Grateful for her small size, Dizzy grabbed her bag, tablet and collar and scuttled around to the other desk. She slipped down underneath it, squeezing herself into the small alcove there and dragging Raze's chair up tight against her shoulder to provide better camouflage.

Curled into a tight little ball, Dizzy sucked the smallest, quietest breaths into her lungs. The door opened with a long squeak. Boots tapped against the floor as a man entered the office. She couldn't remember the last time she had been this scared. Eyes closed, Dizzy prayed Venom would return soon.

The man walked to the desk closest to the door—Venom's desk—and started to rifle though the drawers. He tapped at the computer screen for a few minutes and made annoyed sounds. He wasn't finding what he needed, whatever that was. She heard him moving around the office, digging through cabinets and tapping at keypads.

When he neared Raze's desk, she almost passed out from sheer terror. He was too close. There was no way he would miss her. If he sat down in that chair, she was dead meat.

Suddenly her stomach started to cramp. She couldn't tell if it was a side effect of fear or the fact that she had missed lunch. She clenched her eyes shut and prayed her belly wouldn't make any noise. In a space this small and with the room so quiet, the intruder would never miss it.

Her prayers weren't going to be answered today. As the man walked away from Raze's desk, a loud growl followed by a quick gurgle erupted from her tummy. Dizzy's fingers curled into tight fists. She gulped nervously. *Did he hear that?*

Heavy, quick footsteps pivoted back toward the desk. Before she could move the man roughly shoved the desk out of the way and forced her out into the open. Dropping her bag and tablet, she scrambled to her feet as the sky warrior leered lecherously.

"Well, well, well. Aren't you a pretty little thing?"

"Stay back!" She held up her hands but it was a futile move. This soldier wasn't quite as tall or as solidly built as Venom but he still dwarfed her. "My husband—my mate—will hurt you if you try to touch me."

"What mate? I don't see a collar on that neck."

She gulped and reached up to touch her naked skin. She frantically glanced around the room and spotted it on the floor. Before she could reach it, the soldier cornering her grabbed it and stuffed it in his pocket. She noticed his name tag. Axis was his name. "Give me back my collar!"

Axis shrugged. "What collar? Besides, collar or not, I don't see this mate of yours hanging around here. You're alone—and that makes you fair game."

"If you take one step closer, I'll scream."

A sickeningly triumphant grin stretched his mouth. "Go ahead. No one will hear you. All of the SRU teams are deployed. We're all alone."

Oh god. "Please—just leave me alone. Venom will be back soon. He's going to be furious."

"He should be furious at himself for leaving such a tempting little morsel alone."

The way Axis licked his lips disgusted her. She had no doubt that this brute wanted to get her naked and underneath him as quickly as possible. Well—screw him. She wasn't going down without a fight.

Snatching the closest chair, Dizzy hefted it up with all her might and swung it right at the man who had broken into the office. She caught him off guard and slammed the chair into his shoulder. It knocked him off balance. He stumbled backward, tripped over a stack of ammo boxes and fell flat on his ass.

Dizzy booked it.

Out in the hallway she headed straight for the elevator that had brought her to the SRU offices but she couldn't get it to activate. That was when she remembered her ID chip would only allow her to access certain areas. Cursing the stupid chip, she spun on her heel—and spotted an enraged Axis racing out of the office.

She darted across the hall into the gear room. Slamming the door behind her, she tried to get it to lock but it was activated by a code she didn't have. Grabbing a broom, she fed it through the handles of the double door and raced deeper into the gear room.

There weren't many places to hide—but there were more than enough weapons. She couldn't fire a gun, of course, but there were plenty of heavy things for her to throw and sharp things for her to stab at him.

Axis gave the door three good kicks but couldn't get the metal broom handle to give. He wasn't about to let that stop him. She could see him through the glass wall. At first he looked as though he might try to break the see-through pane but then he ran down to the next entrance.

Shit.

Dizzy hadn't counted on that. His boots hit the floor hard as he raced through the other door and closed the distance between them. Grabbing anything that wasn't nailed down, she chucked things at his head. More often than not, she hit her target. It still wasn't enough to stop him. Axis was a man on a mission and he wasn't leaving emptyhanded.

When she ran out of things to throw, the man snatched for her. She twisted away but he grabbed a handful of her skirt. With one good jerk, he tore the delicate fabric. She kicked out at him and screamed as she realized how very close she was to being assaulted. "Leave me alone!"

"Give it up!" Axis gripped her forearm hard enough to leave bruises and swung her around to face him. "You're mine now."

"Like hell!" She smacked him right in the face. "I belong to Venom."

Axis laughed and pushed her down onto the floor. "Not anymore."

"No!" She put up both hands and shoved at his chest as the man pinned her to the floor. "Get off me!"

"Leave her alone!" Another male voice, this one booming and angry, cut through her panic. She glanced at the doorway and saw a man in exercise clothes standing there. His gleaming silver leg got her attention. She had never seen anything like it.

Despite his injury, the man with the metal leg sprinted across the room with such speed and finesse. As if kicking a ball, he slammed the toe of his metal prosthesis right into the other man's gut. Axis flew off her and hit the floor— but he didn't stay down long.

The man with the missing leg snatched Dizzy up and tossed her onto the closest counter. Squaring off with Axis, he lifted his hands and made a come-and-take me motion. Like two wild street dogs, the men rushed each other and began to brawl.

Crouching on the steel counter, Dizzy decided she was *never* leaving their quarters again. These men were all crazy!

She could hardly stand to watch as the two men pummeled each other with their fists. Every now and then one of them would land a good punch. The sounds of knuckles smacking against flesh sickened her. She had never been able to stomach violence. Seeing it up this close was too much for her.

Over the constant growling and punching and cursing, Dizzy heard the faintest ding of the elevator. She crawled to the very end of the countertop and didn't stop until her face was basically pressed against the transparent wall. The moment she spotted Venom and his team coming down the hall she started to pound on the glass.

"*Venom!* Venom! *Hurry!*"

Her mate's blue eyes widened with shock. She could only imagine what she must have looked like, hiding up on that counter with her hair a mess and dress torn. His gaze flicked over her shoulder to the brawling men behind her. The cold glare that replaced his stunned expression chilled her to the very bone.

Oh, boy. It's about to get ugly.

Chapter Fifteen

"DIZZY!"

The sight of his sweet mate's terrified face and ripped dress enraged Venom. If it hadn't been for Raze's hand clamping down on his shoulder, Venom would have put his boot through the glass to get to her. Instead he managed to shove down the overwhelming urge to protect and defend her so he could think straight.

He sprinted into the room and edged around Mayhem and a sky corps soldier he didn't recognize. Though he wanted so badly to join the brawl and beat on the man who had scared Dizzy, he recognized that she needed to be comforted and reassured more than he needed to satisfy his desire to hurt that bastard for scaring her.

"Come here, sugar." He stepped up to the counter where Dizzy perched like a bird. The moment he was close enough she launched herself at him. He caught her easily and cradled her. Burying his nose in her sweetly scented hair, he whispered, "Are you all right? Did he hurt you?"

She sobbed against his neck. "He tried but I'm okay."

Though her dress was shredded from the waist down, she didn't seem to have been molested any further. It was a small comfort to him. Already her arms were purpling with fingertip-shaped bruises from being grabbed. He gingerly brushed his palm over the spots marking her soft skin. "Oh, honey…"

Guilt wracked Venom. He had promised to protect her but he had left her locked in a room where anyone could have gotten to her.

And someone had.

Still holding Dizzy, Venom glared at the man Mayhem had in a headlock. "Who the fuck is he?"

"Name tag says Axis," Fierce answered in that slow, country-boy drawl of his. "He's not a face I know."

"He's an engineer," Cipher supplied. "From down in the coding department, I think. He works in IT for the ship."

"Is that so?" Raze stood in front of the man and leveled an icy stare. "I suppose that's how he busted the lock on our office."

"I didn't, sir. It was unlocked. She was out in the hall."

Dizzy gasped. "I was not. I was hiding under the desk when he broke into the room!"

Raze used the toe of his boot to lift Axis' bloody chin. "You want to try that again, skyboy?"

Axis swallowed nervously. "Okay. All right. Yes. I hacked the keypad."

"Why?" Raze demanded.

The engineer hesitated. "I heard you were making the shortlist of invitations for the next round of SRU tryouts. I tried to access the list from my work console but your system is walled off from the rest of the ship."

"For good reason, jackass," Cipher retorted with frustration. "It's to keep rubberneckers like you from digging through our highly sensitive files."

Axis didn't respond to Cipher's cutting remark. He turned accusing eyes toward Dizzy. "*She* came on to *me*."

"I did not!" Dizzy's hold on Venom's waist tightened.

"She's not even wearing a collar." Axis gestured toward her. "She practically begged me to take her away from you."

"Enough of the lies," Venom growled. "My mate is shaking with fear. Her dress is torn."

He brushed his gloved fingertips along her bare neck. The sight of her without his collar was like a knife to the heart. It was obvious she had removed it after their argument. There had been no mistaking how upset she was with him back in the elevator. Was she angry enough to want to end their bond? After the wives' meeting she would know that it was a relatively simple procedure to get rid of him.

The thought of losing her punched him in the gut. Sliding his arm across her chest, he pulled her back against him in a public sign of possession. "Collar or no collar, she belongs to me."

Dizzy clasped his forearm in a display of agreement. His fear of her leaving lessened. Hopefully she had simply removed the collar in a fit of anger and not because she truly wanted to leave him for being such an asshole in the elevator.

"He has my collar in his pocket. He took it from me."

Venom loosened his embrace of Dizzy and stalked across the room. He ripped the front pockets on Axis' uniform shirt and Dizzy's collar tumbled into his hand.

"You haven't earned the right to the responsibility that comes with one of these."

Gripping the bridal collar, Venom returned to Dizzy. She clung to his side and he soothingly caressed her back.

"Mayhem, how did you get tangled up in this?" Raze turned his attention to the busted-up soldier hoping to make the next SRU team.

"I was on my way to the gym upstairs and thought I would drop in to talk to you about the upcoming trials. I heard a commotion and found him on top of her. I figured any woman hanging out here had to be the mate of one of the SRU men." Mayhem narrowed his eyes and ran a hand along his swollen jaw. "Mated or not, she needed to be defended from that piece of trash."

"I didn't even hurt her!" Axis continued to dig his hole. "I just wanted to scare her a little."

If Dizzy hadn't been clinging to him Venom would have given in to the desire to slam his fist right into the man's nose. "Get him out of here before I do something very stupid."

Raze nodded. "Secure him in the weight room until the MPs come for him."

Fierce jerked Axis to his feet and roughly shoved him toward the door. "Move."

"Ma'am?" Cipher came forward with a clean shirt he'd grabbed from his locker.

"Would you like this shirt?"

Dizzy smiled gratefully. "Thank you."

Venom took the shirt and pulled it down over her head. Though Cipher wasn't quite as tall as he the length of the shirt was more than enough to cover her ripped skirt. He cupped the back of Dizzy's head and gazed down into her watery brown eyes. She still seemed a bit dazed by the terrible experience.

Her lower lip trembled. "I want to go home."

Venom's gut clenched painfully. Of course she did. After the way he had snapped at her in the elevator and then left her exposed to that brute Axis, he couldn't blame her for wanting to bail on him. If their situations had been reversed he probably would have wanted to return to his planet too.

But he couldn't let her go without a fight. "I can't let you go now."

Her brows knitted. "Please? Just get someone to escort me to our quarters. I don't want to be here anymore."

The painful ball in his belly stopped throbbing. She didn't want to go home to Calyx. She wanted to return to *their* home. Maybe there was still time for him salvage this. "I would prefer for you to wait here while I debrief."

"She can wait in my office," Cipher offered. "It's comfortable and quiet. We'll take turns standing guard if that will make you feel more secure, ma'am."

Dizzy hesitated but eventually nodded. "Okay."

Raze led the way out of the gear room. Venom kept his arm around Dizzy's shoulders while Cipher trailed them. Threat stayed behind with the rest of the team to put the room back together.

Venom's stomach soured when they stopped at the office he shared with Raze to gather Dizzy's things. Seeing the furniture moved haphazardly around the space told him the story of the altercation Dizzy had survived. Raze touched his desk that had been shoved about four feet out of the way and shot a questioning glance her way.

"I was hiding under there," she explained quietly. "I had been listening to a message from Ella when I heard someone at the door. I thought maybe it was you," she looked up at him, "but then he tried the handle and I knew it was someone trying to break in to the office. I couldn't get out so I hid—but he found me. I threw that chair at him and ran."

Listening to Dizzy recount her ordeal only added to his guilt. He pressed his lips to the crown of her head in a silent apology.

Raze picked up her bag and tablet and handed them over. "Get her situated in Cipher's office and then meet me in the debriefing suite."

When they were alone, Venom tried to wrap his collar back around Dizzy's neck. Her hand flew up and blocked him. "No, Venom. I can't stand it anymore."

Taken aback, he reminded her, "Dizzy, this is the way we do things here."

"But it hurts me."

At first he thought she meant it was hurting her emotionally or mentally but then she gestured to her neck. The red, irritated skin surrounding her scars just added to his pile of guilt. How the hell had he missed that?

"I'm sorry." He carefully brushed his fingertips over her chafed skin. "I didn't realize—"

"I didn't want to make a big deal out of it," she interjected. "I thought I could get used to it."

"You never have to get used to pain, Dizzy. I should have recognized that your scars and the collar weren't going to play nice but apparently I'm dense. Next time you have a problem like this you tell me."

"I will."

"Hold out your wrist." When she followed his order, he wrapped the collar around it twice before securing the latch. "We'll make do with this until I can figure out something else."

"Maybe I could only wear it outside our home?"

He didn't like the idea of her skin being irritated and chafed every time she left their quarters but it was the easiest solution. "We can try that."

Her small hands moved across his tactical vest, tracing the ammo magazines and cuffs and other gear tucked into the myriad pockets. "You look really scary in this getup."

His cheek twitched. "That's sort of the point."

Her lopsided smile melted some of his tension. "I figured."

When her gaze moved to his shoulder he sensed she wanted to ask about the rifle strapped to his back but she didn't. She rubbed his chest. "You should go to your debriefing. I'll be fine in your friend's office."

He didn't want to leave her but it had to be done. Holding her hand, he led her to Cipher's office. He spotted a bottle of berry-flavored rehydrating water and a candy bar waiting for her on the desk there. That was just like Cipher to be so considerate and accommodating.

"I won't be long. An hour tops," he said while guiding her onto the small couch along the wall. He picked up the snack and presented it to her. "Eat this. I'm sure you're hungry after missing lunch."

"Thank you." She set aside the bottled drink and bar and reached for his gloved hand. "Venom, are you mad at me?"

"What?" He crouched down in front of her and put both hands on her thighs. "No, of course not! What happened with Axis wasn't your fault. Collar or no collar, he had no right to attack you like that."

"It's just that you seem very...cold. I thought maybe you were mad at me for embarrassing you with the collar thing or—"

"No." He caressed her cheek with his thumb, all the while wishing the fabric of his glove wasn't between his skin and hers. "The call we were on didn't end well."

"Oh." Her eyes sparked with understand. "*Oh.*"

"After a call like this, it's better for me to disengage myself from you until my head is back in the right space."

"Okay. Whatever you need, just tell me, Venom. I can't even begin to understand what you're feeling but I'll do whatever I can to help you."

Her sweet kindness made his heart swell. She didn't seem horrified by the revelation that he had just ended a man's life. Perhaps her experiences during the bombing had given her a glimpse of the awful choices that often had to be made to save innocent lives.

Even so, he didn't want her exposed to any more harshness today. She had seen enough. The last thing she needed to hear were the details of the hostage situation he had ended with deadly force.

"I'll be back as quickly as possible."

She leaned forward and captured his mouth in a tender kiss. "I'll be here waiting for you."

As Venom backed away and left the office, he wondered if Dizzy would ever comprehend how much those six simple words meant to him.

LATER THAT EVENING Dizzy reclined against a pillow and tried to focus on the book opened up on her tablet. She was reading a title Raze had recommended on understanding siege-shock and trauma bonds. Her worried gaze flitted from the screen to the open doorway of their bedroom. Venom still hadn't come to bed and she was concerned about him.

During Venom's debriefing, Raze had come into the office to chat with her. Even though he seemed uncomfortable alone with her, the great big beast of a man had taken the time to explain more about the hostage situation. He had given her a list of signs to watch for in Venom and made sure his private communications number was programmed into her tablet.

Since returning to their quarters she had watched Venom like a hawk. Thankfully he didn't seem to be showing any of the troubling signs. Raze had assured her that Venom had his own ways of dealing with the emotional punch of taking a life in the line of duty but he had warned that Venom might be thrown off by having a new mate to contend with in the midst of it all.

Refusing to let Venom pull away from her, Dizzy

flipped back the covers and set her tablet on the bedside table. She quietly exited the bedroom and found him sitting in the living area, watching the large entertainment screen fixed on the wall. The lights were totally dimmed and the sports show he was watching cast a strange bluish glow about him.

His alert gaze snapped toward her the moment she appeared in the doorway. He quickly twisted in his seat to face her and raised his voice high enough for the audio sensors in the entertainment console to hear him. "Mute."

Dizzy stopped at the edge of the couch. "Are you coming to bed?"

"Not for a while, sugar. Go on back to sleep."

"I wasn't asleep."

A flash of guilt crossed his face. "I'll keep the volume down."

She shook her head. "That's not what kept me awake."

"Is it because of Axis? Are you having nightmares?"

"No." She shrugged. "Oddly enough I'm not nearly as upset about that whole mess as I expected to be. Maybe I'm finally toughening up some."

"You don't need to toughen up." The rough edge to his voice surprised her. "You should be able to sit in an office and wait for your husband without having to worry about some asshole trying to steal or molest you."

"In a perfect world," she softly replied. Extending her hand, she wiggled her fingers. "Come to bed with me."

Venom swallowed nervously. "I don't think that's a good idea."

His rejection surprised her more than it hurt. "Why

not?"

He exhaled a harsh breath and glanced away from her. "It's not safe for you."

The hard set to his jaw convinced her that he was feeling raw and emotionally exposed. Unwilling to allow Venom to wall himself off from her, Dizzy bravely skirted the side of the couch and knelt on the cushion next to him. Putting her hands on his shoulders, she gazed into his haunted eyes. "You have never hurt me. You will never hurt me."

"You can't know that."

"Venom—"

"Dizzy, if you could feel the way I want to fuck you right now, you would be running back in that bedroom and locking the door."

His blunt remark had the opposite effect that he intended. The dangerous glint in his eyes excited her. Since their first time together Venom had been so incredibly gentle with her when they made love. He brought her so much pleasure—sometimes she could hardly breathe as the rapturous spasms of the orgasms he coaxed forth rocked her—but she sensed he had been holding back a part of him.

What was it that Raze had suggested? Touch him. Show him affection. Help him reconnect.

She slowly stood and moved in front of Venom. Gripping the bottom of her nightdress, she peeled it off and presented her naked body to him. She grasped his big, scarred hands and brought them to her bare breasts. Looking him right in the eye, she decided to be brave.

Using harsh language that would shock him, she ordered, "Fuck me, Venom. Be rough with me."

His nostrils flared. He squeezed her soft flesh with enough force to make her rise up on her toes. Pinching her nipples, he warned, "You don't know what you're asking for, Dizzy."

"I know that I want you." She whimpered at the delicious arc of delight that accompanied the continued tweaking of her nipples. "I want to know all of you, Venom."

In a flash of movement, Venom wrapped his brawny arm around her waist and flipped her onto her stomach. The couch softened the unexpected tumble. She gasped when he gripped her hips and dragged her knees up onto the cushion.

Gathering her hair in his hand, he pulled just hard enough to make her chin lift. His lips touched the shell of her ear. "Do you still want to know this side of me?"

Heart racing and belly wobbling, Dizzy had never been more excited in her life. Venom's rough manhandling shouldn't have been so arousing—but it was. Her clitoris pulsed and her pussy ached to be filled by him. Dizzy pushed back against the steely length of him trapped in those shorts. "Yes."

"You don't have to prove anything to me, Dizzy." The arm clamped around her body loosened some.

"I'm not trying to prove anything." Certain she was playing with fire, she ground her backside against the erection jammed against her body. "Fuck me."

He clicked his teeth and whispered against her neck,

"Such a dirty mouth."

A little breathlessly, she taunted, "I'm sure you can think of a good use for it."

"Tease." In the next instant, he bit down on the sensitive curve there. She yelped but instead of feeling fear, she experienced only the heightened awareness of how good the flash of pain felt against the backdrop of arousal saturating her body.

Those rough yet loving hands roamed her naked skin. His fingers swept down her spine, followed the curve of her bottom and disappeared between her thighs. While he nipped and kissed at her shoulders, Venom probed her pussy. She could feel him holding back and using all the willpower he could muster to be gentle with her.

The slick wetness seeping from her core must have assured him that she wanted him, wanted this. She heard him push down his shorts before grasping her wrists and dragging them to the small of her back. With another pull, he pulled her down until her knees were dangling a few inches above the floor. The furniture here simply wasn't built to accommodate her short stature.

Contorted and unable to hold up her body weight, she relied on the couch for support. Relaxing her shoulders and arms, she surrendered to his controlling touch. The head of his cock nudged her pussy. He swiveled his hips while stabbing at her entrance, teasing her with the promise of the coupling to come.

When he finally thrust into her, Dizzy cried out and closed her eyes. She couldn't explain it but the rough way he loved her seemed to activate something hidden and secret within her. Venom took her with fast, hard strokes that made the couch shudder beneath them. Every plunging thrust of his cock made her body sing.

With a growl of frustration or lust—she couldn't tell—Venom flipped her onto her back. She bounced a little on the couch cushion and was still trying to get her bearings when Venom gripped her inner thighs and dropped his mouth right down on her clit. "Oh!"

The wholly unexpected change in his tactic burned her right up. Dizzy cupped the back of his shaved head as he went wild between her thighs. His tongue fluttered over her throbbing bundle of nerves with such speed that she began to pant and rock her hips. "Oh! Oh! *Oh!*"

The explosive climax ripped a scream from her throat. Bucking her hips, Dizzy rode the vacillating waves of her orgasm while clawing at Venom's shoulders. She was still reeling from the unbelievably good vibrations of it when he straightened up and thrust back into her slick sheath.

Head thrown back, Dizzy delighted in the love bites he made on her neck and breasts. Venom pounded her pussy like a man gone feral. She gripped his rippling biceps and held on for dear life as he jackhammered her with that massive tool.

"Dizzy." He uttered her name again and again. "Mine. *Mine.*"

"I'm yours." She sensed he needed the reassurance as he chased his release. "I'm all yours."

Lowering his head, he branded her mouth with a punishing, searing kiss. Slamming hard and deep, Venom went perfectly still for a second before shuddering against her. She lovingly caressed his arms and back as he filled her with his blazing-hot seed.

After the wicked, passionate things he had done to her, Dizzy didn't know how she ever could have imagined one of those staid, white-collar types down in The City would make her happy. Venom had awakened desires within her that would never be sated by anyone but him.

"Are you all right?" he asked sometime later as they cuddled together on the couch. She had burrowed into his comforting heat and didn't want to move.

"Yes. Are you?"

"Yes." He gently tilted her face and kissed her with such sweet tenderness. "Did I hurt you?"

"No."

"You're sure?" He sounded so worried.

"I'm sure." Hoping to set his mind at ease, she admitted, "I enjoyed that a lot. The roughness, I mean."

Seemingly pensive, Venom wound her hair around his finger. "It's probably the Harcos blood running through your veins."

"What do you mean?"

"Did you read the pamphlet about why our people do sex differently than yours?"

"I sort of skimmed it."

"Tomorrow you need to read the entire thing. Then we'll talk about it. The short version? The biochemistry of our bodies is different. Harcos women needed a little pain to find pleasure."

She considered that piece of information. "Do you think that's why I crave deep pressure to feel secure or calm?"

"It's probably the reason. I'm sure Risk could tell you if there's any research on it."

He wound and unwound her hair around his finger. She could practically hear the gears turning in his head. "What's bothering you?"

With some reluctance, he finally answered her. "I don't want you to think that I was turned on by ending that man's life today."

Aghast, she pushed up and stared down into his haunted eyes. "Venom, I don't think that. I know how badly it affected you. I know that you don't take pleasure in what you did."

"I don't. I *hate* that some calls end that way. I wish that we could save every single life we come in contact with—but we can't. We *can't*."

"I know." She caressed his jaw. "You don't have to justify yourself to me. I understand that your line of work is filled with senseless violence. I don't, however, think that *you* are senselessly cruel."

"When I came home today after the debriefing, I was so grateful that you gave me some space to work things out and to decompress. I needed to work through the call a few times to make sure—absolutely sure—that we did everything we could to end it peacefully."

She didn't speak but continued to gently brush her hand down his neck and across his chest.

"Once I worked through all that head shit, I felt so agitated and antsy. All the adrenaline I had suppressed during the call just sort of rushed through me. I thought about checking out of here to go run until I dropped but then I realized that all I wanted was you. I wanted to feel connected to you again—but I was so afraid you would be disgusted by me."

"Venom." She ached for him. It couldn't be easy to be the man everyone else relied on to end difficult and dangerous situations.

"I know," he said softly and pushed into a sitting position. "I know you could never feel that way."

"Never."

He brought her hand to his lips and kissed her fingertips. "You ready for bed?"

Smiling, she confessed, "I'm not sure my shaky legs can make it that far."

"That's okay, sugar." Venom swept her up into his arms and headed for the bedroom. "Sometimes I have to carry you and sometimes I need you to carry me."

He meant emotionally of course but she decided to coax a smile from him with a teasing comeback. "Maybe I should start hitting the gym with Mayhem because I'm going to need to bulk up like Raze to lift your big behind like this."

Venom grinned. "You let me handle your workouts. I'll get you whipped into shape in no time."

A quiver of anticipation struck her. "Maybe we could go a little light on the whipping."

Venom placed her on the bed and pinned her in place with his big, sexy body. "No promises, sugar."

Chapter Sixteen

THE NEXT EVENING, Venom entered their bedroom in search of Dizzy. It was nearly an hour before they were expected to arrive for Menace and Naya's wedding ceremony but he had something special planned for her. He placed the long coil of his softest, lightest rope next to the dress she had laid out on the bed.

His fingertips ghosted down the strikingly beautiful fabric. She had paired a feminine salmon pink with a creamy white lace and bright ocean-blue ribbon accents. He marveled at the construction of the dress. She had told him this was a one-of-a-kind design she had sewn herself. Venom couldn't wait to see it on her.

The sight of undies next to the dress made him frown. He had made an exception by letting her wear them to her wives' club meeting but tonight? Oh no. Picking up her silky panties, he carried them back to the closet and tucked them into the drawer she had claimed.

His ears perked to the sounds she made while getting ready. The mysteries of this ritual still confounded him. Curious, he walked to the open door and leaned against the frame. For a long time he simply enjoyed the sight of her totally naked, her skin still pink and warm from their steamy shower.

"I thought I told you that you were forbidden from coming in here until I was finished."

He grinned at her playful scolding. After pinning her to the wall of their shower for some hot, soapy sex, she had banished him from the bathroom. It was a smart move considering he was always craving her. Even now he had to give his dick an at ease rather than indulging his desire to bury it in her slick, snug sheath again.

"I heard strange sounds and decided to investigate."

"Uh-huh." She smiled at his reflection in the mirror but didn't pause the application of her eye makeup.

The tiny brushes she used to paint color on her eyelids and lips fascinated him but he thought it was a waste of her time. "You don't need that. You're already the most beautiful woman I've ever seen."

She lowered the brush and turned to face him with the sweetest expression on her face. "Thank you."

He shrugged. "It's true."

She turned back to the mirror. "I don't wear it because I think I'm not pretty enough. I wear it because it's a complement to my outfit. A little sweep of color on my cheeks and smokiness around my eyes completes the picture."

"If you say so…"

"I do." Her smile turned a little wistful. "I used to sit on my mother's vanity to watch her put on her makeup. She would let me play with the eye shadow and lipstick. I always think about her when I'm getting ready."

The mention of her mother spurred thoughts of the message from her friend Ella. After Dizzy had let him listen to it he had put in a private call to Pierce because he was concerned Jack Lane might be in real danger. If there was any chance Jack could be useful to the cause the Shadow Force would snap him up and put him in protective custody. Venom didn't dare tell Dizzy what he had done. He hated the idea of getting her hopes up about contacting her father just yet.

"That's a snazzy uniform." Dizzy closed up her makeup pots and tubes and stuffed them back in their small case. "Is it a dress uniform?"

"Yes." He smoothed his hand down the front of the formal uniform shirt. "I haven't pulled this one out of the closet since Vee and Hallie exchanged rings." He rolled his neck and grimaced at the heaviness of the uniform. "It's not my favorite thing to wear."

"You look so handsome." She rested her hands on his chest. "You have a lot of medals and stripes."

He hoped she wouldn't ask how he had earned most of them. They weren't memories he wanted to dredge up before such a happy occasion as witnessing Menace and Naya's wedding ceremony. "Are you finished in here?"

"I am."

He clasped her hand and pulled her toward the door. "Come with me. I want to do something special before the wedding."

She tugged back on his hand. "Venom, I don't want to mess up my hair."

He laughed as he realized she thought he meant another tumble in the sack. Stepping toward her, he slid his hand along the curve of her back to cup her plump bottom. Brushing their mouths together, he murmured, "Sugar, I can think of a dozen different ways to have you that wouldn't knock a single hair out of place."

She gulped. "A dozen, huh?"

Chuckling, he kissed her swollen pout. "I'll show you later. Right now I have other plans for you."

She didn't fight him this time as he led her back into their bedroom. When her gaze fell on the bed, she scowled. "Where are my panties?"

"You should know the rules by now." He reached down to cup her bare sex. "This is always available to me."

She rolled her eyes and teasingly pinched his arm. "Venom, it's one thing for me to run around our quarters like this but I can't go out in public with my bottom uncovered."

Certain it would frustrate her, Venom insisted, "You can and you will. End of discussion."

Dizzy huffed but didn't press the argument. "Whatever."

The blush of excitement staining her cheeks convinced him that she wasn't *that* put out by his order. Picking up the rope, he said, "I'm going to bind you for the wedding."

"What? You mean under my clothing?"

"Yes."

She eyed the rope critically. "But what if someone sees the ropes under my clothing? My dress is lined but if the fabric pulls tight…"

He swept his fingertips along the swell of her breast. "Then they'll know you belong to me and that you're pleasing me by wearing something I created."

The submissive smile she offered did funny things to his heart. From the moment he had spied her that snowy morning, Venom had suspected he would be the first to fall in love. He had been preparing himself for taking a bride and starting a family for much longer than Dizzy so it was only natural that his feelings for her would take a serious turn much more quickly.

As she lifted her arms and relaxed her shoulders to accept his intricate rope work, Dizzy showed that her trust in him was growing. The way she had sought him out last night convinced him that she cared for him. Their easy friendship was slowly morphing into something much more intimate and powerful. It would be some time before either felt comfortable proclaiming their love for the other—but he had no doubt it would happen.

Venom lost himself in the focused intensity of wrapping her petite body in the rope. He crafted a flat body harness, tucking and looping the long lengths of rope rather than using knots to secure it. The diamond shapes he created on her soft skin looked so incredibly beautiful. Always mindful of her comfort and safety, he tested the tautness of the rope and ensured her ability to move freely remained.

When he finished fashioning the corset, he took a step back to study his work. Her flushed skin and pebbled nipples assured him that Dizzy loved the gentle embrace of her bindings. Venom traced her full bottom lip. "You're gorgeous, Dizzy."

She glanced up at him with a mischievous glimmer in her brown eyes. "I'm pretty sure a rope harness isn't going to meet the formal dress code."

A chuckle rumbled through his chest. Dipping his head, he claimed her mouth with a loving kiss. He picked up the dress and helped her step into it. The enticing shimmy of her hips enlivened his cock. Indulging his desire to enjoy her lush body, Venom allowed his hands to caress her bare skin as he dragged her dress into place and slowly tugged the zipper up.

He bent down and picked up the heels she had chosen. Clasping her ankle, he slid the first one on her foot. Dizzy put her hands on his shoulders to steady herself. He had to fight the clamoring desire to flip up her skirt and bury his face between her thighs. The idea of taking her to the wedding with her face still flushed from an orgasm was ever so tempting—but there simply wasn't time to do it right.

Dizzy popped into the bathroom one final time to primp. After he slid into his jacket, she checked over his uniform for any stray pieces of lint or fuzz before grabbing a sleek evening bag. He didn't quite understand the rules of which purses went with which outfits but he assumed there was some science behind her choice.

Spotting her collar on the bedside table, he crossed the room to retrieve it. When he picked it up, he noticed the new lining she had added. "Did you do this while I was at my second debriefing this morning?"

"Yes." She joined him next to their bed and took the collar from him. Looking a bit sheepish, she explained, "I sort of ripped open one of the throw pillows from the couch.

I hope you don't mind."

His eyebrow arched. "It's a bit late to ask about that, isn't it?"

"There's a saying down in The City. Ask first, do penance later."

"Penance, huh?" He easily spun her around, lifted her skirt and popped her bare bottom with his palm. "Like this?"

"Venom!"

Her shocked outburst made him laugh but when she reached around to smack his backside his jaw dropped. "Dizzy!"

She put a hand on her hip. "It's not so funny when you're the one with a stinging butt, is it?"

"That's not the way this works. *I* spank *you*, not the other way around."

"Says who?"

"Says everyone."

"The first night we were together you told me that we're the ones who set the rules for our relationship. I think that if you get to spank me I should get to return the favor."

Her spunky reply curved his mouth with amusement. "Sugar, there is exactly zero chance of you ever turning me across your knee."

"Well yeah, because you would crush me!" Dizzy retorted as she rubbed her bottom.

His brow furrowed. He had barely applied any force to his whack but maybe he had miscalculated. "Did I hurt you?"

"No. It's just hot."

Stepping into her personal space, he slid his hand under her skirt and palmed her naked flesh. "You've got that right." His mouth grazed hers. "This is the hottest ass I've ever had the pleasure of spanking."

A look of annoyance flitted across her face. "Spanked a lot of asses, have you?"

"More than enough to know yours is the very best."

She rolled her eyes. "Smooth save."

He laughed and coaxed a hungry kiss from her. "We'll talk about this spanking thing later. I didn't mean to cross a line with you. It was a spontaneous thing and I probably should have asked before I hit you."

She ran her finger over one of the shiny buttons on his uniform. "You didn't *hit* me. Hit has such an ugly, abusive connotation and that wasn't what happened here. I know it was a playful smack, Venom." She pinched the button between her fingers. "I think I might want to try it again—but with some warning first."

His mouth went dry as visions of Dizzy draped across his lap filled his head. He would take his time warming up her bottom with his cracking palm and then spread her thighs to reach that secret place hidden there. He could almost feel the slick, wet heat of her painting his fingers as he probed her pussy and rubbed her clit. She would come like crazy after a thorough spanking.

Stepping back from her, he inhaled a long breath to clear his lust-riddled thoughts. "We really should go."

A knowing smile played upon her lips. Dizzy handed him the collar. He draped it around her neck and latched it in place. Sweeping aside the silky waves of her pale hair, he dotted a teasing line of kisses from the collar up to her earlobe. "I'm glad you're here with me tonight."

She glanced over her shoulder and smiled at him. "Being Grabbed wasn't the ideal way to meet you, Venom, but I'm so glad our paths crossed out there in that snowy forest."

Taking her hand, Venom led her out of their quarters and down the hall to the elevator bank. It was a short ride down to the banquet and event rooms where the brass typically hosted promotions and official dinners.

When they turned the corner of a hallway leading to the room where Menace and Naya's wedding was scheduled to take place, Hallie bounded toward them. "Thank goodness you're here, Dizzy! We have a major emergency and we need your help."

Dizzy seemed taken aback by the sight of Hallie. "You're wearing one of my dresses."

Hallie blinked. "Really?" She looked down at the delicate lacy dress she wore. "Naya ordered them from a vendor in The City. I had no idea it was one of your designs."

"It must have been the boutique on Quayle Street. It's the only place I sold that particular design." She tilted her head. "You did a nice job taking in the bodice. You know your way around a needle and thread."

"I'm okay," Hallie agreed, "but Naya needs more help than I can give. The elevator caught her dress and I don't know how to fix it."

Dizzy grimaced. "Let me take a look." She took a step

away from him before turning back. "Do you mind?"

"No. Please. Go." He gestured toward the door that Hallie had rushed through. "I'll see if there's anything I can do to help with the ceremony delay."

Certain Dizzy was safe with Hallie, Venom searched out Vicious and Menace. They were fully apprised of the situation with the dress but it seemed that wasn't the only problem.

"Naya's friend Dankirk still hasn't arrived," Vicious explained. "He's supposed to walk her down the aisle. Orion is fast-tracking the transport ship through arrivals but it's taking forever."

Agitated, Menace rubbed his face. "I promised her a perfect wedding day. After everything she's been through, she deserves a perfect wedding day."

"It will be perfect," Vicious assured him. "Venom's mate is a talented seamstress. She'll have that dress fixed in no time. Orion never breaks a promise. He'll get Dankirk here even if he has to suit up, borrow a dart and intercept them out in space."

"I should go to her." Menace stared at the door. "She needs me."

"You can't." Vicious squeezed his friend's shoulder. "The marital customs of Calyx indicate it's bad luck if the groom sees the bride before the ceremony begins."

"I'll pop in and check on her, Menace." Venom clapped the gunner on his back. On his way to rejoin Dizzy, Venom was stopped by Risk. "Is everything okay?"

"There's some sort of an emergency with Naya's wedding dress."

"Maybe I can help," Risk said and locked step with him.

Venom shot him a strange look. "I doubt the bride is so upset she needs to be sedated."

"Ha-ha-ha," Risk intoned dryly. "I can sew, Venom."

Venom doubted sewing fabric and suturing used the same techniques but it wouldn't be the first time he had been proven wrong. Darting inside the dressing room, he found Dizzy kneeling on the floor behind a distraught Naya. His mate held out the badly ripped fabric along the back of the dress and chattered back and forth with Hallie as they searched for a solution.

"The small scissors in my emergency sewing kit aren't nearly big enough for this," Dizzy said tightly. She had the contents of the kit from her clutch spread out on the floor around her.

"I've got you covered, Dizzy." Risk hurried to the medical kit safely stowed behind a glass panel on the far wall. He dragged the big soft-sided bag out of its nesting place and carried it over to Dizzy and Hallie. Crouching down, he unzipped a main compartment and retrieved large trauma shears. "Will these work?"

"Yes!" Dizzy snatched them from his hand. "I don't suppose you have any extra thread or needles in there, do you?"

"Needles, suturing thread and glue coming right at you," he said and started digging again.

"Glue?" Dizzy frowned at the doctor as she started to cut away the shredded back of the gown.

"We use quick-drying suture glue in emergencies."

"How quick?"

"Five seconds maximum."

"Sold!" She glanced at Hallie. "Strip the lace from this bottom part and we'll use it to cover a quick and dirty hem here using that glue. This dress has enough extra fabric in the skirt for me to pull it tighter to form a sheath silhouette and make a bustle." She reached up and patted Naya's arm. "It won't be perfect but it'll be beautiful."

Enthralled by this industrious Dizzy who confidently and calmly gave orders, Venom watched as she transformed the battered gown. She wore the most serious expression as she snipped, sewed and glued. When she clicked her teeth at Risk and made him redo a section he had sewn, Venom didn't even try to hide his smile.

Half an hour later, Dizzy sat back on her heels and studied their work. "I like it."

"Oh, it's terrific!" Hallie breathed excitedly. "You look fantastic, Naya."

"Yeah?" She peered over her shoulder but couldn't see the back of her dress very well. Risk snapped a photo with the pocket tablet he carried everywhere and showed it to her. Her face brightened and the concerned lines around her mouth and eyes vanished. "It's so pretty."

Venom experienced a surge of pride as Naya dragged Dizzy into a bear hug and thanked her profusely. "You saved my wedding!"

"Be careful if you're going to dance," Dizzy warned. "I'll have that tube of suture glue in my purse, just in case."

Naya snorted. "They don't dance here."

"What?" Dizzy sounded scandalized.

Hallie shook her head. "The receptions here are sort of…"

"Boring," Naya interjected with a pointed look to her best friend. Then, with a shrug, she added, "I'd rather have Menace than a party anyway. Well," her mouth curved with a smart-ass grin, "most days, at least."

Venom couldn't help but laugh at that one. He couldn't imagine how tense things had been between Naya and Menace after she had finally made it out of the hospital. He had noticed that she started wearing her collar again right around the time Menace had announced they were going to make a commitment to each other in the way of her people. Their ability to work through that mess and build a stronger relationship filled with trust inspired him to do the same when it came to Dizzy.

The dress crisis averted, Venom waited for Dizzy to pack up her purse. They entered the ceremony room hand in hand and took seats on Menace's side of the room.

Looking a bit out of breath, Orion stood at the front and tapped at his tablet. After performing Vicious and Hallie's ceremony, the admiral seemed to have added a new duty to the long list he already juggled. Venom supposed that Orion's presence meant Dankirk had finally arrived.

"Venom?"

"Yes?"

"Who is that man with the scarred face?"

Her whispered question caused him to crane his neck in the direction she was looking. He had to blink twice to be sure the vision of Terror at the back of the room wasn't a mirage. *Shit.*

Snapping his alert gaze to Menace, Venom started to lift out of his seat in anticipation of a brawl. As far as he knew, the two men hadn't spoken since the night Venom had stood as Menace's second while he and Terror beat the shit out of each other in the ancestral ring to settle their feud. This was a hell of a time for Terror to make a gesture of reconciliation.

The general put his hand on Menace's chest and spoke softly to the gunner. Had Vicious arranged this? Venom glanced at Orion who stood with a clenched jaw and glared in the Shadow Force operative's direction. He wasn't calling for security to yank Terror out of the room and vent him. Venom figured that was a good sign.

Whatever Vicious said caused the tense set of Menace's face to soften. The groom nodded and started across the room. Venom noticed that he wasn't the only one watching Menace's movements with extreme interest. Every eye in the damn room was glued on the weapons expert.

"Venom?"

Lowering his lips until they were almost touching her ear, he explained, "The man with the scarred face is Terror. He's the deadliest Shadow Force operative you'll ever meet—and I hope you never meet one again. A few months ago, he nearly killed Naya."

"What?" Her sharp hiss of outrage came out louder than she had intended. Her cheeks turned the prettiest shade of pink as the soldiers surrounding them looked at her.

Caressing her face, he kept his voice quiet and said, "He used her to flush out the Sixers and Splinters who had hijacked an arms shipment."

"Wait? You mean that shootout in the old battery factory? *That* was how Naya got hurt? But—she said it was a family thing."

"It was. Her mother is the head of the Sixer gang."

"No way!"

He nodded. "Naya's mother survived the skirmish but we haven't been able to locate her. She's still out there somewhere, just as dangerous as ever."

"So Menace and Terror...?"

"Menace, Terror and Vicious are best friends but it's been...tense since that awful day."

"Are they going to fight?"

Venom watched Menace approach Terror. Their body language didn't scream altercation but they warily eyed each other. "No."

Terror was the first to make a move. He extended his hand, exposing himself to ridicule or shame if Menace turned his back. Venom held his breath as he waited to see if Menace would publicly cut his old friend.

But Menace proved himself an honorable man by grasping Terror's hand. Though Venom was sure Menace still harbored hard feelings toward his friend they were making amends. Something told Venom that Terror had already made a conciliatory overture toward Naya. Terror could be a raging asshole—but he wasn't cruel. He would never show up at her wedding and upset her.

Terror trailed Menace up the aisle. While the gunner

continued to the front of the room, Terror moved into the empty seat right next to Dizzy. Venom slipped his arm around her shoulder in a comforting gesture but she didn't seem to be the least bit fazed by the scarred and one-eyed Shadow Force operative. To his surprise, she held out her hand. "Dizzy Lane."

"I know." Terror glanced at Venom for permission to shake her hand before touching his mate. "I'm sorry you ran into a bit of trouble down in the SRU headquarters. Rest assured it's been taken care of."

"Oh. Um…thanks?"

The spook nodded at Venom. "Our paths intersect again."

He remembered Terror's parting words the last time he had seen him. "Not bringing bad news, I hope?"

"Not tonight," Terror replied. His hand sneaked inside his dress jacket and retrieved a crumpled envelope. Holding it out to Dizzy, he said, "For you."

"Me?" She cautiously accepted it. Her finger traced the letters of her name printed on the front. When she didn't ask who had sent it Venom assumed she recognized the handwriting.

"Dizzy?"

She swallowed and tucked the letter inside her purse. "It's from my dad."

Venom's gaze jumped to Terror's face. He had only spoken to Pierce that morning about Jack Lane and the strange message from Ella. There was no way the Shadow Force assets on the ground had been able to track him down and get a message for Dizzy that quickly. No, this had been in the works for a few days at least.

Sensing his inquisitive stare, the black ops soldier rolled his shoulders and stretched out his long legs. "We have a friend of a friend of a friend in common."

"I bet you do."

Before Venom could question him further, gentle music signaled the start of the ceremony. They stood with the rest of the gathered celebrants. Venom had never been an overly sentimental sort of guy but he had to admit there was something rather touching about these wedding ceremonies. To stand in front of friends and publicly exchange vows added a level of solemnity to a mate bond that catching and claiming a woman with a collar lacked.

As Menace and Naya spoke their vows, Dizzy reached for his hand, clasping it between both of hers. He kissed her temple and let himself imagine the two of them taking the place of their friends. Someday.

Chapter Seventeen

"BOY, NAYA WASN'T joking about these wedding receptions being a little on the lame side!"

Dizzy glanced up at the man addressing her with such a languid, easy drawl. She didn't know Dankirk all that well but he was a friendly face from home. "Hi, Danny."

"I brought you some dessert." Bearing cake, he settled into the open seat next to her. The circular table where she and Venom had been assigned seats for dinner was mostly vacant now. Her mate had been dragged away by Raze to another side of the room where a loud group of men had congregated. They were telling stories, it seemed. Very animated stories.

"This cake is pretty good." He pushed a plate with a small slice her way. "I can't believe they didn't do a proper cake cutting with the bride and groom."

Dizzy picked up a clean fork from her roll of silverware and poked at the spongy confection. "They've only been doing weddings here for a little while. Give them time. The most important customs have migrated. That's something."

"I guess." He took a drink of the fizzy champagne that had been imported from one of the wineries in the colonies. "No music and no dancing—but damn. They've got some good booze."

Dizzy smiled at the Red Feather fixer. "You've known Naya a long time?"

He nodded and cut into his cake. "She's the closest thing I've ever had to a best friend."

She didn't miss his wistfully sad expression. She suspected Danny felt more than friendship toward Naya.

"Speaking of best friends," Danny swirled the alcohol in his glass, "Ella tried to reach me before I came up here. I didn't realize she was trying to get a message to a friend or I would have found a way to meet with her. If there's anything you want me to tell her I'll make sure to look her up as soon as I hit the ground."

"Tell her I'm happy and I miss her." She thought of Ella's message. "Let her know that I've already added her name to the visitation list."

"Will do." He took a long sip. "Look—I know this ain't the time or place to talk about serious things...but we should chat about your daddy."

Dizzy eyed her purse. She still hadn't read the letter Terror had given her. "Just lay it out for me, Danny."

"I don't know the specifics, Dizzy. I've heard that someone was putting pressure on him to get a shipment together."

"Who?"

"Take your pick on the who, kiddo. Fat Pete, the Sixers, the Splinters?" He shrugged. "There's a shit-ton of shady operating in The City these days. Everybody's looking for a bigger piece of that nasty little pie—and your daddy has black market connections that everyone wants."

"But he sold my lottery number, Danny. He said—"

"A father will say anything to protect his child," Danny cut in wisely. "I've known Jack for years. If he thought you were in danger and there was no way else to get you out, he would have pushed you toward a Grab. Nothing from back home can touch you here."

Dizzy watched Menace licking a bit of frosting from Naya's fingertip. The passionate love those two shared radiated across the room. Had Naya escaped to the *Valiant* believing nothing from her past, from Connor's Run or The City, could ever touch her again? How wrong she had been!

"I'm not so sure about that, Danny."

He followed her gaze and made a *humph* sound before smashing his cake with his fork. "That situation was different. Naya never would have ended up back on Calyx if that one-eyed bastard hadn't dredged up ancient history." Danny glared at Terror who sat with Vicious and Hallie at a nearby table. "You stay far away from that guy. Understand? He's a shit magnet if I've ever seen one."

Dizzy doubted she had ever heard such colorful descriptions. Considering the Shadow Force men she had encountered so far—Terror, Pierce and Torment—she was incredibly thankful Venom wasn't in that line of work. His spot on the SRU team was dangerous enough but the men who carried out covert operations put their lives on the line in ways even more dangerous than Venom. At least he always had his team to back him up and support him. Just by looking at Terror's scarred face, Dizzy could tell these Shadow Force men were on their own out there.

"When I get back to The City I'll sniff around and see if I can't find your dad. There's a story here. Who knows? It might be something important enough to get him a ticket off Calyx and out to the colonies."

Dizzy perked up. "Do you think the Harcos would make him a deal?"

"They've been doing it for years." Danny swigged down the last of his champagne. "They started cultivating their 'assets' in the colonies and on Calyx more than twenty years ago. Even before their civil war kicked off, there were rumblings. Good intelligence means having boots on the ground."

"I don't know that I would want my dad to be an asset."

Danny shrugged. "He might not have a choice. If Fat Pete or the Splinters were trying to pressure Jack to do something for them and he said no?" He shook his head and sighed. "Jack will want to get the hell off Calyx as quickly as possible. Spending a weekend with some sky warrior interrogators and spilling his guts for a ticket and a new identity in the colonies? That's a mighty fine trade."

Dizzy conceded that the fixer had a point. Thinking of how stressed and weary her father must have been to betray her, she started to feel so incredibly sad. Their relationship had been rocky since her mother's death. They had both said and done things that left her feeling a bit of shame. She remembered the way she had screamed at him, telling him she hated him, that evening he had confessed to losing her to the loan shark and selling her lottery number. What if Danny was right? What if he had been trying to protect her?

"Sugar, are you all right?" Venom had sneaked up on them without her even realizing it. He must have seen the sadness on her face because he caressed her jaw.

She started to lie and say she was perfectly fine. Venom had asked her to always be honest with him so she didn't. "I'm not feeling so well. Can we go home?"

"Of course."

She gathered up her purse and gave Danny's hand a squeeze. "Thanks for the cake. If you see my dad…" Her voice drifted off as the painful clump in her throat made her eyes water.

"I know what you want to say," Danny said gently. "You can count on me."

"Thank you."

Venom placed his hand against the small of her back and walked her out of the reception. There were four soldiers waiting for an elevator and they all ended up in the same car. Venom silently communicated his concern for her by rubbing the spot between her shoulder blades. He didn't say anything until they were safely locked inside their quarters.

Pinning her between the door and his hard body, Venom placed both of his hands against the wall and lowered his face until their breaths mingled. "What has you so upset?"

"I'm just thinking about my dad. I'm worried that he's in real trouble. Between what Ella said and what Danny told me tonight, I can't stop thinking that he's caught up in something really big." Her stomach roiled and she swallowed hard. "Then I start thinking about that stupid blood test. Somewhere out there my biological father is lurking. Is he a good guy? Is he a jerk? Did my mother love him? Did he hurt her? Did he abandon her? Why didn't he stick around? Why didn't he want us?"

"Dizzy," Venom whispered, the sound pained. "Honey, you're going to make yourself sick thinking about all this. Whatever happened back then—it's in the past. I know it's hard to let it go but you can't dwell on the what-ifs. You may never track down your biological father. Even if you get Jack—your dad—to talk to you about your mother, he may not even know the details. There's a possibility—however slim—that he doesn't even know you're not his biological child." Venom touched their foreheads together. "You've got a letter in your purse from your father. Start there."

The envelope shoved into her purse suddenly felt so heavy. What if the letter held truths she didn't want to face? "I can't. Not tonight."

"That's fine. There's no rush." Venom tugged her purse from her grasp and placed it on the entryway table. Interlacing their fingers, he led her into the living area. He left her standing next to the couch while he flicked through the buttons of his uniform jacket and peeled out of it. Crouching down, he unzipped and toed off his boots.

Dizzy followed his lead and kicked off her heels. Standing barefoot, she asked, "Now what?"

"Now," he said with a little smile, "you're going to teach me how to dance."

"What?" A nervous laugh escaped her at the idea of

being held in his arms and swaying with him in their living room. "You don't know how to dance?"

"I do not."

"But—you know how to do *everything*."

Venom chuckled. "You know how to stroke my ego."

"I'm not stroking your ego." Dizzy took his huge paw and placed it on her hip. "You have to be the most capable and skilled man I've ever met."

He studied her for a long minute. "You're serious."

"Yes. Now—this would be easier with music but just match my steps." She clasped his other hand and took one step back but Venom didn't budge. Gazing up into his curious face, she realized that he had no idea how incredibly special he was. "You don't even know, do you?"

"Know what, sugar?"

"How damn amazing you are," she said with a touch of awe in her voice. "Venom, you're an elite soldier who serves with a highly skilled unit—yet you're the kindest, sweetest, gentlest mate." An erotic heat quivered between her thighs as she added, "You're a wonderful and patient lover."

"To be fair, you don't have much to compare me to."

Dizzy frowned at him and playfully kicked his shin. "Don't discount me just because you're my first and only. I may not have other lovers to compare you to but I know that you make me feel *so* good. You leave me breathless and trembling and feeling like I've touched heaven."

Venom's breaths grew heavy. His hard cock jutted against her upper belly as she tried to get him to sway with her. "I've changed my mind about this dancing thing."

She licked her lips as a wicked frisson of anticipation raced through her core. "Oh?"

"Strip for me."

With a saucy grin, she flicked her fingers against his chest. "You first."

His deep, gruff laugh made her thighs clench. After jerking on the buttons of his dress shirt, he shrugged out of the garment and tossed it aside. His undershirt quickly followed. She let her needy gaze rake his ridiculously sexy chest. Her fingers burned to touch all that hard, hot flesh.

Giving in to the urge, she attacked him with her hands and mouth. She followed the ridges of his abdomen while kissing and licking his chest. When she flicked her tongue against the dark disk of his nipple, Venom gasped. She scratched at his belly and suckled him, drawing a long, needful groan from him.

"Out of that dress," he growled. "Now."

She spun around and presented her back so Venom could unzip her. While she shimmied out of the dress, he tore off his pants. By the time she was free of the garment, he was stark naked and reaching for her.

Venom fell back on the couch and dragged her down with him. She straddled his hips and sighed with pleasure as he caressed her skin. The rope harness he had fashioned for her had been like an unending embrace during the wedding ceremony and reception. Even when he was away from her it felt as if he were right there, holding and protecting her.

"You're so beautiful, Dizzy." He spoke with such awe as he gazed upon her corseted body. "So beautiful." He kissed her breasts and ran his fingers over the ropes decorating her body. "I can't believe you're mine."

Dizzy ran her greedy hands over his sculpted body. "I can't believe you're mine."

"But I am." Always looking out for her comfort, Venom unlatched the collar and tossed it aside. He brushed his lips across her scars. "Are you sore?"

"No. The lining helped."

"I'm glad." Cupping her bottom, Venom lined up their bodies and thrust up into her. She moaned as he sucked her nipple between his lips and laved it with his soft tongue. "Let's dance my way."

Chapter Eighteen

THOUGH HE WAS still on leave for his honeymoon, Venom decided to head in to the SRU for the team workout the next morning—but not until he had woken Dizzy with a very pleasurable start to her day.

Leaning against the wall of the elevator, he let his thoughts drift back to her cries of pleasure as he lashed her sweet cunt with his tongue. After their long night of lovemaking—first in the living room and then again in the bedroom—Venom hadn't expected to wake with such a raging hard-on. Dizzy had become his own personal aphrodisiac. The scent of her hair and the feel of her supple, lithe body curled against his was enough to shift his lust into overdrive.

She had whimpered in her sleep and roused only a very little as he had kissed and nibbled his way down her luscious body. He had even managed to part her thighs with his broad shoulders without fully waking her. It wasn't until his tongue had fluttered over that enticing pink clit of hers that she had bolted awake.

Gripping his head, she had come long and hard with his mouth on her pussy and then welcomed his pounding cock. His back was still marked by her fingernails. He wore those red scratches like a badge of honor.

He had left her in bed with a satisfied smile on her face and expected she was already fast asleep again. He liked the idea of her living a comfortable, pampered life and hoped she enjoyed the lifestyle he provided her.

But as the elevator shot down to the main housing floor and Venom crossed to a different bank of elevators that would take him to the SRU section of the ship, he couldn't shake the idea that Dizzy needed more than simply being his kept mate.

There had been no mistaking the utter joy on her face when Naya had proclaimed her wedding saved yesterday evening. He had never doubted Dizzy's skill as a designer and seamstress but seeing her employ the craft she had practiced for so many years drove home a point he hadn't wanted to acknowledge.

Dizzy needed to work.

It didn't jibe with his traditional upbringing or the dominant culture of the Harcos but it couldn't be ignored. She needed to design and create as much as he needed to fulfill his duty as a land corps soldier. Menace didn't seem to mind Naya having a career of her own but Menace probably hadn't spent his entire childhood listening to his mother berate his father for being a poor provider.

The elevator paused seven floors down from the SRU headquarters and Mayhem stepped into the car. "Captain," Mayhem greeted respectfully.

"Sergeant." Venom remembered that he hadn't properly thanked Mayhem for helping Dizzy. "I owe you a debt of honor for coming to my mate's aid the other day."

Mayhem waved his hand. "I would have done that for

any woman. It was my honor that demanded my action."

"Even so, if you ever need a favor, come to me."

Mayhem's dark brow lifted. "Does that extend to a good word for the upcoming SRU tryouts?"

"You don't need it. You're a damn good soldier. You have excellent test scores. You're very well liked. As long as your trials go well, you should have no problem earning a slot."

"With the alpha team?" His hopeful tone came through loud and clear.

"Possibly," Venom answered. "Raze and I are currently considering breaking out some of the more senior members of the established teams to form foundation units for the newer teams we need to create. If that happens, we'll have open slots on alpha squad."

"If I earn a position with SRU, I would like to be considered for one of those slots."

"I'll throw your name in the hat."

"Thank you, sir."

Venom let his gaze drift to Mayhem's bionic prosthesis. "Is that a prototype?"

"Yes. The engineers and rehab staff on the *Mercy* designed this one based on the newest research. It's amazing." He flexed the limb and Venom was surprised at the way it reacted and moved like a natural leg. "They inserted an implant here." Mayhem touched a spot on his lower back. "It helps my brain and my leg talk."

"That's incredible. Are they going to roll this out to more injured soldiers?"

Mayhem nodded. "There are three dozen of us using

them right now. The initial reports are excellent. I think the war council understands how important it is to retain their best soldiers. We aren't useless just because we're injured."

Venom heard Mayhem's bitterness. "The old ideas are changing. Better medical technology is making things possible today that never would have happened when our fathers were active."

Mayhem shifted his gym bag. "I realize I pissed off a lot of people with my lawsuit but the old ways were changing too slowly. I didn't have any say in having my damn leg blown off—but I sure as hell have the right to make choices about my future. The Splinters took my leg but they aren't taking my career."

The elevator slowed to a stop and the doors parted. Mayhem nodded in his direction before stepping out and heading down the long hallway to the SRU private gym. A bit dazed by the man's strident defense of his lawsuit, Venom exited the elevator. Instead of following Mayhem to the gym, he hesitated in the hallway.

Mayhem's words ricocheted in his brain. Was that how Dizzy felt? Her career and her life as a single, independent woman had been snatched from her. She had seemed so excited by the prospect of selling her designs in Naya's shop—and he had stomped on it, crushing her excitement with his own insecurities.

Thinking of the way she had called him an amazing man last night made his heart ache so painfully. She had accepted him for the man he was—scars, emotional baggage and all. She had allowed him to exert dominance over her. She had trusted him with his ropes and restraints. She had supported and reached out to him when he had taken Ben's life to end the hostage situation.

And what had he done? He had crushed her dreams of continuing her work here on the *Valiant*. Didn't she have the right to make choices for her future?

For our future.

Venom took a hard right and strode down the hallway to the SRU offices. He waved at Raze as he passed their shared space but kept right on walking until he reached Cipher's spot. The door was wide open as usual and the engineer was on his back under a bomb-sniffing unit, tinkering with its internal parts.

"Hey, Ven," Cipher greeted, his voice muffled by the metal box sitting over him. "What do you need, man?"

He leaned against the doorframe. "What do you know about sewing machines?"

The wheels on the creeper squealed as Cipher slid out from underneath the bombsniffing device. He sat up and set aside his screwdriver. "You'll have to repeat that. Did you ask me about a sewing machine?"

"Who needs a sewing machine?" Raze elbowed Venom aside so he could get in on the conversation.

"I do. It needs to be a good one, Cipher. One that can make really pretty things."

Raze snorted. "Ven, I realize I opened the floor at last month's meeting to a discussion of new uniforms for the SRU—but let's try to keep the ruffles and lace at a minimum, okay?"

Venom knocked into Raze's shoulder. "Shut up. It's

for Dizzy. I've decided she can continue designing and selling her clothes up here."

Raze offered an approving, if sad, smile. "That's a smart move." Clearing his throat, he pushed off the door-frame. "You two hurry this discussion up, okay? We're in the gym in ten."

"Sure thing, boss." Venom watched his best friend disappear down the hallway. He sensed Raze was still unsettled from the dark turn the hostage call had taken. It was something they needed to talk about but first he wanted to get things squared away with Cipher. "Well?"

"If you want her to be able to produce commercially—say five or ten copies of each design—you'll want to go with one of those fabric printers." Cipher shuffled around the tools and empty drink bottles on his desk to find a tablet. He tapped away at the screen and finally spun it around. "Something like this, you know?"

"It looks like the printers we use to make repair parts for weapons," he said, studying the specs. "Where can I get one of these?" He considered how pricey they were. "What's the hit to my account going to be like?"

"Give me a couple of hours," Cipher replied. "I know a guy down in the recycling department. He lets me source parts from all the broken-down shit that gets routed his way. The uniform shop just upgraded to new clothing printer models. A hundred credits says I can find one free and clear down in the bin."

Venom considered Cipher's outstretched hand. "Okay. I'll take that action."

Their deal made, Venom hurried to the locker room

to change into workout clothes. Every single member of the land or sky corps was required to meet extreme physical fitness standards but the SRU pushed those standards even higher. Every team worked out together at the beginning of their shift as a way to enhance unit cohesiveness.

Today, Raze was brutal as he pushed them through their circuits. By the time their two hours of torture ended, Venom was sweating and exhausted. On legs like jelly, he stumbled into the locker room and peeled out of his soaking-wet clothing. A cool shower helped lower his body temperature but one glance at Raze's clenched jaw told him the same wasn't true for his friend.

"You want to talk?" No man wanted to be ambushed about emotional issues with his dick swinging in the wind so Venom had waited until they were dressed and out of the locker room to ask Raze the obvious question. "Is this about Ben?"

Raze shot him an annoyed glare but didn't lie. "I lost him. Somewhere in that negotiation, I fucked up."

"It wasn't you, Raze. It was the added complication of a hostage. We couldn't control what came out of her mouth. If there had been a way to keep her quiet, to keep Ben's attention away from her, things might have gone differently." Venom squeezed Raze's shoulder. "For what it's worth, I think that guy came on this ship with a death wish. He was either the stupidest man in all of creation to come onto a Harcos warship and shoot four people—or he was suicidal."

Raze made a humming sound of agreement but wouldn't commit one way or the other. Lowering his voice, Raze said, "I heard that Axis was pulled from the central lockup and dragged down to the Shadow Force sector in the middle of the night."

"I assumed something like that had happened. Terror made a comment to Dizzy that made me think he had taken an interest in Axis." Venom rubbed his jaw as he considered the implications of that development. "You have to admit it's a pretty big coincidence that he just happened to come by the offices to ask about the SRU tryout invitations when every single one of our teams was away."

"My thoughts exactly," Raze replied and gestured for Venom to join him on the walk to their shared office. "I asked Cipher to dig around and see what Axis was trying to access when he was on our consoles. Apparently the lying bastard didn't even try to find that SRU invitations file. He was looking for our escort schematics."

"Was he now?" The muscles in his neck tightened. "Trying out for the team, my ass! He was on a recon, wasn't he?"

"Sounds that way, doesn't it?" Raze shook his head. "They never caught the mole who framed Naya. Remember how they suspected that she had used Menace's office to send an information blast out into space by plugging into one of the communication conduits running through that closet down there?"

"Yeah." Venom remembered, all right. He had been part of the team that rousted Naya and Menace from their bed and hauled them in as terrorists. It hadn't been pretty. "You think Axis is the mole?"

"It's possible. He works in IT right? Hell, for all we know, there are dozens of those traitors on this ship." Raze's expression darkened. "I had wanted to grab Terror for a chat last night but he cut out of the wedding pretty damn quick." He shot a sideways glance Venom's way. "I noticed the two of you left early too."

"Dizzy wasn't feeling well."

"Let me guess. She had a fever?" Raze slyly grinned. "But I bet you had the right prescription, huh?"

Venom whacked Raze. "You sound jealous."

Raze chortled. "Hardly. Been there, done that. Remember?"

"I remember," Venom said softly. "I also remember how excited you were in the days leading up to the collaring ceremony you shared with Shelly. I can't for the life of me understand why you're so afraid to try again."

Raze pinned him in place with a look. "Don't, Venom."

The cold, harsh tone should have stopped Venom from pushing the issue but he was sick and tired of watching his best friend deny himself even a chance at happiness.

"I'm your best friend and that means I get to say things to you that no one else has the balls to even bring up in your presence."

"Venom—"

"No. You need to do the math, Raze. It's been over a decade since she walked out on you. It's time for you to move forward. So she didn't love you. It happens, okay? Your first bond was a mess but that doesn't mean you give up, Raze. You were both younger and selfish but you're a smarter man today. You could have what I have with Dizzy."

"And what do you have with her, Venom? You chased a terrified woman down in the snow, put your collar around her neck and dragged her back to your ship where she's virtually your prisoner for thirty days. Sure, everything is going great now—because she's probably afraid of pissing you off and meeting the vicious soldier under that mask of friendliness."

Venom recoiled at Raze's cruel remark. The insinuation that he would ever abuse or harm Dizzy infuriated him. "Fuck. You."

"No thanks." Raze spun on his heel. "Besides, don't you have a mate waiting back in your quarters to service you, warden?"

Venom flinched when Raze slammed the door to their shared office. He ignored his instinct to shove the door open and demand an apology. Venom had poked a damn bear and gotten bitten. There was no point going back in there to jam a pointy stick in the bear's face.

Pivoting away from the door, Venom caught SRU members scattering like bugs under a bright light. He wanted to snap at them for eavesdropping but it wouldn't have been right. He and Raze should have taken their heated discussion behind closed doors if they wanted to avoid gossip.

Annoyed but no longer angry, he waited for an elevator to take him home to Dizzy. Raze would cool down soon enough and come looking for him when he was ready to apologize. Venom figured he probably owed Raze an apology too. He should have respected Raze's direction to let it go but he had pushed too far.

As he leaned against the cold metal wall of the elevator, Venom wondered if today's theme was making amends. Raze wasn't the only one who needed to hear sorry from him. Dizzy, the most important person of all, was at the very top of his list.

AFTER A SIMPLE breakfast of fruit and crunchy cereal, Dizzy wandered around their apartment looking for something to do. Venom wouldn't be home for quite a while.

She vaguely remembered him telling her that SRU workouts were two hours in duration. Well…she thought that might have been what he said. Maybe?

Truthfully she had been panting so hard and was so blissed out from out from three wickedly intense orgasms in a row that it had been hard to understand a word that came out of that sexy mouth of his. Hell, he could have said the ship was on fire and she probably wouldn't have even blinked.

Standing in their room, she opened the closet. Working on Naya's dress last night had reignited her passion for design. She wanted to get her hands on some fabric and make something beautiful and flirty.

But the yards and yards of gray and black uniforms were less than inspiring. Back in The City, Dizzy wouldn't have thought twice of taking a dress that had fallen out of favor, tearing it apart and making it into something cute and new. She didn't dare do that here.

Until she could secure fabric and notions, she was too afraid to risk the fashionforward clothing she had brought with her. What she had seen of women's fashions aboard the *Valiant* terrified her. Everything was so damn boxy and drab. Some of the wives had been doing their own alterations and jazzing up their outfits—but the garments they started with lacked proper form.

Her gaze drifted to the uniform pants Venom had been complaining about the other day while she had been whip-stitching those rope ends for him. She took them down from their hanger and inspected the pocket that had him so riled up. What had he called it? *Oh, right. Janky.*

The description brought a smile to her face. He was right, of course. The pocket sat in a strange position along the thigh. After seeing Venom decked out in his SRU gear she understood better how these pants needed to function. This pocket was too big and it puffed out too far. No doubt Venom and other men wearing them snagged that pocket in tight spots.

An idea formed. She eyed her sewing kit. What would Venom say if she removed the pocket and made some alterations to this pair of pants?

Her bottom tingled with the memory of that swat she had earned after cutting up the throw pillow without asking permission. Instead of diminishing her enthusiasm, Dizzy found herself oddly excited by the idea of Venom giving her a *real* spanking. Knowing her big, sexy sky warrior, he would find a way to make the experience incredibly erotic, arousing and addictive.

Her mind settled, Dizzy picked up her sewing kit and carried the pants to the kitchen table. She examined the seams and the construction of the garment before sketching out her idea on the back of one of the pamphlets she had been given at the wives' club meeting. Scratch paper was impossible to come by up here. She was just lucky she had a pencil in her kit.

As Dizzy carefully ripped the seam of the pouch pocket, she wondered if she would ever get used to the paperless society Venom inhabited. She had always been a tactile person. Even though she could design on her tablet it simply felt different. She was so used to putting together a design board with swatches of fabric and samples of ribbons and laces. To virtually pin a photograph to a virtual board? It wasn't ever going to be the same.

But she had to adapt. There was no going back to The City or her old life.

Sometime later, Dizzy heard the front door open. She had only basted the first redesigned pocket into place when Venom rounded the corner of the kitchen. He scanned the scene before him and his brow furrowed. "You cut up my pants?"

"Are you angry?" Her stomach clenched as she waited for his answer.

He shot her a bewildered look. "Over a pair of pants? No. I would appreciate it if you would ask the next time." His gaze narrowed. "Unless of course you were hoping for a repeat of that swat I gave you last night for tearing up the pillow?"

Ears hot, she dropped her gaze to the pants. "Of course not. What kind of a weirdo do you think I am?"

Venom slipped his fingers under her chin and tipped her head back. His icy-blue eyes bored into her. "The truth, Dizzy."

She swallowed. "So…maybe I sort of thought about you spanking me again."

His thumb brushed her lower lip. A playful smile curved his mouth. "You didn't have to cut up my favorite pants. All you had to do was ask."

She gasped. "Oh no! Were these really your favorite pants?"

He chuckled. "No. I was teasing." He picked up the pants and looked them over. "I like this."

"When I was at the SRU headquarters with you I noticed that you were carrying a lot of weight in that pocket. It looked as if everything had settled down into the bottom.

I can't imagine how hard it is to dig things out of there when you need them."

"It's a real pain in the ass."

"I thought it would be more useful to have two or three shallower pockets. I think a modified welt-style with some hook-and-loop closure maybe…"

"Yeah. I don't understand any of that." He slid into the seat across from her. "In the middle of all that chaos you noticed my pants?"

"It's what I do," she said with a shrug. "I also noticed that the tailor you guys use doesn't hem your pants uniformly. Yours have a quarter break. Raze wears his with a full break. Just about everyone else had no break at all."

"A what?"

She reached down and gave the cuff of his pants a little shake. "A break? It describes the way the pants sit on top of your shoes. See how yours touch the laces on your boot and there is just the tiniest bit of extra fabric that sort of kinks up right here? That's a quarter break."

"Huh." He lifted his leg to study his pants. "I guess you learn something new every day."

She smiled at him. "Your tailor needs to learn how to fit pants better. Raze's pants are too slim."

"How can you tell?"

"The seat is too tight and it makes the pockets flare."

Venom frowned at her. "I don't think I like you looking at Raze's ass."

She rolled her eyes. "Yes dear."

He laughed. "Now that? I could get used to that."

She snorted. "Fat chance, Venom."

As Dizzy measured and marked the spot where the next two pockets would go, she asked, "How was your workout?"

"Fine." He picked up a scrap of fabric and worked it between his fingers. "You get enough rest?"

She didn't meet his intense stare. "Yes—after you left."

"I think that might be the way we start our mornings from now on. What do you think?"

She squirmed in her seat. "If that's what you want…"

"I'm asking what you want."

She finally worked up the courage to look at him. His smoldering gaze made her insides quiver. "I want you."

"Just me?"

"What more could I possibly want?"

He shrugged. "You grew up extremely wealthy. Maybe you dreamed of marrying a rich man and having servants and a mansion and—"

"Venom," Dizzy sighed and stabbed her needle into the pincushion. "Let's get something straight once and for all. Yes, I was born into a rich family. I lived a luxurious life until the bombing and the recession. After that? Well—as the people on my planet like to say—I was so poor I didn't have a pot to piss in."

"Why would you want to piss in a pot?"

She rolled her eyes again. "It's just a saying. It means— look, never mind, okay? Basically I was hand-to-mouth poor. Eventually I got back on my feet and made a nice life for myself. You know what all of that taught me?"

"No."

"It taught me that money doesn't give you happiness. It just gives you money and better stuff." She reached for his hand and gripped the long, rough fingers that had caressed her so lovingly that morning. "Venom, I just want a good man in my corner. I want a man I can love and support who loves and supports me right back."

He mulled over her statement before exhaling loudly. "My father was never good enough for my mother. She constantly harangued him for not advancing high enough or fast enough. Every time I was home on a school break, I had to listen to her berating him. It was—"

"Painful," Dizzy guessed softly.

"Yes."

She leaned forward and kissed his knuckles. "Venom, I'm not your mom."

"I know that now."

She traced one of the gnarly scars on his hand. "Is this why you flipped your lid when I brought up the possibility of selling my designs in Naya's shop? You thought I doubted your ability to provide for me?"

"It was my parents all over again with my mother threatening to shame my father by taking a job in one of the munitions factories." Venom grimaced. "It was awful of me to hurt you like that. I shouldn't have let my insecurities kill your happiness."

She could tell he was upset about his behavior by the deep set of the lines around his mouth. "You didn't kill my happiness. You pissed me off," she said with a little laugh that he matched with a snort. "You said we would figure it out—and this is us figuring it out."

"I'm trying to get my hands on a garment printer for you."

"A what?"

"It's like the sewing machines down on your planet only better. Cipher is working on sourcing one right now."

"Venom, you don't have to do something so extravagant."

"It's hardly extravagant to give you something that will make you happy."

Although his sweet words made her heart flutter wildly, she didn't want him going into debt. "The expense—"

"Cipher has a connection that can get me printer at a very affordable price. Besides," Venom sat forward and cupped her face with his big hand, "like most men in the corps, I've been throwing my salary into a savings account since my first payday." He nuzzled their noses together but didn't try to kiss her yet. "There wasn't anything worth spending it on until now."

She stroked his square jaw. "I appreciate this so much, Venom. I recognize what a huge compromise this is for you. In the spirit of compromise I'll agree to confine my work hours to the times that you're at work. When you're home I'm all yours."

"Thank you." Venom's fingertips trailed along her cheek. "I don't want your dreams to end simply because I Grabbed you."

"They haven't ended." She gazed into the bright blue of his eyes. It was quickly becoming her favorite color. "They're expanding and growing and changing. Now I don't simply dream of what I can build if I work hard. I'm dreaming of what *we* can build *together*."

"Dizzy…" Venom seemed to choke up. Unable to find the right words, he captured her mouth in a kiss filled with the promise of their future. A future she couldn't wait to meet hand in hand with him.

Chapter Nineteen

L ATER THAT EVENING, Dizzy tidied up after dinner. She was finally getting used to the lights around their quarters that operated on a timer to mimic a day of natural sunlight and darkness. She hadn't quite worked up the courage to visit the observation deck for a peek at the vast emptiness of space but so far living off-planet wasn't too bad.

When the doorbell chime sounded, she stepped out of the kitchen. "Venom?"

"I'll get it." He exited their bedroom still pulling on his shirt. After dinner he had disappeared to take a shower. He had that wicked gleam in his eye that promised her a night bound up in his ropes and completely at his mercy.

But the sound of Raze's deep, gruff voice echoing off the walls of their quarters meant a delay to whatever delightfully kinky plans Venom had in store for her. With a disappointed sigh, she finished scraping the last bits of food into the trash compartment and hit the button that swooshed it away to heaven only knew where. She loaded the dishes into the cleaning unit and pressed a few buttons to make it start.

Turning off the lights, she left the kitchen—but stopped short when she heard Venom and Raze talking.

She hesitated, uncertain whether she should cross the hallway where they were discussing something in serious tones or return to the kitchen so they could have their privacy.

"Are we okay?" Raze sounded hopeful.

"We're fine. I shouldn't have pushed so hard on the mating thing."

"Sure, but I shouldn't have talked to you like that. It was totally wrong of me to insinuate that Dizzy is afraid of you or that you would harm her."

"It's water under the bridge."

"You're sure?"

"Raze, we've been friends since we were five. I think I can forgive this."

"Good. I'm glad." Raze cleared his throat. "I should go. It's late and I'm sure you two have plans."

"As a matter of fact," Venom replied, displaying his comfort with being open about their sex life with his friend.

Raze laughed, the sound growing softer as he moved toward the entrance of their quarters. "You two about to practice for demonstration night?"

Demonstration night? Dizzy didn't like the sound of that at all.

"Shit." Venom swore with frustration. "I signed up to teach that rope class almost two months ago. It completely slipped my mind."

"You've got time to put something together. You think she'll enjoy it?"

"We're not going to find out. It's too soon for her. I'll

just use one of the poppies."

Poppies? Something told her Venom wasn't talking about the pretty red flowers that her ancestors had brought from Earth and nurtured into a wild crop on Calyx. She slipped back into the living room and grabbed her tablet off the coffee table. While Venom and Raze finished up their talk, she opened the search browser and typed in *demonstration night*. The ship's calendar was the first result so she double-tapped it.

Her eyes nearly popped out of her head as she read the description. At the wives' meeting, she had heard the officers' club mentioned in passing. The hushed whispers and gossipy remarks about the place had given her a certain feeling about it. Now she understood what it really was—and what Venom was planning to do there.

Without her.

"You all right, sugar?" Used to operating with stealth, Venom had come into the living room without garnering her attention.

Peering at his handsome, kind face, Dizzy refused to believe what she had heard. Surely she had misunderstood. "What is demonstration night?"

"Oh. That. You know about the officers' club?"

"Sort of."

"It's basically a social club open to officers. Most nights of the week it's only open for drinks or dinner. A few nights a month it's open as an adult playground."

"Playground?"

"Men who are mated take their wives there to explore and enjoy the sensual side of our lifestyle. Men who are unmated come there to learn and practice. Remember how I told you some couples like to share? Well—that's where it often happens."

"And you're going to teach a class there?" She tried to slow her racing heart as she tried very hard not to imagine the very worst thing happening.

"It's hardly as salacious as it sounds. It will be an introductory course. It's not that big of a deal."

"How long will the class last?"

"An hour or two, depending on what types of ties or bondage the students want to see." He shrugged as if it were no big thing. "I'll be home before you finish a movie."

She blinked at him and tried to decide if he was really *that* clueless. "You're not taking me?"

His face hardened. "No. You're not ready for the intensity of that place."

"But how am I supposed to get used to a place like that if you don't take me?"

"I'll take you when I think you're ready."

She swallowed hard. "And just who will you be practicing the rope bondage on?"

"I'll use a poppy."

"What is a poppy?" Knowing the sort of place he was going, they probably had fake women made out of gleaming plastic for demonstrations.

"P-O-P," he spelled it out. "It stands for Property Of Prison. It's the nickname for the paid pleasure women who service events like these and the sky brothels."

Dizzy's mouth gaped. "You mean they're prostitutes?"

His expression turned distasteful. "It's not the same thing in our world as it is in yours. Poppies are very highly paid and skilled. Most of them were born inside the prison system, usually from illicit assignations between guards and female inmates. Going into pleasure work is a way for them to make a place for themselves in society. Most of them retire in their early thirties and are very wealthy. It's not—"

"Stop." Dizzy held up her hand. She couldn't listen to another second of him talking about prostitution as though it was a godsend. "Can you hear yourself? You're talking about women who have to choose between escaping prisons or letting dirty, panting soldiers paw all over them for money."

Venom's lips thinned with irritation. "I told you. It's not like that in my world. To us the women who work in the sky brothels are to be respected. They serve a vital need, especially since it takes so many valor points to earn the right to a mate and a family. Most of us haven't seen home in decades. In case you haven't noticed, there aren't a lot of women in space. It's the poppies—or nothing."

Dizzy didn't know what to say to that. Maybe he was right. Maybe in Venom's world being a prostitute wasn't as shameful and exploitative as it was in The City.

"Are you angry with me?" She gawked at him. "Yes!"

"Because I've slept with prostitutes in the past?"

"What? No." She huffed at him. "I'm not thrilled by the idea—but I understand that your culture does things differently than mine. I get that you guys have...needs. If satisfying them with paid pleasure women is your way…well…whatever. It was before me."

"Yes, it was." Venom took a cautious step toward her. "Please don't ever think that the brief moments I shared with any of those women compares to anything we've shared. With them, it was a business transaction. With you—it's *real*."

"If what you've shared with me is so fantastic why aren't you taking me to the demonstration night?"

Venom exhaled roughly. She sensed his patience was thinning. "I've already told you, Dizzy. You aren't ready."

She decided she was done arguing with him. Lifting her chin, she declared, "I'm going with you."

"No," he said sternly. "You. Are. Not."

Dizzy gritted her teeth and stared at him. She had so many ugly things burning the tip of her tongue but she refused to make this situation any worse than it already was.

Overcome with anger and disappointment, she headed for their bedroom, giving Venom a very wide berth in the process. She stopped in the bathroom to brush her teeth and wash her face before changing into a nightgown. The thought of sleeping in their bed made her stomach churn.

Grabbing her pillow, she stormed out of their bedroom and shoved by Venom who stood just outside the doorway. He clasped her wrist to stop her from getting away from him. Even though he was upset with her his touch was surprisingly gentle—and that just infuriated her even more!

They glared at each other for a few seconds before his gaze drifted to the pillow.

"Are you throwing me out of my own bedroom?"

"No." She jerked her wrist free. "I'm sleeping on the couch tonight."

"You're not serious." He seemed shocked. "You're going to throw a fit over something so ridiculous?"

"Ridiculous, huh?" Dizzy threw her pillow on the couch. "Would it be ridiculous if I said that I was going to go to a party without you and let a man who wasn't you put his hands all over my naked body? That I was going to let him wrap ropes around my breasts and pull them between my thighs?"

"That isn't even remotely the same thing. You're talking about infidelity. I'm talking about teaching with a paid volunteer."

"You're talking out of your ass," Dizzy snapped. "And I'm so over it."

Venom crossed his arms. "Come to bed, Dizzy."

"No." She moved to the couch and fluffed her pillow. "I would love to…but I just don't think you're ready for the intensity of it. Maybe I'll see if I can hire a gigolo from the Low Side to come up here and snuggle me tonight."

"Suit yourself." Venom spun on his heel and headed toward the main household control console. He turned off all the lights except the one in the entryway that he dimmed to its lowest setting. At their bedroom door, he paused and turned back to her. "When you're ready to be reasonable—"

"When *I'm* ready to be reasonable?" Infuriated with him, she flopped down on the couch and lifted her hand in his direction. She gave him a bold one-finger salute.

His sharp intake of breath told her that he had seen her flip him off so crudely. "Yeah—that's real ladylike, Dizzy."

"Ladylike this," she grumbled and punched her pillow into submission. Hot tears burned her eyes as she listened to Venom get ready for bed. Her lower lip wobbled but she gulped down the warring emotions and refused to cry.

Dizzy couldn't reconcile Venom's unyielding position on the officers' club with the sweet and loving gesture he had made earlier that day. He had gone out of his way to make her happy. Why in the world was he being so obstinate about this?

Why didn't he understand how it clawed at her heart to think of him touching another woman? Even if it was simply a demonstration of technique it wasn't right. He loved to remind her that she belonged to him. Hell—she wore a collar for him!

Shouldn't that road go both ways? Didn't he belong to her? If he could make up rules for her shouldn't she have the chance to set hard limits for him?

She was still trying to untangle the jumbled mess of thoughts when Venom appeared next to the couch. She stiffened defensively, unsure what he wanted or planned to do. If he saw her rigid body he didn't comment on it.

"Come to bed, Dizzy."

"No."

"You won't get any sleep here. This couch isn't comfortable."

"I'll deal."

He sighed loudly. "Will you *please* come to bed, Dizzy?"

Refusing to budge, she asked, "Will you take me to the club with you?"

"You're not ready."

"Well, then, I guess I'm not ready to come to bed."

"Fine."

After delivering his clipped response, he stepped closer to the couch. For a second, she thought he was going to scoop her up and force her back into the bedroom. Instead he snapped his arms and unfurled one of the heavy extra blankets he kept in the closet. Holding her breath, Dizzy warily watched him. He shocked her by covering her with the blanket and tucking it tightly under her body, almost cocooning her in place.

"It's not your weighted blanket but it will do." He hesitated before brushing his lips across her forehead. "Good night."

Bewildered by his compassion, Dizzy watched him leave. Alone on the couch, she hadn't expected to get any sleep tonight. Since Venom had Grabbed her she had grown accustomed to the feel of his strong, heavy arms cradling her to sleep.

Lying there alone in the dark but embraced by the blanket, Dizzy wondered at Venom's gentleness toward her, even when they were fighting. His desire to take care of her never wavered. So why couldn't he see how much it hurt her to be left behind while he went to the club?

You're not ready.

Was he afraid she would embarrass him? Is that why he didn't want to use her in his class? She didn't have nearly as much experience as he did—or as the poppies, obviously—but how the hell was she supposed to gain that experience if he locked her away in their quarters? Learning to love the way these Harcos men did—with their collars, spanking, ropes and discipline—took some serious hands-on training. She needed to be in his element to learn how to please him.

Dizzy stared at the dark ceiling and tried to decide what to do. Deep down, she didn't believe Venom was purposely trying to hurt her. He was simply caught in that alpha-male mindset of knowing that his way was the best way—even if he was dead wrong.

It had to have been two hours from the time Venom tucked the blanket around her when Dizzy finally dug deep and found enough bravery to twist and wiggle free from her cocoon. She sat up slowly and listened to their quiet apartment. She didn't hear any sounds coming from their bedroom. Was Venom already asleep?

The thought of him drifting off peacefully while she was alone and on the verge of tears angered and hurt her. She feared setting a bad precedent if she capitulated first but what was the alternative? Morning would come and they would still be upset with each other. Staying in here was only delaying the inevitable.

Rubbing her face, Dizzy was reminded of the last few fights she had overheard between her parents. The one that had sent her mother flying out of the house the morning of the bombing had been a doozy. It was the first and only time she had ever seen her dad lose his cool. That vase smashing against the wall had been a symbol of their imploding marriage.

She remembered the nasty words her parents had traded as her father practically chased her mother to the front door. It had been so very ugly. So much of that day she had blocked out but the pain inspired by Venom's refusal to include her in every part of his life seemed to be dredging everything back up.

Glancing at the open doorway of their bedroom, Dizzy decided she didn't want any regrets when it came to her marriage. It was so early in their relationship and they were still building the foundation for years to come. One badly placed brick and the whole damn thing would come crumbling down.

Shoving off the couch, Dizzy silently padded across the living room. She had taken exactly one step into the pitch-black bedroom before the light built into the wall above the bed switched on. She raised a hand to shield her eyes as Venom adjusted the brightness to a setting easier on their eyes.

When she could see clearly, she found him sitting up against his pillow. The sheet sat low enough around his hips that she could tell he was totally naked. Her gaze moved from his trim waist across his chiseled chest to his handsome but concerned face.

"I was waiting for you to fall asleep," he admitted finally. "I planned to come in and get you."

That didn't surprise her at all. Wringing her hands, she took a cautious step forward. Slowly and still trying to decide what to say, she made her way to the bed. Venom held out his hands, opening his arms in a silent gesture of welcome. If he thought she was going to forgive and forget that easily, he had another think coming.

But she couldn't deny that she craved his body heat. Climbing onto the bed, she slid one leg over his and straddled his thighs. The sheet trapped between their bodies kept them from touching too intimately. Knowing Venom, he probably planned to use those masterful hands and his skilled mouth to make her forget about their spat.

Venom cupped the tops of her knees and glided his hands along her bare thighs until they disappeared under her nightgown. The fabric bunched around her waist as his fingers spanned her hips. "Talk to me."

She braced her hands on his broad shoulders. It would be so easy to make a threat to deny him her body or her affection if he didn't take her with him but she refused to start down that petty path. It wasn't going to solve anything.

Deciding that this was one time when she needed to be brave and bold, she stated very clearly, "I'm going with you and you're going to use me to help teach this class."

His sigh of frustration buffeted her neck. "Dizzy, I don't—"

She touched his lips. "I'm not done yet."

His eyebrow quirked but he didn't try to speak over her again. She traced the outline of his mouth and then let her finger trail down a long, thin scar running along the edge of his jaw. "I'm coming with you because I want to learn everything you have to teach me. I'm coming with you because I am your mate, *your wife*, and I belong with you."

She gulped but found the courage to be totally honest. Taking one of his hands, she dragged it out from under her nightgown and brought it up to her chest. He palmed her small breast and she covered his hand with hers. "I'm going because I won't be able to breathe if I have to sit here and imagine these hands that I love so much running along another woman's naked skin."

His pained expression and the rough inhale that accompanied it convinced Dizzy that Venom hadn't realized how badly he had hurt her. She gasped as he expertly and swiftly flipped her onto her back and came down on top of her. "Venom!"

"I wanted to protect you." Kicking the sheet back toward the foot of the bed, Venom insinuated his hips between her thighs and pinned her to the mattress. His huge erection rubbed against her but he didn't try to penetrate her—yet.

She pressed her hands against his chest. "Protect me from what?"

"The club isn't like our playroom, Dizzy. We haven't even begun to scratch the surface of all the erotic possibilities. You will see things on demonstration night that will make you uncomfortable or even frightened. I refuse to push you too fast or too far." His thumb outlined the shell of her ear. "You are so precious to me."

Caressing his hot skin, she pointed out the obvious. "You could have told me that."

"I did tell you that. I told you that you aren't ready."

"That's not what I heard." Her cheeks grew heated. "I thought you were afraid I might embarrass you because

I'm not up to par."

"Never," he swore. He lowered his face and peered intently down at her. The depth of his adoration made her heart swell. "I chose you, Dizzy. I don't want to touch another woman ever again. You're the only one I want."

Rocking her hips in a flirtatious, inviting way, she commanded huskily, "Prove it." Venom crashed their mouths together in a kiss so wickedly passionate her head spun. His tongue stabbed between her lips and flicked against hers before he dragged his mouth along her jaw and down her neck. He nibbled and nipped his way down to the dipping front of her nightgown, leaving a trail of goose bumps in his wake.

He grasped the neckline of her delicate nightgown but he didn't allow her time to protest. With two hard jerks, he ripped her gown right down the front and exposed her breasts and belly. An illicit thrill coursed through her. The damp, throbbing heat between her thighs matched the buzzing pull as her nipples drew tight.

"You like that, don't you?" Venom knew she did but he wanted to hear her say it. He laved her nipple before he suckled her hard enough to cause her hips to buck off the mattress.

"Yes." She didn't even try to hide it. "I like it when you're rough with me."

He groaned against her breast. "Remember that you asked for this."

Her head pounded and her heart thundered against her rib cage. His eyes had gone smoky with desire—and danger. She could hardly breathe as he shredded her nightgown with his big, strong hands and used the long lengths of the fabric to bind her wrists and then tether them to the headboard. There was hardly any give in her new bonds. Panic gripped her.

"Look at me." Venom commanded her attention. "You're safe with me."

She peered up into his handsome, loving face. "I trust you."

He claimed her mouth so sweetly. Her lips were still pulsing from that kiss when he began his lazy travels down her body, exploring her breasts and belly with his hands and tongue. He playfully bit her, leaving aching, red splotches on her skin.

When his shoulders nudged her thighs wider apart, Dizzy experienced a delightful ripple of anticipation. The wicked things Venom did with his tongue were probably criminal on her planet—but she would have gladly taken an indecency charge and a public whipping for the chance to experience it even once.

Venom moaned hungrily as he rubbed his soft lips side to side against her pussy. He slid down flat on his stomach and let long arms rest along her rib cage. Nuzzling his face between her thighs, Venom probed her womanly heat with his pliable tongue. Dizzy threw her head back at the very first touch to her clitoris. "Oh!"

He hummed, the sound both enthusiastic and excited, as he started a languid circling motion. In their short time together, he had discovered that she liked that technique best. The gentle, easy lapping gradually morphed to a pace that made her lower belly quake.

Because he knew all the secrets of her body, Venom anticipated her approaching climax. At the perfect moment, he sucked her clit between his lips and worked his tongue across the engorged bud. Dizzy tumbled over the edge into the blissful abyss. "Yes!"

Tugging at her bonds, Dizzy cried out again and again, the rapturous sounds echoing in their bedroom as Venom continued to sensually torment her. His tongue dipped inside her and then swirled back to her pulsing clitoris. Lashing the pink pearl, he drove her right up to the heights of climax again—but didn't give her enough stimulation to give her what she wanted.

"*Venom.*" She groaned his name with frustration.

"Soon," he promised, smiling so wickedly. Shifting his position, Venom planted his hands against the mattress and angled his hips just perfectly. Dizzy wrapped her legs around his waist and moaned with sheer delight as his steely shaft finally penetrated her. Her body welcomed every last inch of his massive cock, sheathing him tightly and slicking him with her silken heat.

Their foreheads touched as Venom, now fully impaling her, closed his eyes. "Every time," he whispered. "It feels like coming home every single time."

Dizzy had finally begun to understand how much she truly meant to him. By taking her out of that forest and putting his collar on her, Venom had finally gained something that belonged solely to him. In this harsh, militaristic world of his, a wife and mate was the ultimate reward. All he wanted to do was protect and care for her.

And show her such intense pleasure.

When he rocked against her, Dizzy's exposed clitoris rubbed against him in the most delicious way. Venom cupped her backside with one hand and used the other to balance against the mattress as he drove into her again and again.

Tied to his headboard, Dizzy could do nothing but take what he gave her. Over and over, she accepted his thrusting, the blunt tip of him stroking so deeply inside her. When he framed her clit between his fingers, she gasped and swiveled her hips. "Venom!"

"I'm falling in love with you, Briarlina Lane." His steady gaze and hard, long thrusts didn't ease up as he spoke so tenderly. "I'm losing myself in you—and I've never been happier."

Tears spilled from her eyes and dripped down her face as Venom gazed at her with the promise of so much love. He didn't wait for a reply before kissing her. She sensed he understood how much she cared for him. This giant sky warrior had captured her heart the moment he brushed the cold snow from her freezing feet and tended to her rather than asking for help with the trap threatening to cripple him. In that moment she had witnessed the goodness and selflessness within him.

As they kissed, Venom's fingertips danced across her the inflamed bundle of nerves between her thighs. One thrust, two thrusts—and she surrendered to the wild climax he coaxed from her writhing, needy body. His blazing seed seared her tender flesh as he buried himself as deeply as possible and shuddered against her.

With her arms bound overhead, she couldn't embrace

him or rub his back. As their shared aftershocks rocked their joined bodies, Dizzy peppered soft kisses along the side of his neck and down his cheek. She couldn't help but smile at the way Venom nuzzled her like a puppy seeking comfort. Considering all his previous sexual experiences were with women paid to provide him release, she imagined he craved the gentle softness that she willingly gave.

When he finally rolled onto his side, Venom curled up against her. He threw his long leg across her thighs and traced shapes on her rapidly cooling skin. "I am sorry that I upset you. My instinct to shield you got the best of me."

Dizzy shifted as much as her fabric cuffs would allow. "I am thankful that you're looking out for me, Venom. I understand what you mean about pushing me too far too fast. The thing is…I have to experience it before I can tell you if we're moving too quickly."

He silently considered her point while running his finger around her pebbled nipple. "I'll take you with me for the class and to let you get a feel for the place, but we aren't staying after my demonstration ends. There are certain demonstrations scheduled that you don't need to see."

She frowned at him. "Venom, I'm not a child who needs to be protected from everything."

"I didn't say you were a child." Venom massaged her breast and caused warmth to spread through her chest. "I agree there are things you might want to see that would interest you. I worry that it might be difficult for you the next time you attend a wives' club meeting if you run into one of these mates at the club and see them in…extreme play."

"Extreme?"

Reluctance darkened his eyes. "You'll soon learn that I expect very little from you when it comes to submission. You will also gain a better understanding of how very deep this world of mine sometimes digs. There are fetishes and kinks encouraged and practiced here that would probably make you run screaming from the room."

She gulped. "Like?"

"Later," he said in that annoying way he sometimes did. "Right now we need to discuss your punishment."

She narrowed her eyes at him. "For what?"

"Shooting me the bird? Does that ring a bell?"

"You were being an ass."

The corners of his mouth slanted upward but he didn't allow a full smile to curve his lips. "You aren't helping your case."

"You better not even think about punishing me for flipping you off when you deserved it, Venom."

"Or what?" He reached up and flicked the strips of fabric binding her to the bed. "You're my prisoner to-night."

Her jaw dropped. "Venom—"

"Hush," he whispered with a little smile. The kiss he planted on her lips left her reeling and panting for air. Showing his strength, he easily turned her onto her belly. There was enough length in the tether between her roped wrists and the headboard to allow the fabric to twist.

"What are you doing?" Her eyes widened as Venom pushed her up onto her knees.

"Punishing you, of course." His hand unexpectedly smacked her bare bottom. Her gasp of outrage and shock was covered by the crack echoing in the room. A second later, the fingertips of his other hand discovered her clitoris. He expertly manipulated that bundle of nerves while spanking her twice more. "But I have a feeling you're going to enjoy it."

Chapter Twenty

A FEW NIGHTS later, Venom exited their playroom with his bag of selected equipment and tossed it onto the bed. He could hear Dizzy humming to herself in the bathroom as she finished getting dressed. Because he knew how she liked to dally when it came to her makeup and hair, he gently prodded her to hurry along. "Are you nearly ready to go?"

"Almost!"

He doubted that very much. Almost in his lexicon meant a minute or two maximum. To Dizzy, almost seemed to mean a quarter of an hour. "I don't want to be late."

"We have forty-five minutes, Venom. The ship isn't *that* big."

"You know, for a woman who is about to be tied up and completely at the mercy of my whims, you sure are sassy tonight."

Her soft snort and amused giggle traveled out of the bathroom. If he wasn't so damn infatuated with her, he would use this as a teaching moment to instill some discipline. Considering the way her punishment had gone the other night, he knew that he simply didn't have it in him to mold her into a more obedient, more typical Harcos wife. No, he liked her just the way she was.

When she appeared in the doorway of the bathroom, his brain threatened to explode. His cock started to fill and his heart raced. Dizzy had convinced him to allow Hallie to take her costume shopping for their first night at the club. He wondered if that was such a good idea now.

Swallowing hard, he asked, "Where did you get that shirt?"

"At the uniform shop," she answered while slowly advancing toward him. "The costume shop didn't have anything I liked so I decided to make something fun." As if reading his mind, she quickly added, "I checked with the regulations before cutting up the shirt. I was assured there weren't any rules against it."

Venom eyed the naughty little outfit she had crafted. He had a feeling a pile of complaints were going to be stacking up on Vicious and Orion's desks tonight. "There probably will be by morning."

Spinning slowly, she asked, "What do you think?"

His lecherous gaze raked her sexy body. She had cut a land corps uniform shirt in half and altered the top to be formfitting. It tied in the front and she had done something to the sleeves to make them puffy and pleated. The flirty, feminine take on the top was definitely going to turn heads.

Dizzy had used the remainder of the fabric to make a skirt. The hem barely covered her sweet little ass. The garter belt and black thigh-highs he had chosen for her looked sinfully sexy. He was glad that he had indulged her request to wear panties tonight. Though he didn't mind other men looking at his gorgeous bride, he didn't want them getting a peek at the parts of her that belonged only to him.

"I think I should probably toss a weapon or two into my bag because I'm probably going to have to fight off every swinging dick in that place to get you out of there."

Dizzy's mischievous grin made his heart flutter. "Then I guess I did well."

"Very well," he said and reached for her. He only allowed a quick kiss because he knew how easily he was distracted by her sweet mouth. When he pulled back, he studied her hair. She had pulled it up into a high ponytail but that wasn't going to work. "I'm going to braid this."

"I can do that."

He shook his head. "I would like to do it."

"Okay." She seemed a little nervous as she sat on the spot he indicated next to the bed. "Why does it need to be braided?"

"It doesn't need to be braided but I would prefer to know that it's totally out of the way when I'm working tonight." He sank down onto the mattress and pulled her back between his knees. "Braided hair looks beautiful next to rope work. I'm fond of the aesthetic side of bondage too."

"I could tell," Dizzy murmured as he uncurled the elastic binding her hair and combed his fingers through it. "When you put the rope corset on me before the wedding, I noticed the way you made sure the diamonds were spaced so evenly. I figured some of that was about balancing the tautness of the rope but it looked too pretty to be totally practical."

"Yes," he agreed while gathering her hair between his fingers and starting the braid. The silky pale strands felt so incredibly soft in his hands. He enjoyed the light, feminine fragrance wafting from them. "One of these nights I'll tie your hair into the restraints."

"That sounds intriguing." Judging by the prickly bumps of excitement raising along her shoulders and neck, Dizzy found the idea much more than simply intriguing.

When he finished braiding her hair, he helped her stand and kissed her cheek. He wrapped her bridal collar around her neck and made sure it was loose enough to cut down on any chafing. She stepped into her heels and adjusted her thigh-highs.

As she clung to his hand and followed him out of their quarters, she asked, "So, um, how much clothing do I get to keep on during the demonstration?"

Sensing her anxiety, Venom smoothed his hand down her back to cup her bottom and drag her against him. "I won't allow anyone to see you naked. I like to remind you that your body belongs to me—but I would never force you to bare yourself to anyone."

She relaxed in his arms. "Thank you."

He brushed his lips across her temple and gave her backside a loving pat. "It's about respect, Dizzy. You don't have to thank me for that."

Despite her insistence on accompanying him tonight, Venom could tell Dizzy was second-guessing herself as they entered the double doors of the club. She slowed her walk and gripped his hand between both of hers.

Low, thudding music greeted them when they stopped at the registration desk. The man behind the desk actually got up out of his seat to look Dizzy over. He shot Venom an envious smile. "Nice catch, Captain."

Venom grunted and put his hand between Dizzy's shoulders. He hitched his equipment bag higher on his shoulder and gently pushed her forward. She hesitated a few steps inside the club. There were couples and unmated officers lounging around the bar area.

She lifted her questioning gaze to his face. "I thought your people don't dance. What's with the music?"

"The music isn't here for dancing."

As if on cue, a shrill cry erupted from deeper into the club. It wasn't the sound of a woman keening with pleasure but pain. Next to him, Dizzy swayed a bit and pressed tightly to his side. "Oh my god."

Venom cupped her beautiful face and held her gaze. "Sugar, do you want to leave? We'll go right now. I'll cancel this class in a heartbeat and take you home."

She swallowed nervously but shook her head. "I want to stay. But...I don't want to see whatever the hell is making that woman scream like that."

"Truthfully? I don't want to see it either." He caressed her face in a way that he hoped was reassuring. "I respect every couple's right to indulge whatever kinks rev their engines but I'm not a fan of play that causes enough pain for a woman to let loose a cry like that. It doesn't sit well with me."

"Or Raze either, apparently," Dizzy said thoughtfully.

He followed her gaze and spotted Raze storming across the club. He disappeared down the steps that led into the dungeon-like area where the whipping posts were hidden. Apparently those cries of pain weren't the consensual kind.

"He doesn't," Venom confirmed, "but that's not why he's heading that way. Did you see the device lighting up on his arm?"

"That bright-red box?"

He nodded. "It's a device that the monitors wear to keep everyone safe. Within the club, the universal safeword is red but most couples have a word they use whenever their play gets too intense. During check-in, the word is added to a database and tied to our chips. It allows the monitors to keep an eye on couples who are playing near them."

Dizzy frowned up at him. "We don't have one of those words."

"We don't need one."

Her eyebrows bunched together. "And why is that?"

"If you ask me to stop, I stop. I'm not playing games with you or trying to edge you or push you. I asked for complete honesty when we're together and you've given it. You trust me to keep you safe and I trust you to know when you've had enough." He gave her braid a tug. "Do you want a safeword? You can pick one if it would make you feel more secure."

She considered his offer for a few seconds. "No thank you. I think we're fine just the way we are."

Glad that she agreed with him, Venom took her hand

and led her through the gathering crowd. A few times, Dizzy stopped to gawk at the public play stations they passed. He thought her eyes were going to bug out of her head when she spotted a woman down on all fours and the line of men waiting to have their chance with her.

"Venom! Is that—I mean—what the hell?"

Before answering her, he tilted his head to see if the woman was a mate or a poppy. The black collar around her neck answered that question quickly enough. Venom wondered at the motives of her husband. "It's probably a gangbang fantasy."

"That's *gross!*"

"No," he calmly scolded her. "It's not gross. It's their choice. Remember—it's not our place to judge. For all we know, that couple thinks we're crazy because I tie you up."

Dizzy gasped when the next man in line rammed his cock into the woman's ass. The woman cried out with pleasure but Dizzy didn't see it that way. She was too shocked by what she was witnessing to actually *see* the scene. The woman was pushing back and egging on the man taking her from behind.

Venom winced when Dizzy gripped his hand tightly enough to cause pain. When she lifted her terrified eyes to his face, he kissed her forehead and tugged her along. "Let's go."

They weaved in and out of the mingling bodies toward the private rooms in the back. His class tonight was relatively small—only six couples and ten single officers—so he had been given a moderate-sized room equipped for hardcore rope bondage, including reinforced suspension rings from the ceiling and a pulley system and a leather bondage table.

Venom grasped Dizzy by the waist and lifted her onto the table. He took a moment to study her beautiful face. Her shaken expression confirmed his worst fear. "This is why I didn't want to bring you."

"I know." She clasped his arms. "You're sure that woman enjoyed that?"

"Yes. There were monitors there. Her mate would have discussed the scene with them before it began. The monitors would have questioned her to make sure she was open to the scenario."

Dizzy gulped. "Is that how all women are shared?"

"*No,*" he answered emphatically. "That was an extremely unique and hard thing that you witnessed. Many couples who share do it in a gentler, more loving way. That couple seems to have very distinct tastes."

Her face turned bright red as she asked, "Do a lot of women like to...you know...*there*?"

"Are you asking me if women enjoy anal sex?"

She looked as though she was about to slide off the table in embarrassment. He often forgot that despite her age and her success as an independent woman, Dizzy had come into his life incredibly inexperienced when it came to sex.

"Yes," she finally managed.

"Lots of women enjoy anal sex and lots of them don't." He shrugged. "I suspect it has to do with their introduction to it."

Her cheeks still stained red, she asked, "Do you want

to do that to me?"

"I've thought about it," he admitted. Cupping her face, he teased their mouths together. "Rest assured, sugar, if we decide to try that, we'll do it my way. It will be gentle and slow and you'll be the one in charge."

"Me?"

"You." He tapped the tip of her nose. "Sit here while I get everything ready."

She nodded but didn't say anything. Her wide eyes scanned the room. Slowly couples and single officers started to file into the space. He could almost smell her nervousness. It shouldn't have excited him but it did. He liked having her off-kilter because her responses were so much sweeter.

But as her mate, as the man who was falling head over heels in love with her, his first priority was always going to be her well-being. No matter how much he wanted to publicly bind and decorate her supple body, he would never do anything to harm her mentally or emotionally.

Using his body to block out the gathering crowd, Venom braced his hands on either side of her thighs and peered right into her eyes. "Be honest with me. Do you want to go home?"

She licked her lips. "Yes."

"Do you also want to stay and give this a try?"

She nodded. "I do."

"So what's it going to be, sugar? Do we stay? Or do we go?"

Dizzy ran her hands from his wrists to his shoulders and back down again. "We stay."

"All right." He leaned forward and kissed her. Instead of a simple, easy kiss, he plundered her mouth, taking what he wanted from her and reminding her how much he desired and needed her. He backed off just a little before swiping their tongues together one last time.

Venom enjoyed the sight of her swollen, pink pout and lust-darkened eyes for a few seconds before turning around and clapping his hands together. "Okay. Let's get started…"

WHAT THE HELL am I doing here?

The only things keeping Dizzy from bolting from the room were her shaky legs—and Venom's commanding presence. As she sat there in her flirty outfit waiting for him to strip her down to her undies and tie her up with rope in front of three dozen or so people, she wondered where this burst of courage had originated. All it took was one encouraging smile from Venom and her anxiety fled.

It finally occurred to her that she wasn't just falling in love with Venom. No, she had *already* fallen in love with him.

As Venom talked about ensuring the safety of the submissive partner and then choosing the right ropes for the right scenes, Dizzy tried to figure out when her heart had become his. It had come upon her so slowly that she couldn't pinpoint the exact moment. She could only say with certainty that it had happened.

The logical side of her brain screamed that less than two weeks with a man was way too quick to fall in love. Her heart thudded wildly and basically told her brain to shut up. Right, wrong, fast or slow—she loved Venom.

When he came closer to grab short lengths of rope he had prepared so his students could learn to knot, he reached out and playfully pinched her thigh. It took every ounce of her self-control not to throw her arms around him and tell him what she had just discovered. For now, she allowed herself to smile at him and hoped that he could see just how much he meant to her.

Venom's expression registered a bit of surprise but he didn't say anything. This obviously wasn't the time for him to interrogate her as to what had put that sappy smile on her face. Instead he turned around and started handing out the ropes while talking about bites and loops and all sorts of other bondage-related vocabulary.

As Dizzy gleefully enjoyed the realization that she loved Venom, she looked out over the crowd of students following his instructions. She spotted Raze hovering in the doorway. Though he seemed to have a permanently pissed-off expression on that mean-looking face of his, he showed his lighter side by winking at her. She suspected he was like Venom. Beneath that rough exterior, he was soft and sweet.

While she counted up the attendees, Dizzy realized two more women had appeared. They wore expensive-looking lingerie with lots of lace and ribbon. Brightyellow bands squeezed their upper arms. She quickly ascertained that these were the paid pleasure women—the poppies— who had been brought in to provide the single officers a chance to enjoy themselves.

Sneaking discreet glances at the poppies, Dizzy decided that Venom's assertion that his culture treated these women with respect was true. Unlike the scrawny, malnourished women who pandered down in Low Town, these prostitutes looked well-fed and healthy with shiny hair and bright eyes and gorgeous skin. There was none of the haunted sadness in their eyes that Dizzy had witnessed in the hookers who hung around the gritty street corners of The City.

Or maybe these women were simply better actresses. It was probably easier to pretend that you enjoyed your line of work when you had nice housing, clean clothing, adequate food and medical attention provided. These poppies weren't scrounging for scraps in the garbage or bruising their knees to make grocery money for their babies.

When she first thought of Venom sleeping with other women, her jealousy had flared but the more she thought about it the sadder she became. She thought of the way Venom had described their relationship as being real. How cold and lonely was it for these sky warriors and their pleasure girls?

There were so few choices afforded to them. The men in the military couldn't have girlfriends or wives unless they survived enough battles to earn the valor points required. They could either arrange a marriage through their families or a matchmaking service or wait for an open Grab slot.

And these women? They had grown up in the harsh environment of the Kovark prison system, a place where most criminals didn't even survive. Their choices were to stay there forever, marry a guard or go into pleasure work where they could somewhat control their destinies.

For all the internal whining and angst Dizzy had in-dulged in, she couldn't deny that she had been given more choices than most women of her generation. When her family had lost everything, she had been able to fall back on a trade that just happened to be her passion. The connections of her childhood had allowed her to build a small but steady income and enjoy independence.

When Venom had been caught in that trap, she had chosen to go back and help him. She had taken the collar he offered her. Yes, her father had put her in an impossible position, but she had been allowed to make the choices that changed her life—for the better.

"Dizzy, get down." Venom's firm voice snapped her right out of her thoughts.

"Yes sir." He hadn't asked her to use the honorific but Hallie had given her some tips for navigating her first night here. The pleased look on Venom's face was abso-lutely priceless as she slid to her feet.

"Strip for me."

Her fingers shook as she untied the front of the uni-form shirt she had altered to be so sexy and peeled out of it. Her belly clenched as she unbuttoned the skirt and slipped it down her legs. Stepping out of her heels, she set them aside with her folded clothing.

Venom held out his hand and she joined him in front of the class. He spun her around to face the students and pulled her back against his hard body. His huge hand flattened against her chest and his fingers covered the swells of her breasts. The lacy push-up bra with pink ribbon accents was the sexiest thing she had packed. Venom seemed to like it just fine.

"Your woman's body is a blank canvas. You want to adorn her, to make her beautiful and enticing, but you don't want to harm her." His hand glided over her skin, leaving a searing path of tingling heat. "I'm sure it seems as if I'm harping on safety but you must remember that she can be seriously injured."

Dizzy shivered as his fingertips trailed down her arm. He clasped her hand and lifted it to show it to the students. "Look at her wrist. Do you think this dainty little thing could hold up her body weight if she was bound with her arms overhead and one of my knots or ties slipped or a suspension hook gave way?"

He shook his head. "No. Instead of enjoying some fun together, we would be making a trip to the infirmary to have her shoulder put back into place and her wrist braced." He lowered her hand and kissed the side of her neck. "This is serious business. It's fun and sexy—but it's dangerous if you're not paying attention and planning for the worst scenarios."

Amid the murmuring, Venom glided his hands along her belly. "It's not just a fall that will badly hurt your sub. Remember what I said about circulation and avoiding nerve damage?"

She inhaled a shuddery breath as Venom crouched down beside her to point out all the tricky spots on her body where care had to be taken. His warm, strong hands moved over her ankles and knees while he talked. She delighted in his sensual, possessive caress.

With the nitty-gritty details out of the way, Venom picked up four shorter lengths of rope and began to demonstrate simple ankle and wrist cuffs. The single officers who hadn't paid for time with one of the poppies practiced on each other—which Dizzy couldn't help but smile at. Raze caught her amusement because he shot her a playful but scolding glance. Rolling her lips under, Dizzy stifled the giggle that threatened to erupt.

Once they had mastered cuffs, Venom walked them through creating the rope bra, once without knots and once with the knots. When a couple of the mated officers ran into problems, Venom helped them redo the rope work—but he never touched their wives. He stood close by and gave pointers but he kept his hands to himself. Whether that was to make her happy or simply a sign of respect for the men and their wives, she couldn't tell. Dizzy suspected it was both.

"Now that you have this bra part finished, you can carry the rest of the rope down the body to create a corset with or without knots." Venom stood off to the side as he demonstrated how to make the beautiful diamond-shaped patterns by looping and tucking and weaving the rope.

She studied his handsome face, marveling at his focus and attention to detail. After hearing him discuss all those safety points, she realized how much concern and care he took with her. A few times, his gaze would drift from a knot or a looping motion to her face. She enjoyed the private glances they shared as the class practiced all around them.

"If we're doing knots, where do we put the one in the

crotch area?"

Dizzy didn't see the man who asked the blunt question. She tried not to show her annoyance that the intimate gaze she had been sharing with Venom had been broken.

Venom seemed to welcome the question. "You have a couple of options." He moved behind her and framed her hips with his hands. "You can place the knot against her anus or perineum. Some women enjoy having it right against the entrance of their pussy and others like some pressure against their clitoris."

Dizzy swayed a little as Venom's fingertips touched all the places he described. She was very glad for the panties he had allowed her to wear tonight. She could feel the throbbing, wet heat between her thighs spreading. She was certain Venom discovered just how aroused she was he ran his fingers over her panties.

Caressing her skin, he said, "This is an incredibly erogenous area so you want to place the knot in a spot that keeps your mate centered in the experience. Keep in mind that erogenous zones means lots of nerve endings so be careful. You want this to be a thrilling experience—not one that's so painful she'll never agree to play again." He tapped the spot right over her pubic bone. "Avoid this area. I've seen subs bruised by knots here."

"What if you plan to suspend your mate? Does that factor into your design?"

Venom stroked her braid. "It does. You have to think about weight distribution and pressure points. Things that look beautiful and feel good when she's standing might not feel so hot when she's dangling from the ceiling. If you intend to fuck her while she's suspended—and I assume you do," he said amid chuckles, "you'll want to plan ahead to ensure all the important areas are easily accessible."

"Will you show us a suspension tonight?"

Dizzy gulped hard. They hadn't discussed that possibility at all but she trusted Venom's judgment.

"Not tonight," Venom said, causing a few of the single officers to grunt with frustration. "We're nearly out of time. Suspensions shouldn't be rushed."

"Will you consider another class soon?"

"Sure." Venom massaged her neck with his thumbs. "We'll pick up right here and I'll make sure that you get to see a proper suspension." He gave her backside a pop that made her hiss and lift on her tiptoes. As chuckles erupted around them, he asked, "Would you like that, sugar?"

Buzzing with excitement, she glanced over her shoulder. "Yes. Very much."

Actually she wanted to do that, like, *right now*. This whole class had been foreplay. The white-hot need blossoming in her lower belly wouldn't be satisfied until Venom consumed her with his dominant, powerful style of lovemaking.

With the demonstration at an end, students filed out of the room. Most of the couples stopped for pointers. Venom stepped away from her side to show one of his fellow officers how to better accentuate his wife's fuller figure. Enviously eying the other woman's voluptuous bosom, Dizzy didn't even notice the single officer who had cozied up close to her until he reached out to flick one of the tiny bows adorning the cup of her bra.

With lightning speed, Venom snatched the officer's hand in a deadly grip that drove the other man to his knees. "Never touch my mate." He pushed the grabby man's finger back toward his wrist, lurching a strangled cry from the other man's throat.

"Apologize."

"I'm sorry, Captain. I didn't—"

"Not to me," he said through gritted teeth. "To my wife." The man didn't look pleased but he did it. "I'm sorry, ma'am."

"Are you satisfied with that apology, Dizzy?"

She nodded and finally found her voice. "Yes."

Venom released the other guy's hand. "You're lucky she's so gentle-hearted. Other mates might have requested that you get sent to the wall."

Dizzy had no idea what that meant but didn't ask. Still on his knees, the officer with one stripe shaved into his hair rubbed his hand. She had learned to differentiate the land corps from the sky corps by their hairstyles. The pilots seemed to favor those stripes.

Raze gripped the back of the airman's shirt and dragged him to his feet. "Guess what, flyboy? You just earned yourself a two-month suspension from the club and a chat with the admiral. Say goodbye to some of those valor points."

Venom gathered her close and soothingly caressed her shoulder. His anger dwarfed her irritation with the unwanted touch. He calmly finished helping the other officer with his question and bid the couple a good night.

When the door closed behind them, Venom turned toward her and gently gripped her shoulders. He bent down to peer into her eyes. "Are you all right?"

"I'm fine. Honestly I've been jostled and touched more intimately than that at the Subterranean."

"The what?"

"It's a club underground that a friend of ours—of mine and Ella's—runs." When his eyes narrowed, she quickly explained, "A dance club, not one of these kinky clubs like yours."

"Ah." He slipped his finger under one of the ropes crisscrossing her body and tugged. "You did very well tonight. Did you like it?"

She drew her initials on his chest. "You know I did."

As if to confirm his earlier findings, Venom pushed aside the damp fabric guarding her pussy and slipped two fingers between her labia. "Yes, you did."

She pressed against him. "Take me home."

"To do what, sugar?"

"You know what I want." But he was going to make her say it.

"I know what *I* want. I'm only guessing when it comes to you." His fingers slowly manipulated her throbbing clitoris.

"Bull," she said with a little snort. "I don't think you've guessed once when it comes to making love to me." She gazed up at him with such awe. "I think you figured me out that first time you put your hands on me."

He grinned and started to speak but they were interrupted by a loud knock at the door. Venom removed his hand from her panties just as the door swung open. Raze appeared with such fury burning in his eyes that Dizzy was taken aback. As she tried to figure out what had made him so mad she finally realized that men were running down the hall behind him.

"You'd better get her untied and taken back to your quarters." The foreboding edge to Raze's voice filled her with dread. "The Splinters hit one of our cargo ships—and it's bad."

Chapter Twenty-One

V ENOM DIDN'T MISS a beat. "How many dead?"

"Dozens," Raze growled. "There will be more, of course. We've only just received preliminary reports. They're not good."

His instincts as a soldier immediately overwhelmed him. Jerking the knife out of the sheath at his waist, Venom started slitting the ropes decorating Dizzy's beautiful body. He hated to end things so abruptly but an attack on a cargo ship was serious business. With a mole still running loose on the *Valiant* and that mess with Axis, Venom feared the Splinters might try to attack this battleship as well. A one-two punch if there ever was one.

"Which ship was it, Raze?"

"The *Night Bird*," he answered solemnly.

Venom's eyes closed briefly. The escort team with that ship had been the second SRU team off the *Arctis*. Even worse? The *Night Bird* had been scheduled to carry the extremely powerful fuel rods used to power the fleet. "Our guys?"

Raze shook his head. "It doesn't look promising."

Dizzy placed a comforting hand against his neck. She surprised him by suppressing her curious nature and asking no questions. The second she was freed from the corset, she grabbed her clothing. The haunted look in her pretty brown eyes caused him such pain. He had promised that he would keep her safe and protect her from the horror and terror she had known back in The City. Now those same terrorists were threatening her life here.

Venom brushed his thumb across her mouth before kissing her forehead. He refused to make empty promises about how safe the *Valiant* was. Despite being a massive warship and a floating fortress surrounded by dozens of guard ships, the *Valiant* was just as vulnerable as every other vessel.

He didn't bother cleaning up his mess. Grabbing his bag, he put his hand against her back and guided her forward. She carried her high-heeled shoes so she could keep up with his long strides. At the elevator bank he broke away from Raze, who hurried to join the men cramming into the cars that serviced the operations decks instead of the housing wings.

Once inside the elevator Venom tapped the communication screen mounted on the wall to read the up-to-the-minute briefings provided. His gut lurched as he scanned the reports coming in from the *Redemption*, the ship tasked with picking up the rescue pods.

"What does neutralize the ship mean?"

Venom hesitated before answering her because he was certain it would upset her. "It means the *Night Bird* has lost control and is drifting into your planet's gravitational field. It's going to fall and it's going to fall hard. To protect life on Calyx, the ships in the vicinity are ordered to fire at will. The goal is to reduce the ship to the smallest pieces possible so the bulk will burn up during reentry."

"But…what about the rescue pods? What about the men who might still be trapped on the ship?"

"Collateral damage," he said gruffly.

"That's so awful." She sounded as though she might start crying.

"That's war, Dizzy." He hated to be so cold with her but he didn't have time to coddle her right now.

When they reached their floor, he rushed her out of the elevator and into their quarters. Dropping his bag, he pulled her into his arms and tried to decide what to tell her. The truth was he didn't know what to expect once they deployed. The mop-up could take days or weeks.

Terror's warning from their fitting room meetup chilled him. He refused to believe this was the last time he would see her. He'd survived too much to lose it all now. "I'll be back as soon as possible."

"I'll be fine. Please don't worry about me. Just focus on your work. I'm a big girl, remember? I've done this winging-it-on-my-own thing before and made a success of it."

His stomach clenched painfully. Her urge to protect him by setting his mind at ease made him love her even more.

And he did love her. It wasn't simple infatuation and lust that made him feel as if his heart were being ripped out of his chest right now. They had been given nearly two weeks of impossibly perfect bliss—he refused to even acknowledge the bumps along the way—and he wanted so much more with her.

But duty called. His brothers-in-arms needed him.

For the first time in his life, he resented his unwavering loyalty to the men who bled with him on the battlefield. He had never before been tempted to say fuck it to an official order...until faced with leaving Dizzy behind.

"You should go." She must have sensed his warring emotions. Smiling so bravely, she rubbed his chest and lifted up to kiss him. "I'll be here, waiting for you."

He met her seeking mouth with much tenderness. Though he wanted nothing more than to lift her up against the nearest wall and make love to her one last time, Venom wrenched free from Dizzy and stalked to the door. He didn't dare look back after separating from her. Raze and the rest of his team were waiting. He couldn't let them down—even if every step away from Dizzy tore at him.

Stepping into the elevator, he tapped at the screen. The doors had nearly closed when her smaller hand gripped the metal and prevented it from closing. The door slid back on its track. "Obstruction detected. Please clear."

Grinning mischievously, Dizzy appeared before him as the authoritative male voice boomed from the speakers. "I've been called worse things than an obstruction, I guess."

"What are you doing?"

"I decided that I had to tell you something." She gripped the front of his shirt and hauled him down until their noses were nearly touching. "I love you."

The words he had dreamed of one day hearing washed over him like sunshine, blazing away the gut-wrenching pain of leaving her behind. His own love for her left him trembling and feeling nearly giddy. "I love you so much, Dizzy."

"Good. I hear it works better when two people in a marriage share that love thing."

He laughed while his heart felt as if it were doing wild flips in his chest. "Yeah. I've heard that too."

She pressed her lips to his in a lingering kiss. "I love you. I'll see you soon. Be safe, okay?"

"I will." He brushed his knuckles down her cheek. "I love you."

Dizzy stepped back and the elevator door slid slowly closed. He tried to burn the image of her happy, blushing face right into his brain. It was a vision that would sustain him through whatever awaited him on this mission.

When he hit the SRU floor, Venom discovered Raze had already set out his weapon and gear. He swapped his play clothes for his uniform and strapped on his vest and holsters. He entered the briefing room just as Cipher was starting their mic and radio checks.

Taking his place next to Raze, Venom looked over the information flooding the intelligence screens mounted on the wall. He saw that fighter pilots including Zephyr and Blaze had been in hot pursuit of the three Splinter ships that had attacked the *Night Bird*.

"Shit." Venom watched the radar blips as one of the smaller Splinter craft spiraled toward Calyx after being hit hard by Zephyr. "That's going to be a hell of an impact."

"Thankfully most of that backward little planet is un-inhabited," Raze grumbled. "Not that there aren't a couple of villages down there that wouldn't be better of being obliterated."

Venom's mouth settled into a frown at Raze's callous remarks. "What are our orders?"

"To aid the Shadow Force in recovering the fuel rods," Raze answered. "A fighter contingent has boxed in the ship suspected of holding the stolen cargo. They've disabled their engines and left them adrift. We'll breach and board and run a quadrant search." Raze lifted his voice. "Boys, let's move out!"

As they filed toward the door, Raze put a hand on his shoulder. Venom met his best friend's intense stare. "What?"

"Ven, you're technically still on honeymoon leave. It's well within your rights to call off on this one and stay behind. None of us would consider you dishonorable for choosing to stay with Dizzy."

"I know you wouldn't—but I would." Venom clapped Raze on the back. "This is my job. She understands that." He inclined his head toward the door. "Let's go. We have fuel rods to recover and Splinters to kill."

On the deployment deck, Risk waited with one of his injection guns. They all groaned but dutifully rolled up their sleeves and bared their necks. The pressurized guns injected anti-radiation pellets under their skin. Venom winced as the painful little bastards were thrust into him.

"You've got about seventy-two hours of protection under low-dose exposure," Risk reminded them. "Make sure your meters are calibrated, Cipher."

"You don't have to tell me twice," Cipher muttered. "It's my balls on the line."

Venom snorted at Cipher's colorful response. Risk clapped him on the back. "Good luck, Ven."

Certain that Risk would remain onboard the *Valiant* even if further units were deployed, Venom asked, "Will you look in on Dizzy for me? She trusts you and enjoys your company."

"Yes. Of course. I'll look after her exactly as you would."

Venom's mouth slanted. "Well—maybe not *exactly* as I would."

Risk chuckled. "Obviously."

Moments later, as Venom buckled into his seat aboard the waiting strike ship, he touched his mouth. His gloved fingers grazed the still-buzzing spot where Dizzy had kissed him after declaring her love. For the first time in his life, he had a reason greater than the bonds he shared with his teammates to keep him alive.

Come hell or high water, he was going home to Dizzy.

Chapter Twenty-Two

REFUSING TO DWELL on everything that could go wrong with Venom's mission, Dizzy stripped out of the sexy outfit, removed her makeup and stepped into a warm shower. Keeping an eye on the digital display that logged their daily water ration, she made sure it was a short one. Wrapped in a towel, she brushed her teeth and rubbed on some lotion to guard against the dryness of the air onboard the *Valiant*.

Rather than her usual nightgown, Dizzy opted to pull on one of Venom's undershirts. With her short stature, it fit her like a nightdress anyway. Certain sleep would evade her without his heavy arms wrapped around her, Dizzy decided to read on the living room couch until exhaustion gripped her.

But as she stepped out of their bedroom into the main living area of their home, Dizzy spotted a strange figure out of the corner of her eye—and freaked the fuck out.

Her shrill shriek of terror startled the man hovering near the entryway. She realized he was going through her purse. He snapped upright and ate up the floor between them with powerful strides. When he stepped out of the shadows, Dizzy recognized him as Torment, the Shadow Force interrogator.

"Stay back!" She jumped out of the way and put a chair between them. "If you touch me—"

"You'll do what?" Smugly amused, Torment crossed his arms. "You realize I'm about twice as tall as you and three times as heavy, right?"

She swallowed hard. Oh she realized her limitations, all right. "What do you want?"

"Not what you're thinking," he said with clear annoyance. "I've never forced myself on a woman in my life. Don't insult me by questioning my honor."

"Honor, huh? How honorable is it for a man to break into someone's home?"

"I didn't break in. I have the codes to every door on this ship."

"*That's* your comeback?"

"It's the defense I'll use when Venom files a complaint against me when he returns." Torment's harsh expression softened a bit. "He will return, in a little bit. Venom is among the most tenacious soldiers I've ever met."

His reassurance eased her fear some. "Why are you here?"

"A few days ago, Terror gave you a letter from the man you think is your father."

"He *is* my father."

"I'm not here to argue about your DNA. I need to know what was in that letter."

She suspiciously narrowed her eyes. "Why?"

Torment studied her for an unnervingly long moment. "Would you like to meet your real father?"

"What?" she asked, taken aback. "What do you mean?

How?"

"His flagship was rerouted here for his safety after the Splinter attack on the *Night Bird*. He's currently in the war room. I'll take you to him and let him tell you the truth." Torment took a step toward her. His cold, unfeeling eyes made chills race along her spine. "It's time someone finally told you who you really are—and what your mother was."

A shuddery, trembling sensation gripped her belly. *What my mother really was? Who I really am?*

Dizzy recognized that this was one of those moments in her life where everything was going to change. Torment's intriguing but potentially dangerous offer promised answers that she desperately wanted.

"I need to change."

He nodded. "Hurry."

Dizzy rushed into the bedroom and quickly got dressed. She picked up the corner of the mattress and retrieved the still-sealed envelope she had stuffed under there for safekeeping. She hadn't yet worked up the courage to read what her dad had written to her out of fear that it might be a final goodbye—a goodbye she wasn't willing to concede.

Out in the living room, Torment zeroed in on the envelope. She gripped it tightly against her chest. "You take me to my biological father first. Then you get the envelope."

Even as she spoke, Dizzy recognized that Torment could take the envelope from her without much of a fight. Proving that he was an honorable man, he nodded. "Fair enough."

They left the apartment and stepped into the elevator. She noticed that certain sections of ship on the navigational screen were blinking orange. He must have seen her curious gaze as he scanned his wrist and gained access to an unblocked screen. "We're in lockdown. Only authorized personnel are allowed to move about the ship until the admiral lifts the orders."

The serious, no-nonsense set to his jaw discouraged her from asking the myriad questions burning the tip of her tongue. Where Venom would have been only too happy to tell her everything she needed to know about lockdown procedures, Dizzy sensed that Torment wasn't about to indulge her curiosity.

After switching elevators and bypassing four different security checkpoints, they reached a heavily guarded entrance. One of the soldiers guarding the door stepped forward to frisk her but Torment blocked him. He shot the man a withering look.

"Don't touch Venom's bride."

The soldier paled and cleared the path to the double doors. "You can go into the war room, sir."

The doors hissed and separated. Despite his intimidating presence, Dizzy stayed close to Torment. This was clearly an area where a woman like her had no business intruding and she didn't want anyone to think she was snooping.

They progressed down a dark hall to a massive dimly lit room filled with computer equipment. The three-story-high walls were covered in screens that projected all sorts of data—radar images, troop and aircraft movement, radio traffic and more. Her gaze drifted to the live feeds from the rescue mission currently being mounted for the crew of the *Night Bird* who were floating in pods.

"What the hell is that woman doing in here?"

It was a voice she had only heard once before—at the wives' meeting—that drew Dizzy's stunned attention. Orion, the harried admiral and commander of the *Valiant*, glared from his perch atop a raised balcony overlooking the war room. A moment later, General Vicious approached the railing, glanced down at her and frowned.

But it was the third face that appeared between the two men that almost sent Dizzy into a full swoon. Torment steadied her with a hand pressed between her shoulder blades. Her knees knocked as she stared into the eyes of the man she had last seen arguing with her mother on that fateful morning of the embassy explosion. He had aged since that day but those brilliantly blue eyes looked exactly the same.

The man who Dizzy was now certain was her biological father finally spoke. "Bring her to me, Torment."

Both the admiral and the general glanced at the man between them with confusion but neither questioned his order. It occurred to her then that this man—her father—outranked both of them.

Up on the raised platform, Torment stood behind her, preventing her from fleeing down the short flight of stairs. Orion flicked his fingers and sent the lingering support staff back down to the main floor. Dizzy engaged in a staring match with her father. She counted the five stars on his uniform and realized he was one of the highest-ranking generals in the entire Harcos military.

"Thorn?" Vicious carefully questioned his superior. "How do you know Venom's bride?"

Thorn? Of course, she thought sadly. Briarlina. Thorn and Lina. It had been right there in front of her the entire time.

Her father closed the distance between them. His eyes reflected the strangest mix of sadness and happiness. When he reached out to stroke her cheek, Dizzy held still and allowed him the small intimacy. "She is my daughter."

Orion's face slackened with shock. "Your daughter?"

"Yes." Thorn's hand fell from her face. "She is mine."

Dizzy supposed she should find comfort in his public acknowledgment of her. He could have easily refuted her lineage.

Vicious looked downright angry. "You abandoned a female child on a planet where most women don't even see their fortieth birthdays? Where childbirth deaths are nearly forty percent?"

Thorn took the criticism in stride. "I didn't even know she existed until a few days before the embassy bombing in The City. I *should* have known. There's no excuse for the way I abandoned sweet Lina."

At the mention of her mother's name, Dizzy finally found her voice. "How did you know my mother?"

Thorn sighed heavily and glanced at Torment. "Did you tell her?"

The Shadow Force operative shook his head. "I felt it was best to hear this type of truth from you."

Thorn motioned to a nearby chair. Dizzy gratefully sat

down, certain her legs wouldn't hold up through the story she was about to hear. Her father leaned back against a table and gripped the edge with his hands. She spotted the bright-red cuff encircling his thick wrist. It was similar to the white cuff Vicious wore on his left wrist—a cuff that matched Hallie's collar.

"You're married?"

Thorn nodded. "Yes, but that came after your mother—and you." She guessed that was better than the alternative.

"You know that your mother was a stewardess with Cross Colony Air, yes?"

"I do."

"What you don't know is that Lina was recruited as an asset for the Shadow Force within weeks of gaining employment there. Her position with the airline gave her a good clean cover for ferrying information to undercover agents. It allowed her to complete secret surveillance on passengers we suspected of being Splinter sympathizers or terrorists themselves."

Dizzy's mind reeled. What had Danny said at the wedding reception? Hadn't he mentioned something about the Shadow Force cultivating contacts and assets in this sector for decades? "My mother was an agent for your government?"

"A very good one," Thorn confirmed. "People saw that beautiful face of hers and immediately discounted her as being nothing more than a pretty girl. She used that to her advantage." His mouth curved in a wistful smile. "They had no idea how incredibly brilliant and talented she was."

Dizzy tried to reconcile this new information with the memories of her mother. She couldn't believe that a woman who ran a muse agency had been a highly skilled operative for a foreign government. "How did you two…?"

"At the time, I headed a small forward operating base on Safe Harbor. That was my official cover. Truthfully we were running a covert operation to build the foundation of the Shadow Force in this sector. We sensed the small Splinter movement gaining ground at the time would soon spiral out of control. This end of the solar system was so wild and unknown. We believed it would be the one place they would look to hide so we wanted boots on the ground and agents in play. Your mother was one of those foundation agents."

Thorn's gaze skipped over her shoulder. He seemed to be reliving the memories of her mother as he spoke. "I tried to ignore my attraction to her but it was futile. She ensnared me with one smile."

Dizzy hoped he wasn't going to get very specific about their affair. She didn't think she could handle *that* much truth.

"I loved that woman." He caught and held her gaze. "You are never to doubt that you were created in love. You weren't a mistake or an unwanted inconvenience. You are the natural product of a love so deep and so strong it spanned decades."

Dizzy blinked as tears welled in her eyes. "If you loved my mother so much, why did you bail? Why weren't you around when I was a baby? Why am I only meeting you now?"

"Our love was forbidden. Operatives are never supposed to cross that line—and I damn sure never should have crossed it with a subordinate and a native. When I was promoted and moved to the front lines, I couldn't take her with me. I didn't have enough points. If I had taken her as my mate they would have demoted me or bounced me out of the force entirely."

"So you chose your career over my mother?"

"At the time I planned to come back for her when I had the points. By then though, she had married Jack Lane. Once I learned she had married, I stopped digging and Grabbed a mate from a different planet. I didn't ask about any children in their marriage. It wasn't until I came to this sector with the *Indefatigable* that I learned you even existed. I realized then that she had married Jack to protect you." Thorn hung his head with such deep shame. "I won't stand here and make excuses. I own that mistake—and it was a mistake. It's the biggest regret of my life." His mouth slanted with sadness. "Not that hearing that makes any difference to you."

"Not really," she said crossly. "For what it's worth, my dad—my *real* dad—more than made up for your absence."

Thorn flinched. "I'm glad to hear that he was the man I couldn't be."

"Touching as this family reunion is," Orion carefully interjected, "we are in the middle of a Splinter attack. If this can wait—"

"It can't," Torment interrupted. "What General Thorn hasn't told Dizzy is that her mother was never deactivated as an agent. When she married Jack Lane and moved to The City, she continued to operate as an in-country asset for the Shadow Force. Her position as a wealthy banker's wife and as a business owner allowed her to mix and mingle with the government and social elite of Calyx."

"My mother was spying the whole time?"

Torment nodded. "She correctly projected that the League of Concerned Citizens would develop as a front for the Splinters. Over the years, she mapped out the connections between members of your government, the Sixer gang and the Splinter forces. So much of the intelligence framework for our current mission came through Lina. When she was killed, we scrambled to fill her spot. We needed someone who could keep his finger on the pulse of the Splinter movement, someone with the right connections."

Dizzy's mouth gaped as it all started to make sense. "You used my dad."

"He didn't know," Torment explained. "Not exactly," he added. "We used one of our other undercover assets to provide him with the seed money to start his black market operation. We were able to keep tabs on the Splinters through the movements of supplies along his chain. He's been incredibly useful to us—until now."

She narrowed her eyes at Torment. "What does that mean?"

"It means I made a colossal mistake," Thorn answered instead. "A few weeks ago, Jack tried to contact me. We hadn't spoken since you were in the infirmary aboard my ship. When we parted, it was not on good terms."

"Meaning?"

"He told me that I owed it to you to give you a better life but I didn't know how to do that without hurting my wife so very much." He gulped. "She had recently lost a child and I didn't know how to tell her that I had a daughter down on the planet. I couldn't reveal your existence without revealing everything about Lina and my earlier connections with Shadow Force." He shook his head. "And then it was too late. You had been discharged to Jack and I convinced myself you were better off never knowing the truth."

Dizzy's stomach pitched. For a man who insisted she was created with love and not something he considered a mistake, he sure as hell had taken every opportunity to deny her very existence.

"Jack's most recent messages to me were mishandled and jumbled. I thought he was trying to blackmail me into giving him money. What I realize now is that *he* was being blackmailed by someone who knew that I was your father. He needed money to pay them off and get the heat off you."

"Selling my lottery number was just a smoke screen, wasn't it? He wanted me off the planet. He wanted me to be safe."

"Yes," Thorn agreed. "Jack knew that if you were Grabbed our link would be discovered during the intake physical. He knew I would protect you."

Dizzy kneaded her temples as the horror of it all hit her. "What were they blackmailing him to do?"

"Jack was making inquiries about hiring a transport

ship for a cargo run between Calyx and a planet called Ryzina," Torment explained. "It's a planet inside Splinter territory. Our man on the inside doesn't know the details but he confirms the transport arrangements were made. If we fail to recover the fuel rods before they're moved to your planet, we must be able to intercept them before they reach Ryzina."

"Well—what the hell do you want me to do?" Dizzy gawked at Torment. "I haven't spoken to my dad in weeks."

"Jack has gone off the grid," Torment said. "No one can find him, not even Danny. After the wedding, he tried to touch base with Jack but he had vanished. The letter Terror passed to you reached him through four or five sets of hands. If Jack is still alive, he's only going to reveal himself to you."

"*No!*" Thorn's voice echoed like a whip crack. "You are not sending my only child down there as bait."

Torment turned that dead gaze of his to his superior officer. "With all due respect, General Thorn, you aren't in Shadow Force anymore. This is a call *we* make."

"Gentlemen!" Vicious stepped between the two men before things got any more heated. The admiral slid out a stealthy hand and carefully dragged her back behind him, tucking her out of the way in a protective maneuver.

Vicious pointed to the screen covering the far wall. "The SRU alpha team is preparing to breach and sweep the Splinter ship suspected of carrying the fuel rods. If the rods are there, my men will find them." He glanced at her before fixing Torment with a glare. "And this is a call that

Venom will make. This woman belongs to one of my men. I won't allow another bride to be risked for one of your missions."

Dizzy gulped nervously but remained hidden behind Orion. She thought of the story Venom had told her about Naya and Terror. *Please, not me too.*

She stiffened at the unexpected sound of Venom's voice hissing across the sound system. Stepping away from Orion, she glued her gaze to the screen as a live feed from the SRU mission played across it. Her heart stuttered when she realized he was leading the team into the enemy ship. Leaning against the table for support, Dizzy tried to breathe as she watched Venom and his team moving deeper and deeper into the ship.

When they started to trade fire with insurgents, Dizzy gasped. It was Thorn, her father, who put a settling hand on her shoulder. Lowering his voice, he commented, "I realize how frightening this is for you to see but this is a routine mission for Venom and his crew. He's done this a hundred times or more."

That didn't make her feel any better. By the time they finished clearing the vessel, Dizzy was on the verge of vomiting from the stress of it. How Venom could handle this type of work day after day she would never understand. Watching him utilize his skills reminded her how incredibly deadly he could be—and emphasized the tender sweetness with which he had always treated her.

"Raze, report." Vicious addressed the team via the communications link.

"Zero SRU wounded or killed in action. Seven combatants confirmed kills. Four combatants critically wounded and expected to perish. Thirteen combatants taken prisoner. The package is missing. Repeat, fuel rods are not among the cargo."

"Where the hell are they?" Vicious wondered with frustration.

"Admiral?" A voice from below called to the sky fleet commander. "We have Commander Zephyr on the com."

"Patch him through," Orion ordered. "Commander?"

"Admiral, we have a problem." Some sort of radio interference made his connection scratchy. "That ship I hit that started spiraling toward Calyx? I followed it into the atmosphere to ensure the safety of the civilians on the ground. It broke up during reentry but I witnessed seven pressurized pods pop off with chutes that deployed at survivable altitude. I'm picking up a huge and very red-hot G42 trail. The fuel rods are on the planet, Admiral. They're in the pods."

A flurry of activity erupted in the war room. She didn't understand most of the lingo being bandied about but the tense tone of the conversations swirling around her told her it wasn't good. The main screen switched from the live feed of Venom's SRU team to an aerial view of the multiple pods Zephyr had followed onto the planet. He hovered above the smoking craters where the pods had impacted.

"Skyhawk 06 to *Valiant*—I am currently detecting a life-sign sensor on the ground." Panic edged into Zephyr's voice. "Can you confirm?"

"*Valiant* to Skyhawk 06," a voice from down in the pit

replied, "we detect the life sign. ID Number is A7131416."

Vicious strode to the railing. "Repeat that."

"ID Number is A7131416."

The general's rigid stance didn't bode well. "It's Terror. Is he alive?"

"Affirmative."

"Is he moving?"

"Negative, sir."

Looking absolutely stricken, Vicious spun toward Torment. "What the hell is Terror doing with those rods?"

"His job," Torment answered matter-of-factly. "He hitched a ride on the *Night Bird* in the engineering division. There was enough Splinter chatter during the last month to put us on high alert. We hoped the SRU team and extra guard ships would be enough of a deterrent but Terror was tasked with protecting those rods in the event of an attack."

"Did we shoot down our own man?" Thorn asked the question everyone was thinking. Now Dizzy understood the panic filling Zephyr's voice. He had just fired upon and nearly killed one of their own.

"Skyhawk 06 to *Valiant*—I have company. Request immediate assistance. Repeat immediate assistance required."

The aerial surveillance picked up an advancing column of heavy-duty trucks. Dizzy's eyes widened when she noticed the surface-to-air missiles mounted in the beds of two of them. She had heard rumors about the arms dealers operating in The City but she had no idea they were bringing hardware like that to the planet.

Suddenly Orion and Vicious were shouting orders. Dizzy smartly got out of the way and melted into the background.

"Incoming!" Zephyr performed evasive maneuvers before firing on the convoy rushing toward the pods. He was badly outnumbered but refused to leave his position or leave Terror exposed.

Her gut clenched as she realized the sky corps pilots rushing to his aid were too far away. Zephyr was never going to abandon Terror, even if it meant certain death. Though he managed to take out four of the trucks, two missiles fired simultaneously outmaneuvered him. His aircraft was badly clipped and began to spin.

"Skyhawk 06 to *Valiant*, I'm hit. Repeat. I am hit."

The calmness with which he described his situation shocked Dizzy. The pilot had shown more fear upon realizing that he had fired upon Terror than he did when faced with his the very real possibility he was about to die in a fiery crash.

"I'm going down. Skyhawk 06 is hit. I am going down."

Horrified, Dizzy watched the aircraft spiral toward the ground. She flinched as the ship continued to take hits. The cover of the cockpit exploded as Zephyr ejected. She didn't know how he would survive the fall through the debris field.

As the crippled aircraft slammed into the ground, the Splinters used the massive explosion to their advantage. The bright fireball lit up the night. Mostly hidden by the smoke and darkness, the Splinters gathered up the large pods and loaded them into trucks. Dizzy cupped a hand over her mouth at the sight of Terror's lifeless body being dragged out of a crumpled life pod.

By the time the rescue squad of aircraft descended, the Splinters had raced away from the scene and disappeared into the heavily wooded area near the crash site. From Torment and Vicious' frustrated shouts, she deduced the terrorists had disabled any sort of tracking on the pods and cut Terror's ID chip out of his arm. Knocked unconscious by his sudden ejection, Zephyr was collected by another aircraft and reported to be in good condition.

"How could they have known to have their trucks in that vicinity?" Vicious asked the question Dizzy had been wondering. "How did they know the aircraft would go down there?"

"Zephyr dinged the aircraft after it had already locked on to its reentry trajectory," Orion answered. "This was probably the landing site they had picked to transfer the rods to Calyx for safekeeping until the heat abated. They had to have realized the ships they've cobbled together would never outrun us. Stowing the rods on Calyx for a few weeks? That's a better plan."

"Knowing Terror," Torment said, "he probably followed the fuel rods onto that ship and waited to make his move to secure the rods and kill the Splinter pilots after they had performed the trickiest part of the reentry procedure. Once they were locked into their landing location, the onboard navigation system would have attempted to bring them down as close as possible to the original landing site after they were hit."

Thorn's voice deepened to a deadly serious rasp. "I want the full might of our forces mobilized immediately. Our top priority is recovering those rods and our operative."

While the men around her continued to talk battle strategy, Dizzy stared at the envelope she still clutched in her hand. She used her fingernail to tear the sealed edge and slipped her finger inside to rip it open. Instead of a letter as she had expected, there was only a torn postcard tucked inside.

"They could be taking those rods anywhere." Vicious reached out to tap the touchscreen tabletop where the surface of Calyx was mapped out in quadrants.

"They have to know we can follow the radioactive trail. They'll take them to a safe location," Orion guessed.

"A building of some kind," Thorn interjected. "Maybe even a warehouse that has been lined and retrofitted?"

Dizzy rubbed her thumb across the vintage postcard. The picture on the front was so faded she could barely make out the words and the image of the subway as it had been imagined and advertised during the government's push for public support. She flipped over the card and read the simple message scrawled in her father's handwriting.

I tried.

Her eyes closed as she experienced a surge of such soul-crushing sadness. Guilt soured her belly when she thought of the way she and her father had fought the last time she had seen him. He had been trying to save her life and she had treated him so abominably.

"They'll take them underground." Dizzy raised her voice to be heard over the din. "The rods are going underground."

Torment strode toward her and snatched the postcard out of her hand. "Do you know where this is?"

She nodded. "The City started building a massive subway system, like, seventy years ago, but they ran out of money. There were all sorts of scandals surrounding the build and it was never completed. The tunnels are abandoned but they're used by homeless people and street kids and for illegal dance parties."

Torment showed the postcard to Vicious. "It's the perfect place to hide a shipment of fuel rods until a transport ship can sneak them off the planet."

"Do we even have specs of these?" Vicious took the card from Torment. "I can't send my men in blind. There's no telling what the Splinters could have waiting for the SRU."

Dizzy refused to allow Venom to go into such a dangerous place without any intel. "I have a friend who knows the tunnels better than anyone. If you can get me to The City, I'll take you to Hopper."

"Hopper?" Orion repeated with a frown. "What kind of name is that?"

Dizzy shot him an *oh really* look. "It's her nickname. No one knows the tunnels like her. That's why they call her Hopper. You know? Like a rabbit in a warren?"

"You're not going down there." Thorn slashed his hand through the air.

Dizzy calmly stood. "It's a little late for you to pop into

my life and start thinking you can make decisions for me."

"Actually he can," Vicious cut in gently. "You're his offspring, which means you're one of us. Technically you weren't eligible to be Grabbed. Venom had no right to claim you so your classification aboard this ship is—"

"Our laws say you belong to me," Thorn interrupted. "I'm not risking your life. You could be walking into an ambush or worse. Those damn fuel rods may be leaking. You're staying here where I can keep an eye on you."

"I don't care what your law says." Dizzy ripped the postcard from Thorn's hand. "My dad is missing. You know? The man who actually raised me. The man who taught me how to ride a bike and tie my shoes. The man who stayed up with me when I was sick and rocked me when I had nightmares."

Every word etched such pain into Thorn's face. She hated to be so cruel but the fear of losing her dad and Venom demolished any control she had over her mouth.

"I won't be sent to my room to wait like a good little girl while my dad and my husband are fighting for their lives. You need those fuel rods and you need Terror. I'm the best chance you've got at finding them—and you know it."

"I also know that you are irreplaceable. We can build more fuel rods and there will always be more men filing into the ranks of the Shadow Force." Thorn touched her face. "There is only one of you in the entire universe."

"There is only one Venom in the entire universe," she countered. "He's the most amazing thing that has ever happened to me. If I lose him…" She couldn't even bear to finish the thought.

Tension stretched taut between them like razor wire. Thorn finally growled at Torment. "If she comes back with even one hair missing from her head—"

"Understood, sir." Torment clasped her upper arm and dragged her toward the stairs.

While she raced to keep up with Torment, Dizzy couldn't stop thinking about the way her mother had died at the hands of the Splinters. She prayed that her love story with Venom wasn't going to share the same terrible end.

Chapter Twenty-Three

"**O**UR LESS-LETHAL OPTIONS are severely limited in an underground space," Venom said as he checked and rechecked the seal on his gas mask. They had been on Calyx for three hours, two of them spent clearing the woods around the crash site and ensuring there was nothing left behind that might be salvaged or sold.

Now their transport ship sat in a field two miles outside The City. With their cloaking shields on, they waited for their orders from the *Valiant*. The debris field from the *Night Bird* had just begun to reach the outer atmosphere of the planet and was causing major communication interference. Two of their communications satellites had been clipped and were out of operation.

Threat, their infiltration and breaching specialist, sketched out various scenarios for entering the subway system they would soon be searching. So far their intelligence was severely limited. Raze had been attempting to make contact with the *Valiant* but Cipher couldn't establish a com-link.

"One canister of tear gas in a space that confined?" Fierce shook his head as he tested his night-vision gear. "It's going to be fucking pandemonium."

"The real issue is going to be accessing the subway

without garnering the attention of half the damn city," Venom grumbled. "Cipher, how long until sunrise?"

"Four hours," he said absently, his focus trained on the communication equipment in front of him. "Hey, boss? I think I've secured a short window on the com."

Raze tapped his throat mic and moved into a quiet corner of the ship. "SRU Alpha Squad to *Valiant*?" A moment later, Raze nodded at Cipher and gave him a thumbs-up. "We read you loud and clear. Ready to receive orders."

"While the boss is talking to the mother ship," Venom said with a crooked smile, "let's discuss the contamination issue. We all saw the craters left by those pods. Some or all of these fuel rods may be leaking. Contain. Isolate. Neutralize. Understood?"

Amid the agreeing nods, Raze rejoined them. He had an odd look on his face that Venom couldn't place. "Shadow Force reinforcements arrived via darts one hour ago. The team will be here in two minutes. We'll be using native assets on this one." Raze squeezed his shoulder. "Uh, Ven, let's talk over here for a second."

Confused by his friend's strange behavior, Venom followed him to the opposite side of the cargo bay. "What's up?"

Raze hesitated. "Yeah—there's no easy way to say this and you're probably going to lose your shit regardless of how nicely I deliver the news so I'm just going to throw it out there." He paused and seemed to be bracing himself for a blowup. "In about sixty seconds, Torment is going to knock on that cargo door—and you're going to see Dizzy standing next to him."

Venom thought for sure he had misheard Raze. The eerie silence surrounding him told him that he hadn't. Every single SRU member in the cargo bay held perfectly still as they seemed to wait on bated breath for Venom's response.

"Shadow Force reinforcements are in view, Major Raze." The ship pilot's voice came across the speakers. "Lowering shield. Contact in ten, nine, eight…"

Seething with fury at the very thought of Dizzy being placed in such extreme danger, Venom crossed to the rear cargo entrance and punched the button. The cargo loading ramp that doubled as a door slowly lowered.

As in some kind of bad fucking dream, Dizzy appeared between Torment and Pierce. Even in the dark of night, her pale hair, whipping so wildly in the wind, was visible. She looked so out of place in her pretty dress. The second she spotted him, she raced up the ramp and right into his arms.

"What are you doing here, sugar?" He tried not to squeeze her too tightly because the grenades and flashbangs tucked into pockets lining the front of his vest might hurt her.

"It's a really long story and we don't have time, Venom." She gripped his gloved hand. "Short version? My biological dad is General Thorn. My mother was a Shadow Force asset. My dad took her place when she died. He's being blackmailed to move the fuel rods that are probably in the subway and my friend Hopper is going to help us find them."

Venom blinked a few times as he tried to take it all in. Her mother was a spy? General Thorn, one of the most highly respected members of the military, a member of the war council and a man expected to someday be president, was his father-in-law? Unable to think of anything smart to say, he simply replied, "I see."

"Yeah. I know. It's crazy, and we don't have time to hash it all out right now. We'll figure it out later."

Gripping her hand, he tugged her out of the way as the cargo door closed. Thinking of the superfast descent she had taken in the dart, he began to worry. "Dizzy, you weren't supposed to fly for weeks because of your ears. How do you feel?"

She rubbed his arm. "I'm fine. Risk had them put me in this weird pressurized box that the medics use to evacuate head-trauma victims. It wasn't the most comfortable experience but I survived it."

Venom didn't like risking her health. Thinking of the fuel rods waiting for them and the possibility of a leak, he turned his attention to the Shadow Force operatives with her. "What the hell are the two of you thinking? She has no business in a situation like this."

Pierce wouldn't meet his pissed-off glare but Torment simply shrugged. "We're running low on options, Venom. We have to stop the fuel rods from leaving this planet.

Saving Terror would be nice too."

Venom could only imagine what Torment and Pierce were feeling at the moment. Their brother-in-arms was missing and sure to face horrendous torture at the hands of the Splinters who had taken him.

Dizzy soothingly caressed his neck and drew his attention. "Venom, I'm just going to find Hopper and get her to draw some maps. That's it."

"It's never that simple." Venom gritted his teeth and tried to stem his rising anger. He didn't want Dizzy to think he was upset with her. She had no doubt been sweettalked into this by Torment or Pierce. Knowing those two they had likely used her love for him to manipulate her.

"I'll be with her the entire time, Venom," Pierce tried to reassure him but it didn't work. "She'll be safe."

"You'll have to excuse me if I don't believe you. You seem to be forgetting that I watched Naya get tagged in the gut three times and nearly bleed to death on that filthy warehouse floor."

The haunted flash of regret in Pierce's eyes said otherwise. "No, Venom, I haven't forgotten. If there was any other way—"

"There isn't," Torment interjected. "This is the best and safest option for the SRU team. If we don't send Dizzy out to find her friend and get a layout of these tunnels, your team goes in blind, Venom. We're talking miles and miles of dark, subterranean hell."

Venom's jaw worked back and forth as he reluctantly accepted that Dizzy's contact was the best way to get the intel they needed. Possessiveness overwhelmed him and he held her tighter. "I should go with her."

"No." Dizzy shot down his idea. "You're too big. You are, like, the epitome of a Harcos male. Anyone who sees us walking down the street together is going to be suspicious." She gestured to Pierce. "He's leaner and shorter. He'll fit in better."

He considered the spook. The man was a damn killing machine. "If anything happens to my mate—"

Pierce touched his chest. "My life for hers," he swore.

"Guys," Cipher cautiously entered the conversation, "we have a bigger problem than sending an untrained woman into the field. What the hell are we going to do about communication?" He pointed toward the sky. "That debris field is too thick. Most of it is burning up in the atmosphere but I'm finding it impossible to route communications through our satellites. We'll be virtually cut off from the *Valiant* and I have no idea how we're going to relay our signals."

"I don't know much about your technology," Dizzy said nervously, "but what about tapping into the pirate radio relays? Everyone has wireless equipment here. Most of it is cobbled together but they're reliable."

"Pirate radio?" Cipher brightened. "Yeah. Sure!"

"What happens when we're in the tunnels?" Raze asked.

"There are transceivers in the tunnels," Dizzy assured them. "The last time I went to one of Hopper's parties at the Subterranean—her tunnel hotspot—we listened to the Mouth's live show." She noticed their curious looks. "The Mouth from the South? She has a pirate radio show that comes on at night. It's extremely popular."

Cipher flicked his fingers. "Come give me a list of frequencies."

Nodding, Dizzy followed Cipher to his communication equipment. With his wife out of earshot, Venom put a finger in Torment's chest and hissed, "You crossed the line on this one."

"Probably," Torment agreed, "but she wanted to come. She wanted to help you and save her father."

Venom's anger eased some but the uneasy feeling continued to bubble in the pit of his stomach. "What's the deal with Jack Lane?"

"He's either being held captive or he's hiding." Torment lowered his voice so Dizzy wouldn't hear. "Or he's already dead."

Venom's eyes shut briefly. He hoped like hell that wasn't the case. "After she gets the maps and the info from this Hopper woman, I want her secured and back on this damn ship."

"Understood," Pierce replied with a nod.

With the communications issue squared away, Dizzy returned to his side. Feeling absolutely sick to his stomach, Venom walked her over to a corner and boxed her in with his bigger body. Her hands rested on his bare forearms as they peered intently at each other.

There was so much he wanted to tell her, so many pointers he thought she could use while out in the field, but he didn't want to overwhelm her with information she wouldn't retain under such stressful circumstances. Instead he touched his forehead to hers and said, "I love you so much, Dizzy."

"I love you too."

"Please be careful. Do exactly what Pierce says."

"I will."

He cupped her beautiful face and kissed her ever so gently. "When we get home…"

"Yes?" she asked breathlessly.

"I'm going to put you across my lap and wallop your backside for this stunt."

Her sweet mouth curved with happiness. Rising up on tiptoes, she kissed him lovingly. "Yes Master."

Before he could recover from hearing her claim him as her master, Dizzy slipped away from him and followed Pierce to the cargo door. She smiled back and waved as if she were simply headed out to the market rather than into the unknown danger that awaited her. Her bravery filled him with such pride.

"She'll be fine." Raze clapped him on his back. "You need to clear your head and get back in the game. She's got two of the deadliest men in the entire Harcos arsenal on either side of her. She's the safest of all of us."

"She better be," Venom murmured before turning back to the team. Inhaling a cleansing breath, he refocused on the mission that awaited him. Dizzy was in safe hands. Now he had to make sure he survived this mission to take her home.

AS SHE LED Pierce through the mucky, dark streets of Low Town, Dizzy's gaze jumped to the night sky. As the bits and pieces of the *Night Bird* burned up in the atmosphere, the brilliant streaks lit up the inky blackness like a meteor shower.

"It's almost beautiful, isn't it?" Pierce said, keeping close to her side. Before leaving the *Valiant*, he had changed out of his uniform into civilian clothing that looked as if it had been purchased from somewhere in The City. He blended in perfectly and easily played the role of boyfriend or husband to her.

"Almost," Dizzy agreed as they hurried along.

"How much farther?"

"Hopper likes this little all-night café where the arts-and-music crowd hangs. It's only a few more blocks."

"Good. We're running out of time."

"I know." She tried not to think about the mission that awaited Venom and the SRU team. The Splinters had already killed dozens of men trying to get hold of those rods. They weren't going to give them up without a fight.

"There," she said, pointing out the café with a lift of her chin.

"I'll let you do all the talking but I'm not letting you out of my sight. Venom will have my balls in a vise if anything happens to you."

She didn't doubt that in the least. Halting on the sidewalk, she studied Pierce with a critical eye. Unlike Venom who had tattoos snaking down toward his wrist and knuckles and up along his neck, Pierce seemed unmarked. It was probably something they did to fit in as spies. Even so, his haircut was too neat. She lifted the hood of his black jacket into place. "Cover your hair."

Hoping they would look like a couple out for a very late cup of coffee, Dizzy grasped his hand and tugged him along. It felt so very strange to interlace her fingers with another man but she tried to remember that she was putting on this charade to save *her* man.

When they entered the bustling, candlelit café, Dizzy ignored the odd sensation of Pierce pressed against her back. He wasn't trying to come on to her or be inappropriate. The cramped and packed space necessitated such close touching.

"What's with the candles?"

"The power grid has failed again," she explained. With a swift tug on his hand, Dizzy steered him toward the back corner where Hopper liked to hold court. She spotted Hopper's shockingly orange hair. "There she is."

Pierce lowered his face so he could whisper against her ear. "What's with the hair?"

"She's a misfit with a fondness for hair dye."

"She looks like she's about twelve. Are you sure she can help us?"

Dizzy rolled her eyes. "Yes. I'm sure. And she's not twelve. She's only a few years younger than me."

"If you say so," he grumbled.

Across the shadowed café, Dizzy met Hopper's gaze. It wasn't surprise that crossed Hopper's face but relief. Smoothly and without alerting anyone, Hopper left her corner spot and headed for the rear exit of the café. Dizzy and Pierce wound their way through the jostling crowd and finally made it to the back door.

When they stepped into the alley, Hopper was waiting for them. "I figured I would see you soon."

Pierce immediately stepped between them and pushed Dizzy back toward the wall of the café to protect her. "How did you know we were coming?"

"Uh, dude, I'm not freaking blind." Hopper pointed

toward the sky. "I can also hear." She fished a small radio from her pocket. "The Red Feather chain has been lit up tonight. Mouth swears you guys kicked her off her usual frequency. She's using a backup to give out information."

"Great," Pierce growled. "That's all we need."

Dizzy squeezed out from behind Pierce. "Look, Hopper, we don't have a lot of time. I need your help. My dad is missing—"

"He's not missing. He's a prisoner." Hopper flipped up the hood of her purple hoodie to cover her hair. "We need to move. The Splinter rats are everywhere tonight. I don't need that kind of trouble."

"Neither do we." Pierce gave Dizzy a push forward and followed close behind as they navigated the intersecting alleys of Low Town. Hopper led them to one of the more remote access spots for the abandoned subway tunnels. She pushed aside a heavy slab of wood to reveal a small manhole.

"It's an abandoned water-testing checkpoint," Hopper explained. Sizing up Pierce, she added, "Unless you want to get stuck, you'd better suck it in."

"Ha-ha," Pierce replied dryly.

Dizzy smiled as she followed Hopper through the small access panel and into the underground room. It smelled so musty and wet. She didn't know how anyone could stand to live in these dank, dark sections of the tunnels.

Hopper snapped on a couple of battery-operated lanterns to illuminate the space, sat on an overturned bucket and gestured to another one for Dizzy. "Not far from here, there's a subway tunnel section that runs parallel to the Low Town sewers. The section has been blocked off for a few months. I had heard from some of the moles—"

"Moles?" Pierce interrupted.

"Old-timers who have lived in these tunnels for decades," she clarified. "Most of them can't even see above ground anymore. They've all got wet lung." She waved her hand. "Anyway. The moles were saying that certain sections of their tunnels were caved in and blocked. I was concerned about instability because there are a lot of kids coming down here for refuge at night, especially whenever the snatcher rumors start."

"Snatchers?" Pierce sounded curious.

"Sex slavers," Dizzy explained. "They snatch street kids because they won't be missed. There have been rumors about the sex trade off the colonies."

Hopper huffed with disgust. "Apparently it's a growing business for the Splinters."

Dizzy perched on the edge of the bucket. "What did you find when you went looking for the blocked tunnels?"

"What do you think?" Hopper shook her head. "The Splinters and Sixers were using that section as an underground warehouse. Ever since the food riots and that bust-up at the battery factory, they've been looking for alternative places to conduct their business, especially now that the government is doing public crackdowns for publicity. There are crates stacked all over the place down there."

"Weapons? Food?"

She nodded in response to Pierce's question. "I think they may be experimenting too."

"Experimenting?" Dizzy asked, aghast. "With what?"

Hopper pushed down her hood and combed her fingers through her brightly hued hair. "About a month ago, I was walking the tunnels and I found a pile of bodies in an old storage compartment. The smell…" Her eyes closed and she looked sick. "I don't know what they did to them but they weren't killed with guns or knives."

Pierce crouched down between them. "Gas?"

She shrugged. "Maybe? I wouldn't know what that kind of death looks like. All I know is that these people were packed into that room and it seemed like they'd all dropped dead on top of one another." Hopper shrugged. "After that, I put that area on quarantine. I told everyone to stay away from that section and they have."

"But?" Dizzy sensed Hopper was about to drop something important.

"Right after you were Grabbed, I saw your dad hanging around one of the tunnel junctions. I thought that was weird because, I mean, I never see him down here. He's always kept his business up top. Then—a few days ago—Ella comes to see me, right? And she tells me that she ran into your dad and he looked panicked. She thought this loan shark story was bogus."

"It was," Dizzy assured her. "There's so much more to it."

"I figured." Hopper held out her hand to Pierce. "You want me to start drawing or what?"

"Do you know how to use a tablet?" Pierce retrieved one from an interior pocket of his jacket.

"Yes."

Pierce tapped at the screen before handing it to her. "It doesn't have to be precise but I need details. I need to know approximate dimensions, ingress and egress routes, blind spots—"

"Yeah. I got it." Hopper started to draw. "So—anyway—two nights ago, I'm trying to help Molly Mack hunt down one of her wayward twins and what do I see? Your dad with two Splinter dickheads. He was cuffed and gagged and they were pushing him toward that back section. I knew right then that this thing—whatever the hell it is—was so much bigger than I had ever imagined."

Dizzy's stomach churned violently. Was her dad still alive? Had the Splinters gotten what they wanted from him and killed him already? She couldn't stand the thought of the nasty things she had said to him being the last words ever spoken between them.

After twenty minutes of sketching and scribbling, Hopper handed over the tablet. Pierce tapped the mic hidden in his watch and lifted it to his mouth. "Cherry 1 to SRU Alpha. Cherry 1 to SRU Alpha."

Dizzy could only hear Pierce's side of the conversation but it sounded as though it was going well as he transferred the schematics. She prayed Hopper's intel would keep Venom safe and help them locate her father, the fuel rods and Terror. Hopper tapped Dizzy's knee. "So what's it like up there?"

"Different," she said.

"Different good or different bad?"

"Different good."

"What's the ship like? Huge?"

"It's incredibly huge. Everything is so clean and neat. There's ample food, good water and doctors. It's so easy to forget that I'm floating in space."

"And the men?" Hopper raised an eyebrow and tilted her head in Pierce's direction.

"They're…interesting."

"I bet." Hopper looked hopeful. "But you're happy? I mean, your guy treats you well?"

"I'm very happy. My guy treats me very, very well."

"That's good. I worried that you might—"

An overhead sound interrupted their discussion. Immediately Hopper was on her feet. She snatched the lanterns from the shelf, switched off all but one and pressed a finger to her mouth, indicating silence. Pierce gently pushed Dizzy out of the way as men's voices grew louder above them. Hopper pointed down the dimly lit horizontal shaft and the Shadow Force operative nodded.

Hot on Hopper's heels, Dizzy rushed after her friend. The manhole cover made a scraping sound as it was moved. Pierce was right behind them and whispering into his radio mic. Her heart was pounding so hard Dizzy couldn't make out any of the words he hissed. She thought he might have said Torment's name but all she could hear clearly was the *whoosh* of blood thundering against her eardrums.

Suddenly the darkened tunnel lit up as electricity was restored to the section they were running down. A man behind them shouted, "There! Up ahead! We've got them!"

Pierce cursed before ordering, "Move it, ladies."

"There's a ground-access shaft not far ahead."

"Faster!"

Dizzy kicked it into high gear, racing after Hopper. She made the mistake of glancing back and saw a group of heavily armed men chasing them. They had weapons that were older, projectile-firing models unlike the highly advanced energy burst weaponry of the Harcos. Pierce had pistols in the holsters under his jacket but she doubted one man could protect them against the seven she counted.

A second later, Pierce proved her doubts were misplaced. With all the ease and skill of a covert operative, he spun around and fired upon the group. Looking back, she watched two men drop like rocks. Another one fell to his knees and clutched his bleeding gut.

Though he had narrowed the odds considerably in their favor, there were still four armed-to-the-teeth men in hot pursuit. Bullets fired from behind them snapped against the concrete walls. She heard a sharp gasp and glanced back to see that a pair of ricochets had clipped Pierce. Bloody spots blossomed on his pant leg and his gray shirt. Shockingly the wounds didn't seem to slow him down.

Pierce traded shots with the crew chasing them and dropped another two men. As they rounded a corner, Hopper snatched Dizzy's hand and dragged her into a cutout section of the wall. Pierce used his body to box them into the space. While Pierce ripped a knife from his waist sheath, she held her breath in anticipation of the two men who would soon appear.

Showing his deadly skills, Pierce stabbed the first man

to come around the corner right in the neck and slashed backward. With his other hand, he lifted his weapon and fired at the dying man's stunned companion. The bright burst popped him in the temple and put him down instantly.

Aghast and horrified by the violence, Dizzy could hardly breathe. Shocked into silence, she watched Pierce rifle through the pockets of the two men in search of useful intelligence. He slipped a few things into his own pockets before gesturing ahead. "Get us out of here, Hopper."

She dragged her wide-eyed gaze from the bloody carnage and nodded. "Yeah. Um...okay. This way."

Swallowing hard, Dizzy touched his arm. "Pierce, you're bleeding. We need to do something about your wounds."

He shook his head. "They'll keep. These seven probably weren't alone. We've got to get out of these tunnels." He touched his bleeding side. "A couple of grazes will be the least of my worries if I don't get you back to Venom and General Thorn in one piece."

"Hey! Come on!" Hopper sounded as though she wanted to get the hell out of there and Dizzy didn't blame her. This was way more than she had bargained for when she had offered to help.

They raced along the tunnels for another ten minutes or so before finally reaching an access shaft. The busted-out lights overhead plunged them into darkness but Hopper still had the battery-operated lantern with her. It barely illuminated the dark space. Dizzy tried not to think about what sorts of creepy, crawly things might be hiding around the ladder in the grungy tube.

Hopper climbed out on the surface first and tugged Dizzy up after her. Pierce had just cleared his head when all hell broke loose.

A man rushed from the shadows and snatched Hopper. Another one grabbed Dizzy's arms and dragged her clear of the shaft. She screamed as a third man kicked Pierce in the back of the head, instantly knocking him unconscious.

"Pierce!" There was nothing to catch his slack body and he dropped down the ladder shaft, knocking into the rungs before hitting the concrete floor with a sickening thud. Was the fall survivable? She prayed so.

A black hood covered her head and someone taped her wrists together. From the spitting-mad sounds coming from Hopper, she figured her friend had just endured the same thing. A cruel hand gripped the back of her neck and propelled her forward.

Dizzy had no choice but to walk. If she didn't, these men wouldn't hesitate to put a bullet between her eyes or Hopper's. She figured they had a reason for keeping them both alive. Sooner or later Venom would find her—and she intended to be alive when that happened.

Chapter Twenty-Four

JAW TENSE, VENOM slowly crept along the pitch-black tunnels. The team followed slow-moving robotic balls that mapped the tunnels in real time and relayed the information to their headsets and combat glasses.

The hand-drawn maps and information Dizzy's friend had provided had proven invaluable so far. Though the advantage remained with the Splinter crew that had taken over this tunnel section, the SRU team outmatched them when it came to training and firepower.

"I'm picking up a G42 trail." Cipher's voice dinged Venom's ear via the bud firmly planted there.

"Do we have a leak?" Raze continued moving forward despite the danger.

"Yes. The levels are extremely low and within the safety limits but let's try not to stick around any longer than necessary."

"Copy that," Raze muttered.

"At least we know we're in the right place," Fierce hissed.

"We should expect a heavily armed presence," Venom added. "Let's keep it tight. Weapons hot."

Following the path they had memorized, they took two left turns and a right. At the end of the hall, they would take one more left to reach the last door that allowed for easy access to the Splinter-controlled section.

"Skyhawk 97 to SRU Alpha."

"SRU Alpha," Raze answered the call from the pilots of the stealth ship that had brought them to the surface and served as the command center for the mission.

"The debris field has cleared substantially. Satellite coms are back in action. Support teams are in place. Hazardous material crew is on standby to retrieve rods when secured."

"Copy."

When they reached the end of the hall, they hugged the wall so Cipher could perform recon on the door down to the left. He scanned with his penetrating and heatseeking radar to create a better picture of what they faced.

Venom eyed the real-time feed on his glasses. Eleven men, most of them sitting around in chairs, seemed to be guarding the ceiling-high stack of fuel rods. The cases containing the rods showed up white-hot on Cipher's scan.

In another corner, a huddled body lit up the scan. Judging by the size, it was a man but his arms looked forced behind his back and his legs looked tightly bound.

"Looks like we have a prisoner," Cipher said. "He's breathing but not moving."

"Is it Terror?" Hope filled Raze's voice.

"I can't tell."

"It doesn't matter," Venom interjected. As the tactical operations man, it was his decision to make. "Scenario one remains in play. Threat, when we breach, you cover the prisoner. Cipher, stick with the fuel rods. Fierce, Raze, you're with me. Threat, get that door ready to blow."

"On it," Threat said and hurried forward with his bag of explosive tricks.

While Threat applied discs for controlled mini-bursts to the door's frame, Venom ran the various scenarios in his head. These dynamic situations could quickly spiral out of control. They trained for every possibility, running the same exercises twenty different ways. Whatever happened once that door was blown, Venom knew that the team would respond appropriately and efficiently.

"Charges primed," Threat said as he hurried back to rejoin the team against the wall. "Execute in five, four—"

"Hold! Raze, damn it! Hold!" Torment's breathless voice suddenly echoed in their ears.

"Holding!" Raze hissed. "SRU Alpha to Cherry 2, you better have a damn good reason for stopping us."

"Pierce is down." Torment sounded as if he were running. "Bad guys have Dizzy and the friend. I'm on foot pursuit but they're headed your way. We're underground. I'm closing on your position."

Venom's heart stammered. He leaned against the wall for support as Torment's words registered in the most awful way. They had Dizzy. His sweet, precious, beautiful Dizzy.

"Ven?" Raze addressed him roughly. "Shake it off. She's no different than any other hostage."

But she was. She meant the world to him.

Gulping down the fear and panic clogging his throat, Venom got a handle on his emotions. He cleared his mind and focused on the task at hand. The only way Dizzy was getting out of that room alive was if the team did everything right. He refused to be the weak link that put her life at risk.

"I'm good, boss."

"They're entering a door," Torment apprised them of the movements of Dizzy and her captors.

"They're here," Cipher whispered. The scanning device he'd attached to the wall allowed them to see the door opening and a stream of new people entering the room. The two smaller heat signatures trapped between three men were obviously Dizzy and her friend Hopper.

Closing his eyes, Venom pushed all thoughts of Dizzy as his wife out of his mind. She was a hostage. She was like the dozens of nameless, faceless hostages he had rescued in his career with the SRU. This was a mission like any other mission.

"Threat," he said calmly. "Prepare to execute to breach."

"Execute in five, four, three..."

For Venom, the next sixty seconds blew by as if in hyperspeed. The controlled explosions ripped a hole in the hall and caused the door to fall forward. Before the dust and smoke had even cleared, Raze fired two concussive grenades into the room. Venom and Fierce were through the door first but Raze, Cipher and Threat were hot on their heels.

"On the ground!"

"Get down!"

"Hands in the air!"

"Put down your weapons!"

"On the ground!"

Disoriented by the explosion and concussive grenades, six of the men dropped to their bellies and raised their hands high overhead. Only four were dumb enough to lift their weapons and take aim at the team. Venom, Fierce and Raze neutralized them with precision shots.

One man, the dumbest of them all, grabbed Dizzy. The sight of her hooded head and dirty, ripped dress infuriated Venom. The bastard using her as a shield whipped a hunting knife from a sheath at his waist and started to lift it toward Dizzy's throat. Venom reacted on instinct, squeezing his trigger and popping off a perfectly placed burst that ended the threat.

Splattered with blood, Dizzy fell forward onto her knees and flattened onto her belly before covering her hooded head with her bound arms. Though the urge to rush to her aid was strong, he muscled it down and finished securing the men who had surrendered first. Being shot in the back wasn't high on his list of priorities.

Once the scene was safe, he raced to Dizzy and crouched down in front of her. She flinched when he gently grasped her upper arms and hauled her into a kneeling position. Grimacing at the blood spray on her shoulder and arm, he was strangely glad for the hood that had protected her face and hair. It would be easier for her to deal with the aftermath of being taken hostage without the gore.

Carefully he slit the tape binding her wrists and dragged the hood from her head. She had her eyes squeezed shut as if expecting to be hit. Tossing aside the hood, he placed his gloved hand against her face. "Sugar, look at me."

At the sound of his voice, her eyelids fluttered open. Dazed and disoriented from the concussive blast, she blinked and inhaled shaky breaths. Tears soaked her long lashes and made them clump together. With a ragged sob, she flung her arms around his neck and squeezed him tight. "Venom!"

"Honey, you're all right. I've got you."

"Please don't let go."

"I won't, sugar. Not yet." He rubbed her back and kissed the top of her head. "You're okay. I've got you."

Jerking back, she glanced around frantically. "Hopper!"

"I'm okay." The young woman in question sat against a wall while Fierce knelt next to her and cut the tape binding her wrists. "My ears are ringing like crazy."

"It will fade. We'll have the medics check you, just in case." Venom rubbed Dizzy's earlobes between his fingers. "How are your ears, baby?"

"Ringing." She winced. "I've got a headache too."

"As soon as we get back to *Valiant* I'll have Risk check you over." He was very concerned about the effect of the flash-bangs on her delicate ears, especially after having surgery so recently.

"Oh Venom, what about Pierce?" She looked absolutely stricken. "He fell so hard. I don't how he could have survived hitting the concrete that hard."

"He's alive." Torment stepped into the room. His

mouth was fixed in a grim line as he surveyed the scene. "They're about to evacuate him on a dart. One of the support teams—the SRU beta squad—got to him a few minutes after I made chase to catch you two."

Though Venom had a million questions that needed answers, this absolutely was not the time to ask them. "We need to move these prisoners and get Dizzy and her friend out of here immediately. One of these cases is leaking and the women aren't immunized."

"Go." Torment stepped aside to clear the way. "I've already given the hazardous materials team the green light."

Venom scooped up Dizzy and carried her out of the room. He ran her down the hall to a safe distance and gently deposited her on the ground. Fierce carried Hopper to the same spot. Venom unzipped one of his pockets and retrieved one of the compactly folded and super-thin warming sheets used for treating shock.

"You and your pockets," Dizzy said with a laugh. Her teeth chattered as adrenaline saturated her bloodstream and caused havoc inside her body.

Venom snapped open the thin foil-like sheet and wrapped it around shoulders. He tucked it under her bottom and around her legs. "Stay here. I'll be back as soon as possible."

"I don't think I could walk even if I wanted to," she said choppily, her teeth continuing to knock.

Pressing a loving kiss to her forehead, Venom forced himself to leave her behind. Back in the room, he found Cipher and Threat assessing and treating the prisoner they had uncovered. His hopes that it might be Terror were dashed. Moving closer for a better look, he nearly tripped over his boots. "Shit. That's Dizzy's father."

Cipher glanced up at him. "You're sure?"

Venom nodded and studied the bruised face of his father-in-law. "I saw his picture the morning Torment and Pierce dragged her in for questioning. That's Jack Lane."

"We're taking him into custody." Torment gave the order without his usual edge of coldness. "We need his intel and he needs our protection."

"Yes, he does," Venom murmured. There would be no going back for Jack. Whatever had happened here had forever changed the course of his life. Venom could only hope it was for the better.

"The hazardous materials crew is here." Raze stepped away from the prisoners who lined the wall. "They're bringing in a prisoner transport ship. Let's get these guys loaded and get the hell out of here before half The City comes down on us."

Venom didn't think he'd ever heard an order he wanted to follow more. He wanted to get Dizzy safely back on the *Valiant* and put this entire mess behind them.

Chapter Twenty-Five

Dizzy couldn't believe she was back in the hospital wing of the *Valiant* so soon. The minutes following her rescue were still such a blur. More soldiers and medics had swarmed the tunnel. After the line of prisoners had been marched down the hall, two medics carted her father out on a stretcher. She had been shocked by the sight of his battered face but he was breathing and alive.

Despite her protests, Venom had swept her up into his arms and carried her out to the waiting dart. He had reluctantly left her in the care of the medics but not until he'd kissed her so long and hard the medics thought her racing heart was a medical issue.

Somewhere in the ensuing chaos of their rescue, Hopper had sneaked away unnoticed. Dizzy suspected she wanted nothing to do with the Shadow Force interrogators or the Splinters who were probably watching the place. She worried about Hopper but trusted her friend knew what she was doing. Hopper had been on her own since childhood and clearly knew how to survive in a rough and dangerous world.

After being poked and prodded and tested for exposure to the fuel rods, Dizzy had been given a pair of papery-thin hospital pajamas and small white socks to wear. With her legs curled underneath her, she sat in one of the waiting-room chairs and fidgeted anxiously. Risk had promised to deliver news of her dad as soon as possible.

Her emotions vacillated from extreme relief that he was safe here with her and absolute dread at the prospect of dredging up the ancient history that concerned her mother. The idea of hurting him by forcing the discussion made her sick to her stomach.

"Sugar?" Venom stepped out of the elevator and rushed to her side. Sliding into the chair next to her, he scooped her right up and deposited her on his lap. She didn't even try to stop him from kissing her in such a public place. After the dangerous night they had both survived, she would never again turn down the chance to lock lips with the man she loved.

As she gazed into his gorgeous blue eyes, Dizzy stroked her fingertips along the back of his shaved head. "How was the debriefing?"

"Fine." He combed his fingers through her damp hair. "You showered?"

She nodded. "Risk said it would help me feel better."

"Was he right?"

"Yes."

"How's your head?"

"It's okay. He gave me a mild painkiller to help with the discomfort." She shot him an annoyed look. "You guys are *really* loud when you bust in doors."

"It was the concussive grenades or tear gas," he explained. "We went with the least dangerous option."

"And the noisiest."

He smiled. "And the noisiest."

Her thoughts turned more serious. "Did they find Terror?"

Venom's eyes darkened with sadness. "No. The trail is cold. We hope that one of the double agents the Shadow Force has undercover will reveal him to us but it's a long shot."

Dizzy hadn't spent much time at all with Terror but she sensed he was an incredibly complex, complicated yet well-liked man. His loss would be felt by so many of the men Venom called friends.

"Have you heard anything about Pierce? Risk told me they took him to a ship called the *Mercy*."

"He's in good hands there. The trauma surgeons know their stuff." Venom traced the neckline of the loose-fitting shirt. "I saw Torment on the way up here. He said Pierce is expected to make a full recovery. He broke both legs and an arm and had a major concussion. Somehow the lucky bastard managed not to crack and scramble his egg."

She ignored Venom's rather crass way of putting it. "I can't believe that. There's no way he didn't fracture his skull when he hit the ground. I watched some guy kick him in the back of the head!"

"He must have gotten his arm caught up in the ladder when he fell. It probably slowed his speed and tilted him in a strange enough angle that he hit feet first."

"I guess," she said skeptically. "I won't believe it until I see him." She shook her head. "He took two bullets protecting me too."

"So I heard," Venom said, his voice unnaturally tight. Cupping her face, he vowed, "You are *never* leaving this ship without me again. Is that understood?"

"Yes…Master," she added with a teasing grin.

"If you knew what hearing that name does to me…" he said with a low growl.

Wiggling her bottom, she blushed at the sensation of his stiff erection jutting against her. "I can tell what it does to you."

He chuckled softly and kissed her neck. "I can't wait to get you home."

Dizzy stifled a yawn as she snuggled up to her husband. "I may need a nap first."

"We'll see." He caressed her arm and pressed a tender kiss to her forehead. "Is there any word on your father?"

"Risk said he's extremely dehydrated and has a broken cheek and nose but he's in good condition otherwise. When he comes around they're supposed to tell me."

"I hope that's soon. I know how badly you want to speak with him. When he's discharged from the hospital, we'll invite him to stay in one of our extra rooms until he gets settled elsewhere."

Surprised at Venom's incredibly gracious offer, she lifted her head. "Are you sure?"

He frowned down at her. "Of course I'm sure. We're family."

"Are we?" Dizzy suddenly remembered what Vicious and Thorn had said to her in the war room. "General Vicious mentioned that because I'm actually half-Harcos I wasn't ever eligible to be Grabbed. Apparently that means

I'm legally Thorn's and not yours."

"Like fucking hell," he snarled. His brawny arms tightened around her. "I'll take Thorn to the ancestral ring before I allow him to take you from me."

"The ancestral what?"

"It's a fighting pit where Harcos males settle blood feuds."

Dizzy studied Venom's face. From the tight lines around his mouth to his flaring nostrils, it was clear that he was enraged by the idea of losing her. She kissed his cheek to soothe his temper. "Even if some stupid rule says that we aren't mates under your law, I would still choose you again."

Venom framed her chin between his forefinger and thumb. "Again?"

"I could have run away from you out in the woods but I didn't." She played with one of the buttons on his shirt. "There was just something about you that drew me closer. I couldn't walk away from you then—and I sure as hell can't do it now."

"You won't have to walk away from him."

Startled by the unexpected sound of General Thorn's voice, Dizzy nearly fell off Venom's lap. Her mate hesitated before shifting her off his lap so he could stand and salute his superior officer.

"No." Thorn waved his hand. "At ease. Not today, Captain."

"As you wish, sir." Venom remained uncommonly tense even after he sat down and dragged her back down onto his lap.

Thorn took a seat catty-corner to them. He rested his hands on his knees and stared at them for several unnervingly long seconds. "I don't want the two of you worrying about the rules and regulations of the Grabs. I've already started the paperwork required to allow Venom to be your mate."

"What sort of paperwork?" she asked.

"It's basically a betrothal contract," Thorn explained. "It's not that different from the Grab contract you signed after Venom collared you."

"May I stay on the *Valiant* with Venom?" She worried they would force her to leave until the official paperwork was completed.

"Yes. Nothing about your current living situation with Venom will change. It's simply legal ends that need to be neatly tied so there are no questions about your status or those of any children you may have. Later, when the dust from today has settled, we'll sit down and discussion your stipend."

"My *what*?" Dizzy gawked at her biological father.

"Your stipend," Thorn said slowly. "It's your monthly allowance."

Aghast at the idea of taking money from him, she hurriedly shot down that notion.

"I don't need or want a stipend from you."

Thorn frowned. "Have I offended you?"

"No, you haven't offended me." Dizzy suspected she might have just inadvertently offended him. "I don't understand the point. I'm fully capable of supporting myself. Now that I'm married—mated," she corrected,

"I'm well provided for by Venom.

There's no need for you to give me a stipend."

Thorn shook his head. "It's not about need, Dizzy. It's tradition."

She glanced at Venom for confirmation. He nodded stiffly. "It's customary for Harcos fathers to gift their daughters with dowries or stipends."

Her eyebrows arched. Sharing a secret joke with him, she pinched his arm. "Then we had better start saving our pennies since you jinxed us into having a dozen daughters."

The tension fled Venom's face as he seemed to remember their first real conversation and dinner together. His hopeful grin made her belly wildly quiver. "Yes, we probably should."

When Dizzy glanced back at Thorn, she caught him staring at them with amusement and an odd sheen to his eyes. Clearing his throat, he stood up and reached out to give her shoulder a squeeze. "I'll be in the area for the next week or so. I'd like to see you again. Perhaps we might have dinner?"

She wasn't sure what sort of relationship might develop between her and her biological father but Dizzy decided she had to give it a good try. "I'd like that."

"Wonderful." His hand fell from her shoulder. "I hope Jack has a swift recovery. I'll be sure to give him a wide berth while we're inhabiting similar spaces." He nodded in Venom's direction. "Captain."

"General." Venom bid his superior farewell and waited until Thorn had disappeared in an elevator to let loose a pent-up breath. "That went better than I had anticipated."

Dizzy considered Venom's predicament. "I guess it's kind of weird to have someone like General Thorn as a father-in-law."

"Weird is one way of describing it." Then with a snort, Venom added, "I have no idea how I'll handle *two* fathers-in-law."

"I've seen you handle terrorists, Venom. I think you can handle two overprotective dads."

"I hope so," he murmured.

She nuzzled their noses together. "I have faith in you."

"Dizzy?" Risk gently interjected from the edge of the waiting room. "Your dad is awake. He's asking for you."

She slipped off Venom's lap, grabbed his huge paw and tugged him into a standing position. "Come on. It's time you met my dad."

"Is this when I'm supposed to ask for a blessing?"

She laughed. "Venom, I think it's a little late for that considering I've been wearing your collar for weeks."

He brushed his fingers along her bare neck. "That reminds me. We need to get a new collar designed for you with a better lining."

"Actually," she gave him another tug so they could follow Risk, "I don't think I want a new collar."

"Is that so?" Venom's voice held a playful warning. "And how do you intend to let everyone know that you belong to me when we're out in public?"

She decided not to divulge her idea just yet. "You'll see soon enough."

Smiling back at him, she winked and gave him another hard tug to drag him into her dad's hospital room. She gripped his hand and pulled him toward the hospital bed where her father was sitting up and sipping water. "Hey, Dad."

"Hey, sweetheart." He had a number of tubes running from his arms to the medication boxes attached to the wall above the bed. His bruised face seemed even more purple and splotchy under the bright lighting but he grinned at the sight of her and held out his hand. "I look a lot worse than I feel."

She squeezed his fingers. "I'm glad you're okay. You really scared me."

"*You* scared *me*." He shook his head slowly. "Dizzy, why did you come after me? I sent you here so you would be safe."

"But the envelope—"

"I never meant for *you* to come riding to my rescue. I assumed one of your mom's old contacts would intercept the letter and get the message. Never you!"

She eased onto the bed and searched for the right words. "Dad, why didn't you tell me the truth? Why did you let me say all those awful things to you when we fought about Fat Pete and my lottery number?"

Regret flashed across his face. "I didn't know who to trust. I worried that telling you too much would put you in even more danger. Someone down there knew that you were Thorn's daughter. They were threatening to kidnap and ransom you. I tried so hard to get him to speak to me but he blew me off. At that point I knew I couldn't trust him to pay the ransom if you were taken. So I sold your number and bought protection to follow you around until you had been safely Grabbed."

She thought back to the weird men who had been following her around that last day in The City. "I knew I was being tailed! I thought it was Fat Pete's guys keeping tabs on me so they could snatch me up."

"No, they worked for me."

"Dad, what really happened down there?"

He swallowed hard. "I can't tell you everything. I'm sure that the spooks will take me in soon enough for all that—but I can say this. Fat Pete hired me to ship some cargo. I didn't ask what it was until I was given a set of very worrisome instructions. That's when I realized that the men who had hired Fat Pete—the Splinters—were planning to do something very dangerous."

Her dad sipped his water. "I tried to scuttle the transport arrangements but photos of your mother and Thorn—before me and before you—showed up on my doorstep one morning. The next morning, there were pictures of you and pictures of Thorn. I knew then that someone had figured it out."

"Who?" Dizzy racked her brain. "Who could have possibly known about mom and Thorn? That was years ago."

"I assume they've told you about your mother, about what she was."

"Yes. Did you know?"

He nodded. "Not at first. I figured it out when you were about four. I loved her and I trusted that she was trying to do something good and noble so I made sure she was protected and I made sure she had access to the right people." He shrugged. "There's very little you can't accomplish with the right amount of money."

"And me?" Dizzy hated to ask. "Did you know I wasn't yours?"

"I used to travel Cross Colony Air all the time. Your mother was my favorite stewardess. I had the biggest crush on her and when I found her crying one night in a hotel lobby, I knew that I would do anything for her. She told me she was pregnant but I didn't care. I swore to her that I would take care of her and the baby."

Dizzy's eyes closed as her father stroked her cheek. He smiled at her as he said, "The moment the midwife placed you in my arms I fell in love with you. You were my daughter in all the ways that mattered."

With a rough exhale, he added, "I sold your number so you would be safe up here but within a few days of you being Grabbed, I learned that they had someone watching you up here."

"What?" Venom's harshly spoken word drew her father's attention.

Her dad nodded. "Photos of Dizzy on the ship ended up on my kitchen table. I understood the threat. If I didn't come through with the transport arrangements for those fuel rods, they were going to kill her here."

"Not if I kill them first," Venom growled.

Her dad took a few seconds to size up her mate. "So—what do they call you?"

"Venom, sir." He stepped closer to the bed. "It's a

pleasure to finally meet you."

Her father made a disbelieving noise. "What do you do?"

"I'm the tactician expert and lead sniper for the alpha squad of the Special Response Unit."

"I see." He scrutinized Venom some more. "You're an officer?"

"I hold the rank of captain in the land corps, sir."

"Well, I guess that's something. Better an officer than the alternative, I suppose." Her father narrowed his eyes. "You've seen a lot of battles?"

"I have, sir."

"You can drop the sir, Captain. God knows I'm not the type of man who deserves it."

"You are the father of my mate, sir. That's enough for me."

Her dad didn't reply to that. Instead he tapped her hand. "Do you like him? He's bigger and gruffer than the men you normally date."

She smiled. "I do like him."

"Just like?" He had always been able to read her so clearly.

"Maybe a little more than like," she said coyly.

Her father chuckled and touched her neck. "He doesn't make you wear a collar?"

Deciding not to delve into the specifics of their relationship, she shook her head. "He doesn't."

Her dad's estimation of Venom seemed to increase. "Good. I'm happy to hear that." He gulped and guilt made him wince. "I've been consumed with worry about you. I kept imagining the very worst about the type of man who might have Grabbed you."

She clasped his hand between hers. "You can stop worrying, Dad. Venom loves me. He treats me with respect and kindness. We're very happy."

"Sweetheart, even when you're fifty years old and I'm pushing ninety, I'll still worry about you. You're my daughter and I love you."

Dizzy experienced the sweetest sense of relief at the realization that he didn't care one iota about the lack of blood relation between them. Someday when he was fully recovered and she was feeling braver, she would ask him to tell her everything. Today? She was perfectly content to leave things as they were.

"I love you, Dad."

"I know you do, kiddo." He gave her hand a little pat. "You need to get some rest." He glanced at Venom. "Your husband looks like he's dead on his feet. Come see me later, okay?"

"We will." She slid to her feet and watched Venom shake her dad's hand. She didn't think Venom had won him over just yet but he would eventually. After all, Venom had won her heart, hadn't he?

Alone in an elevator with Venom, she leaned against his strong frame for support. She couldn't remember the last time she had been so tired. He wrapped his arms around her and pulled her back against his body. His lips skimmed her temple. "We're almost home."

When they finally entered their quarters, Dizzy started stripping on the way to the bedroom. Venom didn't chide her messiness as he followed her, picking up the pieces of clothing she scattered in her wake. Glancing back at him she expected to see a scowl darkening his handsome face. If anything he looked perfectly happy to tidy up her mess.

As she dragged back the covers and crawled onto the bed, Dizzy wondered if he was simply feeling the same relief she did. They were alive. They were together. They were in love. It was really that easy and that simple.

Rolling onto her side, she watched Venom remove his uniform and boots. She let her adoring gaze roam every inch of his powerful and sculpted frame. Her stare lingered on the bare left side of his body, the side he would soon mark for her.

What would he think about her plan to place a permanent reminder of his ownership on her body instead of a collar? Would he be thrilled in the same way she was about seeing her mark on him?

Standing there naked and sporting a hard-on to rival any other, Venom raked her naked curves with a searing gaze. He crouched down and picked up his belt. Seeing the looped leather in his hand gave her a moment's pause. He'd never once harmed her and the look of utter desire and need on his face told her he wasn't about to start now.

Putting a knee on the bed, Venom stroked his hand down her belly. "I need you, Dizzy." The husky roughness in his voice made her heart race. "Unless you're too tired…"

"I'm never too tired for you." His body heat and obvious desire invigorated Dizzy. She would probably pass out cold after he made love to her but she intended to enjoy every second of him until exhaustion finally took her.

Venom prowled toward her and pinned her to the mattress by placing his knees on either side of her thighs. He gripped her wrists in one hand and pulled them high over her head. "I hope you don't mind the belt."

A wicked frisson sizzled through her belly. "I don't mind."

He smiled at her shaky voice. "No, I'm sure you don't."

With all the ease and skill of a master at restraint, Venom shackled her wrists to the headboard. The leather strap bit into her wrists a little but she relished the slight discomfort. The hint of pain amplified the pleasurable sensation of Venom's hands gliding over her bare breasts.

Dipping his head, he circled the pink buds with his tongue before suckling her. Dizzy's hips lifted off the bed as he pinched her nipples and soothed the little hurts with his mouth. By the time he was done tormenting her so sensually, her breasts ached and felt so heavy.

Down, down, down he went, licking and nibbling her abdomen and hips before forcing her thighs wide open to taste her. By the time his tongue flicked her clitoris, she was already dripping wet for him. Savoring her like a delectable dessert, Venom took his time between her thighs.

He fluttered his tongue over her pink kernel until she couldn't think straight. He kept her there—right there on the edge—but refused to give her the extra bit of stimulation and speed she needed to find release. Twisting her hips and thrusting her pussy against his mouth, Dizzy begged him to give her what she wanted. "Please, Venom. *Please.*"

"Patience," he murmured before dotting kisses along her inner thighs and along the sloping plane of her belly. He crashed their mouths together, teasing her with the musky and erotic scent of her own arousal, and moved into position.

With one swift, hard thrust, he sheathed his huge cock. Dizzy gasped against his mouth and rocked up on her shoulders to meet his strong, deep thrusts. He pounded her slick passage with nearly feral intensity. She tugged at the belt lashing her to the headboard and encouraged him by wrapping her legs around his waist. The leather cut into her skin and would no doubt leave marks but she didn't care.

There was nothing easy or relaxed about their coupling now. Venom took her with the pent-up passion of a man who had nearly lost his wife to crazed terrorists. He seemed intent on reminding her they were both alive to enjoy such fleshly delights.

Cupping her face with one hand, Venom angled his body and tapped the fingers of his other hand against her pulsing clitoris. He rubbed small circles around the throbbing nub while staring into her eyes. Shuddery bursts of rapturous ecstasy began to rock her core.

"Who am I, Dizzy?" He flicked his tongue against hers. "Tell me what I am to you."

Suddenly the entire world fell away and nothing else existed but this man—her husband and mate. Mind, body and soul, Venom had learned her secrets and earned the right to be called her master.

"Who am I, Dizzy?" He asked again, his voice thick with emotion.

"My master," she said on a ragged sob. "You're my master."

He kissed her then, the tenderness of it stealing her breath. When he lifted his gaze his eyes were bright with love. "Do you know what you are to me?"

She shook her head even though she had a pretty good idea what she meant to him. She wanted to hear him say it. "Tell me."

"You are my heart. You are my life." He hastened the pace of his swirling fingertips and thrusting cock. "You're my future and my love."

Head thrown back, Dizzy climaxed with Venom's passionately spoken vow echoing in her mind. Burying his face against her neck, his breath hitched as the jerky spasms of his own orgasm gripped him. Eyes closed, Dizzy relished their shared moment of ecstasy.

Sometime later, after Venom had unleashed her wrists and massaged them in his big hands, he dragged her tight against his chest and brushed his fingers through her hair in a soothing rhythm. "Sleep, sugar. We both need it."

She yawned and snuggled closer to his enticing heat. "Do you have to report for duty soon?"

"Tomorrow morning," he said with a hint of sadness. "They're cutting all unnecessary leave. Apparently honeymoons fall in that category."

"That's okay." She caressed his chest. "The time we've had together is so much more than other married couples

I've known were able to enjoy." She pressed her lips to his jaw. "I think we've managed to build a good foundation."

"A very good one," he agreed. His voice turned solemn as he said, "I feel there may be an uptick in the Splinter activity in this sector. Most of the men stationed out here for long-term deployments were given this duty rotation as a sort of reward. It's quiet out here." He sighed with frustration. "Well, it *was* quiet out here."

"Nothing lasts forever, Venom."

He touched the scars on her neck. "I promised to protect you and to keep you safe from the Splinters who nearly killed you."

She rose up on her elbow and gazed down at him with disbelief. "Are you seriously feeling guilty about what happened last night? Venom, you *saved* my life. I'm the one who volunteered to go down there. You didn't force me."

"You never should have been put in that situation." His eyes closed as pain etched lines into his face. "Do you have any idea what could have happened to you? How many ways that takedown could have gone wrong?" He shook his head. "It makes me sick to even think about how close I came to losing you."

"But you didn't." She kissed him. "Venom, in some strange way, I'm actually glad I went. No, listen," she hurriedly said before he could interrupt. "I faced my fears last night. I faced the boogeymen who have been tormenting me since that morning of the explosion. I did something important and noble last night. I wasn't just running away from danger. I did something to save lives."

He caressed her cheek. "Yes, you did. I wish I could tell you how proud I am of you."

Cuddling up against him, she whispered playfully, "Maybe you can show me later."

He laughed and gave her bottom a pat. "There's no maybe to that one, sugar."

Safe in her mate's arms, Dizzy slowly succumbed to the exhaustion lulling her to sleep. She didn't know what tomorrow would bring but for the first time in years, she was excited to meet each new day.

And she would do it holding the hand of the ruggedly sexy but tender and loving sky warrior who had claimed and saved her.

Chapter Twenty-Six

Five Weeks Later

V ENOM TUGGED ON the double doors leading out to the balcony of their suite. The gauzy, white drapes billowed in the sea breeze rolling in from the ocean. He closed his eyes and enjoyed the unbelievably soothing sound of waves crashing upon the shore.

The images of their wedding ceremony flashed before him. Between Jack and Naya's many contacts, Dizzy had been able to have the day she had always wanted. He had never seen so many flowers or ribbon in his life but the banquet space had been completely transformed. Her dress was the prettiest thing he had ever seen with all that lace and frill.

When Dizzy walked in on Jack's arm, Venom had been struck by the significance of the ceremony. Their public affirmation of their intent to build a life together carried so much more weight than the simple act of collaring her out in the woods. She had picked him then but it had been a decision made out of necessity. Coming down the aisle on her father's arm was a choice she made out of love.

Everything after the moment they exchanged rings and kissed was a blur. There had been dinner and friendly carousing. Dizzy and Jack had shared a dance in the hallway outside the banquet room before Venom had swept her away on their very short second honeymoon.

While he had waited for the touching moment to end, Venom had caught Thorn looking on with such yearning sadness. The older general had been making an effort to get to know Dizzy and she had welcomed his interest—but their relationship would never be as close or as paternal as the one she shared with Jack.

Venom's alert senses detected the slight shift of movement from the next balcony. On instinct he tensed for an attack. Cipher stepped forward from the shadows of the balcony on his right while Fierce gave a little wave from this left. Both men were showing their faces to reassure Venom that they were well-protected while enjoying their two nights at the luxury resort on Blue Shores.

When Cipher stepped back into the shadows, Venom relaxed but a quiver of guilt pierced his chest. He stood on this balcony enjoying the gorgeous view of the three moons reflected off the ocean while somewhere out there Terror remained a hostage.

The trail had gone ice-cold after rescuing Jack Lane and recovering the fuel rods. Or Torment and Pierce were playing their cards awfully close to the chest. If Terror was alive—and Venom hoped he was—there had been no attempt to retrieve him from enemy hands.

He hated to think they would leave him in some backwater rat hole to be tortured just to gain intelligence but it wasn't a possibility he could discount. Terror had already given an eye to help the cause. He wouldn't flinch at giving his life.

And he wasn't the only one who had given his life to a cause. Axis had been found dead in his cell the evening after the botched fuel rod theft. The gruesome details of the airman's self-inflicted wounds had stunned Venom. Presumably Axis had realized what awaited him now that Terror was missing and so many Harcos warriors had been lost in the attack on the *Night Bird*. Rather than fold under intense interrogation, he had taken the cowardly way out.

The unsettling feeling of not knowing who had been watching Dizzy aboard the ship never left him. Cipher had uncovered a tracking program on her tablet but it couldn't be traced any farther back than Axis, who had used the ship's many wireless connection points to transmit the bug to her. He refused to even think about how easy it would have been to snatch her with her every movement mapped.

They couldn't live their lives saturated with paranoia but Venom remained on high alert whenever they were out in the public areas of the ship. He believed the extra precautions taken by him and by General Thorn's orders would keep her safe but his guard would never lower. She depended on him for protection and he would never betray that trust.

Even before Dizzy touched him, Venom sensed her approach. His eyelids drifted together as she wrapped her arms around his waist and lovingly kissed his back. He interlaced their fingers and marveled at the sight of their matching silver wedding bands glinting in the moonlight.

"I thought you were asleep." He lifted her hand to kiss her fingertips.

"I was but the sound of the waves woke me."

"I'm sorry."

"Don't be," she murmured. "It's a beautiful sound. Who knows when we'll hear it again?"

Because of the continuing threat of Splinter attack, this celebratory getaway had only been possible because Thorn had signed the orders himself and arranged for SRU to guard them. Though he had been wary of having a father-in-law so highly ranked, Venom had been forced to admit there were perks to the situation. Bringing Dizzy to Blue Shores to celebrate their wedding never would have been possible without Thorn pulling strings.

Dizzy stepped in front of him and leaned against the balcony. He braced his hands on the railing and nuzzled her neck. He still couldn't believe she had tattooed their family crest on either side of her neck. When they were out in public, there was zero question as to her status. She bore his mark in the most permanent way.

Fully aware of the watching eyes of his SRU team-mates, Venom rejected the primal call to slide his hands under the short nightdress she had donned. Taking her here in the moonlight, with the sounds of the ocean in the background, would have been a beautiful experience but it wasn't one he wanted to share with Cipher and Fierce watching.

"There goes Ella for one of her midnight swims."

Venom lifted his gaze toward the shoreline and

frowned. "It's dangerous."

Dizzy shrugged. "I don't think Ella has ever let a little danger stop her. Anyway, swimming this late is the only way she can enjoy the beach without weirdos trying to mug her for pictures or thinking they can proposition her just because she's a muse."

Venom watched Dizzy's best friend tiptoe in the warm water. She was a strikingly beautiful woman. He hadn't ever imagined it was possible to be too beautiful but he had seen the way Ella was treated by just about everyone. They saw those killer curves and gorgeous face and immediately assumed she was empty and vapid.

He still cringed at the way the soldiers and airmen onboard the *Valiant* had swarmed Ella at the arrivals deck earlier that morning. If it hadn't been for Raze and Threat's help, Venom would never have gotten her secured in their quarters. After that frightening experience, he worried Ella might never want to visit Dizzy again.

Movement on the beach drew his attention. He let the tension ease from his body when he recognized the figure as Raze's hulking form. From this distance, Venom couldn't hear the conversation Raze and Ella were sharing but it seemed friendly enough.

"I think she'll be all right." Dizzy pecked his cheek and tugged him away from the railing. "Come back to bed."

Venom didn't have to be asked twice. He trailed her into the hotel suite and firmly shut the balcony door. By the time he reached the bed, Dizzy had already stripped out of her nightgown and tossed it aside. There was enough moonlight streaming through the thin curtains to light up her skin. She still had a few rope marks from their earlier tryst.

Sliding into bed beside her, Venom traced the lines. "You know, if this little project of ours is successful, we won't be able to play like this for a while."

"Really?" Dizzy clasped his hand and dragged it down between her thighs.

He smiled at her boldness and dotted kisses along the swell of her breast. "I won't take any chances with you or the baby."

"Well…we aren't pregnant yet."

Venom laughed against her breast. "Is that your way of asking me to tie you up and ravish you again?"

"Um…maybe."

He slipped his hand under the pillow and retrieved the small coil of rope he'd hidden there. "Lucky for you, I'm always prepared."

She shivered with delight and giggled. "Don't I know it!"

Pushing up on his knees, Venom captured Dizzy between his chest and the bed. As he gazed down into her sweet face, everything else faded into the background—the war, the Splinters, the threats that awaited them around every corner. When he was with Dizzy, nothing else mattered. There were few guarantees in life but their love was one of them.

While Venom kissed and nibbled his way down the body he craved morning, noon and night, he decided it was time to remind her just how much she meant to him.

"Oh!" Dizzy's pleasured gasp echoed in the stillness of

their hotel room.

Venom grinned triumphantly. *And I think I'll start right about here...*

The End

About Lolita Lopez

The alter ego of *New York Times* and *USA Today* bestselling author Roxie Rivera, I like to write super sexy romances and scorching hot erotica. I live in Texas on five acres with my red-bearded Viking husband, our sweet, mischievous little girl and two crazy Great Danes.

You can find me online at www.lolitalopez.com.

Also by Lolita Lopez

GRABBED

Grabbed by Vicious

Caught by Menace

Saved by Venom

Stolen by Raze – Coming Dec 2015

Dragon Heat

Dead Sexy Dragon

Red Hot Dragon

Wicked Dark Dragon

Renegade Dragon – Coming Soon

Holiday Menage

Be Our Valentine

Margaritas and Mayhem

Fireworks For Three

Trick or Treat Trio – Coming Soon

Mistletoe Menage – Coming Soon

Ringing in the New Year – Coming Soon

58208902R00267

Made in the USA
Columbia, SC
17 May 2019